PRAISE FOR EDNA O'BRIEN

"She has the courage and sureness of vision to derive from the singularity of her character's experience general truths about the world. It is a painful world, a vale of tears where ghosts jostle the beautiful fleshly living for a place in the fanatic heart."

—Mary Gordon, *New York Times Book Review*

"O'Brien's own linguistic power is often quite breathtaking. . . . Edna O' Brien's heart is far from a fanatic's; it is generous, and it is large."

—*The New Leader*

"A landmark collection. . . . The Irish writer's exquisite perceptions and empathy with the women of her country exert an emotional pull, compelling the reader to live the straightened circumstances of their lives."

—*Publishers Weekly*

"Prose like a piece of fine meshwork, a net of perfectly observed sensuous details."

—Philip Roth, *New York Times Book Review*

"Reading Edna O'Brien's fiction, I've been surprised by perceptions of what I thought no one else knew—and I wasn't telling."

—Pauline Kael, *The New Yorker*

EDNA O'BRIEN is the author of eighteen books, including *Lantern Slides, The High Road, The Country Girls Trilogy, House of Splendid Isolation*, and most recently, *Down By the River* (all available in Plume editions). She lives in London.

A Fanatic Heart

ALSO BY EDNA O'BRIEN

Down by the River (1996)
House of Splendid Isolation (1994)
Time and Tide (1992)
Lantern Slides (1990)
The High Road (1988)
Returning (1982)
A Rose in the Heart (1978)
Mrs. Reinhardt & Other Stories (1978)
I Hardly Knew You (1977)
Mother Ireland (1976)
A Scandalous Woman and Other Stories (1974)
Night (1972)
Zee & Co. (1971)
A Pagan Place (1971)
The Love Object and Other Stories (1968)
Casualties of Peace (1966)
August Is a Wicked Month (1964)
Girls in Their Married Bliss (1963)
The Lonely Girl (1962)
The Country Girls (1960)

A Fanatic Heart

SELECTED STORIES OF

Edna O'Brien

A PLUME BOOK

PLUME
Published by the Penguin Group
Penguin Books USA Inc., 375 Hudson Street, New York, New York 10014, U.S.A.
Penguin Books Ltd, 27 Wrights Lane, London W8 5TZ, England
Penguin Books Australia Ltd, Ringwood, Victoria, Australia
Penguin Books Canada Ltd, 10 Alcorn Avenue, Toronto, Ontario, Canada M4V 3B2
Penguin Books (N.Z.) Ltd, 182–190 Wairau Road, Auckland 10, New Zealand

Penguin Books Ltd, Registered Offices: Harmondsworth, Middlesex, England

Published by Plume, an imprint of Dutton NAL, a member of Penguin Putnam Inc. This is an authorized reprint of a hardcover edition published by Farrar, Straus & Giroux. For information address Farrar, Straus & Giroux, 19 Union Square West, New York, N.Y. 10003

First Plume Printing, November, 1985
21 20 19 18 17 16 15 14 13 12 11 10

"Christmas Roses" first appeared in The Atlantic, and "The Doll" in Redbook. Except for "My Mother's Mother," "Tough Men," "Courtship," "The Mouth of the Cave," "Paradise," "A Scandalous Woman," and "Mrs. Reinhardt," all of the other stories in this Volume first appeared in The New Yorker.
Five lines from "Remorse for Intemperate Speech" reprinted with permission of Macmillan Publishing Company from The Poems by W. B. Yeats, edited by Richard J. Finneran. Copyright 1933 by Macmillan Publishing Co., Inc., renewed 1961 by Bertha Georgie Yeats.

REGISTERED TRADEMARK—MARCA REGISTRADA

Library of Congress Cataloging-in-Publication Data:

O'Brien, Edna.
A fanatic heart.
ISBN 0-452-26116-3

I. Title.
[PR6065.B7A6 1985] 823'.914 85-8935

Printed in the United States of America

PUBLISHER'S NOTE
These stories are works of fiction. Names, characters, places, and incidents are either the product of the author's imagination or are used fictitiously, and any resemblance to actual persons, living or dead, events, or locales is entirely coincidental.

Contents

Foreword

You see a country and a culture impressing itself deeply on this writer. The country is Ireland, and from the evidence available, she is more succubus than mother. The need to escape is visceral. There is a sense of protest in these stories, but it is often concealed or channeled into pain, perhaps because the author is a woman. The aggression takes the form of an arresting and unfaltering scream. When the background is rural—even barbaric—there is a rawness and earthiness in Edna O'Brien that some critics have compared with Colette. But she is not like Colette, because the stories are darker and full of conflict. In an essay about James Joyce, Frank Tuohy says that while Joyce, in Dubliners *and* Portrait of the Artist, *was the first Irish Catholic to make his experience and surroundings recognizable, "the world of Nora Barnacle had to wait for the fiction of Edna O'Brien."*

The stories set in the heartland of Ireland almost always depict women—with men, without men, on the make, on the loose, cracking up, women holding to reality by the skin of their teeth. Many are love stories, among them eerily intimate stories relating to sexual love, and these are what people chiefly associate with Edna O'Brien. But her range is wider than that and there is an acute, sometimes searing, social awareness. The worlds depicted are not just those of small farms full of lovelorn women and inebriate men, but also the larger world of cities, of resorts, of estrangement, the world of the very rich and careless. In a long story, a novella really, "Mrs. Reinhardt," there is an idyllic recapture of the countryside of Brittany that ends in disenchantment and havoc; in another story, "Paradise," the narrator says of the fashionable house guests, "All platinum . . . They have a canny sense of self-preservation; they know how much to eat, how much to drink . . . you would think they invented somebody like Shakespeare, so proprietary are they . . . You could easily get filleted. Friends do it to friends."

The sensibility is on two levels and shuttles back and forth, combining the innocence of childhood with the scars of maturity. It is what gives these stories their wounded vigor. The words themselves are chiseled. The welter of emotion is rendered so sparsely that the effect is merciless, like an autopsy.

—Philip Roth

Out of Ireland have we come.
Great hatred, little room,
Maimed us at the start.
I carry from my mother's womb
A fanatic heart.
—W. B. Yeats, "Remorse for Intemperate Speech"

A Fanatic Heart

Returning

1 9 8 1

The Connor Girls

To know them would be to enter an exalted world. To open the stiff green iron gate, to go up their shaded avenue, and to knock on their white hall door was a journey I yearned to make. No one went there except the gardener, the postman, and a cleaning woman who told none of their secrets, merely boasted that the oil paintings on the walls were priceless and the furniture was all antique. They had a flower garden with fountains, a water-lily pond, a kitchen garden, and ornamental trees that they called monkey-puzzle trees. Mr. Connor, the major, and his two daughters lived there. His only son had been killed in a car accident. It was said that the accident was due to his father's bullying of him, always urging him to drive faster since he had the most expensive car in the neighborhood. Not even their tragedy brought them closer to the people in the town, partly because they were aloof, but being Protestants, the Catholics could not attend the service in the church or go to the Protestant graveyard, where they had a vault with steps leading down to it, just like a house. It was smothered in creeper. They never went into mourning and had a party about a month later to which their friends came.

The major had friends who owned a stud farm, and these were invited two or three times a year, along with a surgeon and his wife, from Dublin. The Connor girls were not beauties but they were distinguished, and they talked in an accent that made everyone else's seem flat and sprawling, like some familiar estuary or a puddle in a field. They were dark-haired, with dark eyes and leathery skin. Miss Amy wore her hair in plaits, which she folded over the crown of her head, and Miss Lucy's hair, being more bushy, was kept flattened with brown slides. If they as much as nodded to a local or stopped to admire a new baby in its pram, the news spread throughout the parish and those who had never had a salute felt such a pang of envy, felt left out. We ourselves had been saluted and it was certain that we would become on better terms since they were under a sort of obligation to us. My father had given them permission to walk their dogs over our fields, so that most afternoons we saw the two girls in their white mackintoshes and biscuit-colored walking sticks drawing these fawn unwieldy beasts on leashes. Once they had passed our house they used to let their dogs go, whereupon our own sheepdogs barked fiercely but kept inside our own paling, being, as I think, terrified of the thoroughbreds, who were beagles. Though they had been passing by for almost a year, they never stopped to talk to my mother if they met her returning from the hen house with an empty pail, or going there with the foodstuff. They merely saluted and passed on. They talked to my father, of course, and called him Mick, although his real name was Joseph, and they joked with him about his hunters, which had never won cup or medal. They ignored my mother and she resented this. She longed to bring them in so that they could admire our house with all its knickknacks, and admire the thick wool rugs which she made in the winter nights and which she folded up when no visitors were expected.

"I'll ask them to tea this coming Friday," she said to me. We planned to ask them impromptu, thinking that if we asked them ahead of time they were more likely to refuse. So we made cakes and sausage rolls and sandwiches of egg mayonnaise, some with onion, some without. The milk jelly we had made was whisked and seemed like a bowl of froth with a sweet confectionery smell. I was put on watch by the kitchen window, and as soon as I saw them coming in at the gate I called to Mama.

"They're coming, they're coming."

She swept her hair back, pinned it with her brown tortoiseshell comb, and went out and leaned on the top rung of the gate as if she were posing for a photograph, or looking at a view. I heard her say, "Excuse me, Miss Connor, or rather, Miss Connors," in that exaggerated accent which she had picked up in America, and which she used when strangers came, or when she went to the city. It was like putting on new clothes or new shoes which did not fit her. I saw them shake their heads a couple of times, and long before she had come back into the house I knew that the Connor girls had refused our invitation and that the table which we had laid with such ceremony was a taunt and downright mockery.

Mama came back humming to herself as if to pretend that it hadn't mattered a jot. The Connor girls had walked on, and their dogs, which were off the leashes, were chasing our young turkeys into the woods.

"What will we do with this spread?" I asked Mama as she put on her overall.

"Give it to the men, I expect," she said wearily.

You may know how downcast she was when she was prepared to give iced cake and dainty sandwiches to workmen who were plowing and whose appetites were ferocious.

"They didn't come," I said stupidly, being curious to know how the Connor girls had worded their refusal.

"They never eat between meals," Mama said, quoting their exact phrase in an injured, sarcastic voice.

"Maybe they'll come later on," I said.

"They're as odd as two left shoes," she said, tearing a frayed tea towel in half. When in a temper, she resorted to doing something about the house. Either she took the curtains down, or got on her knees to scrub the floors and the legs and rungs of the wooden chairs.

"They see no one except that madman," she said, mainly to herself.

The Connor girls kept very much to themselves and did most of their shopping in the city. They attended church on Sundays, four Protestant souls comprising the congregation in a stone church that was the oldest in our parish. Moss covered the stones, and various plants grew between the cracks, so that in the distance the side wall of the church was green from both verdure and centuries of rain. Their father did not attend each Sunday, but once a month the girls wheeled him down to the family vault, where his wife and son were interred. Local people who longed to be friends with them would rush out and offer their sympathy, as if the major were the only one to have suffered bereavement. Always he remained brusque and asked his daughters the name of the man or woman who happened to be talking to him. He was known to be crotchety, but this was because of his rheumatism, which he had contracted years before. He could not be persuaded to go to any of the holy wells where other people went, to pray and seek a cure for their ailments. He was a large man with a very red face and he always wore gray mittens. The rector visited him twice a month and in the dapping season sent up two fresh trout on the mail car. Soon after, the Connor girls invited the rector for dinner and some of the toffs who had come for the dapping.

Otherwise they entertained rarely, except for the madman, who visited them every Sunday. He was a retired captain from the next town and he had a brown mustache with a red tint in it and very large bloodshot eyes. People said that he slept with the Connor girls and hence he had been given the nickname of Stallion. It was him my mother referred to as the madman. On Sundays he drove over in his sports car, in time for afternoon tea, which in summertime they had outdoors on an iron table. We children used to go over there to look at them through the trees, and though we could not clearly see them, we could hear their voices, hear the girls' laughter and then the tap of a croquet mallet when they played a game. Their house was approached from the road by a winding avenue that was dense with evergreen trees. Those trees were hundreds of years old, but also there were younger trees that the major had planted for the important occasions in his life—the Coronation, the birth of his children, England's victory in the last war. For his daughters he had planted quinces. What were quinces, we wondered, and never found out. Nailed to the blue cedar, near the gate, was a sign which said BEWARE OF DOGS, and the white pebble-dashed walls that surrounded their acres of garden were topped with broken glass so that children could not climb over and steal from the orchard.

Everyone vetted them when they came out of their stronghold on Sunday evening. Their escort, the Stallion, walked the girls to the

Greyhound Hotel. Miss Amy, who was younger, wore brighter clothes, but they both wore tweed costumes and flat shoes with ornamental tongues that came over the insteps and hid the laces. Miss Amy favored red or maroon, while Miss Lucy wore dark brown with a matching dark-brown beret. In the hotel they had the exclusive use of the sitting room, and sometimes when they were a little intoxicated Miss Lucy played the piano while her sister and the Stallion sang. It was a saucy song, a duet in which the man asked the pretty maid where she was going to, and eventually asked for her hand in marriage. Refusing him, she said, "I will not marry, marry, marry you," and then stamped her feet to emphasize it, whereupon the men in the bar would start laughing and saying Miss Amy was "bucking." There was much speculation about their lives, because the Stallion always spent Sunday night in their house. Hickey, our hired help, said they were all so drunk that they probably tumbled into bed together. Walking home on the frosty nights, Hickey said it was a question of the blind leading the blind, as they slithered all over the road and, according to Hickey, used language that was not ladylike. He would report these things in the morning to my mother, and since they had rebuffed her, she was pleased, and emphasized the fact that they had no breeding. Naturally she thought the very worst of the Stallion and could never bring herself to pronounce his Christian name. To her he was "that madman."

The Stallion was their sole escort until fate sent another man in the form of a temporary bank clerk. We reckoned that he was a Protestant because he didn't go to Mass on the first Sunday. He was most dashing. He had brown hair, he too had a mustache, but it was fuller than the Stallion's and was a soft dark brown. Mostly he wore a tweed jacket and matching plus-fours. Also he had a motorcycle, and when he rode it, he wore goggles. Within two weeks he was walking Miss Amy out and escorting her to the Greyhound Hotel. She began to pay more attention to her clothes, she got two new accordion-pleated skirts and some tight-fitting jumpers that made her bust more pronounced. They were called Sloppy Joes, but although they were long and sloppy, they were also sleek, and they flattered the figure.

Formerly her hair was wound in a staid plait around her head, but now it was allowed to tumble down in thick coils over her shoulders, and she toned down the color in her cheeks with pale powder. No one ever said she was pretty, but certainly she looked handsome when she cycled to the village to collect the morning paper, and hummed to herself as she went freewheel down the hill that led to the town.

The bank clerk and she were in love. Hickey saw them embrace in the porch of the Greyhound Hotel when Miss Lucy had gone back in to get a pack of cigarettes. Later they kissed shamelessly when walking along the towpath, and people said that Miss Amy used to nibble the hairs of his luxurious mustache. One night she took off her sandal in the Greyhound Hotel and put her bare foot into the pocket of his sports jacket, and the two of them giggled at her proceedings. Her sister and the Stallion often tagged along, but Miss Amy and the bank clerk would set off on his motorcycle, down the Shannon Road, for fun. It was said that they swam naked, but no one could verify that, and it was possible that they just paddled their feet.

As it happened, someone brought mischievous news about the bank clerk. A commercial traveler who was familiar with other parts told it on good authority that the bank clerk was a lapsed Catholic and had previously disgraced himself in a seaside town. People were left to guess the nature of the mistake, and most concluded that it concerned a girl or a woman. Instantly the parish turned against him. The next evening when he came out from the bank he found that both wheels of his bicycle had been ripped and punctured, and on the saddle there was an anonymous letter which read "Go to Mass or we'll kill you." His persecutors won. He attended the last Mass the following Sunday, and knelt in the back pew with no beads and no prayer book, with only his fingers to pray on.

However, it did not blight the romance. Those who had predicted that Miss Amy would ditch him because he was a Catholic were proven wrong. Most evenings they went down the Shannon Road, a couple full of glee, her hair and her headscarf flying, and chuckles of laughter from both of them as they frightened a dog or hens that strayed onto the roadside. Much later he saw her home, and the lights were on in their front parlor until all hours. A local person (the undertaker actually) thought of fitting up a telescope to try to see into the parlor, but as soon as he went inside their front gate to reconnoiter, the dogs came rearing down the avenue and he ran for his life.

"Can it be serious, I wonder." So at last my mother admitted to knowing about the romance. She could not abide it, she said that Catholics and Protestants just could not mix. She recalled a grievance held for many years from a time in her girlhood when she and all the others from the national school were invited to the big house to a garden party, and were made to make fools of themselves by doing running jumps and sack races and were then given watery lemonade in which wasps floated. Her mind was firmly made up about the incompatibility of Catholics and Protestants. That very night Miss Amy sported an engagement ring in the Greyhound Hotel and the following morning the engagement was announced in the paper. The ring was star-shaped and comprised of tiny blue stones that sparkled and trembled under the beam of the hanging lamp. People gasped when told that it was insured for a hundred pounds.

"Do we have to give Miss Amy some sort of present?" my mother said grudgingly that evening. She had not forgotten how they snubbed her and how they barely thanked her for the fillets of pork that she gave them every time we killed a pig.

"Indeed we do, and a good present," my father said, so they went to Limerick some time after and got a carving knife and fork that were packed in a velvet-lined box. We presented it to Miss Amy the next time she was walking her dogs past our house.

"It *is* kind of you, thanks awfully," she said, as she smiled at each one of us, and told my father coyly that as she was soon to be hitched up, they ought to have that night out. She was not serious, of course, yet we all laughed and my mother did a *tch tch* in mock disapproval. Miss Amy looked ravishing that day. Her skin was soft and her brown eyes had caught the reflection of her orange neck scarf and gave her a warm theatrical glow. Also she was amiable. It was a damp day, with shreds of mist on the mountains, and the trees dripped quietly as we spoke. Miss Amy held out the palms of her hands to take the drips from the walnut tree and announced to the heavens what a "lucky gal" she was. My mother inquired about her trousseau and was told that she had four pairs of court shoes, two camel-hair coats, a saxe-blue going-away suit, and a bridal dress in voile that was a cross between peach and champagne color. I loved her then, and wanted to know her and wished with all my heart that I could have gone across the fields with her and become her confidante, but I was ten and she was thirty or thirty-five.

There was much speculation about the wedding. No one from the village had been invited, but then that was to be expected. Some said that it was to be in a Registry Office in Dublin, but others said that the bank clerk had assured the parish priest that he would be married in a Catholic church, and had guaranteed a huge sum of money in order to get his letter of freedom. It was even said that Miss Amy was going to take instruction so as to be converted, but that was only wishful thinking. People were stunned the day the bank clerk suddenly left. He left the bank at lunchtime, after a private talk with the manager. Miss Amy drove him to the little railway station ten miles away, and they kissed several times before he jumped onto the moving train. The story was that he had gone ahead to make the plans and that the Connor girls and their father would travel shortly after. But the postman, who was a Protestant, said that the major would not travel one inch to see his daughter marry a Papist.

We watched the house and gate carefully but we did not see Miss Amy emerge throughout the week. No one knows when she left, or what she wore, or in what frame of mind. All we knew was that suddenly Miss Lucy was out walking with the Stallion and Miss Amy was not to be seen.

"And where's the bride-to-be tonight?" inquired Mrs. O'Shea, the hotel proprietor. Miss Lucy's reply was clipped and haughty.

"My sister's gone away, for a change," she said.

The frozen voice made everyone pause, and Mrs. O'Shea gave some sort of untoward gasp that seemed to detect catastrophe.

"Is there anything else you would care to know, Mrs. O'Shea?" Miss Lucy asked, and then turned on her heel and left with the

Stallion. Never again did they drink in the Greyhound Hotel but moved to a public house up the street, where several of the locals soon followed them.

The mystery of Miss Amy was sending people into frenzies of conjecture and curiosity. Everyone thought that everyone else knew something. The postman was asked but he would just nod his head and say, "Time will tell," although it was plain to see that he was pleased with the outcome. The priest, when asked in confidence by my mother, said that the most Christian thing to do would be to go down on one's knees and say a prayer for Miss Amy. The phrase "star-crossed lovers" was used by many of the women, and for a while it even was suggested that Miss Amy had gone berserk and was shut up in an asylum. At last the suspense was ended, as each wedding present was returned, with an obscure but polite note from Miss Lucy. My mother took ours back to the shop and got some dinner plates in exchange. The reason given was that there had been a clash of family interests. Miss Lucy came to the village scarcely at all. The major had got more ill and she was busy nursing him. A night nurse cycled up their avenue every evening at five to nine, and the house itself, without so much coming and going, began to look forlorn. In the summer evenings I used to walk up the road and gaze in at it, admiring the green jalousies, the bird table nailed to the tree, the tall important flowers and shrubs, which for want of tending had grown rampant. I used to wish that I could unlock the gate and go up and be admitted there and find the clue to Miss Amy's whereabouts and her secret.

We did in fact visit the house the following winter, when the major died. It was much more simply furnished than I had imagined, and the loose linen covers on the armchairs were a bit frayed. I was studying the portraits of glum, puffy, grave ancestors when suddenly there was a hush and into the parlor came Miss Amy, wearing a fur coat, looking quite different. She looked older and her face was coarse.

"Miss Amy, Miss Amy," several people said aloud, and flinching she turned to tell the driver to please leave her trunk on the landing upstairs. She had got much fatter and was wearing no engagement ring. When the people sympathized with her, her eyes became cloudy with tears, and then she ran out of the room and up the stairs to sit with the remains.

It did not take long for everyone to realize that Miss Amy had become a drinker. As the coffin was laid in the vault she tried to talk to her father, which everyone knew was irrational. She did not just drink at night in the bar, but drank in the daytime, and would take a miniature bottle out of her bag when she queued in the butcher's shop to get chops and a sheep's head for the dogs. She drank with my father when he was on a drinking bout. In fact, she drank with anyone that would sit with her, and had lost all her snootiness. She sometimes referred to her engagement as "my flutter." Soon after, she was arrested in Limerick for drunken driving, but was not charged, because the superintendent had been a close friend of her father's. Her driving became calamitous. People were afraid to let their children play in the street in case Miss Amy might run them over in her Peugeot car. No one had forgotten that her brother had killed himself driving, and even her sister began to confide to my mother, telling her worries in tense whispers, spelling the words that were the most incriminating.

"It must be a broken heart," my mother said.

"Of course, with Dad gone, there is no one to raise any objections now to the wedding."

"So why don't they marry?" my mother asked, and in one fell swoop surrendered all her prejudices.

"Too late, too late," Miss Lucy said, and then added that Miss Amy could not get the bank clerk out of her system, that she sat in the breakfast room staring at photographs they had taken the day of her engagement and was always looking for an excuse to use his name.

One night the new curate found Miss Amy drunk in a hedge under her bicycle. By then her driving license had been taken away for a year. He picked her up, brought her home in his car, and the next day called on her because he had found a brooch stuck to the fuchsia hedge where she came a cropper. Furthermore, he had put her bicycle in to be repaired. This gesture worked wonders. He was asked to stay to tea, and invited again the following Sunday. Due to his influence, or perhaps secretly due to his prayers, Miss Amy began to drink less. To everyone's amazement the curate went there most Sunday nights and played bridge with the two girls and the Stallion. In no time Miss Amy was overcome with resolve and industry. The garden, which had been neglected, began to look bright and trim again, and she bought bulbs in the hardware shop, whereas formerly she used to send away to a nursery for them. Everyone remarked on how civil she had become. She and my mother exchanged recipes for apple jelly and lemon curd, and just before I went away to boarding school she gave me a present of a bound volume of *Aesop's Fables*. The print was so small that I could not read it, but it was the present that mattered. She handed it to me in the field and then asked if I would like to accompany her to gather some flowers. We went to the swamp to get the yellow irises. It was a close day, the air was thick with midges, and they lay in hosts over the murky water. Holding a small bunch to her chest, she said that she was going to post them to somebody, somebody special.

"Won't they wither?" I said, though what I really wanted to know was who they were meant for.

"Not if I pack them in damp moss," she said, and it seemed that the thought of dispatching this little gift was bringing joy to her, though there was no telling who the recipient would be. She asked me if I'd fallen in love yet or had a "beau." I said that I had liked an actor who had come with the traveling players and had in fact got his autograph.

"Dreams," she said, "dreams," and then, using the flowers as a bat, swatted some midges away. In September I went to boarding school and got involved with nuns and various girl friends, and in time the people in our parish, even the Connor girls, almost disappeared from my memory. I never dreamed of them anymore, and I had no ambitions to go cycling with them or to visit their house. Later when I went to university in Dublin I learned quite by chance that Miss Amy had worked in a beauty parlor in Stephens Green, had drunk heavily, and had joined a golf club. By then the stories of how she teetered on high heels, or wore unmatching stockings or smiled idiotically and took ages to say what she intended to say, had no interest for me.

Somewhat precipitately and unknown to my parents I had become engaged to a man who was not of our religion. Defying threats of severing bonds, I married him and incurred the wrath of family and relatives, just as Miss Amy had done, except that I was not there to bear the brunt of it. Horrible letters, some signed and some anonymous, used to reach me, and my mother had penned an oath that we would never meet again this side of the grave. I did not see my family for a few years, until long after my son was born, and having some change of heart they proposed by letter that my husband, my son, and I pay them a visit. We drove down one blowy autumn afternoon and I read stories aloud as much to distract myself as to pacify my son. I was quaking. The sky was watery and there were pale-green patches like holes or voids in it. I shall never forget the sense of awkwardness, sadness, and dismay when I stepped out of my husband's car and saw the large gaunt cut-stone house with thistles in the front garden. The thistle seed was blowing wildly, as were the leaves, and even those that had already fallen were rising and scattering about. I introduced my husband to my parents and very proudly I asked my little son to shake hands with his grandfather and his grandmother. They admired his gold hair, but he ignored them and ran to cuddle the two sheepdogs. He was going to be the one that would make our visit bearable.

In the best room my mother had laid the table for tea, and we sat and spoke to one another in thin, strained, unforgiving voices. The tea was too strong for my husband, who usually drank China tea anyhow, and instantly my mother jumped to get some hot water. I followed her out to apologize for the inconvenience.

"The house looks lovely and clean," I said.

She had polished everywhere and she had even dusted the artificial flowers, which I remembered as being clogged with dust.

"You'll stay a month," she said in a warm commandeering voice, and she put her arms around me in an embrace.

"We'll see," I said prudently, knowing my husband's restlessness.

"You have a lot of friends to see," she said.

"Not really," I said, with a coldness that I could not conceal.

"Do you know who is going to ask you to tea—the Connor girls." Her voice was urgent and grateful. It meant a victory for her, for me, and an acknowledgment of my husband's non-religion. In her eyes Protestants and atheists were one and the same thing.

"How are they?" I asked.

"They've got very sensible, and aren't half as stuck up," she said, and then ran, as my father was calling for her to cut the iced cake. Next afternoon there was a gymkhana over in the village and my parents insisted that we go.

"I don't want to go to this thing," my husband said to me. He had intended to do some trout fishing in one of the many mountain rivers, and to pass his few days, as he said, without being assailed by barbarians.

"Just for this once," I begged, and I knew that he had consented because he put on his tie, but there was no affability in him. After lunch my father, my husband, my little son, and I set out. My mother did not come, as she had to guard her small chickens. She had told us in the most graphic detail of her immense sorrow one morning upon finding sixty week-old chicks laid out on the flagstone dead, with their necks wrung by weasels.

In the field where the gymkhana was held there were a few caravans, strains of accordion music, a gaudy sign announcing a Welsh clairvoyant, wild restless horses, and groups of self-conscious people in drab clothes, shivering as they waited for the events to begin. It was still windy and the horses looked unmanageable. They were being held in some sort of order by youngsters who had little power over them. I saw people stare in my direction and a few of them gave reluctant half smiles. I felt uneasy and awkward and superior all at once.

"There's the Connor girls," my father said. They were perched on their walking sticks, which opened up to serve as little seats.

"Come on, come on," he said excitedly, and as we approached

them, they hailed me and said my name. They were older but still healthy and handsome, and Miss Amy showed no signs of her past despair. They shook my hand, shook my husband's hand, and were quick to flirt with him, to show him what spirited girls they were.

"And what do you think of this young man?" my father said proudly as he presented his grandson.

"What a sweet little chap," they said together, and I saw my husband wince. Then from the pocket of her fawn coat Miss Amy took two unwrapped jelly sweets and handed them to the little boy. He was on the point of eating them when my husband bent down until their faces were level and said very calmly, "But you don't eat sweets, now give them back." The little boy pouted, then blushed, and held out the palm of his hand, on which rested these absurd two jellies that were dusted over with granular sugar. My father protested, the Connor girls let out exclamations of horror, and I said to my husband, "Let him have them, it's a day out." He gave me a menacing look, and very firmly he repeated to the little boy what he had already said. The sweets were handed back, and with scorn in her eyes Miss Amy looked at my husband and said, "Hasn't the mummy got any say over her own child?"

There was a moment's strain, a moment's silence, and then my father produced a pack of cigarettes and gave them one each. Since we didn't smoke we were totally out of things.

"No vices," Miss Lucy said, and my husband ignored her.

He suggested to me that we take the child across to where a man had a performing monkey clinging to a stick. He raised his cap slightly to say his farewell and I smiled as best I could. My father stayed behind with the Connor girls.

"They were going to ask us to tea," I said to my husband as we walked downhill. I could hear the suction of his galoshes in the soggy ground.

"Don't think we missed much," he said, and at that moment I realized that by choosing his world I had said goodbye to my own and to those in it. By such choices we gradually become exiles, until at last we are quite alone.

My Mother's Mother

I loved my mother, yet I was glad when the time came to go to her mother's house each summer. It was a little house in the mountains and it commanded a fine view of the valley and the great lake below. From the front door, glimpsed through a pair of very old binoculars, one could see the entire Shannon Lake studded with various islands. On a summer's day this was a thrill. I would be put standing on a kitchen chair, while someone held the binoculars, and sometimes I marveled though I could not see at all, as the lenses had not been focused properly. The sunshine made everything better, and though we were not down by the lake, we imagined dipping our feet in it, or seeing people in boats fishing and then stopping to have a picnic. We imagined lake water lapping.

I felt safer in that house. It was different from our house, not so imposing, a cottage really, with no indoor water and no water closet. We went for buckets of water to the well, a different well each summer. These were a source of miracle to me, these deep cold wells, sunk into the ground, in a kitchen garden, or a paddock, or even a long distance away, wells that had been divined since I was last there. There was always a tin scoop nearby so that one could fill the bucket to the very brim. Then of course the full bucket was an occasion of trepidation, because one was supposed not to spill. One often brought the bucket to the very threshold of the kitchen and then out of excitement or clumsiness some water would get splashed onto the concrete floor and there would be admonishments, but it was not like the admonishments in our own house, it was not calamitous.

My grandfather was old and thin and hoary when I first saw him. His skin was the color of a clay pipe. After the market day he would come home in the pony and trap drunk, and then as soon as he stepped out of the trap he would stagger and fall into a drain or whatever. Then he would roar for help, and his grandson, who was in his twenties, would pick him up, or rather, drag him along the ground and through the house and up the stairs to his feather bed, where he moaned and groaned. The bedroom was above the kitchen, and in the night we would be below, around the fire, eating warm soda bread and drinking cocoa. There was nothing like it. The fresh bread would only be an hour out of the pot and cut in thick pieces and dolloped with butter and greengage jam. The greengage jam was a present from the postmistress, who gave it in return for the grazing of a bullock. She gave marmalade at a different time of year and a barmbrack at Halloween. He moaned upstairs, but no one was frightened of him, not even his own wife, who chewed and chewed and said, "Bad cess to them that give him the drink." She meant the publicans. She was a minute woman with a minute face and her thin hair was pinned up tightly. Her little face, though old, was like a bud, and when she was young she had been beautiful. There was a photo of her to prove it.

Sitting with them at night I thought that maybe I would not go home at all. Maybe I would never again lie in bed next to my mother, the two of us shivering with expectancy and with terror. Maybe I would forsake my mother.

"Maybe you'll stay here," my aunt said, as if she had guessed my thoughts.

"I couldn't do that," I said, not knowing why I declined, because indeed the place had definite advantages. I stayed up as late as they did. I ate soda bread and jam to my heart's content, I rambled around the fields all day, admiring sally trees, elder bushes, and the fluttering flowers, I played "shop" or I played teaching in the little dark plantation, and no one interfered or told me to stop doing it. The plantation was where I played secrets, and always I knew the grownups were within shouting distance, if a stranger or a tinker should surprise me there. It was pitch dark and full of young fir trees. The ground was a carpet of bronzed fallen fir needles. I used to kneel on them for punishment, after the playing.

Then when that ritual was done I went into the flower garden, which being full of begonias and lupins was a mass of bright brilliant colors. Each area had its own color, as my aunt planned it that way. I can see them now, those bright reds, like nail varnish, and those yellows like the gauze of a summer dress and those pale blues like old people's eyes, with the bees and the wasps luxuriating in each petal, or each little bell, or each flute, and feel the warmth of the place, and the drone of the bees, and see again tea towels and gray flannelette drawers that were spread out on the hedge to dry. The sun garden, they called it. My aunt got the seeds and just sprinkled them around, causing marvelous blooms to spring up. They even had tulips, whereas at home we had only a diseased rambling rose on a silvered arch and two clumps of devil's pokers. Our garden was sad and windy, the wind had made holes and indentations in the hedges, and the dogs had made further holes where they slept and burrowed. Our house was larger, and there was better linoleum on the floor, there were brass rods on the stairs, and there was a flush lavatory, but it did not have the same cheeriness and it was imbued with doom.

Still, I knew that I would not stay in my grandmother's forever. I knew it for certain when I got into bed and then desperately missed my mother, and missed the little whispering we did, and the chocolate we ate, and I missed the smell of our kind of bedclothes. Theirs were gray flannel, which tickled the skin, as did the loose feathers, and their pointed ends kept irking one. There was a gaudy red quilt that I thought would come to life and turn into a sinister Santa Claus. Except that they had told me that there was no Santa Claus. My aunt told me that, she insisted.

There was my aunt and her two sons, Donal and Joe, and my grandmother and grandfather. My aunt and Joe would tease me each night, say that there was no Santa Claus, until I got up and stamped the floor, and in contradicting them welled up with tears, and then at last, when I was on the point of breaking down, they would say that there was. Then one night they went too far. They said that my mother was not my real mother. My real mother, they said, was in Australia and I was adopted. I could not be told that word. I began to hit the wall and screech, and the more they insisted, the more obstreperous I became. My aunt went into the parlor in search of a box of snaps to find a photo of my real mother and came out triumphant at having found it. She showed me a woman in knickerbockers with a big floppy hat. I could have thrown it in the fire so violent was I. They watched for each new moment of panic and furious disbelief, and then they got the wind up when they saw I was getting out of control. I began to shake like the weather conductor on the chapel chimney and my teeth chattered, and before long I was just this shaking creature, unable to let out any sound, and seeing the room's contents swim away from me, I felt their alarm almost as I felt my own. My aunt took hold of my wrist to feel my pulse, and my grandmother held a spoonful of tonic to my lips, but I spilled it. It was called Parishes Food and was the color of cooked beetroot. My eyes were haywire. My aunt put a big towel around me and sat me on her knee, and as the terror lessened, my tears began to flow and I cried so much that they thought I would choke because of the tears going back down the throat. They said I must never tell anyone and I must never tell my mother.

"She is my mother," I said, and they said, "Yes, darling," but I knew that they were appalled at what had happened.

That night I fell out of bed twice, and my aunt had to put chairs next to it to keep me in. She slept in the same room, and often I used to hear her crying for her dead husband and begging to be reunited with him in heaven. She used to talk to him and say, "Is that you, Michael, is that you?" I often heard her arms striking against the headboard, or heavy movements when she got up to relieve herself. In the daytime we used the fields, but at night we did not go out for fear of ghosts. There was a gutter in the back kitchen that served as a channel, and twice a week she put disinfectant in it. The crux in the daytime was finding a private place and not being found or spied on by anyone. It entailed much walking and then much hesitating so as not to be seen.

The morning after the fright, they pampered me, scrambled

me an egg, and sprinkled nutmeg over it. Then along with that my aunt announced a surprise. Our workman had sent word by the mail-car man that he was coming to see me on Sunday and the postman had delivered the message. Oh, what a glut of happiness. Our workman was called Carnero and I loved him too. I loved his rotting teeth and his curly hair and his strong hands and his big stomach, which people referred to as his "corporation." He was nicknamed Carnero after a boxer. I knew that when he came he would have bars of chocolate, and maybe a letter or a silk hanky from my mother, and that he would lift me up in his arms and swing me around and say "Sugarbush." How many hours were there until Sunday, I asked.

Yet that day, which was Friday, did not pass without event. We had a visitor—a man. I will never know why but my grandfather called him Tim, whereas his real name was Pat, but my grandfather was not to be told that. Tim, it seems, had died and my grandfather was not to know, because if any of the locals died, it brought his own death to his mind and he dreaded death as strenuously as did all the others. Death was some weird journey that you made alone and unbefriended, once you had embarked on it. When my aunt's husband had died, in fact had been shot by the Black and Tans, my aunt had to conceal the death from her own parents, so irrational were they about the subject. She had to stay up at home the evening her husband's remains were brought to the chapel, and when the chapel bell rang out intermittently, as it does for a death, and they asked who it was, again and again, my poor aunt had to conceal her own grief, be silent about her own tragedy, and pretend that she did not know. Next day she went to the funeral on the excuse that it was some forester whom her husband knew. Her husband was supposed to be transferred to a barracks a long way off, and meanwhile she was going to live with her parents and bring her infant sons until her husband found accommodation. She invented a name for the district where her husband was supposed to be, it was in the North of Ireland, and she invented letters that she had received from him, and the news of the Troubles up there. Eventually, I expect, she told them, and I expect they collapsed and broke down. In fact, the man who brought these imaginary letters would have been Tim, since he had been the postman, and it was of his death my grandfather must not be told. So there in the porch, in a worn suit, was a man called Pat answering to the name of Tim, and the news that a Tim would have, such as how were his family and what crops had he put in and what cattle fairs had he been to. I thought that it was peculiar that he could answer for another, but I expect that everyone's life story was identical.

Sunday after Mass I was down by the little green gate skipping and waiting for Carnero. As often happens, the visitor arrives just when we look away. The cuckoo called, and though I knew I would not see her, I looked in a tree where there was a ravaged bird's nest, and at that moment heard Carnero's whistle. I ran down the road, and at once he hefted me up onto the crossbar of his bicycle.

"Oh, Carnero," I cried. There was both joy and sadness in our reunion. He had brought me a bag of tinned sweets, and the most glamorous present—as we got off the bicycle near the little gate he put it on me. It was a toy watch—a most beautiful red, and each bit of the bracelet was the shape and color of a raspberry. It had hands, and though they did not move, that did not matter. One could pull the bracelet part by its elastic thread and cause it to snap in or out. The hands were black and curved like an eyelash. He would not say where he had got it. I had only one craving, to stay down there by the gate with him and admire the watch and talk about home. I could not talk to him in front of them because a child was not supposed to talk or have any wants. He was puffing from having cycled uphill and began to open his tie, and taking it off, he said, "This bloody thing." I wondered who he had put it on for. He was in his Sunday suit and had a fishing feather in his hat.

"Oh, Carnero, turn the bike around and bring me home with you."

Such were my unuttered and unutterable hopes. Later my grandfather teased me and said was it in his backside I saw Carnero's looks, and I said no, in every particle of him.

*

That night as we were saying the Rosary my grandfather let out a shout, slouched forward, knocking the wooden chair and hitting himself on the rungs of it, then falling on the cement floor. He died delirious. He died calling on his Maker. It was ghastly. Joe was out and only my grandmother and aunt were there to assist. They picked him up. His skin was purple, the exact color of the iron tonic, and his eyes rolled so that they were seeing every bit of the room, from the ceiling, to the whitewashed wall, to the cement floor, to the settle bed, to the cans of milk, seeing and bulging. He writhed like an animal and then let out a most beseeching howl, and that was it. At that moment my aunt remembered I was there and told me to go into the parlor and wait. It was worse in there, pitch dark, and I in a place where I did not know my footing or my way around. I'd only been in there once, to fetch a teapot and a sugar tongs when Tim came. Had it been in our own house I would have known what to cling to, the back of a chair, the tassel of a blind, the girth of a plaster statue, but in there I held on to nothing and thought how the thing he dreaded had come to pass and now he was finding out those dire things that all his life his mind had shirked from.

"May he rest in peace, may the souls of the faithful departed rest in peace."

It was that for two days, along with litanies and mourners smoking clay pipes, plates being passed around and glasses filled. My mother and father were there, among the mourners. I was praised for growing, as if it were something I myself had caused to happen. My mother looked older in black, and I wished she had worn a georgette scarf, something to give her a bit of brightness around the throat. She did not like when I said that, and sent me off to say the Confiteor and three Hail Marys. Her eyes were dry. She did not love her own father. Neither did I. Her sister and she would go down into the far room and discuss whether to bring out another bottle of whiskey or another porter cake, or whether it was time to offer the jelly. They were reluctant, the reason being that some provisions had to be held over for the next day, when the special mourners would come up after the funeral. Whereas that night half the parish was there. My grandfather was laid out upstairs in a brown habit. He had stubble on his chin and looked like a frosted plank lying there, gray-white and inanimate. As soon as they had paid their respects, the people hurried down to the kitchen and the parlor, for the eats and the chat. No one wanted to be with the dead man, not even his wife, who had gone a bit funny and was asking my aunt annoying questions about the food and the fire, and how many priests were going to serve at the High Mass.

"Leave that to us," my mother would say, and then my grandmother would retell the world what a palace my mother's house was, and how it was the nicest house in the countryside, and my mother would say "Shhhh," as if she were being disgraced. My father said, "Well, missy," to me twice, and a strange man gave me sixpence. It was a very thin, worn sixpence and I thought it would disappear. I called him Father, out of reverence, because he looked like a priest, but he was in fact a boatman.

The funeral was on an island on the Shannon. Most of the people stayed on the quay, but we, the family, piled into two rowboats and followed the boat that carried the coffin. It was a jolty ride, with big waves coming in over us and our feet getting drenched. The island itself was full of cows. The sudden arrivals made them bawl and race about, and I thought it was quite improper to see that happening while the remains were being lowered and buried. It was totally desolate, and though my aunt sniffled a bit, and my grandmother let out ejaculations, there was no real grief, and that was the saddest thing.

Next day they burned his working clothes and threw his muddy boots on the manure heap. Then my aunt sewed black diamonds of cloth on her clothes, on my grandmother's, and on Joe's. She wrote a long letter to her son in England, and enclosed black diamonds of cloth for him to stitch onto his effects. He worked in Liverpool in a motorcar factory. Whenever they said Liverpool, I thought of a whole mound of bloodied liver, but then I would look down at my watch and be happy again and pretend to tell the time. The house was gloomy. I went off with Joe, who was mowing hay, and sat with him on the mowing machine and fell slightly in love. Indoors was worst, what with my grandmother sighing and recalling old times, such as when her husband tried to kill her with a carving knife, and then she would snivel and miss him and say, "The poor old creature, he wasn't prepared . . ."

Out in the fields Joe fondled my knee and asked was I ticklish. He had a lovely long face and a beautiful whistle. He was probably about twenty-four, but he seemed old, especially because of a slouchy hat and because of a pair of trousers that were several times too big for him. When the mare passed water he nudged me and said, "Want lemonade?" and when she broke wind he made disgraceful plopping sounds with his lips. He and I ate lunch on the headland and lolled for a bit. We had bread and butter, milk from a flask, and some ginger cake that was left over from the funeral. It had gone damp. He sang, "You'll be lonely, little sweetheart, in the spring," and smiled a lot at me, and I felt very privileged. I knew that all he would do was tickle my knees, and the backs of my knees, because at heart he was shy and not like some of the local men who would want to throw you to the ground and press themselves over you so that you would have to ask God for protection. When he lifted me onto the machine, he said that we would bring out a nice little cushion on the morrow so that I would have a soft seat. But on the morrow it rained and he went off to the sawmill to get shelving, and my aunt moaned about the hay getting wet and perhaps getting ruined and possibly there being no fodder for cattle next winter.

That day I got into dire disaster. I was out in the fields playing, talking, and enjoying the rainbows in the puddles, when all of a sudden I decided to run helter-skelter toward the house in case they were cross with me. Coming through a stile that led to the yard, I decided to do a big jump and landed head over heels in the manure heap. I fell so heavily onto it that every bit of clothing got wet and smeared. It was a very massive manure heap, and very squelchy. Each day the cow house was cleaned out and the contents shoveled there, and each week the straw and old nesting from the hen house were dumped there, and so was the pigs' bedding. So it was not like falling into a sack of hay. It was not dry and clean. It was a foul spot I fell into, and as soon as I waded out, I decided it was wise to undress. The pleated skirt was ruined and so was my blouse and my navy cardigan. Damp had gone through to my bodice, and the smell was dreadful. I was trying to wash it off under an outside tap, using a fist of grass as a cloth, when my aunt came out and exclaimed, "Jesus, Mary, and Joseph, glory be to the great God today and tonight, but what have you done to yourself!" I was afraid to tell her that I fell, so I said I was doing washing and she said in the name of God what washing, and then she saw the ruin on the garments. She picked up the skirt and said why on earth had she let me wear it that day, and wasn't it the demon that came with me the day I arrived with my attaché case. I was still trying to wash and not answer this barrage of questions, all beginning with the word "why." As if I knew why! She got a rag and some pumice stone, plus a can of water, and stripped to the skin, I was washed and reprimanded. Then my clothes were put to soak in the can, all except for the skirt, which had to be brought in to dry, and then cleaned with a clothes brush. Mercifully my grandmother was not told.

My aunt forgave me two nights later when she was in the dairy churning and singing. I asked if I could turn the churn handle for a jiff. It was changing from liquid to solid and the handle was becoming stiff. I tried with all my might, but I was not strong enough.

"You will, when you're big," she said, and sang to me. She sang "Far Away in Australia" and then asked what I would like to do when I grew up. I said I would like to marry Carnero, and she laughed and said what a lovely thing it was to be young and carefree. She let me look into the churn to see the mound of yellow butter that had formed. There were drops of water all over its surface, it was like some big bulk that had bathed but had not dried off. She got two sets of wooden pats, and together we began to fashion the butter into dainty shapes. She was quicker at it than I. She made little round balls of butter with prickly surfaces, then she said wouldn't it be lovely if the curate came up for tea. He was a new curate and had rimless spectacles.

The next day she went to the town to sell the butter and I was left to mind the house along with my grandmother. My aunt had promised to bring back a shop cake, and said that, depending on the price, it would be either a sponge cake or an Oxford Lunch, which was a type of fruit cake wrapped in beautiful dun silverish paper. My grandmother donned a big straw hat with a chin strap and looked very distracted. She kept thinking that there was a car or a cart coming into the back yard and had me looking out windows on the alert. Then she got a flush and I had to conduct her into the plantation and sit on the bench next to her, and we were scarcely there when three huge fellows walked in and we knew at once that they were tinkers. The fear is indescribable. I knew that tinkers took one off in their cart, hid one under shawls, and did dire things to one. I knew that they beat their wives and children, got drunk, had fights among themselves, and spent many a night cooling off in the barracks. I jumped up as they came through the gate. My grandmother's mouth fell wide open with shock. One of them carried a shears and the other had a weighing pan in his hand. They asked if we had any sheep's wool and we both said no, no sheep, only cattle. They had evil eyes and gamey looks. There was no knowing what they would do to us. Then they asked if we had any feathers for pillows or mattresses. She was so crazed with fear that she said yes and led the way to the house. As we walked along, I expected a strong hand to be clamped on my shoulder. They were dreadfully silent. Only one had spoken and he had a shocking accent, what my mother would call "a gurrier's." She sent me upstairs to get the two bags of feathers out of the wardrobe, and I knew that she stayed below so that they would not steal a cake or bread or crockery or any other things. She was agreeing on a price when I came down, or rather, requesting a price. The talking member said it was a barter job. We would get a lace cloth in return. She asked how big this cloth was, and he said very big, while his companion put his hand into the bag of feathers to make sure that there was not anything else in there, that we were not trying to fob them off with grass or sawdust or something. She asked where was the cloth. They laughed. They said it was down in the caravan, at the crossroads, ma'am. She knew then she was being cheated, but she tried to stand her ground. She grabbed one end of the bag and said, "You'll not have these."

"D'you think we're mugs?" one of them said, and gestured to the others to pick up the two bags, which they did. Then they looked at us as if they might mutilate us, and I prayed to St. Jude and St. Anthony to keep us from harm. Before going, they insisted on being given new milk. They drank in great slugs.

"Are you afraid of me?" one of the men said to her.

He was the tallest of the three and his shirt was open. I could see the hair on his chest, and he had a very funny look in his eyes as if he was not thinking, as if thinking was beyond him. His eyes had a thickness in them. For some reason he reminded me of meat.

"Why should I be afraid of you," she said, and I was so proud of her I would have clapped, but for the tight shave we were in.

She blessed herself several times when they'd gone and decided that what we did had been the practical thing to do, and in fact our only recourse. But when my aunt came back and began an intensive cross-examination, the main contention was how they learned in the first place that there were feathers in the house. My aunt reasoned that they could not have known unless they had been told, they were not fortune-tellers. Each time I was asked, I would seal my lips, as I did not want to betray my grandmother. Each time she was asked, she described them in detail, the holes in their clothes, the safety pins instead of buttons, their villainous looks, and then she mentioned the child, me, and hinted about the things they might have done and was it not the blessing of God that we had got rid of them peaceably! My aunt's son joked about the lace cloth for weeks. He used to affect to admire it, by picking up one end of the black oilcloth on the table and saying, "Is it Brussels lace or is it Carrickmackross?"

Sunday came and my mother was expected to visit. My aunt had washed me the night before in an aluminum pan. I had to sit in it, and was terrified lest my cousin should peep in. He was in the back kitchen shaving and whistling. It was a question of a "Saturday splash for Sunday's dash." My aunt poured a can of water over my head and down my back. It was scalding hot. Then she poured rainwater over me and by contrast it was freezing. She was not a thorough washer like my mother, but all the time she kept saying that I would be like a new pin.

My mother was not expected until the afternoon. We had washed up the dinner things and given the dogs the potato skins and milk when I started in earnest to look out for her. I went to the gate where I had waited for Carnero, and seeing no sign of her, I sauntered off down the road. I was at the crossroads when I realized how dangerous it was, as I was approaching the spot where the tinkers said their caravan was pitched. So it was back at full speed. The fuchsia was out and so were the elderberries. The fuchsia was like dangling earrings and the riper elderberries were in maroon smudges on the road. I waited in hiding, the better to surprise her. She never came. It was five, and then half past five, and then it was six. I would go back to the kitchen and lift the clock that was face down on the dresser, and then hurry out to my watch post. By seven it was certain that she would not come, although I still held out hope. They hated to see me sniffle, and even hated more when I refused a slice of cake. I could not bear to eat. Might she still come? They said there was no point in my being so spoiled. I was imprisoned at the kitchen table in front of this slice of seed cake. In my mind I lifted the gate hasp a thousand times and saw my mother pass by the kitchen window, as fleeting as a ghost; and by the time we all knelt down to say the Rosary, my imagination had run amuck. I conceived of the worst things, such as she had died, or that my father had killed her, or that she had met a man and eloped. All three were unbearable. In bed I sobbed and chewed on the blanket so as not to be heard, and between tears and with my aunt enjoining me to dry up, I hatched a plan.

On the morrow there was no word or no letter, so I decided to run away. I packed a little satchel with bread, my comb, and, daftly, a spare pair of ankle socks. I told my aunt that I was going on a picnic and affected to be very happy by humming and doing little reels. It was a dry day and the dust rose in whirls under my feet. The dogs followed and I had immense trouble getting them to go back. There were no tinkers' caravans at the crossroads and because of that I was jubilant. I walked and then ran, and then I would have to slow down, and always when I slowed down, I looked back in case someone was following me. While I was running I felt I could elude them, but there was no eluding the loose stones and the bits of rock that were wedged into the dirt road. Twice I tripped. If, coming toward me, I saw two people together, I then felt safe, but if I saw one person it boded ill, as that one person could be mad, or drunk, or likely to accost. On three occasions I had to climb into a field and hide until that one ominous person went by. Fortunately, it was a quiet road, as not many souls lived in that region.

When I came off the dirt road onto the main road, I felt safer, and very soon a man came by in a pony and trap and offered me a lift. He looked a harmless enough person, in a frieze coat and a cloth cap. When I stepped into the trap I was surprised to find two hens clucking and agitating under a seat.

"Would you be one of the Linihans?" he asked, referring to my grandmother's family.

I said no and gave an assumed name. He plied me with questions. To get the most out of me, he even got the pony to slow down, so as to lengthen the journey. We dawdled. The seat of black leather was held down with black buttons. He had a tartan rug over him. He spread it out over us both. Quickly I edged out from under it, complaining about fleas and midges, neither of which there were. It was a desperately lonely road with only a house here and there, a graveyard, and sometimes an orchard. The apples looked tempting on the trees. To see each ripening apple was to see a miracle. He asked if I believed in ghosts and told me that he had seen the riderless horse on the moors.

"If you're a Minnogue," he said, "you should be getting out here," and he pulled on the reins.

I had called myself a Minnogue because I knew a girl of that name who lived with her mother and was separated from her father. I would like to have been her.

"I'm not," I said, and tried to be as innocent as possible. I then had to say who I was, and ask if he would drop me in the village.

"I'm passing your gate," he said, and I was terrified that I would have to ask him up, as my mother dreaded strangers, even dreaded visitors, since these diversions usually gave my father the inclination to drink, and once he drank he was on a drinking bout that would last for weeks, and that was notorious. Therefore I had to conjure up another lie. It was that my parents were both staying with my grandmother and that I had been dispatched home to get a change of clothing for us all. He grumbled at not coming up to our house, but I jumped out of the trap and said we would ask him to a card party for sure, in December.

There was no one at home. The door was locked and the big key in its customary place under the pantry window. The kitchen bore signs of my mother having gone out in a hurry, as the dishes were on the table, and on the table, too, were her powder puff, a near-empty powder box, and a holder of papier-mâché in which her toiletries were kept. Had she gone to the city? My heart was wild with envy. Why had she gone without me? I called upstairs, and then hearing no reply, I went up with a mind that was buzzing with fear, rage, suspicion, and envy. The beds were made. The rooms seemed vast and awesome compared with the little crammed rooms of my grandmother's. I heard someone in the kitchen and hurried down with renewed palpitations. It was my mother. She had been to the shop and got some chocolate. It was rationed because of its being wartime, but she used to coax the shopkeeper to give her some. He was a bachelor. He liked her. Maybe that was why she had put powder on.

"Who brought you home, my lady?" she said stiffly.

She hadn't come on Sunday. I blurted that out. She said did anyone ever hear such nonsense. She said did I not know that I was to stay there until the end of August till school began. She was even more irate when she heard that I had run away. What would they now be thinking but that I was in a bog hole or something. She said had I no consideration and how in heaven's name was she going to get word to them, an SOS.

"Where's my father?" I asked.

"Saving hay," she said.

I gathered the cups off the table so as to make myself useful in her eyes. Seeing the state of my canvas shoes and the marks on the ankle socks, she asked had I come through a river or what. All I wanted to know was why she had not come on Sunday as promised. The bicycle got punctured, she said, and then asked did I think that with bunions, corns, and welts she could walk six miles after doing a day's work. All I thought was that the homecoming was not nearly as tender as I hoped it would be, and there was no embrace and no reunion. She filled the kettle and I laid clean cups. I tried to be civil, to contain the pique and misery that was welling up in me. I told her how many trams of hay they had made in her mother's house, and she said it was a sight more than we had done. She hauled some scones from a colander in the cupboard and told me I had better eat. She did not heat them on the top of the oven, and that meant she was still vexed. I knew that before nightfall she would melt, but where is the use of a thing that comes too late?

I sat at the far end of the table watching the lines on her brow, watching the puckering, as she wrote a letter to my aunt explaining that I had come home. I would have to give it to the mail-car man the following morning and ask the postman to deliver it by hand. She said, God only knows what commotion there would be all that day and into the night looking for me. The ink in her pen gave out, and I held the near-empty ink bottle sideways while she refilled it.

"Go back to your place," she said, and I went back to the far end of the table like someone glued to her post. I thought of fields around my grandmother's house and the various smooth stones that I had put on the windowsill, I thought of the sun garden, of the night my grandfather had died and my vigil in the cold parlor. I thought of many things. Sitting there, I wanted both to be in our house and to be back in my grandmother's missing my mother. It was as if I could taste my pain better away from her, the excruciating pain that told me how much I loved her. I thought how much I needed to be without her so that I could think of her, dwell on her, and fashion her into the perfect person that she clearly was not. I resolved that for certain I would grow up and one day go away. It was a sweet thought, and it was packed with punishment.

Tough Men

"Throw more paraffin in it," Morgan said as he went out to the shop to serve Mrs. Gleeson for the sixth time that morning. Hickey threw paraffin and a fist of matches onto the gray cinders, then put the top back on the stove quickly in case the flames leaped into his face. The skewers of curled-up bills on the shelf overhead were scorched, having almost caught fire many a time before. It was a small office, partitioned off from the shop, where Morgan did his accounts and kept himself warm in the winter. A cozy place with two chairs, a sloping wooden desk, and ledgers going back so far that most of the names entered in the early ones were the names of dead people. There was a safe as well, and everything had the air of being undisturbed, because the ashes and dust had congealed evenly on things. It was called The Snug.

"Bloody nuisance, that Gleeson woman," Morgan said as he came in from the counter and touched the top of the iron stove to see if it was warming up.

"She doesn't do a tap of work; hubby over in England earning money, all the young ones out stealing firewood and milk, and anything else they can lay hands on," Hickey said.

Mrs. Gleeson was an inquisitive woman, always dressed in black, with a black kerchief over her head and a white, miserable, nosy face.

"We'll need to get a good fire up," Morgan said. "That's one thing we'll need," and he popped a new candle into the stove to get it going. He swore by candle grease and paraffin for lighting fires, and neither cost him anything, because he sold them, along with every other commodity that country people needed—tea, flour, hen food, hardware, Wellington boots, and gaberdine coats. In the summer he hung the coats outside the door on a window ledge, and once a coat had fallen into a puddle. He offered it to Hickey cheap, but was rejected.

"Will they miss you?" Morgan said.

"Miss, my eye! Isn't poor man in bed with hot-water bottles and Sloan's liniment all over Christmas, and she's so murdered minding him, she doesn't know what time of day it is."

"Poor man" was Hickey's name for his boss, Mr. James Brady, a gentleman farmer who was given to drink, rheumatic aches, and a scalding temper.

"Say the separating machine got banjaxed up at the creamery," Morgan said.

"Of course," said Hickey, as if any fool would know enough to say that. It was simple; Hickey had been to the creamery with Brady's milk, and when he got home he could say he had been held up because a machine broke down.

"Of course I'll tell them that," he said again, and winked at Morgan. They were having an important caller that morning and a lot of strategy was required. Morgan opened the lower flap door of the stove and a clutter of ashes fell onto his boots. The grating was choked with ashes too, and Hickey began to clean it out with a stick, so that they could at least make the place presentable. Then he rooted in the turf basket, and finding two logs, he popped them in and emptied whatever shavings and turf dust were in the basket over them.

"That stove must be thirty years old," Morgan said, remembering how he used to light it with balls of paper and dry sticks when he first came to work in the shop as an apprentice. He lit it all the years he served his time and he still lit it when he began to get wise to fiddling money and giving short weight. That was when he was saving to buy the shop from the mean blackguard who owned it. He even lit it when he hired the new shopgirl, because she was useless at it. She had chilblains and hence wore a dress down to her ankles, and he pitied her for her foolishness. Finally he married her. Now he had a shopboy who usually lit the stove for him.

"His nibs is off again today," he said to Hickey, remembering the squint-eyed shopboy whom he hired but did not trust.

"He'd stay at home with a gumboil, he would," Hickey said, though neither of them objected very much, as they needed the privacy. Also, business was slack just after Christmas.

"If this thing comes off we'll go to the dogs, Fridays and Saturdays," Morgan said.

"Shanks' mare?" Hickey asked with a grin.

"We'll hire a car," Morgan said, and the dreams of these pleasant outings began to buoy him up and make him smile in anticipation. He liked the dogs and already envisaged the crowds, the excitement, the tote board, the tracks artificially lit up, and the six or seven sleek hounds following the hare with such grace as if it were wind and not their own legs that propelled them.

"Let's do our sums," he said, and together Hickey and himself counted the number of big farmers who had hay sheds. Not having been up the country for many a day, Morgan was, as he admitted, hazy about who lived beyond the chapel road, or up the commons, or down the Coolnahilla way and in the byroads and over the hills. In this Hickey was fluent because he did a bit of shooting on Sundays and had walked those godforsaken spots. They counted the farmers and hence the number of hay sheds, and their eyes shone with cupidity and glee. The stranger who was coming to see them had patented a marvelous stuff that, when sprayed on hay sheds, prevented rusting. Morgan was hoping to be given the franchise for the whole damn parish.

"Jaysus, there must be a hundred hay sheds," Hickey said, and marveled at Morgan's good luck at meeting a man who put him on to such a windfall.

" 'Twas pure fluke," Morgan said, and recalled the holiday he took at the spa town and how one day when he was trying to down this horrible sulphur water a man sat next to him and asked him where he was from, and eventually he heard about this substance that was a godsend to farmers.

"Pure fluke," he said again, and lifted the whiskey bottle from its hiding place, behind a holy picture which was laid against the wall. He took a quick slug.

"I think that's him," Hickey said, buttoning his waistcoat so as not to seem like a barbarian. In fact, it was John Ryan, a medical student, who had been asked not for reasons of his education but because he had a bit of pull. He tiptoed toward the entrance and from the outside played on the frosted glass as if it were a piano.

"Come in," said Morgan.

He knew it was John Ryan by the shape of the long eejitty fingers. Ryan was briefed to tell them if any other shopkeepers up the street had been approached by the bloke. Being home on holidays, Ryan did nothing but hatch in houses, drink tea, and click girls in the evening.

"All set," said Ryan as he looked at the two men and the saucepan waiting on the stove. Morgan had decided that they would do a bit of cooking, having reasoned that if a man came all that way, a bit of grub would not go amiss. Hickey, who couldn't even go to the creamery without bringing a large agricultural sandwich in his pocket, declared that no man does good business on an empty stomach. The man was from the North of Ireland.

"Is the bird on yet?" said John Ryan, splaying his hands fanwise to get a bit of heat from the stove.

"We haven't got her yet," said Hickey, and Morgan cursed aloud the farmer that had promised him a cockerel.

"Get us a few logs while you're standing," Morgan said, and John Ryan reluctantly went out. At the back of the shop by a mossy wall he gathered a bundle of damp, roughly sawn logs. He was in dread that he would stain the new fawn Crombie coat that his mother had given him at Christmas.

"Any sign of anyone?" Morgan said. It was important that the man with the chicken got to them before the stranger.

"Not a soul," John Ryan said.

"Bloody clown," Morgan said, and he went to the door to see if there was a sound of a horse and cart. Hickey lifted the lid of the saucepan to show Ryan the little onions that were in it simmering. He had peeled them earlier at the outside tap and had cried buckets. It was a new saucepan that afterward would be cleaned and put back in stock.

"How's the ladies, John?" he asked. Ryan had a great name with ladies and wasn't a bad-looking fellow. He had a long face and a longish nose and a great crop of brown, thick, curly, oily hair. His eyes were a shade of green that Hickey had never seen on any other human being, only in a shade of darning wool.

"I bet you're clicking like mad," said Morgan, coming back to the snug. He wished that he was John Ryan's age and not a middle-aged married man with a flushed face and a rank liver.

"I get places," Ryan boasted, and gave a nervous laugh, because he remembered his date of the night before. He had arranged to meet a girl behind the shop, on the back road which led to the creamery, the same road where Hickey had the mare and cart tethered to a gate and where Morgan kept the logs in a stack against a wall under a tarpaulin. She'd cycled four miles to meet him because he was damned if he was going to put himself out for any girl. No sooner had she arrived than she asked him the time and said that she'd have to be thinking of getting back soon.

"Take off your scarf," he said. She was so muffled with scarf and gloves and things that he couldn't get near her.

"I'm fine this way," she said, standing with her bicycle between them. Half a dozen words were exchanged and she rode off again, making a date for the following Sunday night.

"So 'twas worthwhile," Morgan said, although he had no interest in women anymore. He knew well enough that nothing much went on between men and women. His own wife nearly drove him mad, sitting in front of the kitchen fire saying she could see faces in the flames and then getting up suddenly and running upstairs to see if there was a man under her bed. He had sent her to Lourdes the summer before to see if that would straighten her out, but she came back worse.

"Love, it's all bull . . ." he said. His wife had developed a craze for putting sugar and peaches into every bit of meat she cooked. Then she had a fegary to buy an egg timer. She played with the egg timer at night, turning it upside down and watching the passage of the sand as it flowed down into the underneath tube. Childish she was.

"I wish he'd come," Hickey said.

"Which of them?" said John Ryan.

"Long John with the chicken," said Hickey.

"He sent word yesterday that he'd be here this morning with my Christmas box," Morgan said.

" 'Twill be plucked and all?" John Ryan asked.

"Oh, ready for the oven," Morgan said. "Other years I brought it up home, but I don't want it dolled up with peaches and sugar and that nonsense."

"No man wants food ruined," said Hickey. He pitied Morgan with the wife he had. Everyone could see she was getting more peculiar, talking to herself as she rode on her bicycle to Mass and hiding behind walls if she saw a man coming.

They heard footsteps in the shop, and Ryan opened the door a crack to see who it was.

"Is it him?"

"No, it's a young Gleeson one."

"She can wait," Morgan said, making no effort to get up. He was damned if he'd weigh three pennies' worth of sugar on a cold day like this. The child tapped the counter with a coin, then began to cough to let them know she was there, and finally she hummed a song. In the end she had to go away unserved.

"In a month from now you'll be well away," Hickey said.

"It's not a dead cert," Morgan said. He had to keep some curb on his dreams, because more than once he or his wife had had a promise of a legacy and were diddled out of it. Yet inwardly his spirits were soaring and made better each minute by the great draughts of whiskey which he took from the bottle. The other two men drank from mugs. In that way he was able to ration them a bit.

He had to go out to the shop for the next customer because it was the schoolteacher's maid, and they gave him quite a bit of trade. She wanted particular toilet rolls for her mistress, but he had none.

"Will you order them?" the maid said, and Morgan made a great to-do about entering the request in the day book. Afterward the three men had a great laugh and Morgan said it wasn't so long ago since the teacher had to use grass, but now that she was taking a correspondence course in Latin, there was no stopping of her and her airs.

"And do you know," said Hickey, although he'd probably told them before a hundred times, "she cancels the paper if she's going away for a day, what do you think of that for meanness, a twopenny paper?"

"There he is!" said Hickey suddenly. They heard a cart being drawn up outside and a mare whinny. Hickey knew that mare belonged to Long John Salmon, because like her owner, she went berserk when she got into civilized surroundings.

"Now," said Morgan, raising his short, fat finger in warning. "Sit tight and don't let neither of you stir or he'll be in here boring us about that dead brother of his."

Morgan went out to the shop, shook hands with Long John Salmon, and wished him a Happy New Year. He was relieved to see that Long John had a rush basket under his arm, which no doubt contained the cockerel. They talked about the weather, both uttering the usual rigmarole about how bad it had been. Patches of snow still lodged in the hollows of the field across the road from the shop. The shop was situated between two villages and looked out on a big empty field with a low stone wall surrounding it. Long John said that the black frost was appalling, which was why he had to come at a snail's pace in case the mare slipped. Long John said that Christmas had been quieter than usual and Morgan agreed, though as far as he could remember, Christmas Day was always the most boring day in his married life; the pubs were closed and he was alone with his missus from Mass time until bedtime. This year, of course, she had added peaches and sugar to the turkey, so there wasn't even that to enjoy.

"I had a swim Christmas Day," Long John said. He believed in a daily swim, and flowers of sulphur on Saturdays to purify the blood.

"We had a goose but no plum pudding," Long John added, giving Morgan the cue to hand him a small plum pudding wrapped in red glassette paper.

"Your Christmas box," Morgan said, hoping to God Long John

would hand him the chicken and get it over with. He could hear the men murmuring inside.

"Do you eat honey?" Long John asked.

"No," said Morgan in a testy voice. He knew that Long John kept bees and had a crooked inked sign on his gate which said HONEY FOR SALE.

"No wonder you have no children," said Long John with a grin.

Morgan was tempted to turn on him for a remark like that. He had no children, not because he didn't eat honey, but because Mrs. Morgan screamed the night of their honeymoon and screamed ever after when he went near her. Finally they got separate rooms.

"Well, here's a jar," said Long John, handing over a jar of honey that looked like white wax.

"That's too good altogether," said Morgan, livid with rage in case Long John was trying to do it cheap this Christmas.

"Christ Almighty," Hickey muttered inside. "If he doesn't hand over a chicken, I'll go out the country to his place and flog a goose."

As if prompted, Long John then did it. He handed over the chicken wrapped in newspaper, ordered some meal stuffs, and said he was on his way to the forge to get the mare's shoes off.

"I'll have it all ready for you," said Morgan, almost running from the counter.

"You'd think it was a boar he was giving away," said Hickey as Morgan came in and unwrapped the chicken.

"Don't talk to me," said Morgan, "get it on."

The water had boiled away, so John Ryan had to run in his patent-leather shoes to the pump, which was about a hundred yards up the road. He thought to himself that when he was a qualified doctor he'd run errands for no one, and Hickey and Morgan would be tipping their hats to him.

"It's a nice bird," said Hickey, feeling the breast, "but you'd think he'd wrap it in butter paper."

"Oh, a mountainy man," said Morgan. "What can you expect from a mountainy man."

They put the chicken in and added lashings of salt. In twenty minutes or so it began to simmer and Morgan timed it on his pocket watch. Later Hickey put a few cubes of Oxo in the water to flavor the soup. Morgan was demented from explaining to customers that all he was cooking was a sheep's head for a dog. Hickey and John Ryan sat tight in the snug and smoked ten cigarettes apiece. Hickey got it out of John Ryan that the girl of the night before was a waste of time. He liked knowing these things, because although he did not have many dates with girls, he liked to be sure that a girl was amenable.

"I didn't get within a mile of her," John Ryan said, and regretted telling it two seconds later. He had his name to keep up and most of the local men thought that, because of being a medical student, he did extraordinary things with girls and took terrible risks.

"I didn't fancy her anyhow," John Ryan said, "I've had too many women lately, women have no shame in them nowadays."

"Ah, stop," said Hickey, hoping that John Ryan would tell him some juicy incidents about orgies in Dublin and streetwalkers who wore nothing under their dresses. At that moment Morgan came in from the shop and said they ought to have a drop of the soup. He was getting irritable because he had been so busy at the counter, and the whiskey was going to his head and fuddling him.

"If I could begin my life again I'd be in the demolition business," Morgan said for no reason. He imagined that there must be great satisfaction in destroying houses and breaking up ornamental mantelpieces and smashing windows. He sometimes had a dream in which Mrs. Morgan lay under a load of mortar and white rubble, with her clothes well above her knees. Hickey got three new cups from the shop and lifted out the soup with one of them. By now the stove was so hot that dribbles of spilled soup sizzled on the black iron top. It was the finest soup any of them had ever tasted.

"Whoever comes in now can wait, 'cos I'm not budging," Morgan said as he sat on the principal chair and drank the soup noisily. It was at that very moment Hickey said, "Wisht," and a car was heard to pull up. The three of them were at the door instantly, and saw the rather battered V8 come to a halt close to the wall. The driver was a small butty fellow with red hair and a red beard.

"Oh, Red Hugh of the North," said Hickey, casting aspersions on the car and the rust on the radiator.

"I don't like his attire," said John Ryan.

The man wore no jacket but a grayish jersey that looked like a dishcloth, as it was full of holes.

"Shag his attire," said Morgan, and went forward to greet the stranger and apologize for the state of the weather. It had begun to rain, or rather to hail, and the snow in the field was being turned to slime. The stranger winked at the three of them and gave a little toss of the head to denote how sporting he was. He was by far the smallest of them. He spoke in the clipped accent of the North, and they could see at once that he was briary. He seemed to be looking at them severely, as if he was mentally assessing their characters.

"Matt O'Meara's the name," he said, shaking hands with Morgan but merely nodding to the others. In the snug he was handed a large whiskey without being asked whether he was teetotal or not. He made them uneasy with his silence and his staring blue eyes.

"Knock that back," Morgan said, "and then we'll talk turkey."

He winked at John Ryan. Ryan was briefed to open the proceedings by telling the fellow how rain played havoc with every damned thing, even gates, and how one didn't know whether it was the oxygen or the hydrogen or some trace minerals that did such damage.

"You'd ask yourself what they add to the rain," Ryan said, and secretly congratulated himself for his erudition.

"Like what the priest said about the French cheese," said Hickey, but Morgan did not want Hickey to elaborate on that bloody story before they got things sorted out. It would have been better if Hickey had been given porter, because he had no head for spirits.

"Well, we have plenty of hay sheds," Morgan said, and the man smiled coldly as if that was a foregone conclusion.

"How many have you contracted?" the man asked. He showed no courtesy but, Morgan thought, business is business, and tolerated it.

"If we get the gentlemen farmers, the others will follow suit," Morgan said.

"How many gentlemen farmers are there?" the fellow asked, and by doing a quick count and with much interruption and counter-interruption from Ryan and Hickey, it was concluded that there were at least twenty gentlemen farmers. The man did his sums on the back of his hand with the stub of a pencil and said that that would yield a thousand pounds and stared icily at his future partners. Five hundred each. Morgan could not repress a smile, already in his mind he had reserved the hackney car for Friday and Saturday evenings. He asked if by any chance the man had brought a sample and was told no. There were dozens of hay sheds in the North where it had been used, and if Morgan wanted to go up there and vet them, he was quite welcome. This man had a very abrasive manner.

"If you want, I can go elsewhere," he said.

Hickey saw that the fellow could become obstreperous, and sensing a rift, he said that if they were going to be partners they must all shake on it, and they did.

"Comrades," said the fellow, much to their astonishment. They abhorred that word. Stalin used that word and a woman in South America called Eva Perón. It was the moment for Morgan to remind Hickey to produce the eats, as their visitor must be starving. Hickey sharpened his knife, drew up his sleeves, and began to carve like an expert. He resolved to give Ryan and the visitor a leg each and keep the breast for himself and Morgan. Up at Brady's, where he had worked for seventeen years, he had never tasted a bit of the breast. She always gave it to her husband, even though he drank acres of arable land away, threatened to kill her more than once, and indeed might have, only that he, Hickey, had intervened and swiped the revolver or pitchfork or whatever weapon Brady had to hand. The stranger, deferring food, began to ask a few practical questions, such as where they would get lodging, whose hay shed they ought to do first, and where he could store the ladders and various equipment if they came on Sunday. The plan was that he and his two men would arrive at the weekend and start on Monday. Morgan said he would get them fixed up in digs, and it was agreed that, pest though she was, Mrs. Gleeson wasn't such a bad landlady, being liberal with tea and cake at any hour. The stranger then inquired about the fishing and set Hickey off on a rigmarole about eels.

"We'll take you on the lake when the May fly is up," Morgan said, and boasted about his boat, which was moored down at the pier.

"There is one thing," said the stranger. "It's the deposit." He smiled as he said this and pursed his lips.

Morgan, who had been extremely cordial up to then, looked sour and stared at the newcomer with disbelief. "Do you think I came up the river on a bicycle?"

"I don't," said the stranger, "but do *you* think I came up the river on a bicycle?" and then very matter-of-factly he explained that three men, the lorry, the gallons of the expensive stuff and equipment had to be carted from the North. He then reminded them that farmers all over Ireland were crying out for his services. A brazen fellow he was. "I want a hundred pounds," he said.

"That's a fortune," said Hickey.

"I'll give you fifty," said Morgan flatly, only to be told that it wasn't worth a tinker's curse, that if Morgan & Co. preferred, he would gladly take his business elsewhere. Morgan saw that he had no alternative, so he slowly moved to the safe and undid the creaky brass catch.

"That needs oiling," said Hickey pointlessly. The place seethed with tension and bad feeling.

The money was in small brown envelopes, and the notes were kept together with rubber bands, some of them shredding. Morgan did not go to the bank often, as it only gave people the wrong idea. He did not even like this villain watching him as he parted them and counted.

The man did not seem either embarrassed or exhilarated at receiving the money; he simply made a poor joke about its being dirty. He confirmed the arrangements and said to make only two appointments for the first week in case the weather was bad or there was any other hitch. He put the money into an old mottled wallet and said he'd be off. Despite the fact that Morgan had provided eats, he did not press the fellow to stay. He did not like him. They'd have a better time of it themselves, so he was quite pleased to mouth formalities and shake hands coldly with the blackguard.

Once he had gone, they fled to the snug to devour their dinner and discuss him. John Ryan took an optimistic view, pointing out that he did not want to slinge and was therefore a solid worker. Hickey said that for a small butty he wasn't afraid to stand up to people, but that wasn't it significant that he hadn't cracked a joke. Hickey could see that Morgan was a bit on edge, so he thought to bolster him.

"Anyhow, he'll bring in the spondulicks," and he reminded Morgan to make a note of the fact that he had paid him a hundred pounds, as if Morgan could forget. Morgan dipped the plain pen in the bottle of ink and asked aloud what date it was, though he knew it already.

No sooner had they sat down to eat than John Ryan started sniffing. Every forkful was put to his nose before being consigned to his mouth. Hickey commented on this and on the fact that John Ryan wouldn't eat a shop egg if you paid him.

"It doesn't smell right," John Ryan said.

"God's sake, it's the tastiest chicken I ever ate," Hickey said.

"First class, first class," Morgan said, though he didn't fancy it that much. That blackguard had depressed him and hadn't given him any sense of comradeship, but hoofed it soon as he got the hundred pounds. Had the others not been there, Morgan would have haggled, and he resolved in future to do business alone.

"Are you in, Morgan?" They heard Long John Salmon call from the shop, and sullenly Morgan got up and put his plate of dinner on top of the stove.

"Coming," he said as he wiped his mouth.

Out in the shop he asked Long John if he had any other calls to do, because business had been so brisk he hadn't got around to weighing the meal stuff.

"Nicest chicken I ever had," he then said, humoring Long John.

"They're a good table fowl, the Rhode Islands," said Long John.

"They are," said Morgan, "they're the best."

"If I'd known you were eating it so soon, I'd have got it all ready for you," said Long John.

"It *was* ready, hadn't a thing to do only put it in the pot with some onions and salt, and Bob's your uncle."

" 'Twasn't cleaned," said Long John Salmon.

"What?" said Morgan, not fully understanding.

"Christ, that's what it is," said John Ryan, dropping his plate and making one leap out of the snug and through the shop, around to the back where he could be sick.

"He's in a hurry," said Long John as he saw Ryan go out with his hand clapped across his mouth.

"You mean it wasn't drawn," said Morgan, and he felt queasy. Then he remembered being in Long John's farmyard and he writhed as he contemplated the muck of the place. Sorrows never come in single file. At that moment Guard Tighe came into the shop in uniform, looking agitated.

"Was there a bloke here about spraying hay sheds?" he asked.

"What business is it of yours," Morgan said.

Morgan was thinking that Tighe was nosy and probably wanted the franchise for his wife's people, who had a hardware shop up the street.

"Was he or wasn't he?"

"He was here," said Morgan, and he was on the point of boasting of his new enterprise when the guard forestalled him.

"He's a bounder," he said. "He's going all over the country bamboozling people."

"How do you know that?" Morgan said.

Hickey had come from inside the snug, wild with curiosity.

"I know it because the man who invented the damn stuff got in touch with us, warning us about this bounder, this pretender."

"Jaysus," said Morgan. "Why didn't you tell me sooner."

"We're a guard short," said Tighe, and at that instant Morgan hit the counter with his fist and kept hitting it so that billheads and paper bags flew about.

"You're supposed to protect citizens," he said.

"You didn't give him any money?" said the guard.

"Only *one hundred pounds,*" said Morgan with vehemence, as if the guard were the cause of it all, instead of his own importunity. The guard then asked particulars of the car, the license plate, the man's appearance, dismissing the man's name as fictitious. When the guard asked if the man's beard looked to be dyed, Morgan lost his temper completely and called upon his Maker to wreak vengeance on embezzlers, chancers, bounders, thieves, layabouts, liars, and the Garda Siotchana.

"Christ, I didn't even give myself a Christmas box," Morgan said, and Hickey, sensing that worse was to follow, picked up his cap and said it was heinous, heinous altogether. Outside, he found Ryan, white as a sheet, over near the wall where the mare and cart were tethered.

"Red Hugh of the North was a bounder," he said.

"I don't care what he was," said Ryan, predicting his own demise.

"You're very chicken," said Hickey, thrilled at making such an apt joke.

"If you had stayed inside I was all right," said Ryan, as he commenced to retch again. Hickey looked up and saw that Mrs. Gleeson was crouched behind the other side of the wall observing. In her black garb she looked like a witch. She'd tell the whole country.

"She'll tell my mother," said Ryan, and drew his coat collar up around him to try and disguise his appearance.

"Good, good Bess," Hickey said to the mare as he unknotted the reins. Morgan had come out and like a lunatic was waving his arms in all directions and calling for action. Hickey was damned if he was going to stay for any postmortem. It was obvious that the whole thing was a swindle and the fellow was now in some smart hotel eating his fill or more likely heading for the boat to Holyhead. Exit the gangsters.

"Get rid of this bloody chicken," Morgan called.

"Add peaches to it," said Hickey.

"Come back," said Morgan. "Come back, you hooligan."

But Hickey had already set out and the mare was trotting at a merry pace, having been unaccountably idle for a couple of hours.

The Doll

Every Christmas there came a present of a doll from a lady I scarcely knew. She was a friend of my mother's, and though they only met rarely, or accidentally at a funeral, she kept up the miraculous habit of sending me a doll. It would come on the evening bus shortly before Christmas, and it added to the hectic glow of those days when everything was charged with bustle and excitement. We made potato stuffing, we made mince pies, we made bowls of trifle, we decorated the windowsills with holly and with tinsel, and it was as if untoward happiness was about to befall us.

Each year's doll seemed to be more beautiful, more bewitching, and more sumptuously clad than the previous year's. They were of both sexes. There was a jockey in bright red and saffron, there was a Dutch drummer boy in maroon velvet, there was a sleeping doll in a crinoline, a creature of such fragile beauty that I used to fear for her when my sisters picked her up clumsily or tried to make her flutter her eyelashes. Her eyes were suggestive of beads and small blue flowers, having the haunting color of one and the smooth glaze of the other. She was named Rosalind.

My sisters, of course, were jealous and riled against the unfairness of my getting a doll, whereas they only got the usual dull flannel sock with tiny things in it, necessary things such as pencils, copybooks, plus some toffees and a licorice pipe. Each of my dolls was given a name, and a place of rest, in a corner or on a whatnot, or in an empty biscuit tin, and each had special conversations allotted to them, special endearments, and if necessary special chastisements. They had special times for fresh air—a doll would be brought out and splayed on a windowsill, or sunk down in the high grass and apparently abandoned. I had no favorites until the seventh doll came, and she was to me the living representation of a princess. She too was a sleeping doll, but a sizable one, and she was dressed in a pale-blue dress, with a gauze overdress, a pale-blue bonnet, and white kid button shoes. My sisters—who were older—were as smitten with her as I. She was uncanny. We all agreed that she was almost lifelike and that with coaxing she might speak. Her flaxen hair was like a feather to finger, her little wrists moved on a swivel, her eyelashes were black and sleek and the gaze in her eyes so fetching that we often thought she was not an inanimate creature, that she had a soul and a sense of us. Conversations with her were the most intense and the most incriminating of all.

It so happened that the teacher at school harbored a dislike for me and this for unfathomable reasons. I loved lessons, was first with my homework, always early for class, then always lit the school fire, raked the ashes, and had a basket full of turf and wood when she arrived. In fact, my very diligence was what annoyed her and she would taunt me about it and proclaim what a "goody-goody" I was. She made jokes about my cardigan or my shoelaces or the slide in my hair, and to make the other girls laugh, she referred to me as "It." She would say, "It has a hole in its sock," or "It hasn't got a proper blazer," or "It has a daub on its copybook." I believe she hated me. If in an examination I came first—and I usually did—she would read out everyone's marks, leave mine until last, and say, "We know who swotted the most," as if I were in disgrace. If at cookery classes I made pancakes and offered her one, she would make a face as if I had offered her tripe or strychnine. She once got a big girl to give me fruit laxatives, pretending that they were sweets, and made great fun when I had to go in and out to the closets all day. It was a cruel cross to bear. When the inspector came and praised me, she said that I was brainy but that I lacked versatility. In direct contrast she was lovely to my sisters and would ask them occasionally how my mother was, and when was she going to send over a nice pot of homemade jam or a slab cake. I used to pray and make novenas that one day she would examine her conscience and think about how she wronged me and repent.

One day my prayers seemed on the point of being answered. It was November and already the girls were saving up for Christmas, and we knew that soon there would be the turkey market and soon after hams and candied peel in the grocery shop window. She said that since we'd all done so well in the catechism exam, she was going to get the infants to act in the school play and that we would build a crib and stack it with fresh hay and statues. Somebody said that my doll would make a most beautiful Virgin. Several girls had come home with me to see the doll and had been allowed to peep in at her in her box, which was lined with silver chaff. I brought her next day, and every head in the classroom craned as the teacher lifted the lid of the black lacquered box and looked in.

"She's passable," she said, and told one of the girls to put the doll in the cookery cupboard until such time as she was needed. I grieved at being parted from her, but I was proud of the fact that she would be in the school play and be the cynosure of all. I had made her a cloak, a flowing blue cloak with a sheath of net over it and a little diamante clasp. She was like a creature of moonlight, shimmering, even on dark wet days. The cookery cupboard was not a fit abode for her, but what could I do?

The play did not pass off without incident. The teacher's cousin Milo was drunk, belligerent, and offensive. He called girls up to the fire to pretend to talk to them and then touched the calves of their legs and tickled the backs of their knees. He called me up and asked would I click. He was an auctioneer from the city and unmarried. The teacher's two sons also came to look at the performance, but one of them left in the middle. He was strange and would laugh for no reason, and although over twenty he called the teacher "Mammy." He had very bright-red hair and a peculiar stare in his eyes. For the most part, the infants forgot their lines, lost their heads, and the prompter was always late, so that the wrong girls picked up her cues. She was behind a curtain but could be heard out on the street. The whole thing was a fiasco. My doll was the star of the occasion and everyone raved about her.

Afterward there was tea and scones, and the teacher talked to those few mothers who had come. My mother had not come because at that time she was unable to confront crowds and even dreaded going to Mass on Sundays, but believed that God would preserve her from the dizziness and suffocations that she was suffering from. After they had all left and a few of us had done the washing up, I went to the teacher and to my delight she gave me a wide genial smile. She thanked me for the doll, said that there was no denying but that the doll saved the play, and then, as I reached out, she staved my hand with a ruler and laughed heartily.

"You don't think I'm going to let you have her now, I've got quite fond of her . . . the little mite," she said, and gave the china cheek a tap. At home I was berserk. My mother said the teacher was probably teasing and that she would return the doll in a day or two. My father said that if she didn't she would have to answer to him, or else get a hammering. The days passed and the holidays came, and not only did she not give me my doll, but she took it to her own home and put it in the china cabinet along with cups and ornaments. Passing by their window, I would look in. I could not see her because the china cabinet was in a corner, but I knew where she was, as the maid Lizzie told me. I would press my forehead to the window and call to the doll and say that I was thinking of her and that rescue was being hatched.

Everyone agreed that it was monstrous, but no one talked to the teacher, no one tackled her. The truth is, they were afraid of her. She had a bitter tongue, and also, being superstitious, they felt that she could give us children brains or take them away, as a witch might. It was as if she could lift the brains out of us with a forceps and pickle them in brine. No one did anything, and in time I became reconciled to it. I asked once in a fit of bravura and the teacher said wasn't I becoming impudent. No longer did I halt to look in the window of her house but rather crossed the road, and I did not talk to Lizzie in case she should tell me something upsetting.

Once, I was sent to the teacher's house with a loin of pork and found her by the fire with her queer son, both of them with their stockings down, warming themselves. There were zigzags of heat on their shins. She asked if I wanted to go in and see the doll, but I declined. By then I was preparing to go away to boarding school and I knew that I would be free of her forever, that I would forget her, that I would forget the doll, forget most of what happened, or at least remember it without a quiver.

The years go by and everything and everyone gets replaced. Those we knew, though absent, are yet merged inextricably into new folk, so that each person is to us a sum of many others and the effect is of opening box after box in which the original is forever hidden.

The teacher dies a slow death, wastes to a thread through cancer, yet strives against it and says she is not ready. I hear the amount of money she left and her pitiable last words, but I feel nothing. I feel none of the rage and none of the despair. She does not matter to me anymore. I am on the run from them. I have fled. I live in a city. I am cosmopolitan. People come to my house, all sorts of people, and they do feats like dancing, or jesting, or singing, inventing a sort of private theater where we all play a part. I too play a part. My part is to receive them and disarm them, ply them with food and drink, and secretly be wary of them, be distanced from them. Like them I smile, and drift; like them I smoke or drink to induce a feverishness or a pleasant wandering hallucination. It was not something I cultivated. It developed of its own accord, like a spore that breathes in the darkness. So I am far from those I am with, and far from those I have left. At night I enjoy the farness. In the morning I touch a table or a teacup to make sure that it is a table or a teacup, and I talk to it, and I water the flowers and I talk to them, and I think how tender flowers are, and woods and woodsmoke and possibly how tender are my new friends, but that like me they are intent on concealment. None of us ever says where we come from or what haunts us. Perhaps we are bewildered or ashamed.

I go back. Duty hauls me back to see the remaining relatives, and I play the expected part. I had to call on the teacher's son. He was the undertaker and was in charge of my aunt's burial. I went to pay him, to "fix up," as it is called. His wife, whom I knew to be a bit scattered, admitted me amid peals of laughter. She said she always thought I had jet-black hair, as she ran down the hall calling his name. His name is Denis. He shakes hands with me very formally, asks what kind of wreath I want and if it should be heart-shaped, circular, or in the form of a cross. I leave it all to him. There in the overstuffed china cabinet is my confiscated doll, and if dolls can age, it certainly had. Gray and moldy, the dress and cloak are as a shroud, and I thought, If I was to pick her up she would disintegrate.

"God, my mother was fond of her," he said, as if he were trying to tell me that she had been fond of me, too. Had he said so, I might have challenged. I was older now and it was clear to me that she had kept the doll out of perversity, out of pique and jealousy. In some way she had divined that I would have a life far away from them and adventures such as she herself would never taste. Sensing my chill, he boasted that he had not let his own children play with the doll, thereby implying that she was a sacred object, a treasured souvenir. He hauled out a brandy bottle and winked, expecting me to say yes. I declined.

A sickness had come over me, a sort of nausea for having cared so much about the doll, for having let them maltreat me, and now for no longer caring at all. My abrupt departure puzzled him. He did something untoward. He tried to kiss me. He thought perhaps that in my world it was the expected thing. Except that the kiss was proffered as a sympathy kiss, a kiss of condolence over my aunt's death. His face had the sour smell of a towel that he must have dried himself on, just before he came to welcome me. The kiss was clumsiness personified. I pitied him, but I could not stay, and I could not reminisce, and I could not pretend to be the fast kiss-easy woman he imagined me to be.

Walking down the street, where I walk in memory, morning noon and night, I could not tell what it was, precisely, that reduced me to such wretchedness. Indeed, it was not death but rather the gnawing conviction of not having yet lived. All I could tell was that the stars were as singular and as wondrous as I remembered them and that they still seemed like a link, an enticement to the great heavens, and that one day I would reach them and be absorbed into their glory, and pass from a world that, at that moment, I found to be rife with cruelty and stupidity, a world that had forgotten how to give.

Tomorrow . . . I thought. Tomorrow I shall be gone, and realized that I had not lost the desire to escape or the strenuous habit of hoping.

The Bachelor

In the distance he was often mistaken for a priest, so solemn did he seem in his great long black overcoat and his black squashed hat. His face was grave, too, and very often he had a drip at the end of his pointed nose. It was unusual to see a grown man with tears in his eyes and this even when he told something lighthearted. The tears would start up in his eyes almost as soon as he began to talk, giving him a morose funereal look. He wore striped flannelette shirts and a tattered homespun jacket that he had once shared with his dead brother. When his brother was alive they had to attend Mass separately, as each wanted to be the proud wearer of the oatmeal jacket.

I used to catch fleas for him and keep them in a match box, and my reward was a penny and a glass of raspberry wine. Nothing can, or could, ever quell the thrill of seeing the thick red cordial in the bottom of a tumbler, and then the flurry as he shot out to the yard where the tap was, and then the leisurely joy of watching him dilute it, of watching its redness gradually pale and pale until it was a beautiful light aerated pink, and oh, for its taste, so sweet and so synthetic, that it even surpassed the joyous taste of warm, melting jelly. I don't know what he did with the fleas, but I know that my mother was incensed when she heard of it and forbade me to catch any more, deeming it a disgrace.

Jack owned a wine shop which he called a "taverna." It was dark and huge like a barracks, and even in the daytime, when it was devoid of customers, the air reeked with the smell of stale flat porter, just as the high oak counter had the circular marks of thousands of porter glasses laid down in different humors, in rage, in mirth, and quite often in insupportable melancholia. Jack did not do brisk business, but certain men went there when they wanted to drink quietly and purposefully, and at night a particular crowd went, preferring it to the neighboring bars because there was no woman to harangue them, or gossip, or tell the whole country how much they drank, or what they owed. Jack's sister, Maggie, was an invalid, and lived her days hunched over the kitchen fire, occasionally letting out a moan that sounded like a prayer and alerting him to the fact if a sod fell onto the floor or if she was in need of tea. My mother sometimes took pity on them and sent a gift of a cake, or black puddings, or a pot of marmalade in the spring, when the oranges came from Seville and the women vied with each other as to whose marmalade was the most tempting. Jack would hasten to our house and thank her with extravagant phrases, but suddenly unable to conquer his awkwardness, he would just lift his hat and run away. He loved my mother and used to stroll in our fields to catch sight of her. In the summer mornings on my way to school I would find him, as he said, penning a little ode. One morning, when the horse chestnut tree was in flower and the beautiful cream blooms hung like candles merely waiting to be lit, I came on him reciting excitedly. The brightness and the freshness of the morning, the rustle of the trees, birds scurrying about, and all of nature hell-bent on its bacchanalia must have fired him as greatly as did his secret passion, and all this despite the fact that he was a grown man who had probably never known a handclasp or certainly a kiss.

"Just penning a little poem," he said.

"What sort of poem?" I asked.

"Ah, you're too young to know," he said, and then inquired if my mother ever came down this far.

"Only to follow turkeys," I said, and he moved off, muttering to himself and smiling in a bemused way. I guessed that the poem was composed in Latin, which no one would be likely to read or translate, not even a clerical student, because Jack's Latin was a botch, gleaned partly from his missal and richly embellished. I could have told him that the written word did not move my mother, that she never read anything, only the price of eggs in the daily paper and the big, stained Mrs. Beeton cookery book. Moreover, she believed that books were sinful, that poetry was rubbish, and that such things helped to turn people's minds and deflect them from their true work. I did not tell him, though I do not know why, since it was my habit to blurt.

The following Sunday when I was going in to Mass, Jack grabbed my coat sleeve and whispered that he would call on us that night, as he had a surprise for me. On Sunday evenings my mother always used to soak her feet in hot water and washing soda and then pare her corns with my father's razor blade. It was a formidable and frightening sight. My father usually went to play cards, though it was something we could not afford, being heavily in debt. But after she had done her feet, she smiled a little and said, "To hell with it," she felt like dolling up. So seldom did she ever dress up that it was almost akin to a ceremony to follow her upstairs, go into the Blue Room, see her open the wardrobe and touch the few long dresses that despite their age and their musty smell still conjured up pictures of all-night dances, buffet suppers, music, and merriment. She put on her white georgette blouse, which had patches of vivid red flowers embroidered on the bodice, and a drawstring which could either be tied tightly or allowed to go slack. She did not tie the string very tightly and the effect was perfect: her pale neck, the white gauzy material, and the flowers so real that it seemed they might stir like flowers in a garden. Downstairs in the kitchen we lit the lamp, and her hair, which was red-brown, glinted as she proceeded to make sandwiches from the bacon left over from lunch. I thought then that when I grew up if I could be as fetching as my mother I would be certain to find happiness. For some reason I believed that the troubles of her life were an anomaly, and never did it occur to me that some of her fatality had already grafted itself onto me and determined my disposition.

"Is there company coming?" I asked.

"Hardly," she said, "I expect Jack was only raving."

Yet she showed no surprise when the familiar knock came on the back door, and she jumped to answer it. Jack came in, looked about, but would not take off his hat; he merely lifted it slightly to salute us. We felt sorry for him because he was ashamed of his bald scalp and people said that not one hair grew on it and that it was the color of putty. He took a tin from his pocket and handed it to me with a flourish. It had a picture of a couple in a jaunting car, and inside there were boiled sweets that had adhered together with dirt and dried sugar. Once one sucked them, they tasted of cloves, as they should. He sat down and gradually started to draw his chair nearer to my mother as he began to expound.

"Strange to say, Mrs. O., I was looking forward to my little expedition here, and unfortunately I was detained, a very irksome thing when one prides oneself on one's punctuality."

"It's early, Jack," my mother said flatly.

"The maternity nurse, Mrs. O. . . ."

On hearing this my mother made a face that conveyed her disgust. She had an idea that all nurses were crude, but the maternity nurse was the limit altogether, as she insisted on describing women's labors and the different ways their water broke.

"Trying to get yours truly into her clutches, Mrs. O.," he said, drawing his chair dangerously near. Their bodies were getting closer to each other, and I thought that if he moved again they would have to touch.

"Makes no secret of her intentions," he said, and then he whispered something which must have been wanton, because my mother writhed and put on her injured face.

"I like a woman to be a lady," he said, and he smiled at her in the most bashful but apparent way, and at that instant she jumped up and said she was dying for an apple. The tiled floor of the vestibule was covered with small wrinkled wine-colored apples and these gave a delicious smell to the whole house, and even the rotting ones made one long for stewed apple or a pie. She returned with a dishful of apples, and taking a small knife from the kitchen drawer, she peeled one and gave it to Jack, then she peeled another, and then she sat on the far side of the fire, a distance away from him.

"By the way, Mrs. O."—he paused as he munched—"there's a little gift awaiting you in my taverna. Drop in at your convenience."

"Oh, Jack, you're too good!" she said, and she beamed at him, and I was sure that now she was sorry for having rebuffed him earlier. As she stood up to make the tea, Jack got up too, dropped three apple pips down inside her low-cut blouse, and fled from the kitchen, muttering something about his sister's swooning fits.

"Can't you stay, Jack, and have a cup," she said, but he had already lifted the heavy latch and was gone. She sent me after him with the flashlamp. I saw his figure going down the field, but I didn't call after him, because I hated him using our cups and being so personal with my mother. It was dark and hushed outside, and I could hear the cows and the horses cropping the grass, and from the village came the strains of a piano accordion playing "Danny Boy." I was unsettled for some reason and went inside, followed by the three sheepdogs, who whined for bread and who would not leave the kitchen until they received a crust each.

"He's gone," I said.

"Creature," she said, "gone home to nothing, only tea and loaf bread and poor Maggie rambling."

"I wonder what's the present," I said.

"That's what I was wondering," she said, and I could see that she was intrigued.

"Would you prefer him to Dada?" I asked, and at that very moment my father came in. To my surprise Mama told him that he shouldn't have been so long and that she was bored to tears with Jack, who insisted on telling her smutty stories.

"Bloody clown, who asked him here anyhow," my father said, then shouted and stamped the floor with his boot, a thing he always did to give impetus to his bad temper. He was jealous. I saw it in his wild, unsatiated, protruding eyes, but I did not know what to call it then.

"I'll have that cold meat, I'm hungry," he said, peremptorily.

"I made sandwiches," she said placatingly.

"Damn your sandwiches, a man gets no satisfaction in this house," and suddenly he banged the table with his fist and sent the dish of apples flying.

"Get me my light shoes," he said to me, and I fetched them

from the shoe closet and threw them on the ground near where he stood. I thought I smelled whiskey and then put the thought aside as being just fear, imaginary fear, but Mama thought it too, and that night in bed we both prayed and cried, hoping that he would not go on a batter.

The next evening when I got home from school there was a note propped against the tea caddy to say that I was to keep a kettle boiling as she had gone down to Jack's to collect her gift. I sat by the window and watched for her, and when I saw the gleam of her bicycle coming in at the gate, I ran down the fields eager to know what she had been given, envisaging a georgette scarf or a beaded bag.

"You'll catch cold without a coat," she shouted from halfway up the field.

"What did you get?" I called.

When she was close to me I saw the disappointment. It was a packet of coffee beans and utterly useless, as we never drank coffee, and moreover, we had nothing to grind the beans with.

"You were ages," I said.

"I was looking at jewelry, gorgeous brooches belonging to Maggie, upstairs in a box."

"Were you upstairs?" I said. There was something untoward about that.

"Yes, and you should see the bedroom." She raised her eyes pitifully toward the sky, to emphasize the squalor.

"Bare boards and not a thing in his room, only an iron bed with his rosary beads hanging at the head of it and his good suit on a chair."

She seemed to be very disgruntled, and when we went in she threw the coffee beans into a holdall where we kept useless things, bottle tops, bits of used string, and a rusted can opener.

Two days later when I came home from school, there was a car outside our front door, and I quickened, thinking it was visitors. But as I approached the house I heard shouting and knew once again that we were in trouble.

"You poor child, you," my mother said, hugging me, and then

she told me that the bailiff was inside with my father and that unless we could find money we could be out on the roadside with the tinkers. At that moment the bailiff came into the kitchen and said he wanted a drink of water. He had a bad stomach and was obliged to take tablets every few hours. She offered him tea, which he declined, and he just stood there, frowning, as if he could not comprehend why people like us, with a nice house and furniture, had come to such desperately unhappy straits. She offered tea a second time, and I think he was annoyed that she should mix up hospitality with the odious business on hand. It was then he realized that I was there, and perhaps feeling sorry for me, he asked suddenly, "Who's the best at school?"

"I am," I said, not knowing that I was boasting.

Then the sergeant arrived and my mother begged him to go in and get the revolver from my father. All three of them went in. I looked through the jamb of the door and saw my father standing near the mantelpiece, the revolver in his hand, his hat thrown back on his head and his mouth frothing. It was like a man in a picture, depicting danger. They were trying to reason with him, and the more they tried, the more he foamed. Suddenly my mother left the room and said she would be back in a matter of minutes. She cycled down the drive at wizard speed and presently she was back, accompanied by Jack. She handed the bailiff a brown envelope containing a wad of money. Then the sergeant linked my father and helped him upstairs; though my father fell a few times, he never lost hold of the bottle of whiskey, which had a label with two shades of gold on it. After the sergeant left, Jack stayed with us and spoke about the vale of tears and life's tribulations. Then when my father was asleep, Jack took off his boots and stole upstairs to get the revolver from under the pillow. Also, he emptied most of the whiskey into a jug and filled the whiskey bottle with water. Mama put the retrieved whiskey into a lemonade bottle, saying she would keep it for the Christmas cake. The kitchen was foul with the smell.

"Well, Mrs. O., you know who your friends are, you can rely on Jack," and then he tied his boots and took his leave. Mama stood on the step with him and he said something her reply to which baffled me.

"How could I, Jack," she said pityingly, and then she came back into the kitchen and asked God Almighty what would become of us. She talked of my sisters and brother, who were at boarding school, and said with no money for fees they would no doubt be expelled and have to come home to rough it. I said that when I grew up I would be rich and that I would install us all in a big house where there would be no wrangling and no debt.

"You'll be lucky if you have any education," she said dolefully, and then conjectured about the impossibility of refunding Jack.

"He won't mind," I said, but she was not so sure about that. She said paupers were paupers and people soon wearied of them. The word "pauper" sounded so beautiful, like some kind of Indian flower or fruit. Later when we heard my father shout we ran out of the house and hid in a hollow behind some trees until he had gone. We well knew the pattern, which was that he would be missing for days, and eventually he would be taken to hospital and then he would come home and apologize for everything.

He came home about two weeks later and asked me to come and count his horses with him. I hated going. It had rained a lot and the fields had pools of water in which the clouds were reflected and kept appearing and disappearing. There were three horses and a young foal. I feared them as much as I feared him, because they too stood for unpredictability and massive jerky strength. As we went to the field they came toward us whinnying, and I kept lurking behind for shelter.

"They won't touch you, they won't touch you," he said as the horse kicked the ground with her hoof as if in a temper. First they galloped wildly, but after a bit they quieted down and nuzzled to see if he had brought any oats.

"I'm a good father, good to you and your mother."

You're not, I thought, but did not speak.

"Answer me," he said.

"Yes," I said grudgingly, and he went on to say that the reason for his recent little mishap was that he did not like the way Jack Holland was making free with my mother. He said it was a disgrace and that it would have to end. I said nothing. By now the horses on a whim had all decided to lie down in the pools of water and roll around, so that they became covered in mud, their haunches smeared. They hadn't seen a soul for two weeks and were probably complaining about this, by resorting to antics. Next day Mama wrote Jack a letter and marked it personal. She put SAG (St. Anthony Guide) on the back of the envelope and dispatched me with it. It was my first time in Jack's kitchen. It was a large kitchen with a stone floor and a great hearth fire. There was a smell of fried onions, wet turf, and old ashes. Maggie was dozing in a rocking chair by the fire and Jack was having a mug of tea at the kitchen table.

"Have a little repast," he said as I went in. To read the letter he had to borrow his sister's glasses, so he pulled them off her face and put them on his own. They were rimless glasses and made him look penurious. A few hens had come in from the yard and were picking at a colander in which there had been cold cabbage but was now almost picked clean. They were very intent on this. A sprig of faded palm was stuck beside the globe of the Sacred Heart lamp and I reckoned that it had been there since Palm Sunday. The willow-patterned plates that were wedged into the dresser badly needed a wash. I tried to find a disappointed look on his face as he read the letter, but there was none.

"Tell your mam that Jack understands all, and that Jack will wait for time's eventualities," and I said I would and ran out of the kitchen, because I had some idea that he was going to kiss me. After that he visited us rarely, and when he did he talked mostly to Dada. But often when I was on the way from school he called me by rapping the windows with his knuckles.

"How's your mam?"

"She's well."

Even when she wasn't, I said it out of deference. Then he'd put two bars of chocolate in an envelope and send them to her.

I was twelve when Maggie died; we all sat in the parlor, and the ladies drank port wine and nibbled marietta biscuits. Jack looked sad, a drip on his nose and a black diamond of cloth on the sleeve of his brown jacket. The maternity nurse had sewed it on for him.

"Creature."

"How many years is it in all since she got crippled?"

"She was lucky to have Jack."

"She's gone straight to heaven."

They all said the same things, agreed with each other about Maggie's sainthood, and probably dimly thought of their own deaths. My mother said that she would make tea, and no doubt she was impelled to do it, so as to keep my father from anything alcoholic. In the parlor, where she and I went to get the cups, we found dog daisies in a jug on the sideboard with the water putrid and the daisies themselves shriveled up. She said what was a house without a woman, and as she carried the jug out, the women had to put their handkerchiefs or their gloved hands to their noses. As we walked home she told my father this and said it was a pity that Jack had never married and that perhaps he would now.

"Whoever marries Jack will have Maggie's brooches," I said.

"Maybe he'll wait for you," she said jokingly.

"She'll marry a doctor," said my father proudly, as he hoped that I would better their situation.

"She'll marry Jack," my mother said, and the thought was offensive. It happened to be a time when my girl friends and I secretly talked of nothing but marriage. We skipped to a rhyme that went:

Raspberry, strawberry, blackberry jam,
tell me the name of my young man

and we mused on the film stars who were our idols. So many girls plumped for Clark Gable that several were insanely jealous of each other, and if one said, "Clark," another would say, "Excuse me, are you talking of my friend Clark Gable," and enmity ensued. Daisies were plucked, novenas were said, and spells resorted to. There was one spell that surpassed all others for novelty. In the post came that particular little white box lined with silver paper that contained dark rich wedding cake, so dense with different fruits that it was as if it had no other ingredients but fruits, raisins, and candied peel. Then there was the deep yellow layer of almond icing and above that the white icing, with maybe a silver ball or the shred of an initial where it had been cut off on someone's name or a greeting. The flavor was exotic, but that was secondary. One slept with it under one's pillow in the hope that the initials of one's own future spouse would be delivered up in a dream. If it did not happen that night, then some other night, in a year or two or three, when another piece of wedding cake hopefully would arrive in the post. I was vexed with my mother for suggesting him, even as a joke. I felt defiled.

When I went away to boarding school, Jack gave me a present wrapped in several sheets of damp newspaper. It was a blue propelling pencil whose lead was so weak that at first usage it broke. Later I gave it to a nun who was collecting for the black babies. Within a week he wrote to me, and since our letters were censored, the nun asked who this gentleman was.

"My uncle, Sister," I said, and was surprised that I could lie with such facility. It was almost dark, but as it was not the appointed time to put on the lights, we were obliged to read our letters in the half-light. I went over to the window and pushed aside a castor-oil plant and read his effusion.

> *I hope you are well and attending diligently to your studies. I shall be curious to learn if geometry is your pet subject as it was mine; three cheers for Pythagoras! Your mam and dad are fine, we converse as usual on world affairs, and we miss your bright pertinent contributions.*
>
> *My wine shop is flourishing; a gentleman traveled from the North of Ireland last week to sample, and later to purchase, a particular vintage of mine. It was my very own, concocted from the offerings of the ditches, rhubarb, elderberry, and parsnip mixed to give a subtle bouquet.*

(I knew that if anyone made the wine it was the maternity nurse.)

> *I am still writing poems and brushing up on Swift and Goldsmith, indeed have dialogues with them when I peruse*

the highways and the byways. The name of Holland will one day be illustrious; if not for one thing, then for another. The weather is clement, though there was a downpour yesterday and I was obliged to take precautions.

(I could see him putting basins in the passage and dishcloths on the shop floor to catch some of the rain as it poured through the leaking roof.)

Here is a little surprise with which to supplement your budget. Do not allow the good nuns to twist your head in a fervent direction, and remember your promise to your friend

Jack

He had enclosed a money order for five shillings; I could hardly believe it. Its white crinkled paper with the heavy black lettering assured me that he had indeed sent this amount, but I did not know why.

It was a clear starry night when I came home for my Christmas holidays as I got off the bus and walked up the field. It was a pleasure to feel the darkness again, to smell the wet grass and the rotting toadstools. The dogs jumped on me, licked my face, and were hysterical with welcome. Inside the door Mama stood waiting to embrace me, and beside her was Jack. He grinned foolishly at me and hurt the two fingers next to my ringed finger by giving me an iron handshake. My new friend, Lydia, had loaned me her signet ring, so that I would think of her constantly.

Mama had a table laid in the breakfast room, and there were sausage rolls, mince pies, and iced orange cake. The turf fire sent up rainbow-colored flames, and to smell it again after so many months made me realize how cold and unnatural was our life in the convent.

"Yours truly is a bit of an antiquarian now," Jack said to me across the table.

"Oh" was all I could say in reply.

"Yes, when searching for mushrooms last harvest I found a brooch which proved to be unique. But keep this under your hat, because of course a lot of hooligans would endeavor to imitate me. It's bronze. I've interested some authorities from Dublin and they are traveling to see it early in the new year."

Mama winked at me. "Will you carry a candle upstairs, till we get a pillow that I want to air for you."

We linked as we climbed the stairs, and for once she did not warn me about spilling grease on the old Turkey carpet. Anyhow, we would melt it next day onto a piece of brown paper, either with a hot iron or with a hot knife. I wanted to sit on the landing step and discuss everything, how my hair once got nits in it and the disgrace that the nun had made of me, then ask if Dada had been drinking, and if the harvest had been good and therefore would we be able to pay my fees. When I shone the candle on her face Mama was laughing.

"It's Jack," she said, "he imagines things now. He's not all there. He digs in the Protestant graveyard every night and finds nothing, only old bottles and chamber pots and broken glass domes."

"Has he any friends?" I asked.

"Only us . . ." she said.

Jack beamed at me when I came downstairs, and a little later when he was leaving it was inside the neck of my jumper and not Mama's that he dropped two toffees. I was back in the convent only a month when Mama wrote to tell me that Jack was building a large two-story house three miles outside the village. She also said that there was a rumor he was getting married to a girl from Longford and that the maternity nurse got shingles when she heard it. He was then probably sixty. There was no telling how he made contact with this lady in Longford unless it was by post, but it was said that such a lady existed, and that her name was Cissy. Most afternoons he shut shop and went to build without any help at all, not even a handyman or a plasterer. As a consequence the house took three years, and my mother wrote to tell me what it was like. "Jack's house is at last complete. Your father and I were brought to see it last Sunday. 'Terrible' is the only word I could use. The roof is not slated, the window frames very crooked, and the exterior a bilious yellow color which he called ocher. The road up to it is a swamp. Of course Jack thinks it is marvelous and he has called it Sweet Auburn, no less. He is dying to show it to you."

When I came home on a summer holiday, having finished with the convent, I aspired toward Dublin and resented having to stay at home and listen to depressing conversations. I was sarcastic to my mother, shunned my father, and spent most of the time upstairs fitting on clothes, my own clothes and my mother's clothes. A youngster came from the village to say that Jack wanted to see me at three o'clock. My mother said that she felt it was propitious. I had done well in my examination and she believed that Jack was going to give me ten or twenty pounds. I hoped she was right, as I yearned for the money to buy style. He was waiting for me outside the shop, sitting on the windowsill with an oilskin thrown over one shoulder in jaunty toreador fashion. He looked happy and he waved to me from fifty yards away.

"What a picture," he said as he stood up and with a nod indicated that we weren't going to sit there in view of the village. The blind was down in his shop and I asked if it was the half day.

"No, but yours truly is his own boss," he said, and took great strides up the hill and passed the chapel and the graveyard.

"Where are we going?" I asked.

"To my country abode," he said.

It began to rain; the drops came singly at first and then with a great urgency, and he used this as an excuse for chivalry and placed the oilskin over my shoulders. We walked out that road and then up the track to the damp spectacle of a solitary house. He was impatient to get to it. There being no gate, he lifted a strand of the rusty barbed wire and helped me in, into the rectangular patch which enclosed the house and where the nettles flourished. The house looked haunted and the windows were dirty. A rat slunk deftly through a hole under the privet hedge; if Jack saw it he certainly made no reference to it. Birds flew wildly in and out of the eaves, and chattered as if they were angry with us, as if their occupancy of the place was challenged by our visit. In the field beyond the barbed wire was a very small old donkey whose hairs had come off in patches and who stared at us but did not bray. Jack muttered something about having flower beds made later on and added that he was also partial to an arch over which roses could tumble in June. It was June and all that blossomed was the ragwort and the masses of buttercups, both yellow, both bright.

As we stood there he was pointing to certain features of the house, the fanlight above the hall door, which he described as neo-Georgian, and the door itself, which was made of deal. For all his talk its features were very prosaic and very wanting. It was a square two-story house, its front pebble-dashed and painted over this dark muddy yellow. The curtainless windows were like long mourners looking out onto the neglected garden. Its only feature, if one can call it that, was that it was on an incline and there was a fine view of plowed land and meadow leading to the road. I went to look through one of the long windows, but he intercepted me. The tour had to be done properly and with him as guide. Impatience seized me and I looked anyhow and in the drawing room saw the bare boards spattered with paint and, in the middle of the floor, incongruously, a marble fireplace. Carrara marble, as he said. It was a sign of the grandeur that he aspired to. He conceded that the house needed a bit more work and then declared that what it surely needed was the woman's touch, that seemly eye that would know where to hang a mirror, or where to put a little whatnot, and which portrait to place over the fireplace, so that visitors would sit there with a sense of enrichment. I listened to his ramblings, resenting the fact that the high wet grass was harming my new sandals and draining the beige dye out of them. Did we, I wondered, ever pay him back the money he had given the bailiff? He was probably paid in kind and hunks of cake and bacon, and even an embroidered tablecloth would have to suffice for much of the money. I did not care. Only one thing was uppermost in me and it was flight, and in my fancies I had no idea that no matter how distant the flight or how high I soared, those people were entrenched in me.

I had to say something, so I said, "It's very secluded."

"Not when there's two of us . . ." he said.

He went around to the side to fetch the key, which was kept in a can. I felt chilled by the sight of it all—nettles, thistles, ragwort, and such an emanation of damp from the house itself that it seemed more dismal than any outhouse. Coming back twirling the big key, he winked at me slyly, and then it happened before I had time to repel him. Jack turned the key in the door; then lifted me up in his arms, and carried me over the threshold, triumphantly shouting, "Hallelujah . . . ours, ours, ours." He said for long he had envisaged such a scene and only wished he had brought a ring. His mouth and nose were lowered toward my face, and I saw him as a great vampire about to demand a kiss. I struggled out of his arms and ran toward the barbed wire, accusing him of being a horrible man. Either he was too shocked or too ashamed to follow, but I need not have gone at such a helter-skelter down the dirt track, because as I looked back, I saw that he was standing as stationary and as forlorn as a poplar tree. He did not move or beckon.

Jack stopped visiting our house, crossed the road when he saw my mother, and avoided my father after Mass. It was then the maternity nurse became essential. Now that we were banished, she made him soda bread, and when she delivered it, she collected dirty socks from the table or from a chair where they were slung. She darned them and even began to talk of plans for the unused parlor; she fancied an oil stove to be put in there. Since the girl from Longford had not materialized, everyone thought he would marry the maternity nurse, and indeed, so did she. But after six months of washing and baking and even repairing the lace curtains on the upstairs landing, she asked the parish priest to have a word with Jack. The priest called one Sunday evening, and since the public house was shut, the front door was ceremoniously lifted back. It had swollen in the rain. Jack threw a newspaper over a kitchen chair and asked His Reverence to sit down and to please forgive the humility of the place, and to have a drop of sherry, or better still a glass of malt.

"Well now, Jack, there's none of us getting younger, and time is passing, and you are keeping company with a very nice lady, and isn't it time that you thought of settling down?"

Those were the very words the parish priest used, because he described the incident in detail to my mother the day she had Mass said in our house.

"Marriage, Father," said Jack, "is out of the question. I was betrothed for a long number of years to a certain little lady in this parish, who jilted me. It has embittered my ideals about the opposite sex, it has cauterized me from ever entering on another alliance; indeed, it has ruined my life."

Jack was soon without the ministerings of the maternity nurse, and in time he became more remote and did not even talk to his customers. He just served them the drink and watched while they drank and brooded. He lost interest in his two-story house, and one evening some children who were picking mushrooms saw flames in the front window and hurried to look inside, thinking it had caught fire. Inside, a group of tinkers squatted on the floor, eating and drinking; they had made a big fire in the grate. When told of this, Jack said he would get the sergeant to deal with it, but whenever the tinkers came, they did not sleep out in the fields as before but used the shelter of the house.

The following winter he got shingles and used to open his shop at odd hours, when it suited him. As I got older, I thought of him, of how embarrassed he must have been and how callous I must have seemed. I wanted to talk to him and somehow to make amends. My mother warned me that he was very peculiar and that if I went to the shop he would not let me past the door but would drive me out as he had done to her. I said that I would follow him from Mass. I sat through the coughing and the croaking, inhaling the damp smell of tweed coats, looking at all the faces that I had almost forgotten, faces worn and twisted like the trees. He was bald, stooped, and he prayed feverishly on his black horn rosary beads. His fingers could have been an old woman's so small were they, so gnarled. The chapel itself seemed a smaller and humbler place, and I thought of the missionaries and the terror of their sermons. The parish priest was very slow and at times hesitated as if he had forgotten the words. At the Last Gospel, Jack jumped up and left. Forewarned about this, I too got up, genuflected, and left. He hurried out under the cypress trees and opened the church gate but did not wait to close it. It clanged.

"Jack, Jack." I could not shout lest it be disrespectful to the proceedings in the church. I closed the gate and walked quickly, all the while calling, but he pretended not to hear. He took great strides, and it was clear that he was avoiding me. I caught up with him as he reached his own shop door and was pushing it in.

"Jack, it's lovely to see you."

He heard but did not respond. He went in, pushed the door shut, and immediately drew a bolt. I stood there thinking that he would change his mind. The gray gauze blind that had once had the name VINTNER printed on it was like filament. Any minute it seemed as if it might disintegrate. I tapped and tapped, but he did not relent. Indeed, I did not know if he stood there, vacillating, or if he had gone on tiptoe into the kitchen and was brewing a cup of tea. As I walked down the road and saw the bright red bells of fuchsia and heard the sounds of motorists hooting happily, I thought how untoward his gloom was and how melancholy had cut him off from others. In him I saw a glimpse of my future exiled self.

When he died he left his premises to a cousin whom we had never seen and scarcely knew of. Realizing that he had not remembered us at all in his will, and reciting the motto about "blood being thicker than water," my mother said that she was genuinely surprised that he hadn't left her a decanter or a biscuit barrel. But I think her disappointment was not so much to do with graft as it was deference to hidden romance, which although she stoutly denounced it, in some part of her mysterious being she cherished it and all her life believed that it would come her way.

Savages

Mabel's family lived in a cottage at the end of our avenue and we were forever going back and forth, helping, borrowing tea or sugar or the paper, or liniment, agog for each other's news. We knew of Mabel's homecoming for weeks, but what we did not know was whether she would come by bus or car, and whether she would arrive in daylight or dusk. She was coming from Australia, making most of the journey by ship, and then crossing on the sailboat to Dublin, and then by train to our station, which was indeed rustic and where a passenger seldom got off. She would be tired. She would be excited. She would be full of strange stories and strange impressions. How long would she stay? What would she look like? Would her hair be permed? What presents, or what knickknacks would she bring? Would she have an accent? Oh, what novelty. These and a thousand other questions assailed us, and as the time got nearer, her name and her arrival were on everyone's lips. I was allowed to help her mother on the Saturday and in my eagerness I set out at cockcrow, having brought six fresh eggs and the loan of our egg beater. First task was to clear out the upstairs room. It smelled musty. Mice scrambled there, because her family kept their oats in it. It was an attic room with a skylight window and a slanting ceiling. In fact, it was only half a room, because of the way one kept bumping one's head on the low, distempered ceiling. My job was to scoop oats with a trowel and pour it into a sack. So buoyed up was I with anticipation that now and then I became absentminded and the oats slid out of the sack once again. From time to time her mother would say, "I hope she hasn't an accident," or "I hope she hasn't broke her pledge," but these things were said to disguise or temper her joy. The thing is, Mabel's coming had brought hope and renewal into her life.

Mabel had been gone for ten years, and the only communications in between had been her monthly letter and some photographs. The photos were very dim and they were always with other girls, smirking, so that one didn't see what she was like in repose. Also, she always wore a hat, so that her features were disguised. Mabel worked as a lady's companion, and her letters told of this lady, her wrath, the sunflowers in her garden, and the beauty of her German piano, which was made of cherrywood.

"I expect she'll stay for the summer," her mother said, and I thought that a bit optimistic. Who would want to stay three or four months in our godforsaken townland? Nothing happened except the land was plowed, the crops were put down, there was a harvest, a threshing, then geese were sent to feast on the stubble, and soon the land was bare again. None of the women wore cosmetics, and in the local chemist shop the jars of cold cream and vanishing cream used to go dry because of no demand. Of course, we read about fashions in a magazine and we knew, my sisters and I knew, that ladies wore tweed costumes the color of mulberries, and that they sometimes had silk handkerchiefs steeped in perfume which they wore underneath their bodices for effect. Not for a second did I think Mabel would stay long, but had I said anything, her mother would have sent me home. We carried a trestle bed up, put the clean sheets on and the blankets, and then hung a ribbon of adhesive paper for the flies to stick to. The place still smelled musty, but her mother said that was to be expected and that if Mabel was ashamed of her origins, she had another guess coming.

We went downstairs to get on with the baking. Her mother cracked the six fresh eggs into the bowl and beat them to a frothlike consistency. Then she got out the halves of orange peel and lemon peel, and in the valleys were crusts of sugar that were like ice. I longed for a piece. I was put sieving the flour and I did it so energetically that the flour swirled in the air, making the atmosphere snow-white. At that moment her husband came in and demanded his dinner. She said couldn't he see she was making a cake. She referred him to the little meat safe that was attached to a tree outside in the garden, whereupon he growled and wielded his ash plant. It seems there was nothing in the meat safe, only buttermilk.

"Don't addle me," she said.

"Is it grass you would have me eat?" he said, and I saw that he was in imminent danger of picking up the whisked eggs and pitching them out in the yard, where we would never be able to retrieve them because hens, ducks, and pigs paddled in the muck out there.

"Can't you give me a chance," she said, but seeing that he was about to explode, she stooped, avoiding a possible blow, and then from under a dish she hauled out an ox tongue that she had boiled that morning. It was of course meant for Mabel, but she realized that she had better be expedient. As she cut the tongue he watched, barely containing his rage. As I saw her put the knife to it, I thought, Poor oxen had not much of a life either living or dead. She cut it thinly, as she was trying to economize. In the silence we heard a mouse as it got caught in the trap that we had just put down in Mabel's room. Its screech was both sudden and beseeching. Her husband picked up a slice of the tongue with his hand, being too impatient to wait for it to be handed on the plate. I too wanted to taste it, but not by itself. I would have loved it with a piece of pickle, so that the taste was not like oxen but like something artificial, something out of a jar. He ate by the fire, munching loudly, asking me for another cut of bread, and quick. He drank his tea from an enamel mug, and I could hear it going glug-glug down his gullet. He had never addressed a civil word to me in his life.

The baked cake was the most beautiful sight. It was dark gold in color, it had risen beautifully, and there were small cracks on the top into which she secretly poured a drop of whiskey to give it, as she said, an aroma. I asked if she was going to ice it, but she seemed to resent that question. For some absurd reason I began to wonder who Mabel would marry, because of course she was not yet married and she must not be left on the shelf, as that was a most mortifying role.

"You can go home now," her mother said to me.

I looked at her. If looks can talk, then these should have. My look was an invocation. It was saying, "Let me come for Mabel's arrival." I lingered, thinking that she would say it, but she didn't. I praised the cake! I was lavish in my praise of it, of the clean windows, the floor polish, the three mice caught and consigned to the fire, of everything. It was all in vain. She did not invite me.

The next day was agony. Would I be let go? It was still not broached and I tried a thousand ruses and just as many imprecations. I would pick up the clock that was lying face down, and if I had guessed the time to within minutes, then I would surely go. A butterfly had got caught between the two panes of opened window and I thought, If it finds its way out unaided, then I shall go. In there it struggled and beat its wings, it kept going around in circles to no purpose, yet miraculously shot up and sailed out into the air, a vision of soft, fluttering orange-brown. Not to go would be torture. But worse than that would be if my sisters were let go and I was told to mind the house. It sometimes happened. Why mind a house that was solid and vaster than oneself? Extreme diligence took possession of me and such a spurt of tidiness that my mother said it was to our house Mabel should be arriving. If only that were so!

After the tea, when I had washed up the dishes, I could no longer contain myself and I began to snivel. My mother pretended not to notice. She was changing her clothes in the kitchen. She often changed there and held the good clothes in front of the fire to air them. The rooms upstairs were damp, the wardrobes were damp, and when you put on your good clothes you could feel the damp seeping into your bones. She was brusque. She said why ringlets and why one's best cardigan. I cried more. She said to put it out of one's head and announced that none of the children was going, as the McCann kitchen was far too small for hordes. She said to cut out the sobs and do one's homework instead. While my father shaved I went under the table to pray. It was evident he was in a bad mood because of the way he scraped the stubble off his chin. He said that not even a day like this could be enjoyed. He said why did he have to fodder cattle and my mother said because there was no one else to do it.

After they had gone, my sisters and I decided to make pancakes. As it happened, my older sister nearly set fire to the house because of the amount of paraffin she threw onto the stove. I shall never forget it. It was like the last day, with flames rising out of the stove, panels of orange flame going up the walls, and my other sister and I screaming at her to quench it, quench it. The first thing to hand was a can of milk, which we threw on it in terror. Luckily we conquered it, and all that remained was a smell of paraffin and a terrible smell of burned milk. The pancake project was abandoned and we spent the next hour trying to air the place and clean the stove. Docility had certainly taken hold of us by the time my mother and father returned. It was dark and we could hear the hasp of the gate and then the dogs bounding toward the door and then the latch lifting. My mother was first. She always came first so as to be able to put on the kettle for him and so as to get on with her tasks. First thing we noticed was the parcel under her arm. It was in tissue paper and it had been opened at one end. My sister grabbed it as my mother wrinkled up her nose and said was there something burning. We denied that and harried her to tell, tell. Mabel had come, was tired from her journey, spoke in a funny accent, and said that in Australia wattles meant mimosa trees and not mere sticks or stones.

By then my father had arrived and said that he was a better-looking man than Mabel himself and then did an impersonation of her accent. It was like no accent I had ever heard. My father said that the only interesting thing about her was that she backed horses and had been to race meetings in Sydney. My mother said that she had been marooned out on some sheep station and had met very few people, only the shearers and the lady she worked for. My mother pronounced on her as being haggard and with a skin tough and wizened from the heat. The present turned out to be pale-blue silk pajamas. I could see my mother's reaction—immense disappointment that was bordering on disgust. She had hoped for a dress or a blouse, she had certainly hoped for a wearable. For another thing, pajamas were shameful, sinful. Men wore pajamas, women wore nightgowns. Shame and disgrace. My mother folded them up quickly so as not to let my father see them, in case it gave him ideas. She bundled them into a cupboard and it was plain to see that she was nettled. She would have even liked a remnant so as to be able to make dresses for us. It seemed that the homecoming was something of an anticlimax and that even Mabel's father couldn't understand a word that she had said. It seems that the men who had come to vet her agreed that she wasn't worth tuppence and the women were most disappointed by her attire. They had expected her to be wearing high-heeled court shoes, preferably suede, and it seems she was wearing leather shoes that were almost, but not quite, flat. To make matters worse, they were tan and her stockings were tan and her skin was slightly tan, and along with all that, she was in a bright-red suit. My mother said she looked like a scarecrow and was very loud.

Next day it rained. So fiercely that hailstones beat against the window frames, pelting them like bullets. The sky was ink-black, and even when a cloud broke, the silver inside was dark and oppressive, presaging a storm. I was sent around the house to close the windows and put cloths on the sills in case the rain soaked through. I saw a figure coming up the avenue and thought it might be a begging woman with a coat over her head. When we heard the knocking on the back door, my mother opened it sharply, poised as she was for hostilities.

"Mabel," my mother said, surprised, and I ran to see her. She was a small woman with black bobbed hair, a very long nose, and eyes which were like raisins and darting. She wore rubber overshoes, which she began to remove, and as she held on to the side of the sink, I stood in front of her. She asked me was I me and said that the last time she had seen me I was screaming my head off in a hammock, in the garden. Somehow she expected me to be pleased by this news, or at least to be amused.

What struck me most about her was her abruptness. In no time she was complaining about those two old fogies, her mother and father, and telling us that she was not going to sit by a fire with them all day long and discuss rheumatism. Also, she complained about the house, said it wasn't big enough.

My mother calmed her with tea and cake, and my father asked her what kind of horses they bred in Australia. He wagered a bet that they were not as thoroughbred as the Irish horses. To that my mother gave a grunt, since our horses brought us nothing but disappointment and debt. When pressed for other news, Mabel said that she had seen a thing or two, her eyes had been opened, but she would not say in what way. She hinted at having undergone some terrible shock and I thought that possibly she had been jilted. She described a tea they drank out of glasses, sitting on the veranda at sundown. My mother said it was a wonder the hot tea didn't crack the glasses. Mabel said she should never have come home and that when she woke up that morning and heard the rain on the skylight she had yearned to go back. Yet in no time she was contradicting herself and said it was all "outback" in Australia and who wanted to live in an outback. My father said he'd make a match for her, and gradually she cheered up as she sat at the side of the stove and from time to time popped one or the other foot in the lower oven for warmth. Her stockings were lisle and a very unfortunate color, rather like the color of the stirabout that we gave to the hens and the chickens. She had an accent at certain moments, but she lost it whenever she talked about her own people. She said their house was nothing but a cabin, a thatched cabin. When she said indiscreet things, she laughed and persisted until she got someone to join in.

"Mabel, you're a scream," my mother said, while also pretending to be shocked at the indiscretions.

Very reluctantly my father had gone out to fodder, and Mabel was drinking blackberry wine from a beautiful stemmed glass. When she held the glass up, colors danced on her cheek and then ran down her throat, just as the wine was running down inside. Presently her face got flushed and her eyes teary, and she confessed that she had thought of Ireland night and day for the ten years, had saved to come home, and now realized that she had made a frightful mistake. She sniffled and then took out a spotted handkerchief.

"Faraway hills look green," my mother said, and the two of them sighed as if a wealth of meaning had been exchanged. My mother proposed a few visits they could make on Sundays, and buoyed up by the wine and these promises, Mabel said that she had a second present for my mother but that in the commotion the previous evening she had been unable to find it. She said it must be somewhere in the bottom of her trunk. It was to be a brush and comb set, with matching bone tray. We never saw it.

It took several months before Mabel paid me any attention. She had favored my sisters because they were older and because they had ideas about how to set hair, how to paint toenails, and how to use an emery board or a nail buffer. It was either of them she took on her Sunday excursion, and it was either of them she summoned on the way home from school so as to sit with her in the garden and chat. It proved to be a scorching summer and Mabel had put two deck chairs in their front garden and had planted lupins. She never let anyone pass without hollering, as she was avid for company. In the autumn my sisters went away to school, and suddenly Mabel was in need of a walking companion. My mother had long since ceased to go with her, because Mabel was mad for gallivanting and had worn out her welcome in every house up the town, and in many houses up the country.

One Sunday she chose me. It was the very same as if she had just arrived home, because to me she was still a mysterious stranger. We were calling on a family who lived in the White House. It had been given that name because the money for it had come from relatives in America. It was a yellow, two-story, pebble-dash house set in its own grounds with a heart-shaped lawn in front. At the edge of the lawn there was a flower bed in which there had been dark-red tulips, and at the far end was a little house with an electricity plant. They were the only people in the neighborhood to have electricity, and that plus the tulips, plus the candlework bedspreads, plus the legacies from America, made theirs the most enticing house in the county. As we went up their drive, my white canvas shoes adhered to the tarmac, which was fresh and melting. The house with its lace-edged fawn blinds was quiet and suggested luxury and harmony. Needless to say, they had cross dogs, and at the first sound of a yelp Mabel lagged behind, while telling me to stand my ground and not give off an adrenaline smell. A boy who was clipping the privet hedge saved us by calling the dogs and holding them by their tawny manes. They snarled like lions.

Since we were not expected, a certain coolness ensued. The mistress of the house was lying down, her husband was in bed sick, and the little serving girl, Annie, didn't ask us to cross the threshold. All of a sudden the dummies appeared. They were brother and sister, and though I had often heard of them, and even seen them at Mass devoutly fingering their rosary beads, I had no idea that they would be so effusive. They descended on us. They mauled us. They strove with tongue and lips and every other feature to talk to us, to communicate. The movements of their hands were fluent and wizard. They pulled us into the kitchen, where the female dummy put me up on a chair so she could look at the pleats in my coat, and then the buttons. She herself was dressed in a terrible hempen dress that was almost to her ankles. Her brother was in an ill-fitting coarse suit. They were in-laws of the mistress of the house and it was rumored that she did not like them. She was trying to say something urgent when the mistress, who had risen from her nap, came in and greeted us somewhat reservedly. Soon we were seated around the kitchen table, and while Mabel and the mistress discussed who had been at Mass, and who had taken Holy Communion, and who had new style, the dummies were pestering me and trying to get me to go outside. They would puff their cheeks out in an encouragement to make me puff mine.

Mabel and the mistress of the house began to talk about her husband. They moved closer together. They were like two people conspiring. A terrible word was said. I heard it. It was the word hemorrhage. He was hemorrhaging. Only women did that. I began to go dizzy with dread. I gripped the chair by its sides, then put one hand on the table for further security and began to hum. My face must have been burning, because soon the dummies realized there was something wrong, and thinking only one thing, they pulled me toward a door and down a passage to a lavatory. It was a cold spot and there was a canister of scouring powder left on a ledge, as if Annie had been cleaning and had gone off in a hurry or a sulk. They kept knocking on the door and when I came out inspected me carefully to see that my coat was pulled down. The lady dummy, whose pet name was Babs, drew me into the kitchen, and as we stood in front of the fire, she did a little caper. She had a tea cloth in one hand and held it out as if she were keeping a bull at bay. She was told by the mistress of the house to put it down or she would be sent to the dairy. Her twin brother affected the most terrible huff by letting out moans that were nearly animal, and moving his eyes hither and thither and at such a speed I thought they would drop out. He, too, was threatened with a sojourn in the dairy. At length so chastised were they that they each took a chair and sat with their backs to us and refused when asked to turn around.

The mistress said they needed a good smacking.

After an age the mistress offered us a tour of the house. When she opened the drawing-room door, what one first saw was the sun streaming in through the long panes of glass and bouncing on the polished furniture. She muttered something about having forgotten to draw the blinds. Pictures of cows and ripening corn hung on either side of the marble mantelpiece, and in the tiled fireplace there was an arrangement of artificial flowers—tea roses, yellow, apricot, and gold. Not only that, but the flowers in a round thick rug matched. To look at it you felt certain that no one had stepped on that rug, that it was pristine like a wall hanging. Its pile and its softness made one long to kneel or bask in it. Mabel of course commented on the various things, on the curtains, for instance, which were sumptuous; on the pelmet that matched; on the long plaited cord by which the curtains could be folded or parted. Pulling it, I had a fancy that I was opening the curtains of a theater and that presently through the window would come a troupe of performers. The mistress of the house was pleased at our excitement and as a reward she took something from the china cabinet and let me hold it. It was a miniature cabin made of blackthorn wood. It had a tiny door that opened the merest chink.

Next we saw the breakfast room and then the dining room, which by contrast was dark and somber, save for the gleam of the silver salver on the sideboard. Next we saw the bathroom, with its green bath, matching basin, and candlewick bath mat. But we were not brought up the last flight of stairs, which led to the bedrooms, lest our footsteps waken her husband and make him want to get up. He was craving to get up and go out in the fields. Up there, the darkness was extreme because of a stained-glass window. The hallway seemed a bit sepulchral and quite different from the downstairs room. I could hear the crows cawing ceaselessly, and it occurred to me that before long there would be a death in the house, as I believe it occurred to them, because they looked at one another and shook their heads in silent commiseration.

The kitchen clock chimed five and still we sat in hope of something to eat. Mabel rubbed her stomach to indicate that she was hungry, while the mistress put on her apron and said that soon it would be milking time and time to feed calves and do a million things. Halfheartedly she offered us a cup of tea. There was nothing festive about it, it was just a cup of tea off a tray, four scones, and a slab of strong-smelling yellow country butter. It was not fashioned into little burr balls as I had expected. Mabel kicked me under the table, knowing my disappointment. There was no cake and no cold meat. Mabel judged people's hospitality by whether they gave her cold meat or not.

On the way home she lamented that there was not a bit of lamb, no chicken, no beetroot or freshly made potato salad with scallions.

It was a warm evening and the ripe corn in the fields was a sight to behold. Here and there it had lodged, but for the most part it was high and victorious, ready for the thresher. She said, "I wonder what they're doing in Australia now," and ventured to say that they missed her. She asked did I like those flowers my mother fashioned by putting twirls of silver and gold paper over the ears of corn. When I said no, she hurrahed. It meant that she and I were now friends, allies. Of course, I knew that I had betrayed my mother and would pay for it either by being punished or by having bouts of remorse. She took out her flapjack to apply some powder. It was a tiny gold flapjack and the powder puff was in shreds.

Mabel made a face at herself and then asked if I had a boy yet. The word "boy," like the word "hemorrhage," threatened to make me faint. She said soon I would have a boy and to be careful not to let him lay a finger on me, because it was a well-known fact that one could get a craze for it and end up ruined, imprisoned in the Magdalen Laundry, until you had a baby. She might have launched into more graphic tales but a car came around the corner and she jumped up and waved so as to summon a lift.

In the town we called on a woman to whom Mabel had given a crocheted tea cozy, and our reward was two long glasses of lemonade and a plate of currant-topped biscuits. Mabel was prodigal with her promises. She volunteered to crochet a bedcover and asked the woman if there were any favorite colors, or more important, if there were any colors she could not abide. She burped as we walked down the hill and over the bridge toward home. It was getting dark and the birds were busy with both song and chatter. Every bird in every tree had something to say. As we passed the houses we could hear people banging buckets and dishes, and by the light of a lantern we saw one woman feeding calves at her doorstep. As each calf finished its quota, its head was pulled out to give the next calf a chance. Those whose heads were outside the bucket kept butting and kicking and were in no way satisfied. We knew the woman but we did not linger, as Mabel whispered that it would be dull old blather about new milk and sucking calves. Mabel did not like the country and had no interest in tillage, sunsets, or landscape. She objected to pools of water in the roadside, pools of water in the meadows, the corncrake in the evening, and the cocks crowing at dawn. As we walked along she took my hand and said that henceforth I was to be her walking companion. It was a thrill to feel her gloved hand awkwardly pressing on mine. Untold adventures lay ahead.

Sometimes on our travels we met with a shut door or we were not asked to cross the threshold. But these rebuffs meant nothing to her and she merely designated the people as being ignorant and countrified. As luck would have it, our third Sunday we struck on a most welcoming house. It was a remote house, first along a tarred road, then a dirt road, and then across a stream. Our hosts were two young girls who were home from England, and great was their pleasure in receiving company. They were home for a month but were already aching to go back. The older one, Betty, was a nurse, and Moira, her sister, was a buyer in a shop and consequently they dressed like fashion plates. We went every Sunday, knowing that they would be waiting for us and that they had got their father and mother out of the house visiting cousins. It was such a thrill as we got to the stream and took off our shoes and stockings, then let out raucous sounds about the temperature of the water, but really to alert them. It was clean silvery water with stones beneath, some round and smooth, some pointed. They would hear us and run down the slope to welcome us, while also asking in exaggerated accents if the water was like ice. To hear our names called was the zenith of welcome.

We would be brought through the kitchen into the parlor, while they told Nora, their young sister, to put the kettle on and to be smart about it. The parlor was dark, with red embossed wallpaper, and we all sat very upright on hard horsehair sofas. It so happened that I had begun to do impersonations of the dummies, and immediately they requested them. As a reward I was given a slice of coconut cake that they had brought back from England and that was kept in a tin with a harlequin figure on the lid. It was a bit dry but much more exotic than their homemade cake. Mabel would let her tongue roll over her top and bottom teeth, then ask was there any meat left, whereupon Moira would lift a plate that exactly adhered to another plate and reveal that she had kept Mabel a lunch.

"You sport, you," Mabel said. Her accent would suddenly sound Australian.

"Don't mention it," Moira would say airily.

Our visits sustained them. With us they could discuss fashion and fit on their finery, then later do the Lambeth Walk in the big flagged kitchen. Doing this led to howls of laughter. Always, one of us got the step wrong and the whole thing had to be recommenced. Even their sheepdog thought it was hilarious and moved about in a clumsy way to the strains of the music from the crackling wind-up gramophone. We alternated at being ladies or gents, and we had conversations that ladies and gents have.

"Do you come here often?" or "Next dance, please," or "Care for a mineral?" was what our partners said. Afterward we lounged in the chairs breathless, and then we set out for a walk, or, as they called it, "a ramble." It was on one of these rambles that we met

Matt. An auspicious meeting it proved to be. He had the reputation of being a queer fellow, a recluse. He had gone to Canada, made some money, and had come back to marry his childhood sweetheart, but was jilted on the eve of the wedding. Some said that the marriage was broken off because the two families couldn't agree about land, others said she thought his manners too gruff; at any rate, she fled to England. Matt was a tall man with a thin face, a wart, and longish hair. He looked educated, as if he spent time poring over books and almanacs. It seems he had newfangled ideas about planting trees, whereas most of the farmers just felled them for firewood. There was something original about him. It may have been his gravity or his silence. He could go into a public house and drink a pint of porter without passing a word to anyone, even the publican. He never visited any of his neighbors and had his Christmas dinner at home, with his brother, who was supposed to be a bit missing in the head. Matt met us down by the river. He had a stick in his hand and his hat was pushed back on his head. He must have been driving cattle, because he was perspiring a bit, but he still looked dignified. Moira had picked some sorrel and was eating it, saying it was like lemon juice and very good for one's skin. He stood apart from us, but at the same time he was taking stock. At least that's what one read from his smile. There was mockery in his smile, but there was also scrutiny. Betty and Moira knew him, knew his moods, and pretended not to notice that he was there.

"Wouldn't you all fancy sugar plums?" he said to no one in particular. Mabel was the first to respond.

"Are they ripe?" she asked.

"They're ripe," he said, but in such an insolent way we were not sure if he was telling the truth or just tantalizing us.

"I much prefer damsons," Moira said.

"Damsons are too tart," Mabel said; "damsons are only fit for jam."

"Please yourselves," he said, and sauntered off, letting a whistle escape from his lips. Mabel called out, were we invited or not.

"As you wish," he said, and nodding to each other, we followed. I thought we were like cows ambling across a field, not quite a herd, and not herded but all heading in the same direction and feeling aimless. It was a beautiful autumn evening, with the sun a vivid orb and in the sky around it rivers of red and pink and washed gold. His was a two-story stone house and the front door was closed. It looked very dead and secretive. There was a hand pump in the yard, and as he passed it, he worked the handle a few times to replenish the trough underneath. We could hear the calves lowing, and suddenly the cock started to crow as if disapproving. Hens ran in all directions and there were two small bonhams wallowing in some mud. It was anything but cheerful. He did not invite us in.

In contrast, the orchard was a great tangle of trees and fruit bushes all smothered in convolvulus and the grass needed to be scythed. The apples looked so tempting, blood-red and polished, while the plums were like dusky globes ready to drop off. He put one to his lips. It was the first time that anything approaching pleasure touched his countenance.

"Help yourselves," he said, and I thought, Perhaps he is a generous man, perhaps he is kind inside and only needs four or five girls giggling and gorging to draw him out. Mabel was intrepid as she picked three plums and debated which to sample first. The two girls, having been to England, were much more polite and did not rhapsodize over the taste and did not drip juice onto their chins. Mabel declared that there would be no stopping her now, that she would come Sunday after Sunday while the fruits lasted. He picked up a lid of a tin can that had been lying in the grass, lined it with a few wide leaves, and handed it to me, with the instruction that we were to bring some home. It was obvious that he took great pleasure in the fact that we were so excited.

"No one ever eats them . . . they just rot," he said.

"That's a shame," Mabel said, and she winked at him, and he winked back. It is an odd thing how a face can suddenly alter. It was not that she appeared beautiful, but she had a kind of luster and her glances were knowing and piquant.

"We'll raid you every autumn," she said, and I thought of life as being charmed, a series of autumns just like then, the sun going down, the beautiful globes of fruit like lamps, waiting to be plucked, our happiness undimmed. In my hand I felt the softness of a plum, yet knew the hardness of the stone deep within it, and I knew that my optimism was unwise.

"How long are you home for?" he asked Moira.

"Long enough," she said, and shrugged. Her reply both shocked and dazzled me. I thought, What a wonderful way to talk to a man, to be at once polite and distant, to be scornful without being downright rude, to parry. Then he broached the subject of the carnival. The carnival was to take place at the end of the month. Mabel asked if he'd take her for a ride on the swing-boats or the bumper cars, and he smiled at each one of us and said he hoped he would have the pleasure.

"We'll be gone back," Betty said.

"You ought to stay for the carnival," Mabel said, but I knew that she did not mean it and was looking forward to a time when she would see Matt without the competition of two younger, comelier girls. God knows what fancies were stirred in her then. Perhaps she thought—a bachelor, a two-story house, a man she could cook for, prosperity, a wedding. She clung to his coat sleeve by way of thanking him, but he did not like that. He left abruptly and said to help ourselves to the black plums as well. On our way home the others made fun of him, made fun of his wart and the unmatching buttons on his coat.

"And what about his anatomy?" Mabel said, and we all burst out laughing, though we did not know why.

He appeared the last night of the carnival, danced with the two elderly Protestant girls, excelled himself at the rifle range, and won a jug, which he gave to Mabel. She had been trailing around after him the whole evening and asked him up for the Ladies' Choice. No one knows for sure if they went behind the tent, but they were missing for a while, and the following day Mabel was trembling with excitement. She told everyone that Matt "had what it takes." She had a home perm, which did not suit her, and also she wrote to the woolen mills to ask if they had remnants sufficient to make two-pieces or three-pieces, and in anticipation she reserved the dressmaker. The money for these fripperies came from the few remaining bonds that she cashed. Her mother did not know. Her father did not know. I thought how courageous in a way was her recklessness. She was younger, giddier, and in good spirits with everybody. One morning she met me on my way to school. There was a light frost and the plumes of grass looked like ostrich feathers. Feeling my bare hands, she said that she would knit me gloves before the winter. I wondered why she was so affectionate. Then came the command. I was to get away early from school and I was to tell the teacher that we were expecting visitors, hence I had to help my mother with sausage rolls and dainties. I dreaded telling a lie, but she had a hold over me because of my impersonation of the dummies. She told me where to meet her and what time. There was a downpour after lunch, and when I came upon her she was cursing the rain, cursing the fates, and putting her hands up to protect her frizzled hair. Her hair hung in wet absurd ringlets over her forehead and made her look like a crabbed doll.

"What the hell kept you," she said, and started to walk. Before long I learned that I was to take a letter to Matt. She conveyed me some of the way and then crouched against a wall to wait. There was a roaring wind, and she looked pathetic as she huddled there in suspense.

"Take the shortcut through the woods," she said. It was an old wood and dark as an underworld. In the wind the branches swayed and even the boughs seemed to waver. Every time a bird chirped or every time a branch snapped, I thought it was some monster come to tackle me. I talked out loud to keep things at bay, I shouted, I ran, and at moments doubted if I would ever get there. The thought of her huddled beneath a wall in her good coat, reeking of perfume, drove me on. The perfume was called Californian Poppy and it had a smell of carnations. I could barely distinguish the path through the wood so obscure was it, and briars barred the way. My heart gave a leap of joy when I saw the three chimney pots and realized that I was almost there. The house seemed even lonelier than on the first day. Everything—the hall door, the stone itself, the window frames—everything was green and sodden from rain. It looked a picture of desolation, a house with no other houses to buffet or befriend it and no woman to hang curtains or put pots of geraniums on the sill. It would have been ghostly except for the fowl and the snorting of the pigs. I reckoned they would kill the pigs for Christmas. Matt was not at home. His brother gaped through the window, then drew the bolt back and peered out and said without being asked, "He's gone to Gort and won't be back." I feared now some worse incident, so I thrust the note into his hand, bolted down the yard, did not wait to close the iron gate, and hurried into the woods, which by comparison were safe.

Mabel was livid. She called me every name under the sun. An eejit, a fool, a dunce, an imbecile. She wanted me to go back for the letter, but I said the brother would have read it by now and going back would only show that we were culpable.

"You little poltroon," she said, and I thought she would brain me with the point of a stick which she brandished and prodded in the air. The rain had stopped, but the drops came in sudden bursts from the trees, and each time she ducked to protect her hair. Our walk home was wretched. Not a word passed between us. The only thing I heard was an occasional smack as she clacked her tongue against the roof of her mouth to verify her rage. We parted company as we got to the town, and she said that was the last time we would be seen walking together. I did not plead with her, knowing that it was in vain. Poor Mabel. It was pitiful to think of how she had dressed up and had worn uncomfortable court shoes under her galoshes and had been lavish with the perfume, all to no avail. But I could not tell her I pitied her, as she would have exploded. I don't know what she did then, whether she went back to search for him or went into the chapel to give outlet to her grief. She might even have called on her friend the lady publican for a few glasses of port. All I know is that she stopped speaking to me, and when we met on the road she would give a toss of her head and look in the opposite direction. Sundays reverted to being long dull days when one waited fruitlessly for a caller.

After Christmas there was a ghastly rumor and it was that Mabel was having a baby. It resounded throughout the parish. It was at first hotly denied by Mabel's mother, who was told it in the strictest confidence by my mother. Mabel had grown a bit stout, her mother conceded, but that was because she ate too much griddle bread. The denial and the excuse pacified people, but not for long. Within a month Mabel had swelled, and one day a few of the women set a terrible trap for her. Polly, the ex-midwife and her nearest neighbor, who had fainted upon hearing of Mabel's downfall, enlisted Rita, a young girl, to help in their ruse.

The plan was that they would invite Mabel to tea, flatter her by telling her how thin she looked, and then, having put her off guard, Rita was to steal up on her from behind and put a measuring tape around her waist. It turned out that Mabel was gross, and by nightfall the conclusion was that Mabel was indeed having a baby. After that she was shunned at Mass, shunned on her way down from Mass, and avoided when she went into the shops. People were weird in the punishments they thought should be meted out to her. Throughout all this Mabel did nothing but grin and smile and say what marvelous weather it was. If people were too snooty, she went up to them and said, "Go on, tell me what you're thinking of me." She would dare them to give an opinion. My mother said that it would be a mercy if someone were to take a stick to Mabel, and her mother said that when Mabel's father got to hear of it, he would kick her arse through the town. Mabel had few friends—the lady publican, the postman, who himself had once got a girl into trouble, and the dummies, who mauled her as she came out of Mass, not knowing that she was to be ostracized. She went to the town at all hours and cadged cigarettes off the men once they were drunk.

"Whose is it, Mabel?" she was asked by one of these drunkards.

"Your guess is as good as mine," she said, manifesting no shame at all. She did not go to see Matt and she did not even mention him. He kept to himself and was not seen at Mass. Strange that a posse of men led by her father did not go either. It may have been because Matt was superior, having been to Canada, and also, he kept a shotgun and might fire as they came through the yard. The priest promised her mother that he would go when the weather got finer, but he kept putting it off and instead made a most lurid sermon about impurity. The women in the congregation coughed, blushed, and were deeply affected by it. All Mabel did was smirk and cross her legs, which was a disrespectful thing to do in a holy place. It was decided that she was losing her reason, hence her outrageous behavior. She alternated between being very talkative and being gloomy. She sat in the hen house for hours, smoking and brooding. Getting cigarettes was at that time one of her biggest problems, because she had extended her credit in all the shops. She asked me if ever I got a shilling or found money to get her a packet of fags. Then she made me listen at the wall of her stomach and said wasn't it full of mischief.

My parents were enlisted to help. A stranger was to come to our house and I was not sure what he was to do for Mabel, but he was crucial. A man in a long brown leather coat and matching gauntlet gloves arrived in his motor just before dark. He was shown into the front room, where my parents and Mabel's mother spoke to him. Mabel was with me in the kitchen, where she did nothing but make faces. She had discovered the satisfaction of making faces. She scrunched up her nose, stuck out her tongue, and rolled her eyes in all directions.

"I can paddle my own canoe," she said as she paced back and forth. Watching her I kept imagining the most terrible metamorphosis going on inside her and tried to calculate how old the thing was. She asked if the people up the street ever spoke about her and I lied by saying no. She said a lot of people had a lot of bees in their bonnet, yet when they reproached her she quailed. She went in with bowed head and bowed back. Presently my mother came out and said to lay a tray quickly. She was surprisingly cheerful, as if he had promised to perform a miracle. She bustled about the kitchen and said what a mercy it was that we did not have such a cross to bear. Then she asked me to put a doily on the cake plate and to make sure that the cake knife had no mold or rust.

To this day I do not know whether the stranger was a faith healer or a quack, or perhaps a bachelor in search of a wife. At any rate, after he left, spirits sagged. There was another consortium and it was decided that they would tell Mabel's father that night. His shock upon hearing it was such that he could be heard roaring half a mile away, and it seems it took three people to hold him down as he threatened to go to Mabel's room in order to kill her. Gradually he was mollified with hot whiskey and the assurance that the event had happened in the most untoward and unfortunate way, in short, that Mabel had been molested by a stranger. Thus, rage was transferred to a brute who had come and gone, and now Mabel was told to come down and eat her supper. It seems she sat hunched over the fire sniveling and fiddling with the tongs while her father ranted. He had somehow got it into his head that it was a tinker who had done the deed, and he cursed every member of that fraternity, both male and female. He was made to swear that he would not strike her, and when my parents left, the family was as happy as might be expected under such woeful circumstances.

The next day Mabel's mother went to the town to buy wool, and in her spare time she began to knit vests, matinee coats, and little boots. But it could not be said that she and Mabel became reconciled. Her mother would sit out in the yard scraping the ground with a stone or a stick, making V's and circles, and asking her Maker to take pity on her. Not a word passed between the two women, only growls. When the mother came into the kitchen Mabel went out to the hen house. No one knew where the birth would take place and no one knew when. No arrangements were made. Mabel got highly strung when asked and burst into tears and said that no one in the whole wide world loved or understood her. She was a sight, in a brown tweed coat and a knitted cap. Being large did not become her, and in contrast her face looked minute. She went to the chapel every afternoon as if to atone, and as it got nearer her time, people were less vicious about her.

It was a summer's day and the men were in the hayfield when Mabel's labor commenced. The Angelus had just struck. When her mother heard the first howl, she ran with the tongs still in her hand onto the road for help. She hailed a passing cyclist and told him to get the doctor quick. The doctor, who was a locum, was bound to be in the dispensary at that hour. I was nearby playing shop with two of my friends and we were sent to fetch my mother. Soon pots of water were boiled, Mabel was crying and begging for ether. My friends and I were both drawn to the house and repelled by it. At every sound Mabel's mother asked was it coming, yet she avoided going into the room. She merely called in through the open door. Mabel was becoming delirious as the pains got worse, but mercifully we saw the doctor arrive. He was brusque, asked what the trouble was, and said, "Tch . . . tch . . . tch," when told.

"Why haven't I seen her sooner?" he said, and then frowned as if he decided that everyone in the neighborhood was wanting. Mabel was howling as he entered, but soon after, a calm descended, and we remained in the kitchen, full of suspense and muttering a prayer. It was not long until he came out.

"You can put that stuff away," he said, referring to the swaddling clothes and the aluminum bath that was filled with water. Mabel's mother concluded that the infant was dead and said, "Lord have mercy on its soul."

"There is no *it*," he said. "She's no more pregnant than I am."

My mother and Mabel's mother were aghast. It was as if some terrible trick had been played on them. Naturally they were incredulous.

"There's nothing there, I've examined her."

"But, Doctor, is that possible?" my mother asked accusingly.

"It's all hogwash," he said. He did not know the circumstances and nobody bothered to tell him. He simply said that it was a pity he had not been consulted sooner and then announced that his fee would be two pounds and he'd like it there and then. From the room the crying had stopped and no one took the slightest trouble to go in. No one went near her. It was as if she had taken on the marks of a leper. Her mother glared in that direction and said that her only daughter had brought them nothing but disaster. To have to tell this to the parish was the last straw. The waves in her white hair bristled, and she reminded me of nothing so much as a weasel, poised to spit. Her withheld temper was worse than all her husband's exclaiming.

"Let her break it to him herself," she said, pointing a fist toward the closed door. If one can curse in silence, she did it then, so resolute and so full of hatred was her expression. By way of consolation my mother said that surely Mabel could not be right in the head. Her words were hardly a solace.

From the room now there was a low keen. No doubt Mabel was still lying down, bunched up as she had been in labor and perhaps waiting for a kind word. No one ventured in. Her mother emptied the tea leaves into the front garden and with a swish told my two friends, who had been waiting outside, to vamoose. Back in the kitchen she began to list Mabel's faults and lament the money she had cost them since she came home. Money on tonics, money on style, money on faddish food when she got those cravings at night.

"Tinned salmon, no less," she said sourly, and told my mother that her pension each week had gone toward Mabel's fancies. Then for no reason she recalled a large beautiful hand-painted urn that Mabel had broken when young. It seems that from the confines of her pram Mabel had reached up to embrace it and toppled it instead. This announcement seemed to confirm that Mabel was, from birth, a rotten egg. Mabel's attraction to the opposite sex had been in the nature of a disease.

It would be funny to see her thin, having just seen her that morning large and cumbersome. The rush crib was still on the kitchen table and the sight of it an affront. I wanted to bring her a slice of cake, or tea in her favorite china cup, but I was afraid to disobey them. I felt that this now would be as much a quality of mine as my eyes or my hair, this paralysis in my character, this wanting to step in but not daring to, this dreadful hesitancy. I would, I wouldn't. Thus I wrestled, but the weight and depth of their opprobrium won and I did not go in, nor did they, and the whimpering went on, the chant of a hopeless creature.

We did not lay eyes on Mabel again. Just as the shame of pregnancy had made her brazen and untoward, so now the shame of non-pregnancy had made her withdrawn. She refused to see anyone and barely broke her fast. One evening, after dark, she left as she had once arrived, in a hackney car, and from that moment her memory was banished. The only reminder was that next day on the clothesline were her blankets, her patchwork quilt, and some baby clothes. Her parents had a Mass said in the house, and in time it was as if she had never come home, as if she were still in Australia.

Some said that she was in Dublin working for nuns, others said that she worked in a nursing home, and still others that she was a charwoman. These were just stories. No one ever knew the truth, but it is certain that Mabel withered and finally died without ever having been reinstated with family or friends, and that she is buried in some strange and unmarked place.

Courtship

A favorite school poem was "The Mother" by Patrick Pearce. It was a wrenching poem condoling the plight of a mother who had seen her two strong sons go out and die, "in bloody protest for a glorious thing." Mrs. Flynn had also known tragedy, her husband having died from pleurisy and her youngest son, Frank, having drowned while away on holiday. For a time she wept and gnashed, her fate being similar to the poor distraught mother's in the poem. I did not know her then but there were stories of how she balked at hearing the tragic news. When the guards came to tell her that Frank was drowned, she simply pressed her hands to her ears and ran out of the house, into the garden, saying to leave her alone, to stop pestering people. When at last they made her listen, her screaming was such that the curate heard it two miles away. Her son was eighteen and very brainy.

By the time I met her she seemed calm and reconciled, a busy woman who owned a shop and a mill and who had three other sons, all of whom were over six feet and who seemed gigantic beside her, because she was a diminutive woman with gray permed hair. Her pride in them was obvious and transmitted itself to all who knew her. It was not anything she said, it was just the way she would look up at them as if they were a breed of gods, and sometimes she would take a clothes brush and brush one of their lapels, just to confirm that closeness. They all had dark eyes and thick curly hair, and there was not a girl in the parish who did not dream of being courted by one of them. Of the three, Michael was the most sought after. It was his lovely manner, as the women said; even the old women melted when they described how he put them at their ease when they went to sell eggs or buy groceries. He was a famous hurley player, and the wizard way that he scored a goal was renowned and immortalized in verses that the men carried in their pockets. If his team was ever in danger of losing and he had been put out for a foul—as he often was—the crowd would clamor for him and the referee had no choice but to let him back. His specialty was to score a goal in the very last minute of the game, when the opposing team thought themselves certain of victory; and this goal and the eerie way in which it was scored would be a talking point for weeks. Then after the match the fans would carry him on their shoulders, and the crowd would mill around, trying to touch his feet or his hands, just as in the Gospels the crowd milled about trying to touch Our Lord. That night in a dance hall, girls would vie to dance with him. He had a steady girl called Moira, but when he traveled to hurling matches he met other girls at dances, and for weeks some new girl, some Ellen, or some Dolly, or some Kate, would plague him with love letters. I learned this from Peggy, their maid, when I went there on my first ever holiday. I had yearned to go for many years and at last the chance came, because my sister, who used to go, had set her sights on the city and went instead to cousins in Limerick who had a sweet shop that adjoined a chip shop. As in many other things I had taken her place; I was her substitute, and the realization of this was not without its undercurrent of jealousy and pique.

On my first day in their house I felt very gawky, and kept avoiding the brothers and crying in the passage. I wanted to go home but was too ashamed to mention it. It was Michael who rescued me.

"Will you do me a favor?" he said.

The favor was very simple—it was to make him apple fritters. If there was anything in the world he craved, it was apple fritters. I was to make them surreptitiously, when his mother was not looking.

"Can't," I said.

His mother and Peggy were constantly about and the thought of defying them quite impossible.

"Suppose they went off for a day, would you make them then?"

"Of course."

That "of course," so quick, so yielding, already making it clear that I was eager to serve him.

In a matter of days I had settled in and thought no place on earth so thrilling and so bustling as their house and their shop. They stocked everything—groceries, animal feed, serge for suits, winceyette, cotton, paraffin, cakes, confectionery, boots, Wellingtons, and cable-knit sweaters that were made by spinsters and lonely women up in the mountains. They even sold underwear for ladies and gents, and these were the subject of much innuendo and mirth. The ladies' corsets were of pink broderie Anglaise, and sometimes one of the brothers would take one out of its cellophane and put it on over his trousers, as a joke. Of course, that was when the shop was empty and his mother had gone to confession, or to see a sick neighbor. They respected their mother and in her presence never resorted to shady language.

What I liked about staying there was the jokes, the levity, and the constant activity—cakes being delivered, meal being weighed, eggs being brought in and having to be counted as well as washed, orders having to be got ready, and at any moment a compliment or a pinch in the arm from one of the brothers. It was all so exhilarating. At night more diversion, when the men convened in the back bar, drank porter, and talked in monosyllables until they got drunk, and then ranted and raved and got obstreperous when it came to politics. If they were too unruly Michael would roll up his sleeves, take off his wristwatch, and tell them that unless they "cut out the bull" they would be rudely ejected to the yard outside.

In the morning the brothers joked and made references to the dramas of the night before, while their mother always said it was inviting disaster to have men in after hours. The guards rarely raided because of once having to give the terrible news about Frank, but she was always in fear that she might be raided, disgraced, and brought to court. The brothers used to tease her about being a favorite with the sergeant, and though pretending to resent this, she blushed and got very agitated and looked in all directions so as to avoid their insinuations. I wore a clean dress each day and, to enhance myself, a starched white collar which gave me, I thought, a plaintive look. I was forever plying them with more tea or another fried egg or relish. Michael would touch my wrist and say, "That the girl, that the girl," and I hoped that I would never have to go home. I even harbored a dream about being adopted by his mother, so that I would become his sister and shake hands with him, or even embrace, without any suggestion of shame or sin.

Each morning the oldest brother, William, filled the buggy with provisions in order to go up the country to buy and to sell. He used to coax me to go with him by telling me about the strange people he met. In one house three members of the family were mad and bayed like dogs, and the fourth, sane member had to throw buckets of water on them to calm them down. There was the house, or rather the hovel, where the hunchback, Della, lived, and she constantly invited him in for tea in the hope that he would propose to her. Each time when he refused, Della stamped her foot and said that the invitation wasn't meant anyhow. There was a mother and daughter who never stirred out of bed and who called to him to come upstairs, where he would find them in bed, wearing fancy bed jackets, with rouge and lipstick on them, consulting fashion catalogues.

"Do you ever score?" I heard his cousin Tom ask him one morning, and William put his finger to his lips and smiled as if there were sagas he could tell. But I would not be dragged to these places, because for one thing I had no interest in fields or hay sheds or lakes, and for another I wanted to remain in Michael's orbit and be ready at any moment should he summon me, or just bump into me and give me a sudden thrilling squeeze. He worked in the mill, which was a short distance across the garden. Sometimes I would convey him out there, and if the birds were gorging on the currant bushes, as they usually were, he would flap his hands and make a great to-do as he frightened them away.

"Be seeing you later, alligator," he always said, and lifted his cap once or twice to show that he was a gentleman. I then had to go back and help Peggy to wash the dishes, polish the range, and scrub the kitchen and the back kitchen. Later we made the beds. Making his bed was exciting but untoward. Peggy would flare up as she entered the room, then she would whip the bedclothes off and grumpily shake them out the window. In the yard below the geese cackled when she shook these bedclothes, and the gander hissed and raised his orange beak to defend his tribe.

"I can't wait to get to England," Peggy would say, and her version of life there seemed to envisage a world that did not include geese or the necessity to make beds. The room itself was like all the bedrooms, high-ceilinged, covered with garish carpet and unmatching furniture. There was the dark mahogany wardrobe with a long mirror that looked muddied over and gave back a very poor reflection of the self. There was the double bed with wooden headboard, and there was a cane chair beside the bed on which he flung clothes. His shoes, so big and so important, were laid inside the curb of the tiled fireplace, tan shoes well shone and with shoe trees in them, his fawn coat on a hanger, swaying a little in the dark space of the wardrobe. There were, too, his various ties, the red-tasseled box in which were thrown the several love letters, his scapulars, his missal, and then, most nakedly of all, his pajamas in a heap at the end of the very tossed bed, causing Peggy to be incensed and to ask aloud if he played hurley in his sleep or what. Along the mantelpiece was the row of cups that he had won at hurley and beside them a framed photograph of his mother as a very young girl, with lips pouted, like a rosebud. I would touch the cups and beg of Peggy to tell me when and where each one had been awarded. They were tarnished, and I resolved that one day I would get silver dip and put such a shine on them that when he entered his room that night he would be greeted by the gleam of silver and would wonder who had done it and maybe would even find out.

Once the beds were done, I would then concoct an excuse to go over to the mill. Up to the moment I had yielded I would intend not to go, but then all of a sudden some frenzied need would take hold of me, and though despising myself for such weakness, I succumbed. Crossing the garden, humming some stupid ditty, I would already picture him, his face and jacket dusted over with white grain, his whole being smelling of it, his skin powdered and pale, a feature which made him look older but made his eyes shine like deep pools. I would hear the rush of the little river and see segments of it being splashed and tumbled in the spokes of the big wooden mossy mill wheel, and I would go in trying to appear casual.

"Any news?" he would say, and invariably he asked if the English folk had been to the shop yet. An Englishman and his son had come to the district to shoot and fish, and their accents were a source of mirth to us, as was their amazement about nature. They were most surprised by the fact that they had caught a rabbit, and brought it over to show it to people as if it were a trophy.

One day, however, I found him in a rage, and saw that he was hitting the wooden desk and calling Jock, the boy who helped him, the greatest idiot under the sun. Michael had addressed the bills to his customers and had put *Esquire* after each one, when Jock had come along and put *Mr.* before each name, and now thirty or forty envelopes would have to be readdressed. Despite his fury he had put his arm around me as usual and said what a pity that I couldn't work in the mill, so's he'd send Jock to a reformatory, where he belonged. I was basking in being so close to him when a beautiful older girl sauntered in, on the very flimsy excuse that she was looking for her father. This was Eileen, with blond hair, blue eyes, and great long black lashes, which she knowingly flaunted by repeated fluttering. She worked in Dublin but was home for a few days, and as she came down between the sacks, it was prodigal to see their interest in each other quicken. She walked with a sway and said that her father was supposed to have come with bags of corn for grinding but where on earth had he vanished to? Seeing his arm around me, she pretended to be very haughty and said, "Sorry," then turned on her heel and walked away. She wore a red jacket, a pleated skirt, and wedge-heeled canvas sandals with straps that laced up over her calves.

"What's the big hurry?" he called out to her.

"Have to see a man about a dog," she said, and she turned and smirked. He said that he had not known she was at home and might he ask how long would the parish have the pleasure of her exotic company.

"Until I get the wanderlust," she said, and announced that she might go to a hotel at the seaside for a weekend, as she heard they had singsongs.

"God, you must be rolling in it," he said.

"Correct," she said, and put out her arm to reveal the bone bangles that she wore.

"I suppose we're the country Mohawks," he said.

"You certainly don't know how to pamper a gal," she said, and implied that men in Dublin knew what it was all about. The peals of laughter that she let out were at once sweet and audacious.

"Do you live on the north side?" he said.

"Gosh, no, the south side," she said, and added that if one lived on the north side, one would be roused by the bawling of cattle two mornings a week as they were driven to the cattle market and herded into pens. "The north side is far too countrified," she said.

"So you're sitting pretty on the south side," he said with a sting. By now he had deserted me and was facing her, taking such stock of her as if every detail of her person intrigued him. Though they were saying caustic things, they were playful and reveled in each other's banter.

"Who's the little kid?" she said, looking back at me, and upon being told, she said that she knew my sister, had seen her at dances, and that my sister was full of herself.

"What are you up to tonight?" he asked.

"Fast work," she said, and he biffed her, and then they linked and went outside to confer. Standing next to Jock, who was scratching the *Mr.* off each envelope, I felt foolish, felt outcast just like him. They stood in the doorway close together, and fired with curiosity, I hurried toward them and slipped out without even being noticed. There was a lorry parked to one side and I stood on the running board in order to spy on them. It was awful. His arm was around her waist and she was looking up at him, saying, "What do *you* think you're doing." He said he could do as he pleased, break her ribs if he felt like it.

"Just try, just you try," she said, and with both hands he appeared to mash her ribs as he circled her waist. A few flies droned around the lorry, as there were milk tanks on the back, and there was a smell of sour milk and metal. The driver's seat was torn and bits of spiral spring stuck out of it. I wondered whose lorry it was. Not having looked for a few minutes, I now allowed myself another glance at the bewitched pair. He was standing a little behind her; her pleated skirt was raised so that it came unevenly above her knees, and I could see the top of her legs, the lace of her slip, and her mounting excitement as she stood on tiptoe to accommodate herself to what he was doing. Also, she let out suggestive sounds and was laughing and wriggling until suddenly she became very matter-of-fact, pulled her skirt down, and said what did he think he was up to. Then she ran off, but he caught her and they had a little tug of war. He let go of her on the understanding that they would meet that night, and they made an appointment in the grounds of what had once been a demesne but was now gone to ruin.

By the time they met, and possibly just as he was resting their two bicycles, interlocking them against a tree, or spreading his overcoat on the grass, I was kneeling down to say the Rosary with his mother, whose voice throbbed with devotion. She had decided that night to offer up the Rosary for her dead son and her dead husband. The kitchen flagstones felt hard and grimy; it was as if grit was being ground into our knees as we recited endless Our Fathers, Hail Marys, and Glory Bes. I was thinking of the lovers with a curiosity that bordered on frenzy. I could picture the meeting place, the smell of grass, cows wheezing, their two faces almost featureless in the dark, and by not being able to see, their power of touch so overwhelmingly whetted that their hands reached out, and suddenly they clove together and dared to say each other's Christian name with a hectic urgency. I was thinking this while at the same time mouthing the prayers and hearing the mumbling of the men in the bar outside. I even knew the men who were there, and saw one old man to whom I had an aversion, because the porter froth made gold foam on his gray mustache. Mrs. Flynn was profligate that night with prayers and insisted that we do the Three Mysteries—the Joyful, Sorrowful, and Glorious. It was after ten o'clock when we stood up, and we were both doubled over from the hours of kneeling.

She asked if as a reward I would like a "saussie," and she popped two sausages into the pan that was always lying on the side of the stove in case any of her sons became hungry. In no time the fat was hissing and she was prodding the sausages with a fork and telling them to hurry up, as there were two famished customers. Afterward she gave me little biscuits with colored icing and said that I could come for every holiday and stay for the entire length. Saying it, I think she believed that I would never grow up. I slept with her, and all that I recall of the bedroom is that it was damp, that the flowered wallpaper had become runny and disfigured, and that the feathers in the pillows used to dig into one's flesh. That night, perhaps exalted from so much praying, she did not insist that we go to sleep at once but allowed us to chat. Naturally I brought the subject around to her sons.

"Which of them do you prefer?" I asked.

"They're all the same in my eyes," she said in a very practical voice.

"But isn't Michael a great hurler?" I said, hoping that we could discuss him, hoping she would tell me what he was like as a baby, and as a little boy, what mischief he had done, and maybe even discuss his present behavior, especially his gallivanting.

She said that a gypsy came into the shop one day long ago and predicted that Michael would have a checkered life, and that she prayed hourly that he would never take it into his head to go to England.

"He won't," I said, without any justification.

"Please God not," she said, and added that Michael was a softie with everybody. Little did she know that at that moment he was engaged in a tryst that would make her writhe.

"I think he is your favorite," I said.

"What a little imp you are," she said, and announced that we must go to sleep at once. But I knew that I wouldn't. I knew that I would stay awake until I heard him come up the stairs and go into his room, and that having heard him, I would experience some remote satisfaction, thinking, or rather hoping, that he had tired of Eileen and was now ours again. It was very late when he got back and my mood was dismal because of his whistling. A mad notion took hold of me to go and ask him if he wanted sausages, but mercifully I resisted.

I wondered which of the two girls he would smile at next day at Mass. As it happened, Eileen and his girl friend Moira were in the same seat, but not next to one another. Eileen was all in black, with a black mantilla that shrouded her face. I thought she looked ashamed, but I may have imagined it. Moira had a cardigan knitted in the blackberry stitch and a matching beret that was clapped on the side of her head and secured with a pearled hat pin. During the long sermon she kept turning around, probably to see where Michael was. He stood in the back of the church with the men, and like them skedaddled at the Last Gospel. The two girls came down the aisle very quietly and exchanged a word on the porch. Then Moira went on home with her parents, and Eileen cycled home alone.

At lunchtime Michael was very attentive to me, kept giving me more gravy and more roast potatoes, kept telling me to eat up. It was my last day, as I was leaving very early in the morning on the mail car. Perhaps he was nice to me for that reason, or else it was a silent bribe not to betray his secret. I had already accrued a gift of ten shillings and rosary beads from his mother; in the back of the crucifix was a little cavity containing a special relic.

As we were eating, their cousin Tom rushed into the kitchen and announced that he was taking me to the pictures that night. The brothers let out some hoots, whereupon he said that for two weeks I had helped in the kitchen, helped in the shop, and had had no diversion at all. To my dismay their mother applauded the idea and said what a shame that one of her sons hadn't shown such thought. I disliked Tom; he had a smile that was faintly indecent, and whenever a girl went by, he made licking sounds and gurgles. He had glaring red hair, pale skin with freckles, and often he wore his socks up over his trouser legs to emphasize his calves. His hands were the most revolting, being very white, and his fingers were like long white slugs. Despite the fact that I withered at being invited, he said that he would pick me up at six and that we would have a whale of a time. The cinema was three or four miles away and we were to cycle. I dreaded cycling, as even in the daylight I had a tendency to wobble.

The Angelus was striking as he arrived in a green tweed suit with matching cap. He was unable to conceal his pleasure, and at once I saw his salaciousness from the way he touched the saddle of my bicycle and said oughtn't I to have a little cover on it, as it wasn't soft enough. "You demon," Michael said to him as we set off. The cycling was most unnerving; I bumped into him several times and found myself veering to the ditch whenever a car passed us. He said that had he known of my precariousness he would have put a cushion on the crossbar and conveyed me himself. I could not bear his voice and I could not bear his unctuousness, and what I disliked most of all was the way he kept saying my name, making it clear that he was attracted to me.

When we got to the cinema he linked me up the steps and led me into the foyer. It was a very luxurious place with a wide stairs, and the streams of light from the big chandelier made rainbow prisms on the red carpet. The stair handle had just been polished and it smelt of Brasso. Inside, he settled us into two seats in the second to last row, and once it became dark, he grasped my hand and began to squeeze it. I pretended not to know what was going on. His next ruse was to tickle the palm of my hand slowly with his fingers. A woman had told me that if tickled on the palm of the hand, or behind the knees, one could become wanton and lose control. On the screen Lola Montez was engaged in the most strenuous and alarming scuffles as she tried to escape a villain. Her predicament was not unlike my own. Having attacked the palm of one hand, he then set out on the other, and finding me unwilling, if not to say recalcitrant, he told me to uncross my legs, but I wouldn't. I sealed them together and wound one foot around the other ankle so that I was like something stitched together. I strove to ignore him, and annoyed by this he leaned over and licked my ear and so revolted me that I let out a cry, causing people to turn around in amazement. Naturally he drew away, and when the man behind him thumped his shoulder, he muttered some abject apology about his sister (that was me) being very highly strung.

When we left the cinema he was livid. He said why do such a thing, why egg him on with ringlets and smiles and then make a holy show of him. I said sorry. What with the dark and the long cycle home, I realized that I was at his mercy. I feigned great interest in the plot of the film and began to question him about it, but he saw through this ruse and suddenly swerved his bicycle in front of mine and said, "Halt, halt." I knew what it presaged. He took both bicycles, slung them aside, and then embraced me and said what a little tease I was, and then backed me toward a gateway. The gate rattled and shook under the impact of our joined bodies and from inside the field a cow let out a very lugubrious moan.

"I'm not going in there," I said.

"Not half," he said.

He said he had paid three and sixpence per seat and had had enough codology and wasn't taking any more. I summoned all the temerity I could and said how the priest would kill me and also Mrs. Flynn would kill me.

"They needn't know," he said.

"They would, they would," I said.

He was not going to be fobbed off with excuses.

"Have a heart!" he said as he began to kiss me, and inquire what color underclothes I wore.

"I love Michael, I love Michael," I said vehemently. Foolishly, I thought jealousy might quell his intentions.

"Hasn't he got Moira?" he said, and went on to outline how Michael was at that very moment in the loft above the mill, close to Moira, a rendezvous they kept most Sunday nights.

"That's a lie," I said.

"Is it!" he said, and boasted how Michael described Moira's arrival, her shyness, her chatter, then her capitulation as he removed her coat, her dress, her underclothes, and she lay there with not a stitch. As his advances were now rapid, I knew there was nothing for it but to have a fit. I started to shake all over, to scream, to say disjointed things, indeed to be so delirious that he slapped me on the face and said for Christ's sake to calm down, that no one was going to do anything to me. We could hear a car in the distance, and as its headlights came around the corner, I ran out and waved frantically. It was the vet, who slowed down, wound the window, and shouted, "What's up?"

"Nothing's up," Tom said, and added that I had a puncture but that he had mended it. When the car drove off he picked up his bicycle and said for a long time he had not had such a fiasco of an evening.

Ours was a silent and a sullen journey home. He cycled ahead of me and never once turned around to see if I followed. As we neared the village, he cycled on downhill, and I got off because my brakes were faulty. I felt full of shame and blunder and did not know what I would say if Mrs. Flynn or the brothers asked me if I had enjoyed myself. I felt disgraced and dearly wished that I could go home there and then.

Michael confronted me in the hall as I was hanging up my coat. He said had I seen a ghost or what, as I was white as a sheet. Soon he guessed.

"The pup, the blackguard," he said as he brought me into the kitchen. He put me in the big armchair, sat beside me, and started to stroke my hair, all the while iterating what injury he would do to Tom. Suddenly he kissed me, and this kiss being a comfort, he followed it with a shower of kisses, embraces, and fond fugitive words.

"I love you," I said bluntly.

"Ditto," he said. His voice and expression were quite different now, young and unguarded. I was seeing the man for whom Moira, Eileen, and a host of girls would tear one another's eyes out. We heard a stir and he drew back, stood up sharply, and opened the kitchen door very casually, while also winking at me.

"Who goes there?" he said in a stern voice, and then went into the well of the hall, but no one answered. He crossed over into the shop and all of a sudden the kitchen became dark, either because he had interfered with the mains or their electricity plant had gone wrong. I was like someone in a trance. I could feel him coming back by his soft quick steps and then by the glow of a cigarette. Just as I had once imagined the lure of his voice in the dark saying a name, he now said mine, and his arms reached out to me with a sweet, almost a childlike supplicatingness. What had been disgusting and repellent an hour before was now a transport, and there was nothing for it but to be glad; that wild and frightened gladness that comes from breaking out of one's lonely crust, and just as with the swimmer who first braves the depths, the fear is secondary to the sense of prodigal adventure. He said that he would get some cider and two glasses and that we could go over to the loft, where no one would bother us. Whatever he proposed I would have agreed to. We went out like thieves, and crossing the yard, he picked me up so's I wouldn't spoil my shoes.

In the morning he stuck his tousled head out of his bedroom door, and in front of his mother gave me a quick kiss, then whispered, "I'll be waiting for you." It was not true, but it was all I wanted to hear, and on the drive home, the blue misted hills, the cold lakes, the songs of the birds, and the shiny laurel hedges around the grand estates all seemed startlingly beautiful and energized, and it was as if they had just been inhabited by some new and invigorating pulse of life.

Ghosts

Three women. They represent defiance, glamour, and a kind of innocence that I miss in my later world. They were all tall and if I had to liken them to anything it would be to those paintings of winter trees, with scarcely a leaf left, trees shorn by the wind.

The first of them went periodically mad, and one day, during one of those bouts, she walked into our kitchen wielding an ash plant. Our back door was always open, and there was an odd Wellington boot against it to keep it ajar. She was called Delia, and at once she struck out at everything she could see. Her consummate anger was vented on our pale elm dresser, and I worried for the beautiful plates that were wedged in along the back. They were plates that my mother had won at a carnival in Coney Island long before. They were the nicest thing in the whole kitchen. They were white china plates with a different flower on each one. The plate I loved most had a strange mauve spiral flower that was not like the flowers that grew in the fields. I feared for all of them, but principally for it. Delia lashed out and said that they were dirty, filthy, said that the whole place was a dive and full of muck and that she was going to see to it that we cleaned our premises. I went in under the table, a place I often resorted to, and where pups or dogs often followed.

On she went, expressing her dislike of our way of life, of my mother's brown bread—she made horrible faces, as if she were taking cascara—of the oilcloth on the table, of the dust in the brown corduroy cushions on the armchair. As far as we knew, her own house was a pigsty. She lived there with her two brothers and an invalid mother, and no one ever cleaned it. The veterinary surgeon used to say that he had to fumigate himself after he had been to their back kitchen to get hot water or his fee. Their house was called Bracken House, and there was a river nearby. It flooded in the winter, and their fields were swampy. They had an old piano in the sitting room, and there they kept bags of sugar and flour and also a machine in which they pulped mangels and turnips. Their voices were forever raised. That was all we knew about them, and when we children had occasion to pass their gateway, we would run and tell each other that the maddies had come to catch us. Her brother Dinny used to chase girls and ask them into the hay shed to romp. He, too, used to be carted to the asylum.

Now Delia was in our house and behaving as if she were a governess, as if she had a right to open cupboards and object to spilled sugar or spilled oatmeal, and to say "disgusting" and repeat it until she was singing it on a very high wavery note. It was just as well we did not own a piano or have our concertina. The local sergeant had borrowed it for a wedding.

My mother calmed her by sitting her down and giving her a mug of tea and cake. It was a marble cake, and Delia marveled at the three colors that composed each slice. They were like a painting, with more brown than green, the plain egg color in the center acting as a barrier between the two other tempting colors. My mother then showed her the green essence that she had used, and suddenly Delia became soft-spoken and our house became the loveliest nest in the world. She brooded for a moment as she chewed. She chewed very determinedly, as if she were tasting each crumb. She was a thin creature, and she wore high-heeled, laced shoes.

All of a sudden she ventured to say that her mother and father should never have married, because they were misfits. She said that her mother had only married him because he had given her "coaxyorum." My mother asked what that was, and Delia lowered her head and pointed to the little bottle of essence and asked if she could have a drop. After taking a spoonful of green syrup, she was all soppy and babyish, rubbing her chest in slow circular strokes. "Coaxyorum," she said, was like that. Long ago, her father had got up on a ladder, had gone into her mother's bedroom, had given her mother this potion, and before she knew where she was, the mother was being carried down the ladder and into a sidecar and off to the father's house—in fact, to Bracken House. Her mother's family had disowned her and never spoke to her again.

Delia became so happy that at dusk she refused to go home. My mother bribed her by putting a hunk of cake in clean greaseproof paper and by giving her a pompon that she had taken a fancy to, but she would not budge. I remember how she clung to the brown polished bars of the chair when our workman tried to shift her, and eventually he had to threaten her with the poker, for by now we were dire enemies again and our house was a pigsty. She flounced off, threw the cake on the cement flags outside, trampled on it, and got into the cart the workman had brought round, shouting with the utmost vehemence, "We don't need you, we don't need you, we don't bloody need you!" The last I saw of her, she was standing in the cart and then, as he got the mare into a gallop, falling down, but all the while continuing her shout of defiance. "We don't need you, we don't bloody need you!"

The next of these women, Nancy, was a dream figure in a long motor coat, and dangling from her arm a lizard handbag with a beautiful amber clasp. I can even now hear it being opened and shut as she would take out her cigarette case or her lace-edged hankie, or look in it for no reason—though perhaps it was to gaze in the little mirror in the side pocket. Every time she came to our house, she brought her own box camera, so her visits and her lovely clothes were all perpetuated, though many of them came out blurred. She was a flirt. I did not know all that it meant, but I knew that she was a flirt. She would look at men, she would drink them in, and then make a movement, or a flurry of movements, with her swallow, and she would gulp as if it were sherbet or lemonade or something fizzy. She came to our house whenever there was a dress dance in the village; she would arrive a day or two before and stay a day or two after.

The day before, she would put oatmeal packs on her face and then a beaten egg white, and my mother and she would laugh and pose as they tried on her clothes. She always brought an attaché case full of style. There would be at least two dance dresses, her fur stole with the dark stripes that seemed in danger of coming alive or purring, two or three purses, dance shoes, and a beautiful perfume spray. I would be let hold it in my hand, let squeeze its soft, thick rubber nozzle, and presently the air of the room would be imbued with this near-religious smell and I, at least, was transported elsewhere. Sometimes she brought clothes that were on approval, and these, being new, were the most coveted and the most beautiful. She brought an astrakhan coat that she and my mother took turns trying on; they must have tried it on ten or fifteen times one wet morning. Then I was allowed to try it on, but at once had to take it off, because it was trailing along the floor, and what with their diversion, the floor had not been swept that day and the tiles were smudged from the dogs and the men. It suited Nancy best. Her hair was auburn and copious, and this brown curly astrakhan was a perfect complement to it. She always brought her curling tongs, and when, before a dance, she started to curl her hair, she would sometimes threaten to put my nose between the two warm pincers. Then her eyes would narrow and she would laugh. She was inscrutable.

She and my mother often discussed possible marriages, though she could see from my mother's life, and infer from their conversation, that marriage was not an ideal state. Still, each new man that came to the neighborhood was a source of supreme interest to her. Not many new men came, but from time to time there was a change of staff at the bank or at the creamery, or, more rarely, a new curate. In these men she manifested great interest before she had met them at all or had any inkling what they looked like. The local county councillor was too staid for her, but my father would insist that he was a good catch, had good land and a stock of cattle. Nancy dreamed of being a receptionist in a grand hotel, of making friends with people from different walks of life and being snatched up by a foreign count or baron.

She was lazy and stayed in bed till noon. I would bring her tea and toast, and she would get me to pass her the red woolly dressing gown, and then she would lie back with her head lolled against the brass rungs and say what a lazybones she was. I lived in dread that I might see her breasts, but mercifully her nightdress was not sheer. Her toast would be cut in neat fingers by my mother, and they seemed more mouth-watering than anything we might have downstairs. Usually we had to have brown bread, because my mother made it and it was our duty to have plain things. Toast was from shop bread and was a definite luxury. I would eat the crusts that she had left.

The new curate, who had come fresh from the seminary, was the admiration of all. Girls blushed at the mention of his name. Nancy and he became inseparable. They would go to the shops in his baby Ford to get mutton or a sheep's head or their favorite cigarettes, and when they came back they did not get out of the car immediately but sat laughing and smoking. They chain-smoked. I never saw them touch, but as they walked toward the house, it often was as if they were on the point of touching and therefore all the more tantalizing. Her hand would come out of her coat pocket, or his hand might gesture toward the gate, or lift the rose briar as she stooped and stepped under it, and it needed but one more fraction for them to be in a clasp. Once, each carrying a handle of a wide straw basket, they dropped it, so that the grapefruit, the sugar cubes, and the tins of peas were rolling all over the flagstones. The grapefruit was for him, because my mother said that after the long fast for holy Mass he needed something delicate before he tackled a proper breakfast.

When Nancy was with us, he came to our house directly after Mass and stayed the whole day, until it was time to leave for the evening devotions. They would sit in the kitchen and they would talk and laugh, and Nancy would show him her style. One Sunday, she went so far as to cut his hair. It was quite a ceremony—draping him with the white towel, putting newspaper underneath, and then putting the big rusted brown scissors to his temple and going snip-snip. He was begging her to let him look in the mirror, so that he could see if she was clipping too much, but she laughed and said to trust her. As a joke, she put one of the locks of hair into a little lavaliere that she wore around her neck. The rest was swept up onto a piece of cardboard and tossed over the hedge, as tea leaves might be. He did not like the haircut, said the congregation would now see his big ears, and so she called him Big Ears, and smiled at him, and swallowed intensely. As she commiserated with him, her eyes filled up with the most glistening tears, which she did not shed. They were like glycerine.

Sometimes she and he would call me into the kitchen and ask me to recite or tell some story about the schoolteacher—how she thumped us and called us ugly names—and then just as unaccountably they would ask me to leave the kitchen at once and go outside and not come back till I was called. Those exiles into the garden were agony. They made me think of Christ in Gethsemane, and I would kneel down and ask my Maker to let such agony pass, knowing that it would not. The garden was big and windy: there was just the privet hedge, some devil's pokers, a few shrubs, and two granite pedestals that served as decoration. They were like giant mushrooms, and one of them had come unstuck from its base. I would shake it, hoping it would fall, yet dreading the fact that it might fall and yearning for a tap on the window or a "yoo-hoo"—the signal that said come back.

The curate escorted her to the Halloween dance, and there their friendship underwent a breach. It seems he stood inside the dance-hall door, holding her fur stole, not daring to commit it to the ladies' room, lest it be stolen or tried on by the woman who minded the coats and who was dopey and lackadaisical. The dance floor was like an ice rink, and the band from County Offaly was reputed to be the best that ever came. Nancy danced with all and sundry, and each time she came to the door she smiled or gave some recognition to the curate, who was taking stock of all the dancers but particularly of her.

For the Ladies' Choice she asked the county councillor, knowing that it could not give offense to her new admirer. Her new admirer was the crooner, who wore a fawn gaberdine suit and had a lot of oil in his hair. It seems that the moment he caught sight of her in her raspberry-colored dress he stopped singing, in mid-song, let out a whistle, and then pointed the microphone in her direction. After that, he made a point of singling her out when she approached the bandstand, and he sang the song "Jealousy" with a special lady in mind. When the supper break came, she did not go down to the end of the hall and join the curate for lemonade and queen cakes; rather, she sneaked out by an upper door, which was a fire exit, and was followed by the crooner, who providently brought his Crombie overcoat. No one knew for certain what ensued out there, save that they were not on the grounds of the dance hall but had gone along the road and lurked in a gateway. Nancy herself assured my mother that it was the most harmless little thing—that they sat on the wet wall while the crooner taught her the words of a song she loved. She sang a bit of the chorus of it:

After the ball was over
Just at the break of day
Many's the heart that was aching
If I could read them all
Many's the heart that was broken
Af . . . ter the ball.

It could have been the theme song for the injured curate, because he did not wait to see her home. She got a lift on the crossbar of a bicycle and got oil all over her long dress. He did not come the next morning. My mother said that probably he would never come, and became snappy, as she, too, loved his visits, because they lessened the undercurrent of despair that permeated our house.

Nancy said, "Care to bet?" And they bet sixpence. Nancy's prediction was that he would come on the third day, and so sure was she of this that she postponed going home until then, even though she was needed in the city in her parents' shop. Her parents owned a confectionery shop in Limerick and sold the most beautiful cakes and buns. When she came to us, she always brought a lemon cake or a chocolate cake, and once there was an almond-flavored cake with almond icing and a little almond chicken. She realized there was some pique on my mother's part and took to tidying two cupboards and lined them with newspaper. She picked out all the old socks too, and they looked ridiculous on the kitchen table, gray or flecked socks, all looking for a partner and most of them full of holes.

On the third morning, as the dogs ran joyously from the back steps and chased down the fields, she knew—we all knew—that it was he. She ran to the front window to make sure it was his car. My mother volunteered to go to the yard to feed the fowl, and told Nancy to lay a tray and make him feel at home.

"Hello, stranger" was what Nancy said, and she put her hand out, but he did not shake it. Her nail varnish was a rose pink and the cuticles were very defined. He sat near the range, scowling like a boy. She was all the time smiling, waiting for his rebuke so that she could dismiss it. Her hair was tied up in a big soft roll that stretched from ear to ear, and it made her look older and more sedate. It was like a big sausage. She told me to make myself scarce.

Out in the garden, I wondered what they were saying, or if they had moved nearer, or if as she marched about the kitchen to prepare his repast he was shocked by the slits in her skirt. There was a front and a back slit, and as she moved she took uncommonly large strides, so that one saw above the backs of her knees—saw the flesh covered in beige silk stockings, saw the seam going right up. I was holding the stone mushroom and was about to tilt it to one side, but the next moment I let go of it and it was bending like the Tower of Pisa. In the front room, with its long French window opening onto the garden, the most terrible thing had transpired. They had gone in there and he was stripped to the waist. He had his back to the window. She was looking at his body, as if examining it for spots or a mole or something. But what? I had to come closer in order to find out. His head was turned half around, perhaps to say darling, or what are you doing. At the very same moment, my mother was coming from the farmyard with two empty buckets. My mother was always carrying buckets, always busy, always modest, and was now about to witness the most profane scene—the half-naked curate and Nancy laughing. Nancy bent and said something to his back, and then they must have heard my mother in the kitchen, because suddenly he was putting his shirt on and she was leaving the room. I do not know what she said to him or what caused him to undress. All I know is that I realized she had some secret with men, and that it was a secret I would never grasp, and never quite understand.

The third woman, Mrs. Keogh, did not set foot in our house ever, being too shy. She came once a week, Fridays, after she had drawn her pension, and sat on the back step and drank a cup of buttermilk. She wore heavy serge clothes, the same ones winter and summer, and the same brown velour hat with the two hat pins, one being a huge dented pearl and the other of false emerald stones, many of which were missing. There were holes where the stones should be. She lived across the fields from us and only saw civilization on Sundays, when she went to Mass, and on Fridays, when she drew her old-age pension. She would sit on the back step and say eagerly to my mother, "Any news?" She had a habit of lifting her face and the tip of her nose, as if she were a bird about to take off into the air. If she saw my father or a workman coming toward the house, she would run off and leave the unfinished buttermilk. There was seldom any news, and yet she would ask and ask, as if she could be told something that would fill her up until the next week.

She suffered from shingles. She said she hoped that my mother would never get shingles, and in a strange way my mother knew that one day she would. It was as if, out of consolation, one person eventually got another person's ailment, and what they all dreaded getting was cancer.

Mrs. Keogh had only two ambitions in her life, and we knew them. The first was that her husband might be persuaded to build a new house up near the main road, so that she could see people as they went by. All she wanted was to see them and to see whom they were with, and to see what kind of bicycles they rode, or to see the occasional motorcar. Motorcars were still a novelty, and she expressed a great fear of them—said they were dangerous bulls and could easily get out of hand. My mother said nonsense and that they had brakes, just like a bicycle, but we were all vastly ignorant of their workings. One man carried his toolbox on the running board of his car, and it was said to be crammed with implements. Mrs. Keogh said to just imagine how many things could go wrong with a car, and my mother said that they need not worry, as it would be shanks' mare for them until they died. Her second wish—and this was a terrible secret—was that her husband would die before her. In that way, she imagined she could also achieve her first wish. She thought she would sell the house to people with young children, and being a widow, she might get a county-council cottage and grow flowers in a window box. She told this only one time, when she was racked with pain and was discussing with my mother a new ointment. The ointment was in a little round box, and together they smelled it and were dubious about it. She lifted her bodice and there we saw, like stigmata, a huge crop of sores, and while we were looking at them, the terrible wish tumbled out of her mouth and she retracted it at once.

Her life had no variety. They said the Rosary every evening after their tea. They were in bed while it was still bright in summer, and she was up at five or six washing. She was a powerful washer. She washed tables, chairs, the milk tankard, she washed the outhouses, she washed the windows and the sills of windows, and she would have washed the roof of the hay shed if she had had a ladder long enough. She disliked cooking; her standby was potatoes, bacon, and cabbage; and nothing else.

Their dogs were savages, so one did not venture there unless it was an emergency. After she had been missing from Mass, my mother and I set out to call on her one Sunday evening. As we came up the overgrown lane that led to their cement house, two ferocious creatures came bounding over the fields, barking and snarling. When we saw that the distance between us and them was desperately shortening, we backed away and jumped over a fence, capsizing the uppermost loose plank. They were upon us—two mangy creatures, baring their teeth so that we could see their torn gums. My mother told me to pick up a stone, and while I did she pushed them backward with the plank, making sure that at least the fence was between our feet and their carnivorousness. Pelting them with sod and stones made them worse, and had not Mrs. Keogh's son, Patrick, come to call them, we would have been eaten to death. He dragged them away, and still they snarled and still they conspired to get back to us and have their revenge. He did not invite us in.

Mrs. Keogh came down the field in a man's hat. She always kept her head covered because of the shingles, so the air could never get to her scalp. Wiping her hands on her apron, she then shook hands with us and begged us to sit down on the loose wall. She did not dare ask us in, as her husband was moody and talked only to the sheep and never kept his money anywhere but under his mattress. He thought that any visitors would be apt to steal or borrow from him.

Mrs. Keogh and my mother talked about a new motorcar that Mrs. Sparling had got; they raved about it. There were six motorcars in the neighborhood, but Mrs. Sparling's was unique. It was a French car, and she had been given it as a gift by her brothers in America. Her brothers owned big stores there and gave employment to lots of local people who emigrated. My mother said that Mrs. Sparling had been born with a silver spoon in her mouth and had kept it there ever since. The car was dark purple, almost maroon, with huge head-lamps that gave off two lights, a bright-yellow light and a dimmer, smokier light. I had written my name in dust on the bonnet, the day Mrs. Sparling, the proud owner, had come to show it off. I had sat in it; I had touched and smelled the red leather seats; I had wielded the steering wheel and zanily imagined going this way and that; I had inadvisedly blown the horn and sent my father's horses into a frenzy. I put my initials on the dusty metal and thought how in a sense I would be traveling all over the countryside.

Mrs. Keogh asked about the car in such detail—how big it was, how many could fit comfortably, and if when it was moving, the guts and stomach rumbled. We could not answer these things, because we had not driven in it, though of course we aspired to. By way of apologizing for not asking us in, she slipped me half a crown and from under her skirt produced a carnival jug for my mother. It was a beautiful orange color and it was almost opaque; yet when my mother held it up in the sunset, it gleamed and caught fire. It was like something from a far-off bazaar, completely unlike the dreariness of the surroundings. There were the big piles of cloud, the ragged fields, the hazel trees with their unripe green-skinned nuts, and the little stream that seemed to say tra-la-la tra-la-la tra-la-la.

Thrilled by the gift, my mother made a rash promise. She said that she would ask Mrs. Sparling if we could all go for a drive. It was as if the request had been magically made and magically answered, because Mrs. Keogh jumped up in excitement, gushed like the stream, and asked what would she wear and when would it be.

As we walked home, my mother regretted her promise, because Mrs. Sparling was a snob and made fun of Mrs. Keogh, with her long idiotic clothes, her birdlike snout, and her nervous singsong voice. Called her a Mohawk. My mother said she would not ask just yet; she would bide her time. It was because of that we had to start avoiding Mrs. Keogh. We had to hide when we saw her coming across the fields on Friday, and after Mass my mother rushed out at the Last Gospel, before the rest of the congregation. Mrs. Keogh never left the chapel until the throng went out, and so it was easy enough to avoid her. It bothered us one day when she left a sweater on the back step. It was wrapped in old newspaper. It was a beautiful sweater, with a special zigzag pattern, and it must have taken her weeks to knit. It was for me. It had many colors and reminded me of Joseph and the dream coat. Yet getting it put us under an obligation, and I could enjoy it only in spasms.

It was a few weeks later that we heard how Mrs. Keogh was seen in the village, in the forester's car, and that she was waving to everyone as they sped by. They went through the village, past the school and down the very steep hill that led to the lower road, and we learned that they stopped in the next village and went into the lovely hotel with the pale-green walls, green blinds, and, on the veranda, green glass-topped tables and green bamboo chairs. To our astonishment, Mrs. Keogh and the forester took a cup of tea in there and Mrs. Keogh had the clientele in stitches describing the drive, describing how hedges and houses slid past, saying that it was too quick, was like seeing the tail of a fox as he vanished. Then the forester—he was a distant relation of hers—bought a box of matches, counted them, found there were four missing, reluctantly paid for the two teas, and rose to go home.

At the gateway that led to their little stile, and thence led to a walk across four fields, Mrs. Keogh was loath to leave him. She even suggested going to the village where he lodged and walking home. He could only get rid of her with the guarantee that he would bring her out again. As she crossed the fields, she took off her hat and coat. She and her husband and son always did that. They would always be stripped of their good clothes by the time they got to the house, so that they could start work straightaway. She hurried in to put on the kettle, to get the feed for the hens, to oil and light the lamp, while gabbing to her son about the drive, her vertigo, the way the car swerved at a very bad corner, the forester's presence of mind. Then all of a sudden she dropped the cup with which she was filling the kettle and said she must go out, as she felt dizzy.

Outside, she stood under the hazel tree and clung to a bough, lowered her head onto it, and, without a word, slouched down as her feet had given way, and softly fell and died. There was a seraphic smile on her face, as if the car ride had been the crowning joy of her life. It was what everyone remarked on when they sat in the downstairs room and looked at her remains. Perhaps they found solace in it. I myself could not help thinking of the evening when we sat on the loose wall and the clouds heaved dully by and the little giddy stream went tra-la-la. It was November now, the squirrels had eaten the hazelnuts, and the husks were trampled into the ground and were rotting and nourishing the earth. I could not imagine her dead. I still can't. I still can't imagine any of them dead. They live on; they are fixed in that far-off region called childhood, where nothing ever dies, not even oneself.

Sister Imelda

Sister Imelda did not take classes on her first day back in the convent but we spotted her in the grounds after the evening Rosary. Excitement and curiosity impelled us to follow her and try to see what she looked like, but she thwarted us by walking with head bent and eyelids down. All we could be certain of was that she was tall and limber and that she prayed while she walked. No looking at nature for her, or no curiosity about seventy boarders in gaberdine coats and black shoes and stockings. We might just as well have been crows, so impervious was she to our stares and to abortive attempts at trying to say "Hello, Sister."

We had returned from our long summer holiday and we were all wretched. The convent, with its high stone wall and green iron gates enfolding us again, seemed more of a prison than ever—for after our spell in the outside world we all felt very much older and more sophisticated, and my friend Baba and I were dreaming of our final escape, which would be in a year. And so, on that damp autumn evening when I saw the chrysanthemums and saw the new nun intent on prayer I pitied her and thought how alone she must be, cut off from her friends and conversation, with only God as her intangible spouse.

The next day she came into our classroom to take geometry. Her pale, slightly long face I saw as formidable, but her eyes were different, being blue-black and full of verve. Her lips were very purple, as if she had put puce pencil on them. They were the lips of a woman who might sing in a cabaret, and unconsciously she had formed the habit of turning them inward, as if she, too, was aware of their provocativeness. She had spent the last four years—the same span that Baba and I had spent in the convent—at the university in Dublin, where she studied languages. We couldn't understand how she had resisted the temptations of the hectic world and willingly come back to this. Her spell in the outside world made her different from the other nuns; there was more bounce in her walk, more excitement in the way she tackled teaching, reminding us that it was the most important thing in the world as she uttered the phrase "Praise be the Incarnate World." She began each day's class by reading from Cardinal Newman, who was a favorite of hers. She read how God dwelt in light unapproachable, and how with Him there was neither change nor shadow of alteration. It was amazing how her looks changed. Some days, when her eyes were flashing, she looked almost profane and made me wonder what events inside the precincts of the convent caused her to be suddenly so excited. She might have been a girl going to a dance, except for her habit.

"Hasn't she wonderful eyes," I said to Baba. That particular day they were like blackberries, large and soft and shiny.

"Something wrong in her upstairs department," Baba said, and added that with makeup Imelda would be a cinch.

"Still, she has a vocation!" I said, and even aired the idiotic view that I might have one. At certain moments it did seem enticing to become a nun, to lead a life unspotted by sin, never to have to have babies, and to wear a ring that singled one out as the Bride of Christ. But there was the other side to it, the silence, the gravity of it, having to get up two or three times a night to pray and, above all, never having the opportunity of leaving the confines of the place except for the funeral of one's parents. For us boarders it was torture, but for the nuns it was nothing short of doom. Also, we could complain to each other, and we did, food being the source of the greatest grumbles. Lunch was either bacon and cabbage or a peculiar stringy meat followed by tapioca pudding; tea consisted of bread dolloped with lard and occasionally, as a treat, fairly green rhubarb jam, which did not have enough sugar. Through the long curtainless windows we saw the conifer trees and a sky that was scarcely ever without the promise of rain or a downpour.

She was a right lunatic, then, Baba said, having gone to university for four years and willingly come back to incarceration, to poverty, chastity, and obedience. We concocted scenes of agony in some Dublin hostel, while a boy, or even a young man, stood beneath her bedroom window throwing up chunks of clay or whistles or a supplication. In our version of it he was slightly older than her, and possibly a medical student, since medical students had a knack with women, because of studying diagrams and skeletons. His advances, like those of a sudden storm, would intermittently rise and overwhelm her, and the memory of these sudden flaying advances of his would haunt her until she died, and if ever she contracted fever, these secrets would out. It was also rumored that she possessed a fierce temper and that, while a postulant, she had hit a girl so badly with her leather strap that the girl had to be put to bed because of wounds. Yet another black mark against Sister Imelda was that her brother Ambrose had been sued by a nurse for breach of promise.

That first morning when she came into our classroom and modestly introduced herself, I had no idea how terribly she would infiltrate my life, how in time she would be not just one of those teachers or nuns but rather a special one, almost like a ghost who passed the boundaries of common exchange and who crept inside one, devouring so much of one's thoughts, so much of one's passion, invading the place that was called one's heart. She talked in a low voice, as if she did not want her words to go beyond the bounds of the wall, and constantly she stressed the value of work both to enlarge the mind and to discipline the thought. One of her eyelids was red and swollen, as if she was getting a sty. I reckoned that she overmortified herself by not eating at all. I saw in her some terrible premonition of sacrifice which I would have to emulate. Then, in direct contrast, she absently held the stick of chalk between her first and second fingers, the very same as if it were a cigarette, and Baba whispered to me that she might have been a smoker when in Dublin. Sister Imelda looked down sharply at me and said what was the secret and would I like to share it, since it seemed so comical. I said, "Nothing, Sister, nothing," and her dark eyes exuded such vehemence that I prayed she would never have occasion to punish me.

November came and the tiled walls of the recreation hall oozed moisture and gloom. Most girls had sore throats and were told to suffer this inconvenience to mortify themselves in order to lend a glorious hand in that communion of spirit that linked the living with the dead. It was the month of the Suffering Souls in Purgatory, and as we heard of their twofold agony, the yearning for Christ and the ferocity of the leaping flames that burned and charred their poor limbs, we were asked to make acts of mortification. Some girls gave up jam or sweets and some gave up talking, and so in recreation time they were like dummies making signs with thumb and finger to merely say "How are you?" Baba said that saner people were locked in the lunatic asylum, which was only a mile away. We saw them in the grounds, pacing back and forth, with their mouths agape and dribble coming out of them, like melting icicles. Among our many fears was that one of those lunatics would break out and head straight for the convent and assault some of the girls.

Yet in the thick of all these dreads I found myself becoming dreadfully happy. I had met Sister Imelda outside of class a few times and I felt that there was an attachment between us. Once it was in the grounds, when she did a reckless thing. She broke off a chrysanthemum and offered it to me to smell. It had no smell, or at least only something faint that suggested autumn, and feeling this to be the case herself, she said it was not a gardenia, was it? Another time we met in the chapel porch, and as she drew her shawl more tightly around her body, I felt how human she was, and prey to the cold.

In the classroom things were not so congenial between us. Geometry was my worst subject, indeed, a total mystery to me. She had not taught more than four classes when she realized this and threw a duster at me in a rage. A few girls gasped as she asked me to stand up and make a spectacle of myself. Her face had reddened, and presently she took out her handkerchief and patted the eye which was red and swollen. I not only felt a fool but felt in imminent danger of sneezing as I inhaled the smell of chalk that had fallen onto my gym frock. Suddenly she fled from the room, leaving us ten minutes free until the next class. Some girls said it was a disgrace, said I should write home and say I had been assaulted. Others welcomed the few minutes in which to gabble. All I wanted was to run after her and say that I was sorry to have caused her such distemper, because I knew dimly that it was as much to do with liking as it was with dislike. In me then there came a sort of speechless tenderness for her, and I might have known that I was stirred.

"We could get her defrocked," Baba said, and elbowed me in God's name to sit down.

That evening at Benediction I had the most overwhelming surprise. It was a particularly happy evening, with the choir nuns in full soaring form and the rows of candles like so many little ladders to the golden chalice that glittered all the more because of the beams of fitful flame. I was full of tears when I discovered a new holy picture had been put in my prayer book, and before I dared look on the back to see who had given it to me, I felt and guessed that this was no ordinary picture from an ordinary girl friend, that this was a talisman and a peace offering from Sister Imelda. It was a pale-blue picture, so pale that it was almost gray, like the down of a pigeon, and it showed a mother looking down on the infant child. On the back, in her beautiful ornate handwriting, she had written a verse:

Trust Him when dark doubts assail thee,
Trust Him when thy faith is small,
Trust Him when to simply trust Him
Seems the hardest thing of all.

This was her atonement. To think that she had located the compartment in the chapel where I kept my prayer book and to think that she had been so naked as to write in it and give me a chance to boast about it and to show it to other girls. When I thanked her next day, she bowed but did not speak. Mostly the nuns were on silence and only permitted to talk during class.

In no time I had received another present, a little miniature prayer book with a leather cover and gold edging. The prayers were in French and the lettering so minute it was as if a tiny insect had fashioned them. Soon I was publicly known as her pet. I opened the doors for her, raised the blackboard two pegs higher (she was taller than other nuns), and handed out the exercise books which she had corrected. Now in the margins of my geometry propositions I would find "Good" or "Excellent," when in the past she used to splash "Disgraceful." Baba said it was foul to be a nun's pet and that any girl who sucked up to a nun could not be trusted.

About a month later Sister Imelda asked me to carry her books up four flights of stairs to the cookery kitchen. She taught cookery to a junior class. As she walked ahead of me, I thought how supple she was and how thoroughbred, and when she paused on the landing to look out through the long curtainless window, I too paused. Down below, two women in suede boots were chatting and smoking as they moved along the street with shopping baskets. Nearby a lay nun was on her knees scrubbing the granite steps, and the cold air was full of the raw smell of Jeyes Fluid. There was a potted plant on the landing, and Sister Imelda put her fingers in the earth and went "Tch tch tch," saying it needed water. I said I would water it later on. I was happy in my prison then, happy to be near her, happy to walk behind her as she twirled her beads and bowed to the servile nun. I no longer cried for my mother, no longer counted the days on a pocket calendar until the Christmas holidays.

"Come back at five," she said as she stood on the threshold of the cookery kitchen door. The girls, all in white overalls, were arranged around the long wooden table waiting for her. It was as if every girl was in love with her. Because, as she entered, their faces broke into smiles, and in different tones of audacity they said her name. She must have liked cookery class, because she beamed and called to someone, anyone, to get up a blazing fire. Then she went across to the cast-iron stove and spat on it to test its temperature. It was hot, because her spit rose up and sizzled.

When I got back later, she was sitting on the edge of the table swaying her legs. There was something reckless about her pose, something defiant. It seemed as if any minute she would take out a cigarette case, snap it open, and then archly offer me one. The wonderful smell of baking made me realize how hungry I was, but far more so, it brought back to me my own home, my mother testing orange cakes with a knitting needle and letting me lick the line of half-baked dough down the length of the needle. I wondered if she had supplanted my mother, and I hoped not, because I had aimed to outstep my original world and take my place in a new and hallowed one.

"I bet you have a sweet tooth," she said, and then she got up, crossed the kitchen, and from under a wonderful shining silver cloche she produced two jam tarts with a crisscross design on them where the pastry was latticed over the dark jam. They were still warm.

"What will I do with them?" I asked.

"Eat them, you goose," she said, and she watched me eat as if she herself derived some peculiar pleasure from it, whereas I was embarrassed about the pastry crumbling and the bits of blackberry jam staining my lips. She was amused. It was one of the most awkward yet thrilling moments I had lived, and inherent in the pleasure was the terrible sense of danger. Had we been caught, she, no doubt, would have had to make massive sacrifice. I looked at her and thought how peerless and how brave, and I wondered if she felt hungry. She had a white overall over her black habit and this made her warmer and freer, and caused me to think of the happiness that would be ours, the laissez-faire if we were away from the convent in an ordinary kitchen doing something easy and customary. But we weren't. It was clear to me then that my version of pleasure was inextricable from pain, that they existed side by side and were interdependent, like the two forces of an electric current.

"Had you a friend when you were in Dublin at university?" I asked daringly.

"I shared a desk with a sister from Howth and stayed in the same hostel," she said.

But what about boys? I thought, and what of your life now and do you long to go out into the world? But could not say it.

We knew something about the nuns' routine. It was rumored that they wore itchy wool underwear, ate dry bread for breakfast, rarely had meat, cakes, or dainties, kept certain hours of strict silence with each other, as well as constant vigil on their thoughts; so that if their minds wandered to the subject of food or pleasure, they would quickly revert to thoughts of God and their eternal souls. They slept on hard beds with no sheets and hairy blankets. At four o'clock in the morning while we slept, each nun got out of bed, in her habit—which was also her death habit—and chanting, they all flocked down the wooden stairs like ravens, to fling themselves on the tiled floor of the chapel. Each nun—even the Mother Superior—flung herself in total submission, saying prayers in Latin and offering up the moment to God. Then silently back to their cells for one more hour of rest. It was not difficult to imagine Sister Imelda face downward, arms outstretched, prostrate on the tiled floor. I often heard their chanting when I wakened suddenly from a nightmare, because, although we slept in a different building, both adjoined, and if one wakened one often heard that monotonous Latin chanting, long before the birds began, long before our own bell summoned us to rise at six.

"Do you eat nice food?" I asked.

"Of course," she said, and smiled. She sometimes broke into an eager smile, which she did much to conceal.

"Have you ever thought of what you will be?" she asked.

I shook my head. My design changed from day to day.

She looked at her man's silver pocket watch, closed the damper of the range, and prepared to leave. She checked that all the wall cupboards were locked by running her hand over them.

"Sister," I called, gathering enough courage at last—we must have some secret, something to join us together—"what color hair have you?"

We never saw the nuns' hair, or their eyebrows, or ears, as all that part was covered by a stiff white wimple.

"You shouldn't ask such a thing," she said, getting pink in the face, and then she turned back and whispered, "I'll tell you on your last day here, provided your geometry has improved."

She had scarcely gone when Baba, who had been lurking behind some pillar, stuck her head in the door and said, "Christsake, save me a bit." She finished the second pastry, then went around looking in kitchen drawers. Because of everything being locked, she found only some castor sugar in a china shaker. She ate a little and threw the remainder into the dying fire, so that it flared up for a minute with a yellow spluttering flame. Baba showed her jealousy by putting it around the school that I was in the cookery kitchen every evening, gorging cakes with Sister Imelda and telling tales.

I did not speak to Sister Imelda again in private until the evening of our Christmas theatricals. She came to help us put on makeup and get into our stage clothes and fancy headgear. These clothes were kept in a trunk from one year to the next, and though sumptuous and strewn with braiding and gold, they smelled of camphor. Yet as we donned them we felt different, and as we sponged pancake makeup onto our faces, we became saucy and emphasized these new guises by adding dark pencil to the eyes and making the lips bright carmine. There was only one tube of lipstick and each girl clamored for it. The evening's entertainment was to comprise scenes from Shakespeare and laughing sketches. I had been chosen to recite Mark Antony's lament over Caesar's body, and for this I was to wear a purple toga, white knee-length socks, and patent buckle shoes. The shoes were too big and I moved in them as if in clogs. She said to take them off, to go barefoot. I realized that I was getting nervous and that in an effort to memorize my speech, the words were getting all askew and flying about in my head, like the separate pieces of a jigsaw puzzle. She sensed my panic and very slowly put her hand on my face and enjoined me to look at her. I looked into her eyes, which seemed fathomless, and saw that she was willing me to be calm and obliging me to be master of my fears, and I little knew that one day she would have to do the same as regards the swoop of my feelings for her. As we continued to stare I felt myself becoming calm and the words were restored to me in their right and fluent order. The lights were being lowered out in the recreation hall, and we knew now that all the nuns had arrived, had settled themselves down, and were eagerly awaiting this annual hotchpotch of amateur entertainment. There was that fearsome hush as the hall went dark and the few spotlights were turned on. She kissed her crucifix and I realized that she was saying a prayer for me. Then she raised her arm as if depicting the stance of a Greek goddess; walking onto the stage, I was fired by her ardor.

Baba could say that I bawled like a bloody bull, but Sister Imelda, who stood in the wings, said that temporarily she had felt the streets of Rome, had seen the corpse of Caesar, as I delivered those poignant, distempered lines. When I came off stage she put her arms around me and I was encased in a shower of silent kisses. After we had taken down the decorations and put the fancy clothes back in the trunk, I gave her two half-pound boxes of chocolates—bought for me illicitly by one of the day girls—and she gave me a casket made from the insides of match boxes and covered over with gilt paint and gold dust. It was like holding moths and finding their powder adhering to the fingers.

"What will you do on Christmas Day, Sister?" I said.

"I'll pray for you," she said.

It was useless to say, "Will you have turkey?" or "Will you have plum pudding?" or "Will you loll in bed?" because I believed that Christmas Day would be as bleak and deprived as any other day in her life. Yet she was radiant as if such austerity was joyful. Maybe she was basking in some secret realization involving her and me.

On the cold snowy afternoon three weeks later when we returned from our holidays, Sister Imelda came up to the dormitory to welcome me back. All the other girls had gone down to the recreation hall to do barn dances and I could hear someone banging on the piano. I did not want to go down and clump around with sixty other girls, having nothing to look forward to, only tea and the Rosary and early bed. The beds were damp after our stay at home, and when I put my hand between the sheets, it was like feeling dew but did not have the freshness of outdoors. What depressed me further was that I had seen a mouse in one of the cupboards, seen its tail curl with terror as it slipped away into a crevice. If there was one mouse, there were God knows how many, and the cakes we hid in secret would not be safe. I was still unpacking as she came down the narrow passage between the rows of iron beds and I saw in her walk such agitation.

"Tut, tut, tut, you've curled your hair," she said, offended.

Yes, the world outside was somehow declared in this perm, and for a second I remembered the scalding pain as the trickles of ammonia dribbled down my forehead and then the joy as the hairdresser said that she would make me look like Movita, a Mexican star. Now suddenly that world and those aspirations seemed trite and I wanted to take a brush and straighten my hair and revert to the dark gawky somber girl that I had been. I offered her iced queen cakes that my mother had made, but she refused them and said she could only stay a second. She lent me a notebook of hers, which she had had as a pupil, and into which she had copied favorite quotations, some religious, some not. I read at random:

> *Twice or thrice had I loved thee,*
> *Before I knew thy face or name.*
> *So in a voice, so in a shapeless flame,*
> *Angels affect us oft . . .*

"Are you well?" I asked.

She looked pale. It may have been the day, which was wretched and gray with sleet, or it may have been the white bedspreads, but she appeared to be ailing.

"I missed you," she said.

"Me too," I said.

At home, gorging, eating trifle at all hours, even for breakfast, having little ratafias to dip in cups of tea, fitting on new shoes and silk stockings, I wished that she could be with us, enjoying the fire and the freedom.

"You know it is not proper for us to be so friendly."

"It's not wrong," I said.

I dreaded that she might decide to turn away from me, that she might stamp on our love and might suddenly draw a curtain over it, a black crepe curtain that would denote its death. I dreaded it and knew it was going to happen.

"We must not become attached," she said, and I could not say we already were, no more than I could remind her of the day of the revels and the intimacy between us. Convents were dungeons and no doubt about it.

From then on she treated me as less of a favorite. She said my name sharply in class, and once she said if I must cough, could I wait until class had finished. Baba was delighted, as were the other girls, because they were glad to see me receding in her eyes. Yet I knew that the crispness was part of her love, because no matter how callously she looked at me, she would occasionally soften. Reading her notebook helped me, and I copied out her quotations into my own book, trying as accurately as possible to imitate her handwriting.

But some little time later when she came to supervise our study one evening, I got a smile from her as she sat on the rostrum looking down at us all. I continued to look up at her and by slight frowning indicated that I had a problem with my geometry. She beckoned to me lightly and I went up, bringing my copybook and the pen. Standing close to her, and also because her wimple was crooked, I saw one of her eyebrows for the first time. She saw that I noticed it and said did that satisfy my curiosity. I said not really. She said what else did I want to see, her swan's neck perhaps, and I went scarlet. I was amazed that she would say such a thing in the hearing of other girls, and then she said a worse thing, she said that G. K. Chesterton was very forgetful and had once put on his trousers backward. She expected me to laugh. I was so close to her that a rumble in her stomach seemed to be taking place in my own, and about this she also laughed. It occurred to me for one terrible moment that maybe she had decided to leave the convent, to jump over the wall. Having done the theorem for me, she marked it "100 out of 100" and then asked if I had any other problems. My eyes filled with tears, I wanted her to realize that her recent coolness had wrought havoc with my nerves and my peace of mind.

"What is it?" she said.

I could cry, or I could tremble to try to convey the emotion, but I could not tell her. As if on cue, the Mother Superior came in and saw this glaring intimacy and frowned as she approached the rostrum.

"Would you please go back to your desk," she said, "and in future kindly allow Sister Imelda to get on with her duties."

I tiptoed back and sat with head down, bursting with fear and shame. Then she looked at a tray on which the milk cups were laid, and finding one cup of milk untouched, she asked which girl had not drunk her milk.

"Me, Sister," I said, and I was called up to drink it and stand under the clock as a punishment. The milk was tepid and dusty, and I thought of cows on the fairs days at home and the farmers hitting them as they slid and slithered over the muddy streets.

For weeks I tried to see my nun in private; I even lurked outside doors where I knew she was due, only to be rebuffed again and again. I suspected the Mother Superior had warned her against making a favorite of me. But I still clung to a belief that a bond existed between us and that her coldness and even some glares which I had received were a charade, a mask. I would wonder how she felt alone in bed and what way she slept and if she thought of me, or refusing to think of me, if she dreamed of me as I did of her. She certainly got thinner, because her nun's silver ring slipped easily and sometimes unavoidably off her marriage finger. It occurred to me that she was having a nervous breakdown.

One day in March the sun came out, the radiators were turned off, and, though there was a lashing wind, we were told that officially spring had arrived and that we could play games. We all trooped up to the games field and, to our surprise, saw that Sister Imelda was officiating that day. The daffodils in the field tossed and turned; they were a very bright shocking yellow, but they were not as fetching as the little timid snowdrops that trembled in the wind. We played rounders, and when my turn came to hit the ball with the long wooden pound, I crumbled and missed, fearing that the ball would hit me.

"Champ . . ." said Baba, jeering.

After three such failures Sister Imelda said that if I liked I could sit and watch, and when I was sitting in the greenhouse swallowing my shame, she came in and said that I must not give way to tears, because humiliation was the greatest test of Christ's love, or indeed *any* love.

"When you are a nun you will know that," she said, and instantly I made up my mind that I would be a nun and that though we might never be free to express our feelings, we would be under the same roof, in the same cloister, in mental and spiritual conjunction all our lives.

"Is it very hard at first?" I said.

"It's awful," she said, and she slipped a little medal into my gym-frock pocket. It was warm from being in her pocket, and as I held it, I knew that once again we were near and that in fact we had never severed. Walking down from the playing field to our Sunday lunch of mutton and cabbage, everyone chattered to Sister Imelda. The girls milled around her, linking her, trying to hold her hand, counting the various keys on her bunch of keys, and asking impudent questions.

"Sister, did you ever ride a motorbicycle?"

"Sister, did you ever wear seamless stockings?"

"Sister, who's your favorite film star—male?"

"Sister, what's your favorite food?"

"Sister, if you had a wish, what would it be?"

"Sister, what do you do when you want to scratch your head?"

Yes, she had ridden a motorbicycle, and she had worn silk stockings, but they were seamed. She liked bananas best, and if she had a wish, it would be to go home for a few hours to see her parents and her brother.

That afternoon as we walked through the town, the sight of closed shops with porter barrels outside and mongrel dogs did not dispel my refound ecstasy. The medal was in my pocket, and every other second I would touch it for confirmation. Baba saw a Swiss roll in a confectioner's window laid on a doily and dusted with castor sugar, and it made her cry out with hunger and rail against being in a bloody reformatory, surrounded by drips and mopes. On impulse she took her nail file out of her pocket and dashed across to the window to see if she could cut the glass. The prefect rushed up from the back of the line and asked Baba if she wanted to be locked up.

"I am anyhow," Baba said, and sawed at one of her nails, to maintain her independence and vent her spleen. Baba was the only girl who could stand up to a prefect. When she felt like it, she dropped out of a walk, sat on a stone wall, and waited until we all came back. She said that if there was one thing more boring than studying it was walking. She used to roll down her stockings and examine her calves and say that she could see varicose veins coming from this bloody daily walk. Her legs, like all our legs, were black from the dye of the stockings; we were forbidden to bathe, because baths were immoral. We washed each night in an enamel basin beside our beds. When girls splashed cold water onto their chests, they let out cries, though this was forbidden.

After the walk we wrote home. We were allowed to write home once a week; our letters were always censored. I told my mother that I had made up my mind to be a nun, and asked if she could send me bananas when a batch arrived at our local grocery shop. That evening, perhaps as I wrote to my mother on the ruled white paper, a telegram arrived which said that Sister Imelda's brother had been killed in a van while on his way home from a hurling match. The Mother Superior announced it, and asked us to pray for his soul and write letters of sympathy to Sister Imelda's parents. We all wrote identical letters, because in our first year at school we had been given specimen letters for various occasions, and we all referred back to our specimen letter of sympathy.

Next day the town hire-car drove up to the convent, and Sister Imelda, accompanied by another nun, went home for the funeral. She looked as white as a sheet, with eyes swollen, and she wore a heavy knitted shawl over her shoulders. Although she came back that night (I stayed awake to hear the car), we did not see her for a whole week, except to catch a glimpse of her back, in the chapel. When she resumed class, she was peaky and distant, making no reference at all to her recent tragedy.

The day the bananas came I waited outside the door and gave her a bunch wrapped in tissue paper. Some were still a little green, and she said that Mother Superior would put them in the glasshouse to ripen. I felt that Sister Imelda would never taste them; they would be kept for a visiting priest or bishop.

"Oh, Sister, I'm sorry about your brother," I said in a burst.

"It will come to us all, sooner or later," Sister Imelda said dolefully.

I dared to touch her wrist to communicate my sadness. She went quickly, probably for fear of breaking down. At times she grew irritable and had a boil on her cheek. She missed some classes and was replaced in the cookery kitchen by a younger nun. She asked me to pray for her brother's soul and to avoid seeing her alone. Each time as she came down a corridor toward me, I was obliged to turn the other way. Now Baba or some other girl moved the blackboard two pegs higher and spread her shawl, when wet, over the radiator to dry.

I got flu and was put to bed. Sickness took the same bleak course, a cup of hot senna delivered in person by the head nun, who stood there while I drank it, tea at lunchtime with thin slices of brown bread (because it was just after the war, food was still rationed, so the butter was mixed with lard and had white streaks running through it and a faintly rancid smell), hours of just lying there surveying the empty dormitory, the empty iron beds with white counterpanes on each one, and metal crucifixes laid on each white, frilled pillow slip. I knew that she would miss me and hoped that Baba would tell her where I was. I counted the number of tiles from the ceiling to the head of my bed, thought of my mother at home on the farm mixing hen food, thought of my father, losing his temper perhaps and stamping on the kitchen floor with nailed boots, and I recalled the money owing for my school fees and hoped that Sister Imelda would never get to hear of it. During the Christmas holiday I had seen a bill sent by the head nun to my father which said, "Please remit this week without fail." I hated being in bed causing extra trouble and therefore reminding the head nun of the unpaid liability. We had no clock in the dormitory, so there was no way of guessing the time, but the hours dragged.

Marigold, one of the maids, came to take off the counterpanes at five and brought with her two gifts from Sister Imelda—an orange and a pencil sharpener. I kept the orange peel in my hand, smelling it, and planning how I would thank her. Thinking of her I fell into a feverish sleep and was wakened when the girls came to bed at ten and switched on the various ceiling lights.

At Easter Sister Imelda warned me not to give her chocolates, so I got her a flashlamp instead and spare batteries. Pleased with such a useful gift (perhaps she read her letters in bed), she put her arms around me and allowed one cheek to adhere but not to make the sound of a kiss. It made up for the seven weeks of withdrawal, and as I drove down the convent drive with Baba, she waved to me, as she had promised, from the window of her cell.

In the last term at school, studying was intensive because of the examinations which loomed at the end of June. Like all the other nuns, Sister Imelda thought only of these examinations. She crammed us with knowledge, lost her temper every other day, and gritted her teeth whenever the blackboard was too greasy to take the imprint of the chalk. If ever I met her in the corridor, she asked if I knew such and such a thing, and coming down from Sunday games, she went over various questions with us. The fateful examination day arrived and we sat at single desks supervised by some strange woman from Dublin. Opening a locked trunk, she took out the pink examination papers and distributed them around. Geometry was on the fourth day. When we came out from it, Sister Imelda was in the hall with all the answers, so that we could compare our answers with hers. Then she called me aside and we went up toward the cookery kitchen and sat on the stairs while she went over the paper with me, question for question. I knew that I had three right and two wrong, but did not tell her so.

"It is black," she said then, rather suddenly. I thought she meant the dark light where we were sitting.

"It's cool, though," I said.

Summer had come; our white skins baked under the heavy uniform, and dark violet pansies bloomed in the convent grounds. She looked well again, and her pale skin was once more unblemished.

"My hair," she whispered, "is black." And she told me how she had spent her last night before entering the convent. She had gone cycling with a boy and ridden for miles, and they'd lost their way up a mountain, and she became afraid she would be so late home that she would sleep it out the next morning. It was understood between us that I was going to enter the convent in September and that I could have a last fling, too.

*

Two days later we prepared to go home. There were farewells and outlandish promises, and autograph books signed, and girls trudging up the recreation hall, their cases bursting open with clothes and books. Baba scattered biscuit crumbs in the dormitory for the mice and stuffed all her prayer books under a mattress. Her father promised to collect us at four. I had arranged with Sister Imelda secretly that I would meet her in one of the summerhouses around the walks, where we would spend our last half hour together. I expected that she would tell me something of what my life as a postulant would be like. But Baba's father came an hour early. He had something urgent to do later and came at three instead. All I could do was ask Marigold to take a note to Sister Imelda.

Remembrance is all I ask,
But if remembrance should prove a task,
Forget me.

I hated Baba, hated her busy father, hated the thought of my mother standing in the doorway in her good dress, welcoming me home at last. I would have become a nun that minute if I could.

I wrote to my nun that night and again the next day and then every week for a month. Her letters were censored, so I tried to convey my feelings indirectly. In one of her letters to me (they were allowed one letter a month) she said that she looked forward to seeing me in September. But by September Baba and I had left for the university in Dublin. I stopped writing to Sister Imelda then, reluctant to tell her that I no longer wished to be a nun.

In Dublin we enrolled at the college where she had surpassed herself. I saw her maiden name on a list, for having graduated with special honors, and for days was again sad and remorseful. I rushed out and bought batteries for the flashlamp I'd given her, and posted them without any note enclosed. No mention of my missing vocation, no mention of why I had stopped writing.

One Sunday about two years later, Baba and I were going out to Howth on a bus. Baba had met some businessmen who played golf there and she had done a lot of scheming to get us invited out. The bus was packed, mostly mothers with babies and children on their way to Dollymount Strand. We drove along the coast road and saw the sea, bright green and glinting in the sun, and because of the way the water was carved up into millions of little wavelets, its surface seemed like an endless heap of dark-green broken bottles. Near the shore the sand looked warm and was biscuit-colored. We never swam or sunbathed, we never did anything that was good for us. Life was geared to work and to meeting men, and yet one knew that mating could only lead to one's being a mother and hawking obstreperous children out to the seaside on Sunday. "They know not what they do" could surely be said of us.

We were very made up; even the conductor seemed to disapprove and snapped at having to give change of ten shillings. For no reason at all I thought of our makeup rituals before the school play and how innocent it was in comparison, because now our skins were smothered beneath layers of it and we never took it off at night. Thinking of the convent, I suddenly thought of Sister Imelda, and then, as if prey to a dream, I heard the rustle of serge, smelled the Jeyes Fluid and the boiled cabbage, and saw her pale shocked face in the months after her brother died. Then I looked around and saw her in earnest, and at first thought I was imagining things. But no, she had got on accompanied by another nun and they were settling themselves in the back seat nearest the door. She looked older, but she had the same aloof quality and the same eyes, and my heart began to race with a mixture of excitement and dread. At first it raced with a prodigal strength, and then it began to falter and I thought it was going to give out. My fear of her and my love came back in one fell realization. I would have gone through the window except that it was not wide enough. The thing was how to escape her. Baba gurgled with delight, stood up, and in the most flagrant way looked around to make sure that it was Imelda. She recognized the other nun as one with the nickname of Johnny who taught piano lessons. Baba's first thought was revenge, as she enumerated the punishments they had meted out to us and said how nice it would be to go back and shock them and say, "Mud in your eye, Sisters," or "Get lost," or something worse. Baba could not understand why I was quaking, no more than she could understand why I began to wipe off the lipstick. Above all, I knew that I could not confront them.

"You're going to have to," Baba said.

"I can't," I said.

It was not just my attire; it was the fact of my never having written and of my broken promise. Baba kept looking back and said they weren't saying a word and that children were gawking at them. It wasn't often that nuns traveled in buses, and we speculated as to where they might be going.

"They might be off to meet two fellows," Baba said, and visualized them in the golf club getting blotto and hoisting up their skirts. For me it was no laughing matter. She came up with a strategy: it was that as we approached our stop and the bus was still moving, I was to jump up and go down the aisle and pass them without even looking. She said most likely they would not notice us, as their eyes were lowered and they seemed to be praying.

"I can't run down the bus," I said. There was a matter of shaking limbs and already a terrible vertigo.

"You're going to," Baba said, and though insisting that I couldn't, I had already begun to rehearse an apology. While doing this, I kept blessing myself over and over again, and Baba kept reminding me that there was only one more stop before ours. When the dreadful moment came, I jumped up and put on my face what can only be called an apology of a smile. I followed Baba to the rear of the bus. But already they had gone. I saw the back of their two sable, identical figures with their veils being blown wildly about in the wind. They looked so cold and lost as they hurried along the pavement and I wanted to run after them. In some way I felt worse than if I had confronted them. I cannot be certain what I would have said. I knew that there is something sad and faintly distasteful about love's ending, particularly love that has never been fully realized. I might have hinted at that, but I doubt it. In our deepest moments we say the most inadequate things.

FROM

The Love Object

1968

The Love Object

He simply said my name. He said "Martha," and once again I could feel it happening. My legs trembled under the big white cloth and my head became fuzzy, though I was not drunk. It's how I fall in love. He sat opposite. The love object. Elderly. Blue eyes. Khaki hair. The hair was graying on the outside and he had spread the outer gray ribs across the width of his head as if to disguise the khaki, the way some men disguise a patch of baldness. He had what I call a very religious smile. An inner smile that came on and off, governed as it were by his private joy in what he heard or saw: a remark I made, the waiter removing the cold dinner plates that served as ornament and bringing warmed ones of a different design, the nylon curtain blowing inward and brushing my bare, summer-ripened arm. It was the end of a warm London summer.

"I'm not mad about them, either," he said. We were engaged in a bit of backbiting. Discussing a famous couple we both knew. He kept his hands joined all the time as if they were being put to prayer. There were no barriers between us. We were strangers. I am a television announcer; we had met to do a job, and out of courtesy he asked me to dinner. He told me about his wife—who was thirty like me—and how he knew he would marry her the very first moment he set eyes on her. (She was his third wife.) I made no inquiries as to what she looked like. I still don't know. The only memory I have of her is of her arms sheathed in big, mauve, crocheted sleeves; the image runs away with me and I see his pink, praying hands vanishing into those sleeves and the two of them waltzing in some large, grim room, smiling rapturously at their good fortune in being together. But that came much later.

We had a pleasant supper and figs for afters. The first figs I'd ever tasted. He tested them gently with his fingers, then put three on my side plate. I kept staring down at their purple-black skins, because with the shaking I could not trust myself to peel them. He took my mind off my nervousness by telling me a little story about a girl who was being interviewed on the radio and admitted to owning thirty-seven pairs of shoes and buying a new dress every Saturday, which she later endeavored to sell to friends or family. Somehow I knew that it was a story he had specially selected for me and also that he would not risk telling it to many people. He was in his way a serious man, and famous, though that is hardly of interest when one is telling about a love affair. Or is it? Anyhow, without peeling it, I bit into one of the figs.

How do you describe a taste? They were a new food and he was a new man and that night in my bed he was both stranger and lover, which I used to think was the ideal bed partner.

In the morning he was quite formal but unashamed; he even asked for a clothes brush because there was a smudge of powder on his jacket where we had embraced in the taxi coming home. At the time I had no idea whether or not we would sleep together, but on the whole I felt that we would not. I have never owned a clothes brush. I own books and records and various bottles of scent and beautiful clothes, but I never buy cleaning stuffs or aids for prolonging property. I expect it is improvident, but I just throw things away. Anyhow, he dabbed the powder smear with his handkerchief and it came off quite easily. The other thing he needed was a piece of sticking plaster because a new shoe had cut his heel. I looked but there was none left in the tin. My children had cleared it out during the long summer holidays. In fact, for a moment I saw my two sons throughout those summer days, slouched on chairs, reading comics, riding bicycles, wrestling, incurring cuts which they promptly covered with Elastoplast, and afterward, when the plasters fell, flaunting the brown-rimmed marks as proof of their valor. I missed them badly and longed to hold them in my arms—another reason why I welcomed his company. "There's no plaster left," I said, not without shame. I thought how he would think me neglectful. I wondered if I ought to explain why my sons were at boarding school when they were still so young. They were eight and ten. But I didn't. I had ceased to want to tell people the tale of how my marriage had ended and my husband, unable to care for two young boys, insisted on boarding school in order to give them, as he put it, a stabilizing influence. I believed it was done in order to deprive me of the pleasure of their company. I couldn't.

We had breakfast outdoors. The start of another warm day. The dull haze that precedes heat hung from the sky, and in the garden next door the sprinklers were already on. My neighbors are fanatic gardeners. He ate three pieces of toast and some bacon. I ate also, just to put him at his ease, though normally I skip breakfast. "I'll stock up with plaster, clothes brush, and cleaning fluids," I said. My way of saying, "You'll come again?" He saw through it straightaway. Hurrying down the mouthful of toast, he put one of his prayer hands over mine and told me solemnly and nicely that he would not have a mean and squalid little affair with me, but that we would meet in a month or so and he hoped we would become friends. I hadn't thought of us as friends, but it was an interesting possibility. I remembered the earlier part of our evening's conversation and his referring to his earlier wives and his older grown-up children, and I thought how honest and unnostalgic he was. I was really sick of sorrows and people multiplying them even to themselves. Another thing he did that endeared him was to fold back the green silk bedspread, a thing I never do myself.

When he left I felt quite buoyant and in a way relieved. It had been nice and there were no nasty aftereffects. My face was pink from kissing and my hair tossed from our exertions. I looked a little wanton. Feeling tired from such a broken night's sleep, I drew the curtains and got back into bed. I had a nightmare. The usual one, where I am being put to death by a man. People tell me that a nightmare is healthy and from that experience I believe it. I wakened calmer than I had been for months and passed the remainder of the day happily.

Two mornings later he rang and asked was there a chance of our meeting that night. I said yes, because I was not doing anything and it seemed appropriate to have supper and seal our secret decently. But we started recharging.

"We did have a very good time," he said. I could feel myself making little petrified moves denoting love, shyness; opening my eyes wide to look at him, exuding trust. This time he peeled the figs for both of us. We positioned our legs so that they touched and withdrew them shortly afterward, confident that our desires were flowing. He brought me home. I noticed when we were in bed that he had put cologne on his shoulder and that he must have set out to dinner with the hope if not the intention of sleeping with me. I liked the taste of his skin better than the foul chemical and I had to tell him so. He just laughed. Never had I been so at ease with a man. For the record, I had slept with four other men, but there always seemed to be a distance between us, conversation-wise. I mused for a moment on their various smells as I inhaled his, which reminded me of some herb. It was not parsley, not thyme, not mint, but some nonexistent herb compounded of these three smells. On this second occasion our lovemaking was more relaxed.

"What will you do if you make an avaricious woman out of me?" I asked.

"I will pass you on to someone very dear and suitable," he said. We coiled together, and with my head on his shoulder I thought of pigeons under the railway bridge nearby, who passed their nights nestled together, heads folded into mauve breasts. In his sleep we kissed and murmured. I did not sleep. I never do when I am overhappy, overunhappy, or in bed with a strange man.

Neither of us said, "Well, here we are, having a mean and squalid little affair." We just started to meet. Regularly. We stopped going to restaurants because of his being famous. He would come to my house for dinner. I'll never forget the flurry of those preparations —putting flowers in vases, changing the sheets, thumping knots out of pillows, trying to cook, putting on makeup, and keeping a hairbrush nearby in case he arrived early. The agony of it! It was with difficulty that I answered the doorbell when it finally rang.

"You don't know what an oasis this is," he would say. And then in the hallway he would put his hands on my shoulders and squeeze them through my thin dress and say, "Let me look at you," and I would hang my head, both because I was overwhelmed and because I wanted to be. We would kiss, often for a full five minutes. He kissed the inside of my nostrils. Then we would move to the sitting room and sit on the chaise longue still speechless. He would touch the bone of my knee and say what beautiful knees I had. He saw and admired parts of me that no other man had ever bothered with. Soon after supper we went to bed.

Once, he came unexpectedly in the late afternoon when I was dressed to go out. I was going to the theater with another man.

"How I wish I were taking you," he said.

"We'll go to the theater one night?" He bowed his head. We would. It was the first time his eyes looked sad. We did not make love because I was made up and had my false eyelashes on and it seemed impractical. He said, "Has any man ever told you that to see a woman you desire when you cannot do a thing about it leaves you with an ache?"

The ache conveyed itself to me and stayed all through the theater. I felt angry for not having gone to bed with him, and later I regretted it even more, because from that evening onward our meetings were fewer. His wife, who had been in France with their children, returned. I knew this when he arrived one evening in a motorcar and in the course of conversation mentioned that his small daughter had that day peed over an important document. I can tell you now that he was a lawyer.

From then on it was seldom possible to meet at night. He made afternoon dates and at very short notice. Any night he did stay, he arrived with a travel bag containing toothbrush, clothes brush, and a few things a man might need for an overnight, loveless stay in a provincial hotel. I expect she packed it. I thought, How ridiculous. I felt no pity for her. In fact, the mention of her name—it was Helen—made me angry. He said it very harmlessly. He said they'd been burgled in the middle of the night and he'd gone down in his pajamas while his wife telephoned the police from the extension upstairs.

"They only burgle the rich," I said hurriedly, to change the conversation. It was reassuring to find that he wore pajamas with her, when he didn't with me. My jealousy of her was extreme, and of course grossly unfair. Still, I would be giving the wrong impression if I said her existence blighted our relationship at that point. Because it didn't. He took great care to speak like a single man, and he allowed time after our lovemaking to stay for an hour or so and depart at his leisure. In fact, it is one of those after-love sessions that I consider the cream of our affair. We were sitting on the bed, naked, eating smoked-salmon sandwiches. I had lighted the gas fire because it was well into autumn and the afternoons got chilly. The fire made a steady, purring noise. It was the only light in the room. It was the first time he noticed the shape of my face, because he said that up to then my coloring had drawn all of his admiration. His face and the mahogany chest and the pictures also looked better. Not rosy, because the gas fire did not have that kind of glow, but resplendent with a whitish light. The goatskin rug underneath the window had a special luxurious softness. I remarked on it. He happened to say that he had a slight trace of masochism, and that often, unable to sleep at night in a bed, he would go to some other room and lie on the floor with a coat over him and fall fast asleep. A thing he'd done as a boy. The image of the little boy sleeping on the floor moved me to enormous compassion, and without a word from him, I led him across to the goatskin and laid him down. It was the only time our roles were reversed. He was not my father. I became his mother. Soft and totally fearless. Even my nipples, about which I am squeamish, did not shrink from his rabid demands. I wanted to do everything and anything for him. As often happens with lovers, my ardor and inventiveness stimulated his. We stopped at nothing. Afterward, remarking on our achievement—a thing he always did—he reckoned it was the most intimate of all our intimate moments. I was inclined to agree. As we stood up to get dressed, he wiped his armpits with the white blouse I had been wearing and asked which of my lovely dresses I would wear to dinner that night. He chose my black one for me. He said it gave him great pleasure to know that although I was to dine with others my mind would ruminate on what he and I had done. A wife, work, the world, might separate us, but in our thoughts we were betrothed.

"I'll think of you," I said.

"And I, of you."

We were not even sad at parting.

It was after that I had what I can only describe as a dream within a dream. I was coming out of sleep, forcing myself awake, wiping my saliva on the pillow slip, when something pulled me, an enormous weight dragged me down into the bed, and I thought: I have become infirm. I have lost the use of my limbs and this accounts for my listlessness for several months when I've wanted to do nothing except drink tea and stare out the window. I am a cripple. All over. Even my mouth won't move. Only my brain is ticking away. My brain tells me that a woman downstairs doing the ironing is the only one who could locate me, but she might not come upstairs for days, she might think I'm in bed with a man, committing a sin. From time to time I sleep with a man, but normally I sleep alone. She'll leave the ironed clothes on the kitchen table, and the iron itself upright on the floor so that it won't set fire to anything. Blouses will be on hangers, their frilled collars white and fluid like foam. She's the sort of woman who even irons the toes and heels of nylon stockings. She'll slip away, until Thursday, her next day in. I feel something at my back or, strictly speaking, tugging at my bedcovers, which I have mounted right up the length of my back to cover my head. For shelter. And I know now that it's not infirmity that's dragging me down, but a man. How did he get in there? He's on the inside, near the wall. I know what he's going to do to me, and the woman downstairs won't ever come to rescue me, she'd be too ashamed or she might not think I want to be rescued. I don't know which of the men it is, whether it's the big tall bruiser that's at the door every time I open it innocently, expecting it's the laundry boy and find it's Him, with an old black carving knife, its edge glittering because he's just sharpened it on a step. Before I can scream, my tongue isn't mine anymore. Or it might be the Other One. Tall too, he gets me by my bracelet as I slip between the banisters of the stairs. I've forgotten that I am not a little girl anymore and that I don't slip easily between banisters. If the bracelet snapped in two I would have made my escape, leaving him with one half of a gold bracelet in his hand, but my goddamn provident mother had a safety chain put on it because it was nine-carat. Anyhow, he's in the bed. It will go on forever, the thing he wants. I daren't turn around to look at him. Then something gentle about the way the sheet is pulled down suggests that he might be the New One. The man I met a few weeks ago. Not my type at all, tiny broken veins on his cheeks, and red, actually red, hair. We were on a goatskin. But it was raised off the ground, high as a bed. I had been doing most of the loving; breasts, hands, mouth, all yearned to minister to him. I felt so sure, never have I felt so sure of the rightness of what I was doing. Then he started kissing me down there and I came to his lapping tongue and his head was under my buttocks and it was like I was bearing him, only there was pleasure instead of pain. He trusted me. We were two people, I mean, he wasn't someone on me, smothering me, doing something I couldn't see. I could see. I could have shat on his red hair if I wanted. He trusted me. He stretched the come to the very last. And all the things that I loved up to then, like glass or lies, mirrors and feathers, and pearl buttons, and silk, and willow trees, became secondary compared with what he'd done. He was lying so that I could see it: so delicate, so thin, with a bunch of worried blue veins along its sides. Talking to it was like talking to a little child. The light in the room was a white glow. He'd made me very soft and wet, so I put it in. It was quick and hard and forceful, and he said, "I'm not considering you now, I think we've considered you," and I said that was perfectly true and that I liked him roughing away. I said it. I was no longer a hypocrite, no longer a liar. Before that he had often remonstrated with me, he had said, "There are words we are not going to use to each other, words such as 'Sorry' and 'Are you angry?' " I had used these words a lot. So I think from the gentle shuffle of the bedcovers—like a request really—that it might be him, and if it is I want to sink down and down into the warm, dark, sleepy pit of the bed and stay in it forever, coming with him. But I am afraid to look in case it is not Him but One of the Others.

When I finally woke up I was in a panic and I had a dreadful urge to telephone him, but though he never actually forbade it, I knew he would have been most displeased.

When something has been perfect, as our last encounter in the gaslight had been, there is a tendency to try hard to repeat it. Unfortunately, the next occasion was clouded. He came in the afternoon and brought a suitcase containing all the paraphernalia for a dress dinner which he was attending that night. When he arrived he asked if he could hang up his tails, as otherwise they would be very creased. He hooked the hanger on the outer rim of the wardrobe, and I remember being impressed by the row of war medals along the top pocket. Our time in bed was pleasant but hasty. He worried about getting dressed. I just sat and watched him. I wanted to ask about his medals and how he had merited them, and if he remembered the war, and if he'd missed his then wife, and if he'd killed people, and if he still dreamed about it. But I asked nothing. I sat there as if I were paralyzed.

"No braces," he said as he held the wide black trousers around his middle. His other trousers must have been supported by a belt.

"I'll go to Woolworth's for some," I said. But that was impractical because he was already in danger of being late. I got a safety pin and fastened the trousers from the back. It was a difficult operation because the pin was not really sturdy enough.

"You'll bring it back?" I said. I am superstitious about giving people pins. He took some time to reply because he was muttering "Damn" under his breath. Not to me. But to the stiff, inhuman, starched collar, which would not yield to the little gold studs he had wanted to pierce through. I tried. He tried. Each time when one of us failed the other became impatient. He said if we went on, the collar would be grubby from our hands. And that seemed a worse alternative. I thought he must be dining with very critical people, but of course I did not give my thoughts on the matter. In the end we each managed to get a stud through and he had a small sip of whiskey as a celebration. The bow tie was another ordeal. He couldn't do it. I daren't try.

"Haven't you done it before?" I said. I expect his wives—in succession—had done it for him. I felt such a fool. Then a lump of hatred. I thought how ugly and pink his legs were, how repellent the shape of his body, which did not have anything in the way of a waist, how deceitful his eyes, which congratulated himself in the mirror when he succeeded in making a clumsy bow. As he put on the coat the sound of the medals tinkling enabled me to remark on their music. There was so little I could say. Lastly he donned a white silk scarf that came below his middle. He looked like someone I did not know. He left hurriedly. I ran with him down the road to help get a taxi, and trying to keep up with him and chatter was not easy. All I can remember is the ghostly sight of the very white scarf swinging back and forth as we rushed. His shoes, which were patent, creaked unsuitably.

"Is it all-male?" I asked.

"No. Mixed," he replied.

So that was why we hurried. To meet his wife at some appointed place. The hatred began to grow.

He did bring back the safety pin, but my superstition remained, because four straight pins with black rounded tops that had come off his new shirt were on my window ledge. He refused to take them. *He* was not superstitious.

Bad moments, like good ones, tend to be grouped together, and when I think of the dress occasion, I also think of the other time when we were not in utter harmony. It was on a street; we were searching for a restaurant. We had to leave my house because a friend had come to stay and we would have been obliged to tolerate her company. Going along the street—it was October and very windy—I felt that he was angry with me for having drawn us out into the cold where we could not embrace. My heels were very high and I was ashamed of the hollow sound they made. In a way I felt we were enemies. He looked in the windows of restaurants to see if any acquaintances of his were there. Two restaurants he decided against, for reasons best known to himself. One looked to be very attractive. It had orange bulbs inset in the walls and the light came through small squares of iron grating. We crossed the road to look at places on the opposite side. I saw a group of rowdies coming toward us, and for something to say—what with my aggressive heels, the wind, traffic going by, the ugly unromantic street, we had run out of agreeable conversation—I asked if he ever felt apprehensive about encountering noisy groups like that, late at night. He said that in fact a few nights before he had been walking home very late and saw such a group coming toward him, and before he even registered fear, he found that he had splayed his bunch of keys between his fingers and had his hand, armed with the sharp points of the keys, ready to pull out of his pocket should they have threatened him. I suppose he did it again while we were walking along. Curiously enough, I did not feel he was my protector. I only felt that he and I were two people, that there was in the world trouble, violence, sickness, catastrophe, that he faced it in one way and that I faced it—or to be exact, that I shrank from it—in another. We would always be outside one another. In the course of that melancholy thought the group went by, and my conjecture about violence was all for nothing. We found a nice restaurant and drank a lot of wine.

Later our lovemaking, as usual, was perfect. He stayed all night. I used to feel specially privileged on the nights he stayed, and the only little thing that lessened my joy was spasms of anxiety in case he should have told his wife he was at such and such a hotel and her telephoning there and not finding him. More than once I raced into an imaginary narrative where she came and discovered us and I acted silent and ladylike and he told her very crisply to wait outside until he was ready. I felt no pity for her. Sometimes I wondered if we would ever meet or if in fact we had already met on an escalator at some point. Though that was unlikely, because we lived at opposite ends of London.

Then to my great surprise the opportunity came. I was invited to a Thanksgiving party given by an American magazine. He saw the card on my mantelpiece and said, "You're going to that, too?" and I smiled and said maybe. Was he? "Yes," he said. He tried to make me reach a decision there and then but I was too canny. Of course I would go. I was curious to see his wife. I would meet him in public. It shocked me to think that we had never met in the company of any other person. It was like being shut off . . . a little animal locked away. I thought very distinctly of a ferret that a forester used to keep in a wooden box with a sliding top, when I was a child, and of another ferret being brought to mate with it once. The thought made me shiver. I mean, I got it confused; I thought of white ferrets with their little pink nostrils in the same breath as I thought of him sliding a door back and slipping into my box from time to time. His skin had a lot of pink in it.

"I haven't decided," I said, but when the day came I went. I took a lot of trouble with my appearance, had my hair set, and wore virginal attire. Black and white. The party was held in a large room with paneled walls of brown wood; blown-up magazine covers were along the panels. The bar was at one end, under a balcony. The effect was of shrunken barmen in white, lost underneath the cliff of the balcony, which seemed in danger of collapsing on them. A more unlikely room for a party I have never seen. There were women going around with trays, but I had to go to the bar because there was champagne on the trays and I have a preference for whiskey. A man I knew conducted me there, and en route another man placed a kiss on my back. I hoped that he witnessed this, but it was such a large room with hundreds of people around that I had no idea where he was. I noticed a dress I quite admired, a mauve dress with very wide crocheted sleeves. Looking up the length of the sleeves, I saw its owner's eyes directed on me. Perhaps she was admiring my outfit. People with the same tastes often do. I have no idea what her face looked like, but later when I asked a girl friend which was his wife, she pointed to this woman with the crocheted sleeves. The second time I saw her in profile. I still don't know what she looked like, nor do those eyes into which I looked speak to my memory with anything special, except, perhaps, slight covetousness.

Finally, I searched him out. I had a mutual friend walk across with me and apparently introduce me. He was unwelcoming. He looked strange, the flush on his cheekbones vivid and unnatural. He spoke to the mutual friend and virtually ignored me. Possibly to make amends he asked, at length, if I was enjoying myself.

"It's a chilly room," I said. I was referring of course to his manner. Had I wanted to describe the room I would have used "grim," or some such adjective.

"I don't know about you being chilly but I'm certainly not," he said with aggression. Then a very drunk woman in a sack dress came and took his hand and began to slobber over him. I excused myself and went off. He said most pointedly that he hoped he would see me again some time.

I caught his eye just as I left the party, and I felt both sorry for him and angry with him. He looked stunned, as if important news had just been delivered to him. He saw me leave with a group of people and I stared at him without the whimper of a smile. Yes, I was sorry for him. I was also piqued. The very next day when we met and I brought it up, he did not even remember that a mutual friend had introduced us.

"Clement Hastings!" he said, repeating the man's name. Which goes to show how nervous he must have been.

It is impossible to insist that bad news delivered in a certain manner and at a certain time will have a less awful effect. But I feel that I got my walking papers from him at the wrong moment. For one thing, it was morning. The clock went off and I sat up wondering when he had set it. Being on the outside of the bed, he was already attending to the push button.

"I'm sorry, darling," he said.

"Did you set it?" I said, indignant. There was an element of betrayal here, as if he'd wanted to sneak away without saying goodbye.

"I must have," he said. He put his arm around me and we lay back again. It was dark outside and there was a feeling—though this may be memory feeling—of frost.

"Congratulations, you're getting your prize today," he whispered. I was being given an award for my announcing.

"Thank you," I said. I was ashamed of it. It reminded me of being back at school and always coming first in everything and being guilty about this but not disciplined enough to deliberately hold back.

"It's beautiful that you stayed all night," I said. I was stroking him all over. My hands were never still in bed. Awake or asleep, I constantly caressed him. Not to excite him, simply to reassure and comfort him and perhaps to consolidate my ownership. There is something about holding on to things that I find therapeutic. For hours I hold smooth stones in the palm of my hand or I grip the sides of an armchair and feel the better for it. He kissed me. He said he had never known anyone so sweet or so attentive. Encouraged, I began to do something very intimate. I heard his sighs of pleasure, the "oy, oy" of delight when he was both indulging it and telling himself that he mustn't. At first I was unaware of his speaking voice.

"Hey," he said jocularly, just like that. "This can't go on, you know." I thought he was referring to our activity at that moment, because of course it was late and he would have to get up shortly. Then I raised my head from its sunken position between his legs and I looked at him through my hair, which had fallen over my face. I saw that he was serious.

"It just occurred to me that possibly you love me," he said. I nodded and pushed my hair back so that he would read it, my testimony, clear and clean upon my face. He put me lying down so that our heads were side by side and he began:

"I adore you, but I'm not in love with you; with my commitments I don't think I could be in love with anyone, it all started gay and lighthearted . . ." Those last few words offended me. It was not how I saw it or how I remembered it: the numerous telegrams he sent me saying, "I long to see you," or "May the sun shine on you," the first few moments each time when we met and were overcome with passion, shyness, and the shock of being so disturbed by each other's presence. We had even searched in our dictionaries for words to convey the specialness of our regard for each other. He came up with "cense," which meant to adore or cover with the perfume of love. It was a most appropriate word, and we used it over and over again. Now he was negating all this. He was talking about weaving me into his life, his family life . . . becoming a friend. He said it, though, without conviction. I could not think of a single thing to say. I knew that if I spoke I would be pathetic, so I remained silent. When he'd finished I stared straight ahead at the split between the curtains, and looking at the beam of raw light coming through, I said, "I think there's frost outside," and he said that possibly there was, because winter was upon us. We got up, and as usual he took the bulb out of the bedside lamp and plugged in his razor. I went off to get breakfast. That was the only morning I forgot about squeezing orange juice for him and I often wonder if he took it as an insult. He left just before nine.

The sitting room held the traces of his visit. Or, to be precise, the remains of his cigars. In one of the blue, saucer-shaped ashtrays there were thick turds of dark-gray cigar ash. There were also stubs, but it was the ash I kept looking at, thinking that its thickness resembled the thickness of his unlovely legs. And once again I experienced hatred for him. I was about to tip the contents of the ashtray into the fire grate when something stopped me, and what did I do but get an empty lozenge box and with the aid of a sheet of paper lift the clumps of ash in there and carry the tin upstairs. With the movement the turds lost their shape, and whereas they had reminded me of his legs, they were now an even mass of dark-gray ash, probably like the ashes of the dead. I put the tin in a drawer underneath some clothes.

Later in the day I was given my award—a very big silver medallion with my name on it. At the party afterward I got drunk. My friends tell me that I did not actually disgrace myself, but I have a humiliating recollection of beginning a story and not being able to go ahead with it, not because the contents eluded me, but because the words became too difficult to pronounce. A man brought me home, and after I'd made him a cup of tea, I said good night over-properly; then when he was gone I staggered to my bed. When I drink heavily I sleep badly. It was still dark outside when I woke up and straightaway I remembered the previous morning and the suggestion of frost outside, and his cold warning words. I had to agree. Although our meetings were perfect, I had a sense of doom impending, of a chasm opening up between us, of someone telling his wife, of souring love, of destruction. And still we hadn't gone as far as we should have gone. There were peaks of joy and of its opposite that we should have climbed to, but the time was not left to us. He had of course said, "You still have a great physical hold over me," and that in its way I found degrading. To have gone on making love when he had discarded me would have been repellent. It had come to an end. The thing I kept thinking of was a violet in a wood and how a time comes for it to drop off and die. The frost may have had something to do with my thinking, or rather, with my musing. I got up and put on a dressing gown. My head hurt from the hangover, but I knew that I must write to him while I had some resolution. I know my own failings, and I knew that before the day was out I would want to see him again, sit with him, coax him back with sweetness and my overwhelming helplessness.

I wrote the note and left out the bit about the violet. It is not a thing you can put down on paper without seeming fanciful. I said if he didn't think it prudent to see me, then not to see me. I said it had been a nice interlude and that we must entertain good memories of it. It was a remarkably controlled letter. He wrote back promptly. My decision came as a shock, he said. Still, he admitted that I was right. In the middle of the letter he said he must penetrate my composure and to do so he must admit that above and beyond everything he loved me and would always do so. That of course was the word I had been snooping around for, for months. It set me off. I wrote a long letter back to him. I lost my head. I oversaid everything. I testified to loving him, to sitting on the edge of madness in the intervening days, to my hoping for a miracle.

It is just as well that I did not write out the miracle in detail, because possibly it is, or was, rather inhuman. It concerned his family.

He was returning from the funeral of his wife and children, wearing black tails. He also wore the white silk scarf I had seen him with, and there was a black mourning tulip in his buttonhole. When he came toward me I snatched the black tulip and replaced it with a white narcissus, and he in turn put the scarf around my neck and drew me toward him by holding its fringed ends. I kept moving my neck back and forth within the embrace of the scarf. Then we danced divinely on a wooden floor that was white and slippery. At times I thought we would fall, but he said, "You don't have to worry, I'm with you." The dance floor was also a road and we were going somewhere beautiful.

For weeks I waited for a reply to my letter, but there was none. More than once I had my hand on the telephone, but something cautionary—a new sensation for me—in the back of my mind bade me to wait. To give him time. To let regret take charge of his heart. To let him come of his own accord. And then I panicked. I thought that perhaps the letter had gone astray or had fallen into other hands. I'd posted it, of course, to the office in Lincoln's Inn where he worked. I wrote another. This time it was a formal note, and with it I enclosed a postcard with the words YES and NO. I asked if he had received my previous letter to kindly let me know by simply crossing out the word which did not apply on my card, and send it back to me. It came back with the NO crossed out. Nothing else. So he had received my letter. I think I looked at the card for hours. I could not stop shaking, and to calm myself I took several drinks. There was something so brutal about the card, but then you could say that I had asked for it by approaching the situation in that way. I took out the box with his ash in it and wept over it, and wanted both to toss it out of the window and to preserve it forevermore.

In general I behaved very strangely. I rang someone who knew him and asked for no reason at all what she thought his hobbies might be. She said he played the harmonium, which I found unbearable news altogether. Then I entered a black patch, and on the third day I lost control.

Well, from not sleeping and taking pep pills and whiskey, I got very odd. I was shaking all over and breathing very quickly, the way one might after witnessing an accident. I stood at my bedroom window, which is on the second floor, and looked at the concrete underneath. The only flowers left in bloom were the hydrangeas, and they had faded to a soft russet, which was much more fetching than the harsh pink they were all summer. In the garden next door there were frost hats over the fuchsias. Looking first at the hydrangeas, then at the fuchsias, I tried to estimate the consequences of my jumping. I wondered if the drop were great enough. Being physically awkward I could only conceive of injuring myself fatally, which would be worse, because I would then be confined to my bed and imprisoned with the very thoughts that were driving me to desperation. I opened the window and leaned out, but quickly drew back. I had a better idea. There was a plumber downstairs installing central heating—an enterprise I had embarked upon when my lover began to come regularly and we liked walking around naked eating sandwiches and playing records. I decided to gas myself and to seek the help of the plumber in order to do it efficiently. I am aware—someone must have told me—that there comes a point in the middle of the operation when the doer regrets it and tries to withdraw but cannot. That seemed like an extra note of tragedy that I had no wish to experience. So I decided to go downstairs to this man and explain to him that I *wanted* to die, and that I was not telling him simply for him to prevent me, or console me, that I was not looking for pity—there comes a time when pity is of no help—and that I simply wanted his assistance. He could show me what to do, settle me down, and—this is absurd—be around to take care of the telephone and the doorbell for the next few hours. Also to dispose of me with dignity. Above all, I wanted that. I even decided what I would wear: a long dress, which in fact was the same color as the hydrangeas in their russet phase and which I've never worn except for a photograph or on television. Before going downstairs, I wrote a note which said simply: "I am committing suicide through lack of intelligence, and through not knowing, not learning to know, how to live."

You will think I am callous not to have taken the existence of my children into account. But, in fact, I did. Long before the affair began, I had reached the conclusion that they had been parted from me irrevocably by being sent to boarding school. If you like, I felt I had let them down years before. I thought—it was an unhysterical admission—that my being alive or my being dead made little difference to the course of their lives. I ought to say that I had not seen them for a month, and it is a shocking fact that although absence does not make love less, it cools down our physical need for the ones we love. They were due home for their mid-term holiday that very day, but since it was their father's turn to have them, I knew that I would only see them for a few hours one afternoon. And in my despondent state that seemed worse than not seeing them at all.

Well, of course, when I went downstairs the plumber took one look at me and said, "You could do with a cup of tea." He actually had tea made. So I took it and stood there warming my child-sized hands around the barrel of the brown mug. Suddenly, swiftly, I remembered my lover measuring our hands when we were lying in bed and saying that mine were no bigger than his daughter's. And then I had another and less edifying memory about hands. It was the time we met when he was visibly distressed because he'd caught those same daughter's hands in a motorcar door. The fingers had not been broken but were badly bruised, and he felt awful about it and hoped his daughter would forgive him. Upon being told the story, I bolted off into an anecdote about almost losing *my* fingers in the door of someone's Jaguar. It was pointless, although a listener might infer from it that I was a boastful and heartless girl. I would have been sorry for any child whose fingers were caught in a motorcar door, but at that moment I was trying to recall him to the hidden world of him and me. Perhaps it was one of the things that made him like me less. Perhaps it was then he resolved to end the affair. I was about to say this to the plumber, to warn him about so-called love often hardening the heart, but like the violets, it is something that can miss awfully, and when it does two people are mortally embarrassed. He'd put sugar in my tea and I found it sickly.

"I want you to help me," I said.

"Anything," he said. I ought to know that. We were friends. He would do the pipes tastefully. The pipes would be little works of art and the radiators painted to match the walls.

"You may think I will paint these white, but in fact they will be light ivory," he said. The whitewash on the kitchen walls had yellowed a bit.

"I want to do myself in," I said hurriedly.

"Good God," he said, and then burst out laughing. He always knew I was dramatic. Then he looked at me, and obviously my face was a revelation. For one thing I could not control my breathing. He put his arm around me and led me into the sitting room and we had a drink. I knew he liked drink and thought, It's an ill wind that doesn't blow some good. The maddening thing was that I kept thinking a live person's thoughts. He said I had so much to live for. "A young girl like you—people wanting your autograph, a lovely new car," he said.

"It's all . . ." I groped for the word. I had meant to say "meaningless," but "cruel" was the word that came out.

"And your boys," he said. "What about your boys?" He had seen photographs of them, and once I'd read him a letter from one of them. The word "cruel" seemed to be blazing in my head. It screamed at me from every corner of the room. To avoid his glance, I looked down at the sleeve of my angora jersey and methodically began picking off pieces of fluff and rolling them into a little ball.

There was a moment's pause.

"This is an unlucky road. You're the third," he said.

"The third what?" I said, industriously piling the black fluff into my palm.

"A woman farther up; her husband was a bandleader, used to be out late. One night she went to the dance hall and saw him with another girl; she came home and did it straightaway."

"Gas?" I asked, genuinely curious.

"No, sedation," he said, and was off on another story about a girl who'd gassed herself and was found by him because he was in the house treating dry rot at the time. "Naked, except for a jersey," he said, and speculated on why she should be attired like that. His manner changed considerably as he recalled how he went into the house, smelled gas, and searched it out.

I looked at him. His face was grave. He had scaled eyelids. I had never looked at him so closely before. "Poor Michael," I said. A feeble apology. I was thinking that if he had abetted my suicide he would then have been committed to the memory of it.

"A lovely young girl," he said, wistful.

"Poor girl," I said, mustering up pity.

There seemed to be nothing else to say. He had shamed me out of it. I stood up and made an effort at normality—I took some glasses off a side table and moved in the direction of the kitchen. If dirty glasses are any proof of drinking, then quite a lot of it had been done by me over the past few days.

"Well," he said, and rose and sighed. He admitted to feeling pleased with himself.

As it happened, there would have been a secondary crisis that day. Although my children were due to return to their father, he rang to say that the older boy had a temperature, and since—though he did not say this—he could not take care of a sick child, he would be obliged to bring them to my house. They arrived in the afternoon. I was waiting inside the door, with my face heavily made up to disguise my distress. The sick boy had a blanket draped over his tweed coat and one of his father's scarves around his face. When I embraced him, he began to cry. The younger boy went around the house to make sure that everything was as he had last seen it. Normally I had presents for them on their return home, but I had neglected it on this occasion, and consequently they were a little downcast.

"Tomorrow," I said.

"Why are there tears in your eyes?" the sick boy asked as I undressed him.

"Because you are sick," I said, telling a half-truth.

"Oh, Mamsies," he said, calling me by a name he had used for years. He put his arms around me and we both began to cry. I felt he was crying for the numerous unguessed afflictions that the circumstances of a broken home would impose upon him. It was strange and unsatisfying to hold him in my arms, when over the months I had got used to my lover's size—the width of his shoulders, the exact height of his body, which obliged me to stand on tiptoe so that our limbs could correspond perfectly. Holding my son, I was conscious only of how small he was and how tenaciously he clung.

The younger boy and I sat in the bedroom and played a game which entailed reading out questions such as "A river?" "A famous footballer?" and then spinning a disk until it steadied down at one letter and using that letter as the first initial of the river or the famous footballer or whatever the question called for. I was quite slow at it, and so was the sick boy. His brother won easily, although I had asked him to let the invalid win. Children are callous.

We all jumped when the heating came on, because the boiler,

from the basement just underneath, gave an almighty churning noise and made the kind of sudden erupting move I had wanted to make that morning when I stood at the bedroom window and tried to pitch myself out. As a special surprise and to cheer me up, the plumber had called in two of his mates, and among them they got the job finished. To make us warm and happy, as he put it when he came to the bedroom to tell me. It was an awkward moment. I'd avoided him since our morning's drama. At teatime I'd even left his tea on a tray out on the landing. Would he tell other people how I had asked him to be my murderer? Would he have recognized it as that? I gave him and his friends a drink, and they stood uncomfortably in the children's bedroom and looked at the little boy's flushed face and said he would soon be better. What else could they say!

For the remainder of the evening, the boys and I played the quiz game over and over again, and just before they went to sleep I read them an adventure story. In the morning they both had temperatures. I was busy nursing them for the next couple of weeks. I made beef tea a lot and broke bread into it and coaxed them to swallow those sops of savory bread. They were constantly asking to be entertained. The only thing I could think of in the way of facts were particles of nature lore I had gleaned from one of my colleagues in the television canteen. Even with embellishing, it took not more than two minutes to tell my children: of a storm of butterflies in Venezuela, of animals called sloths that are so lazy they hang from trees and become covered with moss, and of how the sparrows in England sing different from the sparrows in Paris.

"More," they would say. "More, more." Then we would have to play that silly game again or embark upon another adventure story.

At these times I did not allow my mind to wander, but in the evenings, when their father came, I used to withdraw to the sitting room and have a drink. Well, that was disastrous. The leisure enabled me to brood; also, I have very weak bulbs in the lamps and the dimness gives the room a quality that induces reminiscence. I would be transported back. I enacted various kinds of reunion with my lover, but my favorite one was an unexpected meeting in one of those tiled, inhuman, pedestrian subways and running toward each other and finding ourselves at a stairway which said (one in London actually does say), TO CENTRAL ISLAND ONLY, and laughing as we leaped up those stairs propelled by miraculous wings. In less indulgent phases, I regretted that we hadn't seen more sunsets, or cigarette advertisements, or something, because in memory our numerous meetings became one long uninterrupted state of lovemaking without the ordinariness of things in between to fasten those peaks. The days, the nights with him, seemed to have been sandwiched into a long, beautiful, but single night, instead of being stretched to the seventeen occasions it actually was. Ah, vanished peaks. Once I was so sure that he had come into the room that I tore off a segment of an orange I had just peeled, and handed it to him.

But from the other room I heard the low, assured voice of the children's father delivering information with the self-importance of a man delivering dogmas, and I shuddered at the degree of poison that lay between us when we'd once professed to love. Plagued love. Then, some of the feeling I had for my husband transferred itself to my lover, and I reasoned with myself that the letter in which he had professed to love me was sham, that he had merely written it when he thought he was free of me, but finding himself saddled once again, he withdrew and let me have the postcard. I was a stranger to myself. Hate was welling up. I wished multitudes of humiliation on him. I even plotted a dinner party that I would attend, having made sure that he was invited, and snubbing him throughout. My thoughts teetered between hate and the hope of something final between us, so that I would be certain of his feelings toward me. Even as I sat in a bus, an advertisement which caught my eye was immediately related to him. It said, DON'T PANIC. WE MEND, WE ADAPT, WE REMODEL. It was an advertisement for pearl stringing. I would mend and with vengeance.

I cannot say when it first began to happen, because that would be too drastic, and anyhow, I do not know. But the children were back at school, and we'd got over Christmas, and he and I had not exchanged cards. But I began to think less harshly of him. They were silly thoughts, really. I hoped he was having little pleasures like eating in restaurants, and clean socks, and red wine the temperature he liked it, and even—yes, even ecstasies in bed with his wife. These thoughts made me smile to myself inwardly, the new kind of smile I had discovered. I shuddered at the risk he'd run by seeing me at all. Of course, the earlier injured thoughts battled with these new ones. It was like carrying a taper along a corridor where the drafts are fierce and the chances of it staying alight pretty meager. I thought of him and my children in the same instant, their little foibles became his: my children telling me elaborate lies about their sporting feats, his slight puffing when we climbed steps and his trying to conceal it. The age difference between us must have saddened him. It was then I think that I really fell in love with him. His courtship of me, his telegrams, his eventual departure, even our lovemaking were nothing compared with this new sensation. It rose like sap within me, it often made me cry, the fact that he could not benefit from it! The temptation to ring him had passed away.

His phone call came quite out of the blue. It was one of those times when I debated about answering it or not, because mostly I let it ring. He asked if we could meet, if, and he said this so gently, my nerves were steady enough. I said my nerves were never better. That was a liberty I had to take. We met in a café for tea. Toast again. Just like the beginning. He asked how I was. Remarked on my good complexion. Neither of us mentioned the incident of the postcard. Nor did he say what impulse had moved him to telephone. It may not have been impulse at all. He talked about his work and how busy he'd been, and then relayed a little story about taking an elderly aunt for a drive and driving so slowly that she asked him to please hurry up because she would have walked there quicker.

"You've recovered," he said then, suddenly. I looked at his face. I could see it was on his mind.

"I'm over it," I said, and dipped my finger into the sugar bowl and let him lick the white crystals off the tip of my finger. Poor man. I could not have told him anything else, he would not have understood. In a way it was like being with someone else. He was not the one who had folded back the bedspread and sucked me dry and left his cigar ash for preserving. He was the representative of that one.

"We'll meet from time to time," he said.

"Of course." I must have looked dubious.

"Perhaps you don't want to?"

"Whenever you feel you would like to." I neither welcomed nor dreaded the thought. It would not make any difference to how I felt. That was the first time it occurred to me that all my life I had feared imprisonment, the nun's cell, the hospital bed, the places where one faced the self without distraction, without the crutches of other people—but sitting there feeding him white sugar, I thought, I now have entered a cell, and this man cannot know what it is for me to love him the way I do, and I cannot weigh him down with it, because he is in another cell confronted with other difficulties.

The cell reminded me of a convent, and for something to say, I mentioned my sister the nun.

"I went to see my sister."

"How is she?" he asked. He had often inquired about her. He used to take an interest in her and ask what she looked like. I even got the impression that he had a fantasy about seducing her.

"She's fine," I said. "We were walking down a corridor and she asked me to look around and make sure that there weren't any other sisters looking, and then she hoisted her skirts up and slid down the banister."

"Dear girl," he said. He liked that story. The smallest things gave him such pleasure.

I enjoyed our tea. It was one of the least fruitless afternoons I'd had in months, and coming out he gripped my arm and said how perfect it would be if we could get away for a few days. Perhaps he meant it.

In fact, we kept our promise. We do meet from time to time. You could say things are back to normal again. By normal I mean a state whereby I notice the moon, trees, fresh spit upon the pavement; I look at strangers and see in their expressions something of my own predicament; I am part of everyday life, I suppose. There is a lamp in my bedroom that gives out a dry crackle each time an electric train goes by, and at night I count those crackles because it is the time he comes back. I mean the real he, not the man who confronts me from time to time across a café table, but the man that dwells somewhere within me. He rises before my eyes—his praying hands, his tongue that liked to suck, his sly eyes, his smile, the veins on his cheeks, the calm voice speaking sense to me. I suppose you wonder why I torment myself like this with details of his presence, but I need it, I cannot let go of him now, because if I did, all our happiness and my subsequent pain—I cannot vouch for his—will all have been nothing, and nothing is a dreadful thing to hold on to.

The Mouth of the Cave

There were two routes to the village. I chose the rougher one, to be beside the mountain rather than the sea. It is a dusty ill-defined stretch of road littered with rocks. The rocks that have fallen from the cliff are a menacing shade of red once they have split open. On the surface the cliff appears to be gray. Here and there on its gray and red face there are small clumps of trees. Parched in summer, tormented by winds in winter, they nevertheless survive, getting no larger or no smaller.

In one such clump of green, just underneath the cliff, I saw a girl stand up. She began to tie her suspenders slowly. She had bad balance because when drawing her knickers on she lost her footing more than once. She put her skirt on by bringing it over her head, and lastly her cardigan, which appeared to have several buttons. As I came closer she walked away. A young girl in a maroon cardigan and a black skirt. She was twenty or thereabouts. Suddenly, and without anticipating it, I turned toward home so as to give the impression that I'd simply been having a stroll. The ridiculousness of this hit me soon after and I turned around again and walked toward the scene of her secret. I was trembling, but these journeys have got to be accomplished.

What a shock to find that nothing lurked there, no man, no animal. The bushes had not risen from the weight of her body. I reckoned that she must have been lying for quite a time. Then I saw that she, too, was returning. Had she forgotten something? Did she want to ask me a favor? Why was she hurrying? I could not see her face, her head was down. I turned and this time I ran toward the private road that led to my rented house. I thought, Why am I running, why am I trembling, why am I afraid? Because she is a woman and so am I. Because, because? I did not know.

When I got to the courtyard I asked the servant, who had been fanning herself, to unchain the dog. Then I sat outdoors and waited. The flowering tree looked particularly dramatic, its petals richly pink, its scent oppressively sweet. The only tree in flower. My servant had warned me about those particular flowers; she had even taken the trouble to get the dictionary to impress the word upon me—*Venodno*, poison, poison petals. Nevertheless I had the table moved in order to be nearer that tree, and we steadied it by putting folded cigarette cartons under two of its legs. I told the servant to lay a place for two. I also decided what we would eat, though normally I don't, in order to give the days some element of surprise. I asked that both wines be put on the table, and also those long sugar-coated biscuits that can be dipped in white wine and sucked until the sweetness is drained from them and redipped and resucked, indefinitely.

She would like the house. It had simplicity despite its grandeur. A white house with green shutters and a fanlight of stone over each of the three downstairs entrances. A sundial, a well, a little chapel. The walls and the ceilings were a milky blue, and this, combined with the sea and sky, had a strange hallucinatory effect, as if sea and sky moved indoors. There were maps instead of pictures. Around the light bulbs pink shells that over the years had got a bit chipped, but this only added to the informality of the place.

We would take a long time over supper. Petals would drop from the tree; some might lodge on the stone table, festooning it. The figs, exquisitely chilled, would be served on a wide platter. We would test them with our fingers. We would know which ones when bitten into would prove to be satisfactory. She, being native, might be more expert at it than I. One or the other of us might bite too avidly and find that the seeds, wet and messy and runny and beautiful, spurted over our chins. I would wipe my chin with my hand. I would do everything to put her at ease. Get drunk if necessary. At first I would talk, but later show hesitation in order to give her a chance.

I changed into an orange robe and put on a long necklace made of a variety of shells. The dog was still loose in order to warn me. At the first bark I would have him brought in and tied up at the back of the house, where even his whimpering would be unheard.

I sat on the terrace. The sun was going down. I moved to another chair in order to get the benefit of it. The crickets had commenced their incessant near-mechanical din and the lizards began to appear from behind the maps. Something about their deft, stealthlike movements reminded me of her, but everything reminded me of her just then. There was such silence that the seconds appeared to record their own passing. There were only the crickets and, in the distance, the sound of sheep bells, more dreamlike than a bleat. In the distance, too, the lighthouse, faithfully signaling. A pair of shorts hanging on a hook began to flutter in the first breeze, and how I welcomed it, knowing that it heralded night. She was waiting for dark, the embracing dark, the sinner's dear accomplice.

My servant waited out of view. I could not see her, but I was conscious of her the way one sometimes is of a prompter in the wings. It irritated me. I could hear her picking up or laying down a plate, and I knew it was being done simply to engage my attention. I had also to battle with the smell of lentil soup. The smell, though gratifying, seemed nothing more than a bribe to hurry the proceedings, and that was impossible. Because, according to my conjecture, once I began to eat the possibility of her coming was ruled out. I had to wait.

The hour that followed had an edgy, predictable, and awful pattern—I walked, sat on various seats, lit cigarettes that I quickly discarded, kept adding to my drink. At moments I forgot the cause of my agitation, but then recalling her in dark clothes and downcast eyes, I thrilled again at the pleasure of receiving her. Across the bay the various settlements of lights came on, outlining towns or villages that are invisible in daylight. The perfection of the stars was loathsome.

Finally, the dog's food was brought forth, and he ate as he always does, at my feet. When the empty plate skated over the smooth cobbles—due to my clumsiness—and the full moon, so near, so red, so oddly hospitable, appeared above the pines, I decided to begin, taking the napkin out of its ring and spreading it slowly and ceremoniously on my lap. I confess that in those few seconds my faith was overwhelming and my hope stronger than it had ever been.

The food was destroyed. I drank a lot.

Next day I set out for the village, but took the sea road. I have not gone the cliff way ever since. I have often wanted to, especially after work, when I know what my itinerary is going to be: I will collect the letters, have one Pernod in the bar where retired colonels play cards, sit and talk to them about nothing. We have long ago accepted our uselessness for each other. New people hardly ever come.

There was an Australian painter whom I invited to supper, having decided that he was moderately attractive. He became offensive after a few drinks and kept telling me how misrepresented his countrymen were. It was sad rather than unpleasant, and the servant and I had to link him home.

On Sundays and feast days girls of about twenty go by, arms around each other, bodies lost inside dark commodious garments. Not one of them looks at me, although by now I am known. She must know me. Yet she never gives me a sign as to which she is. I expect she is too frightened. In my more optimistic moments I like to think that she waits there, expecting me to come and search her out. Yet I always find myself taking the sea road, even though I most desperately desire to go the other way.

Irish Revel

Mary hoped that the rotted front tire would not burst. As it was, the tube had a slow puncture, and twice she had to stop and use the pump, maddening, because the pump had no connection and had to be jammed on over the corner of a handkerchief. For as long as she could remember, she had been pumping bicycles, carting turf, cleaning out houses, doing a man's work. Her father and her two brothers worked for the forestry, so that she and her mother had to do all the odd jobs—there were three children to care for, and fowl and pigs and churning. Theirs was a mountainy farm in Ireland, and life was hard.

But this cold evening in early November she was free. She rode along the mountain road, between the bare thorn hedges, thinking pleasantly about the party. Although she was seventeen, this was her first party. The invitation had come only that morning from Mrs. Rodgers of the Commercial Hotel. The postman brought word that Mrs. Rodgers wanted her down that evening, without fail. At first, her mother did not wish Mary to go, there was too much to be done, gruel to be made, and one of the twins had earache and was likely to cry in the night. Mary slept with the year-old twins, and sometimes she was afraid that she might lie on them or smother them, the bed was so small. She begged to be let go.

"What use would it be?" her mother said. To her mother all outings were unsettling—they gave you a taste of something you couldn't have. But finally she weakened, mainly because Mrs. Rodgers, as owner of the Commercial Hotel, was an important woman and not to be insulted.

"You can go, so long as you're back in time for the milking in the morning; and mind you don't lose your head," her mother warned. Mary was to stay overnight in the village with Mrs. Rodgers. She plaited her hair, and later when she combed it, it fell in dark crinkled waves over her shoulders. She was allowed to wear the black lace dress that had come from America years ago and belonged to no one in particular. Her mother had sprinkled her with Holy Water, conveyed her to the top of the lane, and warned her never to touch alcohol.

Mary felt happy as she rode along slowly, avoiding the potholes that were thinly iced over. The frost had never lifted that day. The ground was hard. If it went on like that, the cattle would have to be brought into the shed and given hay.

The road turned and looped and rose; she turned and looped with it, climbing little hills and descending again toward the next hill. At the descent of the Big Hill she got off the bicycle—the brakes were unreliable—and looked back, out of habit, at her own house. It was the only house back there on the mountain, small, whitewashed, with a few trees around it and a patch at the back which they called a kitchen garden. There was a rhubarb bed, and shrubs over which they emptied tea leaves, and a stretch of grass where in the summer they had a chicken run, moving it from one patch to the next every other day. She looked away. She was now free to think of John Roland. He had come to their district two years before, riding a motorcycle at a ferocious speed; raising dust on the milk cloths spread on the hedge to dry. He stopped to ask the way. He was staying with Mrs. Rodgers in the Commercial Hotel and had come up to see the lake, which was noted for its colors. It changed color rapidly—it was blue and green and black, all within an hour. At sunset it was often a strange burgundy, not like a lake at all, but like wine.

"Down there," she said to the stranger, pointing to the lake below, with the small island in the middle of it. He had taken a wrong turning.

Hills and tiny cornfields descended steeply toward the water. The misery of the hills was clear, from all the boulders. The cornfields were turning, it was midsummer; the ditches throbbing with the blood-red of fuchsia; the milk sour five hours after it had been put in the tanker. He said how exotic it was. She had no interest in views herself. She just looked up at the high sky and saw that a hawk had halted in the air above them. It was like a pause in her life, the hawk above them, perfectly still; and just then her mother came out to see who the stranger was. He took off his helmet and said, "Hello," very courteously. He introduced himself as John Roland, an English painter, who lived in Italy.

She did not remember exactly how it happened, but after a while he walked into their kitchen with them and sat down to tea.

Two long years since; but she had never given up hoping—perhaps this evening. The mail-car man said that someone special in the Commercial Hotel expected her. She felt such happiness. She spoke to her bicycle, and it seemed to her that her happiness somehow glowed in the pearliness of the cold sky, in the frosted fields going blue in the dusk, in the cottage windows she passed. Her father and mother were rich and cheerful; the twin had no earache, the kitchen fire did not smoke. Now and then she smiled at the thought of how she would appear to him—taller and with breasts now, and a dress that could be worn anywhere. She forgot about the rotted tire, got up, and cycled.

The five streetlights were on when she pedaled into the village. There had been a cattle fair that day and the main street was covered with dung. The townspeople had their windows protected with wooden half-shutters and makeshift arrangements of planks and barrels. Some were out scrubbing their own piece of footpath with bucket and brush. There were cattle wandering around, mooing, the way cattle do when they are in a strange street, and drunken farmers with sticks were trying to identify their own cattle in dark corners.

Beyond the shop window of the Commercial Hotel, Mary heard loud conversation and men singing. It was opaque glass, so that she could not identify any of them, she could just see their heads moving about inside. It was a shabby hotel, the yellow-washed walls needed a coat of paint, as they hadn't been done since the time De Valera came to that village during the election campaign five years before. De Valera went upstairs that time and sat in the parlor and wrote his name with a penny pen in an autograph book, and sympathized with Mrs. Rodgers on the recent death of her husband.

Mary thought of resting her bicycle against the porter barrels under the shop window, and then of climbing the three stone steps that led to the hall door, but suddenly the latch of the shop door clicked and she ran in terror up the alley by the side of the shop, afraid it might be someone who knew her father and would say he saw her going in through the public bar. She wheeled her bicycle into a shed and approached the back door. It was open, but she did not enter without knocking.

Two town girls rushed to answer it. One was Doris O'Beirne, the daughter of the harness maker. She was the only Doris in the whole village, and she was famous for that, as well as for the fact that one of her eyes was blue and the other a dark brown. She was learning shorthand and typing at the local technical school, and later she meant to be a secretary to some famous man or other in the government, in Dublin.

"God, I thought it was someone important," she said when she saw Mary standing there, blushing, beholden, and with a bottle of cream in her hand. Another girl! Girls were two a penny in that neighborhood. People said that it had something to do with the limewater that so many girls were born. Girls with pink skins and matching eyes, and girls like Mary, with long, wavy hair and gorgeous figures.

"Come in or stay out," said Eithne Duggan, the second girl, to Mary. It was supposed to be a joke, but neither of them liked her. They hated shy mountainy people.

Mary came in, carrying cream which her mother had sent to Mrs. Rodgers as a present. She put it on the dresser and took off her coat. The girls nudged each other when they saw her dress. In the kitchen was a smell of cow dung from the street, and fried onions from a pan that simmered on the stove.

"Where's Mrs. Rodgers?" Mary asked.

"Serving," Doris said in a saucy voice, as if any fool ought to know. Two old men sat at the table eating.

"I can't chew, I have no teeth," said one of the men to Doris. " 'Tis like leather," he said, holding the plate of burned steak toward her. He had watery eyes and he blinked childishly. Was it so, Mary wondered, that eyes got paler with age, like bluebells in a jar?

"You're not going to charge me for that," the old man was saying to Doris. Tea and steak cost five shillings at the Commercial.

" 'Tis good for you, chewing is," Eithne Duggan said, teasing him.

"I can't chew with my gums," he said again, and the two girls began to giggle. The old man looked pleased that he had made them laugh, and he closed his mouth and munched once or twice on a piece of fresh shop bread. Eithne Duggan laughed so much that she had to put a dishcloth between her teeth. Mary hung up her coat and went through to the shop.

Mrs. Rodgers came from the counter for a moment to speak to her.

"Mary, I'm glad you came, that pair in there are no use at all, always giggling. Now, first thing we have to do is to get the parlor upstairs straightened out. Everything has to come out of it except the piano. We're going to have dancing and everything."

Quickly Mary realized that she was being given work to do, and she blushed with shock and disappointment.

"Pitch everything into the back bedroom, the whole shootin' lot," Mrs. Rodgers was saying, as Mary thought of her good lace dress and of how her mother wouldn't even let her wear it to Mass on Sundays.

"And we have to stuff a goose, too, and get it on," Mrs. Rodgers said, and went on to explain that the party was in honor of the local Customs and Excise Officer, who was retiring because his wife won some money in the sweep. Two thousand pounds. His wife lived thirty miles away at the far side of Limerick, and he lodged in the Commercial Hotel from Monday to Friday, going home for the weekends.

"There's someone here expecting me," Mary said, trembling with the pleasure of being about to hear his name pronounced by someone else. She wondered which room was his, and if he was likely to be in at that moment. Already in imagination she had climbed the rickety stairs and knocked on the door and heard him move around inside.

"Expecting you!" Mrs. Rodgers said, and looked puzzled for a minute. "Oh, that lad from the slate quarry was inquiring about you, he said he saw you at a dance once. He's as odd as two left shoes."

"What lad?" Mary said, as she felt the joy leaking out of her heart.

"Oh, what's his name," Mrs. Rodgers said, and then to the men with empty glasses who were shouting for her, "Oh, all right, I'm coming."

Upstairs Doris and Eithne helped Mary move the heavy pieces of furniture. They dragged the sideboard across the landing, and one of the casters tore the linoleum. She was expiring, because she had the heaviest end, the other two being at the same side. She felt that it was on purpose: they ate sweets without offering her one, and she caught them making faces at her dress. The dress worried her, too, in case anything should happen to it. If one of the lace threads caught in a splinter of wood, or on a porter barrel, she would have no business going home in the morning. They carried out a varnished bamboo whatnot, a small table, knickknacks, and a chamber pot with no handle which held some withered hydrangeas. They smelled awful.

"How much is the doggie in the window, the one with the wag-gledy tail?" Doris O'Beirne sang to a white china dog and swore that there wasn't ten pounds' worth of furniture in the whole shebeen.

"Are you leaving your curlers in, Dot, till it starts?" Eithne Duggan asked her friend.

"Oh, def," Doris O'Beirne said. She wore an assortment of curlers—white pipe cleaners, metal clips, and pink plastic rollers. Eithne had just taken hers out, and her hair, dyed blond, stood out, all frizzed and alarming. She reminded Mary of a molting hen about to attempt flight. She was, God bless her, an unfortunate girl, with a squint, jumbled teeth, and almost no lips; like something put together hurriedly. That was the luck of the draw.

"Take these," Doris O'Beirne said, handing Mary bunches of yellowed bills crammed on skewers.

Do this! Do that! They ordered her around like a maid. She dusted the piano, top and sides, and the yellow and black keys; then the surround and the wainscoting. The dust, thick on everything, had settled into a hard film because of the damp in that room. A party! She'd have been as well off at home, at least it was clean dirt attending to calves and pigs and the like.

Doris and Eithne amused themselves, hitting notes on the piano at random and wandering from one mirror to the next. There were two mirrors in the parlor and one side of the folding fire screen was a blotchy mirror, too. The other two sides were water lilies painted on black cloth, but like everything else in the room it was decrepit.

"What's that?" Doris and Eithne asked each other as they heard a hullabaloo downstairs. They rushed out to see what it was, and Mary followed. Over the banisters they saw that a young bullock had got in the hall door and was slithering over the tiled floor, trying to find his way out again.

"Don't excite her, don't excite her, I tell ye," said the old toothless man to the young boy who tried to drive the black bullock out. Two more boys were having a bet as to whether or not the bullock would do something on the floor, when Mrs. Rodgers came out and dropped a glass of porter. The beast backed out the way he'd come, shaking his head from side to side.

Eithne and Doris clasped each other in laughter, and then Doris drew back so that none of the boys would see her in her curling pins and call her names. Mary had gone back to the room, downcast. Wearily she pushed the chairs back against the wall and swept the linoleumed floor where they were later to dance.

"She's bawling in there," Eithne Duggan told her friend Doris. They had locked themselves into the bathroom with a bottle of cider.

"God, she's a right-looking eejit in the dress," Doris said. "And the length of it!"

"It's her mother's," Eithne said. She had admired the dress before that, when Doris was out of the room, and had asked Mary where she bought it.

"What's she crying about?" Doris wondered aloud.

"She thought some lad would be here. Do you remember that lad stayed here the summer before last and had a motorcycle?"

"He was a Jew," Doris said. "You could tell by his nose. God, she'd shake him in that dress, he'd think she was a scarecrow." She squeezed a blackhead on her chin, tightened a curling pin which had come loose, and said, "Her hair isn't natural either, you can see it's curled."

"I hate that kind of black hair, it's like a gypsy's," Eithne said, drinking the last of the cider. They hid the bottle under the scoured bath.

"Have a cachou, take the smell off your breath," Doris said as she hawed on the bathroom mirror and wondered if she would get off with that fellow O'Toole from the slate quarry, who was coming to the party.

In the front room Mary polished glasses. Tears ran down her cheeks, so she did not put on the light. She foresaw how the party would be; they would all stand around and consume the goose, which was now simmering in the turf range. The men would be drunk, the girls giggling. Having eaten, they would dance and sing and tell ghost stories, and in the morning she would have to get up early and be home in time to milk. She moved toward the dark pane of window with a glass in her hand and looked out at the dirtied streets, remembering how once she had danced with John on the upper road to no music at all, just their hearts beating and the sound of happiness.

He came into their house for tea that summer's day, and on her father's suggestion he lodged with them for four days, helping with the hay and oiling all the farm machinery for her father. He understood machinery. He put back doorknobs that had fallen off. Mary made his bed in the daytime and carried up a ewer of water from the rain barrel every evening, so that he could wash. She washed the checked shirt he wore, and that day his bare back peeled in the sun. She put milk on it. It was his last day with them. After supper he proposed giving each of the grown-up children a ride on the motorbike. Her turn came last; she felt that he had planned it that way, but it may have been that her brothers were more persistent about being first. She would never forget that ride. She warmed from head to foot in wonder and joy. He praised her as a good balancer, and at odd moments he took one hand off the handlebar and gave her clasped hands a comforting pat. The sun went down, and the gorse flowers blazed yellow. They did not talk for miles; she had his stomach encased in the delicate and frantic grasp of a girl in love, and no matter how far they rode, they seemed always to be riding into a golden haze. He saw the lake at its most glorious. They got off at the bridge five miles away and sat on the limestone wall, which was cushioned by moss and lichen. She took a tick out of his neck and touched the spot where the tick had drawn one pinprick of blood; it was then they danced. A sound of larks and running water. The hay in the fields was lying green and ungathered, and the air was sweet with the smell of it. They danced.

"Sweet Mary," he said, looking earnestly into her eyes. Her eyes were a greenish-brown. He confessed that he could not love her, because he already loved his wife and children, and anyhow, he said, "You are too young and too innocent."

Next day, as he was leaving, he asked if he might send her something in the post; it came eleven days later: a black-and-white drawing of her, very like her, except that the girl in the drawing was uglier.

"A fat lot of good, that is," said her mother, who had been expecting a gold bracelet or a brooch. "That wouldn't take you far."

They hung it on a nail in the kitchen for a while, and then one day it fell down and someone (probably her mother) used it to sweep dust onto; ever since it was used for that purpose. Mary had wanted to keep it, to put it away in a trunk, but she was ashamed to. They were hard people, and it was only when someone died that they could give in to sentiment or crying.

"Sweet Mary," he had said. He never wrote. Two summers passed, devil's pokers flowered for two seasons, and thistle seed blew in the wind; the trees in the forest were a foot higher. She had a feeling that he would come back, and a gnawing fear that he might not.

"Oh, it ain't gonna rain no more, no more, it ain't gonna rain no more. How in the hell can the old folks say it ain't gonna rain no more?"

So sang Brogan, whose party it was, in the upstairs room of the Commercial Hotel. Unbuttoning his brown waistcoat, he sat back and said what a fine spread it was. They had carried the goose up on a platter and it lay in the center of the mahogany table, with potato stuffing spilling out of it. There were sausages also and polished glasses rim downward, and plates and forks for everyone.

"A fork supper" was how Mrs. Rodgers described it. She had read about it in the paper; it was all the rage now in posh houses in Dublin, this fork supper where you stood up for your food and ate with a fork only. Mary had brought knives in case anyone got into difficulties.

" 'Tis America at home," Hickey said, putting turf on the smoking fire.

The pub door was bolted downstairs, the shutters across, as the eight guests upstairs watched Mrs. Rodgers carve the goose and then tear the loose pieces away with her fingers. Every so often she wiped her fingers on a tea towel.

"Here you are, Mary, give this to Mr. Brogan, as he's the guest of honor." Mr. Brogan got a lot of breast and some crispy skin as well.

"Don't forget the sausages, Mary," Mrs. Rodgers said. Mary had to do everything: pass the food around, serve the stuffing, ask people whether they wanted paper plates or china ones. Mrs. Rodgers had bought paper plates, thinking they were sophisticated.

"I could eat a young child," Hickey said.

Mary was surprised that people in towns were so coarse and outspoken. When he squeezed her finger, she did not smile at all. She wished that she were at home—she knew what they were doing at home: the boys at their lessons; her mother baking a cake of whole meal bread, because there was never enough time during the day to bake; her father rolling cigarettes and talking to himself. John had taught him how to roll cigarettes, and every night since, he rolled four and smoked four. He was a good man, her father, but dour. In another hour they'd be saying the Rosary in her house and going to bed; the rhythm of their lives never changed, the fresh bread was always cool by morning.

"Ten o'clock," Doris said, listening to the chimes of the landing clock.

The party began late; the men were late getting back from the dogs in Limerick. They killed a pig on the way in their anxiety to get back quickly. The pig had been wandering in the road, and the car came around the corner; it got run over instantly.

"Never heard such a roarin' in all me born days," Hickey said, reaching for a wing of goose, the choicest bit.

"We should have brought it with us," O'Toole said. O'Toole worked in the slate quarry and knew nothing about pigs or farming; he was tall and thin and jagged. He had bright-green eyes and a face like a greyhound's; his hair was so gold that it looked dyed, but in fact it was bleached by the weather. No one had offered him any food.

"A nice way to treat a man," he said.

"God bless us, Mary, didn't you give Mr. O'Toole anything to eat yet?" Mrs. Rodgers said as she thumped Mary on the back to hurry her up. Mary brought him a large helping on a paper plate, and he thanked her and said that they would dance later. To him she looked far prettier than those good-for-nothing town girls—she was tall and thin like himself; she had long black hair that some people might think streelish, but not him; he liked long hair and simple-minded girls; maybe later on he'd get her to go into one of the other rooms where they could do it. She had funny eyes when you looked into them, brown and deep, like a bloody bog hole.

"Have a wish," he said to her as he held the wishbone up. She wished that she were going to America on an airplane, and on second thought she wished that she would win a lot of money and could buy her mother and father a house down near the main road.

"Is that your brother, the bishop?" Eithne Duggan, who knew well that it was, asked Mrs. Rodgers, concerning the flaccid-faced cleric over the fireplace. Unknown to herself, Mary had traced the letter J on the dust of the picture mirror earlier on, and now they all seemed to be looking at it, knowing how it came to be there.

"That's him, poor Charlie," Mrs. Rodgers said proudly, and was about to elaborate, but Brogan began to sing unexpectedly.

"Let the man sing, can't you," O'Toole said, hushing two of

the girls who were having a joke about the armchair they shared; the springs were hanging down underneath and the girls said that any minute the whole thing would collapse.

Mary shivered in her lace dress. The air was cold and damp, even though Hickey had got up a good fire. There hadn't been a fire in that room since the day De Valera signed the autograph book. Steam issued from everything.

O'Toole asked if any of the ladies would care to sing. There were five ladies in all—Mrs. Rodgers, Mary, Doris, Eithne, and Crystal, the local hairdresser, who had a new red rinse in her hair and who insisted that the food was a little heavy for her. The goose was greasy and undercooked, she did not like its raw, pink color. She liked dainty things, little bits of cold chicken breast with sweet pickles. Her real name was Carmel, but when she started up as a hairdresser, she changed it to Crystal and dyed her brown hair red.

"I bet you can sing," O'Toole said to Mary.

"Where she comes from, they can hardly talk," Doris said.

Mary felt the blood rushing to her sallow cheeks. She would not tell them, but her father's name had been in the paper once, because he had seen a pine marten in the forestry plantation; and they ate with a knife and fork at home and had oilcloth on the kitchen table, and kept a tin of coffee in case strangers called. She would not tell them anything. She just hung her head, making it clear that she was not about to sing.

In honor of the bishop, O'Toole put "Far Away in Australia" on the horn gramophone. Mrs. Rodgers had asked for it. The sound issued forth with rasps and scratchings, and Brogan said he could do better than that himself.

"Christ, lads, we forgot the soup!" Mrs. Rodgers said suddenly, as she threw down the fork and went toward the door. There had been soup scheduled to begin with.

"I'll help you," Doris O'Beirne said, stirring herself for the first time that night, and they both went down to get the pot of dark giblet soup which had been simmering all that day.

"Now we need two pounds from each of the gents," said O'Toole, taking the opportunity while Mrs. Rodgers was away to mention the delicate matter of money. The men had agreed to pay two pounds each, to cover the cost of the drink; the ladies did not have to pay anything, but were invited so as to lend a pleasant and decorative atmosphere to the party, and, of course, to help.

O'Toole went around with his cap held out, and Brogan said that as it was *his* party, he ought to give a fiver.

"I ought to give a fiver, but I suppose ye wouldn't hear of that," Brogan said, and handed up two pound notes. Hickey paid up, too, and O'Toole himself and Long John Salmon—who had been silent up to then. O'Toole gave it to Mrs. Rodgers when she returned and told her to clock it up against the damages.

"Sure that's too kind altogether," she said, as she put it behind the stuffed owl on the mantelpiece, under the bishop's watchful eye.

She served the soup in cups, and Mary was asked to pass the cups around. The grease floated like drops of molten gold on the surface of each cup.

"See you later, alligator," Hickey said, as she gave him his; then he asked her for a piece of bread, because he wasn't used to soup without bread.

"Tell us, Brogan," said Hickey to his rich friend, "what'll you do, now that you're a rich man?"

"Oh, go on, tell us," said Doris O'Beirne.

"Well," said Brogan, thinking for a minute, "we're going to make some changes at home." None of them had ever visited Brogan's home because it was situated in Adare, thirty miles away, at the far side of Limerick. None of them had ever seen his wife either, who, it seems, lived there and kept bees.

"What sort of changes?" someone said.

"We're going to do up the drawing room, and we're going to have flower beds," Brogan told them.

"And what else?" Crystal asked, thinking of all the lovely clothes she could buy with that money, clothes and jewelry.

"Well," said Brogan, thinking again, "we might even go to Lourdes. I'm not sure yet, it all depends."

"I'd give my two eyes to go to Lourdes," Mrs. Rodgers said.

"And you'd get 'em back when you arrived there," Hickey said, but no one paid any attention to him.

O'Toole poured out four half tumblers of whiskey and then stood back to examine the glasses to see that each one had the same amount. There was always great anxiety among the men about being fair with drink. Then O'Toole stood bottles of stout in little groups of six and told each man which group was his. The ladies had gin-and-orange.

"Orange for me," Mary said, but O'Toole told her not to be such a goody, and when her back was turned, he put gin in her orange.

They drank a toast to Brogan.

"To Lourdes," Mrs. Rodgers said.

"To Brogan," O'Toole said.

"To myself," Hickey said.

"Mud in your eye," said Doris O'Beirne, who was already unsteady from tippling cider.

"Well, we're not sure about Lourdes," Brogan said. "But we'll get the drawing room done up anyhow, and the flower beds put in."

"We've a drawing room here," Mrs. Rodgers said, "and no one ever sets foot in it."

"Come into the drawing room, Doris," said O'Toole to Mary, who was serving the jelly from the big enamel basin. They'd had no china bowl to put it in. It was red jelly with whipped egg white in it, but something had gone wrong, because it hadn't set properly. She served it in saucers, and thought to herself what a rough-and-ready party it was. There wasn't a proper cloth on the table either, just a plastic one, and no napkins, and that big basin with the jelly in it. Maybe people washed in that basin downstairs.

"Well, someone tell us a bloomin' joke," said Hickey, who was getting fed up with talk about drawing rooms and flower beds.

"I'll tell you a joke," said Long John Salmon, erupting out of his silence.

"Good," said Brogan, as he sipped from his whiskey glass and his stout glass alternately. It was the only way to drink enjoyably.

That was why, in pubs, he'd be much happier if he could buy his own drink and not rely on anyone else's meanness.

"Is it a funny joke?" Hickey asked of Long John Salmon.

"It's about my brother," said Long John Salmon, "my brother Patrick."

"Oh no, don't tell us that old rambling thing again," said Hickey and O'Toole together.

"Oh, let him tell it," said Mrs. Rodgers, who'd never heard the story anyhow.

Long John Salmon began, "I had this brother Patrick and he died; the heart wasn't too good."

"Holy Christ, not this again," said Brogan, recollecting which story it was.

But Long John Salmon went on, undeterred by the abuse from the three men.

"One day I was standing in the shed, about a month after he was buried, and I saw him coming out of the wall, walking across the yard."

"Oh, what would you do if you saw a thing like that?" Doris said to Eithne.

"Let him tell it," Mrs. Rodgers said. "Go on, Long John."

"Well, it was walking toward me, and I said to myself, 'What do I do now?'; 'twas raining heavy, so I said to my brother Patrick, 'Stand in out of the wet or you'll get drenched.' "

"And then?" said one of the girls anxiously.

"He vanished," said Long John Salmon.

"Ah, God, let us have a bit of music," said Hickey, who had heard that story nine or ten times. It had neither a beginning, a middle, nor an end. They put a record on, and O'Toole asked Mary to dance. He did a lot of fancy steps and capering; and now and then he let out a mad "Yippee." Brogan and Mrs. Rodgers were dancing, too, and Crystal said that she'd dance if anyone asked her.

"Come on, knees up, Mother Brown," O'Toole said to Mary, as he jumped around the room, kicking the legs of chairs as he moved. She felt funny: her head was swaying around and around, and in the pit of her stomach there was a nice ticklish feeling that made her want to lie back and stretch her legs. A new feeling that frightened her.

"Come into the drawing room, Doris," he said, dancing her right out of the room and into the cold passage, where he kissed her clumsily.

Inside, Crystal O'Meara had begun to cry. That was how drink affected her; either she cried or talked in a foreign accent and said, "Why am I talking in a foreign accent?"

This time she cried.

"Hickey, there is no joy in life," she said as she sat at the table with her head laid in her arms and her blouse slipping up out of her skirtband.

"What joy?" said Hickey, who had all the drink he needed, and a pound note which he slipped from behind the owl when no one was looking.

Doris and Eithne sat on either side of Long John Salmon, asking if they could go out next year when the sugar plums were ripe. Long John Salmon lived by himself, way up the country, and he had a big orchard. He was odd and silent in himself; he took a swim every day, winter and summer, in the river at the back of his house.

"Two old married people," Brogan said, as he put his arm around Mrs. Rodgers and urged her to sit down because he was out of breath from dancing. He said he'd go away with happy memories of them all, and sitting down, he drew her onto his lap. She was a heavy woman, with straggly brown hair that had once been a nut color.

"There is no joy in life," Crystal sobbed, as the gramophone made crackling noises and Mary ran in from the landing, away from O'Toole.

"I mean business," O'Toole said, and winked.

O'Toole was the first to get quarrelsome.

"Now, ladies, now, gentlemen, a little laughing sketch, are we ready?" he asked.

"Fire ahead," Hickey told him.

"Well, there was these three lads, Paddy th'Irishman, Paddy th'Englishman, and Paddy the Scotsman, and they were badly in need of a . . ."

"Now, no smut," Mrs. Rodgers snapped, before he had uttered a wrong word at all.

"What smut?" asked O'Toole, getting offended. "Smut!" And he asked her to explain an accusation like that.

"Think of the girls," Mrs. Rodgers said.

"Girls," O'Toole sneered, as he picked up the bottle of cream—which they'd forgotten to use with the jelly—and poured it into the carcass of the ravaged goose.

"Christ's sake, man," Hickey said, taking the bottle of cream out of O'Toole's hand.

Mrs. Rodgers said that it was high time everyone went to bed, as the party seemed to be over.

The guests would spend the night in the Commercial. It was too late for them to go home anyhow, and also, Mrs. Rodgers did not want them to be observed staggering out of the house at that hour. The police watched her like hawks, and she didn't want any trouble, until Christmas was over at least. The sleeping arrangements had been decided earlier on—there were three bedrooms vacant. One was Brogan's, the room he always slept in. The other three men were to pitch in together in the second big bedroom, and the girls were to share the back room with Mrs. Rodgers herself.

"Come on, everyone, blanket street," Mrs. Rodgers said, as she put a guard in front of the dying fire and took the money from behind the owl.

"Sugar you," O'Toole said, pouring stout now into the carcass of the goose, and Long John Salmon wished that he had never come. He thought of daylight and of his swim in the mountain river at the back of his gray, stone house.

"Ablution," he said aloud, taking pleasure in the word and in the thought of the cold water touching him. He could do without people, people were waste. He remembered catkins on a tree outside his window, catkins in February as white as snow; who needed people?

"Crystal, stir yourself," Hickey said, as he put on her shoes and patted the calves of her legs.

Brogan kissed the four girls and saw them across the landing to the bedroom. Mary was glad to escape without O'Toole noticing; he was very obstreperous and Hickey was trying to control him.

In the bedroom she sighed; she had forgotten all about the furniture being pitched in there. Wearily they began to unload the things. The room was so crammed that they could hardly move in it. Mary suddenly felt alert and frightened, because O'Toole could be heard yelling and singing out on the landing. There had been gin in her orangeade, she knew now, because she breathed closely onto the palm of her hand and smelled her own breath. She had broken her Confirmation pledge, broken her promise; it would bring her bad luck.

Mrs. Rodgers came in and said that five of them would be too crushed in the bed, so that she herself would sleep on the sofa for one night.

"Two of you at the top and two at the bottom," she said, as she warned them not to break any of the ornaments, and not to stay talking all night.

"Night and God bless," she said, as she shut the door behind her.

"Nice thing," said Doris O'Beirne, "bunging us all in here; I wonder where she's off to."

"Will you loan me curlers?" Crystal asked. To Crystal, hair was the most important thing on earth. She would never get married because you couldn't wear curlers in bed then. Eithne Duggan said she wouldn't put curlers in now if she got five million for doing it, she was that jaded. She threw herself down on the quilt and spread her arms out. She was a noisy, sweaty girl, but Mary liked her better than the other two.

"Ah, me old segotums," O'Toole said, pushing their door in. The girls exclaimed and asked him to go out at once, as they were preparing for bed.

"Come into the drawing room, Doris," he said to Mary, and curled his forefinger at her. He was drunk and couldn't focus on her properly, but he knew that she was standing there somewhere.

"Go to bed, you're drunk," Doris O'Beirne said, and he stood very upright for an instant and asked her to speak for herself.

"Go to bed, Michael, you're tired," Mary said to him. She tried to sound calm because he looked so wild.

"Come into the drawing room, I tell you," he said as he caught her wrist and dragged her toward the door. She let out a cry, and Eithne Duggan said she'd brain him if he didn't leave the girl alone.

"Give me that flowerpot, Doris," Eithne Duggan called, and then Mary began to cry in case there might be a scene. She hated scenes. Once, she heard her father and a neighbor having a row about boundary rights and she'd never forgotten it; they had both been a bit drunk, after a fair.

"Are you cracked or are you mad?" O'Toole said, when he perceived that she was crying.

"I'll give you two seconds," Eithne warned, as she held the flowerpot high, ready to throw it at O'Toole's stupefied face.

"You're a nice bunch of hard-faced aul crows, crows," he said. "Wouldn't give a man a squeeze," and he went out, cursing each one of them. They shut the door very quickly and dragged the sideboard in front of the door, so that he could not break in when they were asleep.

They got into bed in their underwear; Mary and Eithne at one end, with Crystal's feet between their faces.

"You have lovely hair," Eithne whispered to Mary. It was the nicest thing she could think of to say. They each said their prayers and shook hands under the covers and settled down to sleep.

"Hey," Doris O'Beirne said a few seconds later, "I never went to the lav."

"You can't go now," Eithne said, "the sideboard's in front of the door."

"I'll die if I don't go," Doris O'Beirne said.

"And me, too, after all that orange we drank," Crystal said. Mary was shocked that they could talk like that. At home you never spoke of such a thing, you just went out behind the hedge and that was that. Once a workman saw her squatting down, and from that day she never talked to him, or acknowledged that she knew him.

"Maybe we could use that old pot," Doris O'Beirne said, and

Eithne Duggan sat up and said that if anyone used a pot in that room she wasn't going to sleep there.

"We have to use something," Doris said. By now she had got up and had switched on the light. She held the pot up to the naked bulb and saw what looked to be a crack in it.

"Try it," Crystal said, giggling.

They heard feet on the landing, and then the sound of choking and coughing, and later O'Toole cursing and swearing and hitting the wall with his fist. Mary curled down under the bedclothes, thankful for the company of the girls. They stopped talking.

"I was at a party. Now I know what parties are like," Mary said to herself, as she tried to force herself asleep. She heard a sound as of water running, but it did not seem to be raining outside. Later she dozed, but at daybreak she heard the hall door bang and she sat up in bed abruptly. She had to be home early to milk, so she got up, took her shoes and her lace dress, let herself out by dragging the sideboard forward, and opening the door slightly.

There were newspapers spread on the landing floor and in the lavatory, and a heavy smell pervaded. Downstairs, porter had flowed out of the bar into the hall. It was probably O'Toole who had turned on the taps of the five porter barrels; the stone-floored bar and sunken passage outside were swimming with black porter. Mrs. Rodgers would kill somebody. Mary put on her high-heeled shoes and picked her steps carefully across the room to the door. She left without even making a cup of tea.

She wheeled her bicycle down the alley and into the street. The front tire was dead flat. She pumped for half an hour, but it remained flat.

The frost lay like a spell upon the street, upon the sleeping windows and the slate roofs of the narrow houses. It had magically made the dunged street white and clean. She did not feel tired but relieved to be out, and stunned by lack of sleep, she inhaled the beauty of the morning. She walked briskly, sometimes looking back to see the track which her bicycle and her feet made on the white road.

Mrs. Rodgers wakened at eight and stumbled out in her big

nightgown from Brogan's warm bed. She smelled disaster instantly and hurried downstairs to find the porter in the bar and the hall; then she ran to call the others.

"Porter all over the place; every drop of drink in the house is on the floor—Mary Mother of God, help me in my tribulation! Get up, get up." She rapped on their door and called the girls by name.

The girls rubbed their sleepy eyes, yawned, and sat up.

"She's gone," Eithne said, looking at the place on the pillow where Mary's head had been.

"Oh, a sneaky country one," Doris said, as she got into her taffeta dress and went down to see the flood. "If I have to clean that in my good clothes, I'll die," she said. But Mrs. Rodgers had already brought brushes and pails and got to work. They opened the bar door and began to bail the porter into the street. Dogs came to lap it up, and Hickey, who had by then come down, stood and said what a crying shame it was, to waste all that drink. Outside, it washed away an area of frost and revealed the dung of yesterday's fair day. O'Toole, the culprit, had fled since the night; Long John Salmon was gone for his swim, and upstairs in bed Brogan snuggled down for a last-minute warm and deliberated on the joys that he would miss when he left the Commercial for good.

"And where's my lady with the lace dress?" Hickey asked, recalling very little of Mary's face, but distinctly remembering the sleeves of her black dress, which dipped into the plates.

"Sneaked off, before we were up," Doris said. They all agreed that Mary was no bloody use and should never have been asked.

"And 'twas she set O'Toole mad, egging him on and then disappointing him," Doris said, and Mrs. Rodgers swore that O'Toole, or Mary's father, or someone, would pay dear for the wasted drink.

"I suppose she's home by now," Hickey said, as he rooted in his pocket for a butt. He had a new packet, but if he produced that, they'd all be puffing away at his expense.

Mary was half a mile from home, sitting on a bank.

If only I had a sweetheart, something to hold on to, she thought, as she cracked some ice with her high heel and watched the crazy splintered pattern it made. The poor birds could get no food, as the ground was frozen hard. Frost was everywhere; it coated the bare branches and made them like etchings, it starched the grass and blurred the shape of a plow that stood in a field, above all it gave the world an appearance of sanctity.

Walking again, she wondered if and what she would tell her mother and her brothers about it, and if all parties were as bad. She was at the top of the hill now, and could see her own house, like a little white box at the end of the world, waiting to receive her.

The Rug

I went down on my knees upon the brand-new linoleum and smelled the strange smell. It was rich and oily. It first entered and attached itself to something in my memory when I was nine years old. I've since learned that it is the smell of linseed oil, but coming on it unexpectedly can make me both a little disturbed and sad.

I grew up in the west of Ireland, in a gray cut-stone farmhouse which my father inherited from his father. My father came from lowland, better-off farming people, my mother from the windswept hungry hills above a great lake. As children, we played in a small forest of rhododendrons—thickened and tangled and broken under scratching cows—around the house and down the drive. The avenue up from the front gates had such great potholes that cars had to lurch off into the field and out again.

But though all outside was neglect, overgrown with ragwort and thistle, strangers were surprised when they entered the house; my father might fritter his life away watching the slates slip from the outhouse roof—but within, that same, square, lowland house of stone was my mother's pride and joy. It was always spotless. It was stuffed with things—furniture, china dogs, Toby mugs, tall jugs, trays, tapestries, and whatnots. Each of the four bedrooms had holy pictures on the walls and a gold mantelpiece surmounting each fireplace. In the fireplaces there were paper fans or lids of chocolate boxes. Mantelpieces carried their own close-packed array of wax flowers, holy statues, broken alarm clocks, shells, photographs, soft rounded cushions for sticking pins in.

My father was generous, foolish, and so idle that it could only have been some sort of illness. That year in which I was nine and first experienced the wonderful smell, he sold another of the meadows to pay off some debt, and for the first time in many years my mother got a lump of money.

She went out early one morning and caught the bus to the city, and through a summer morning and afternoon she trudged around looking at linoleum. When she came home in the evening, her feet hurting from high heels, she said she had bought some beautiful light-brown linoleum, with orange squares on it.

The day came when the four rolls were delivered to the front gates, and Hickey, our farm help, got the horse and cart ready to bring it up. We all went; we were that excited. The calves followed the cart, thinking that maybe they were to be fed down by the road-side. At times they galloped away but came back again, each calf nudging the other out of the way. It was a warm, still day, the sounds of cars and neighbors' dogs carried very distinctly; and the cow lats on the drive were brown and dry like flake tobacco.

My mother did most of the heaving and shoving to get the rolls onto the cart. She had early accepted that she had been born to do the work.

She may have bribed Hickey with the promise of hens to sell for himself, because that evening he stayed in to help with the floor—he usually went over to the village and drank a pint or two of stout. Mama, of course, always saved newspapers, and she said that the more we laid down under the lino the longer it would wear. On her hands and knees, she looked up once—flushed, delighted, tired—and said, "Mark my words, we'll see a carpet in here yet."

There was calculation and argument before cutting the difficult bits around the door frames, the bay window, and the fireplace. Hickey said that without him my mother would have botched the whole thing. In the quick flow of argument and talk, they did not notice that it was past my bedtime. My father sat outside in the kitchen by the stove all evening while we worked. Later, he came in and said what a grand job we were doing. A grand job, he said. He'd had a headache.

The next day must have been Saturday, for I sat in the sitting room all morning admiring the linoleum, smelling its smell, counting the orange squares. I was supposed to be dusting. Now and then I rearranged the blinds, as the sun moved. We had to keep the sun from fading the bright colors.

The dogs barked and the postman cycled up. I ran out and met him carrying a huge parcel. Mama was away up in the yard with the hens. When the postman had gone, I went up to tell her.

"A parcel?" she said. She was cleaning the hens' trough before putting their food in it. The hens were moiling around, falling in and out of the buckets, pecking at her hands. "It's just binding twine for the baling machine," she said. "Who'd be sending parcels?" She was never one to lose her head.

I said that the parcel had a Dublin postmark—the postman told me that—and that there was some black woolly thing in it. The paper was torn at the corner, and I'd pushed a finger in, fearfully.

Coming down to the house, she wiped her hands with a wad of long grass. "Perhaps somebody in America has remembered us at last." One of her few dreams was to be remembered by relatives who had gone to America. The farm buildings were some way from the house; we ran the last bit. But even in her excitement, her careful nature forced her to unknot every length of string from the parcel and roll it up, for future use. She was the world's most generous woman, but was thrifty about saving twine and paper, and candle stumps, and turkey wings, and empty pill boxes.

"My God," she said reverently, folding back the last piece of paper and revealing a black sheepskin hearthrug. We opened it out. It was a half-moon shape and covered the kitchen table. She could not speak. It was real sheepskin, thick and soft and luxurious. She examined the lining, studied the maker's label in the back, searched through the folds of brown paper for a possible letter, but there was nothing at all to indicate where it had come from.

"Get me my glasses," she said. We read the address again, and the postmark. The parcel had been sent from Dublin two days before. "Call your father," she said. He was in bed with rheumatic pains. Rug or no rug, he demanded a fourth cup of tea before he could get up.

We carried the big black rug into the sitting room and laid it down upon the new linoleum, before the fireplace.

"Isn't it perfect, a perfect color scheme?" she said. The room had suddenly become cozy. She stood back and looked at it with surprise, and a touch of suspicion. Though she was always hoping, she never really expected things to turn out well. At nine years old, I knew enough about my mother's life to say a prayer of thanks that at last she had got something she wanted, and without having to work for it. She had a round, sallow face and a peculiarly uncertain, timid smile. The suspicion soon left her, and the smile came out. That was one of her happiest days; I remember it as I remember her unhappiest day to my knowledge—the day the bailiff came, a year later. I hoped she would sit in the newly appointed room on Sundays for tea, without her apron, with her brown hair combed out, looking calm and beautiful. Outside, the rhododendrons, though wild and broken, would bloom red and purple, and inside, the new rug would lie upon the richly smelling linoleum. She hugged me suddenly, as if I were the one to thank for it all; the hen mash had dried on her hands and they had the mealy smell I knew so well.

For spells during the next few days, my mother racked her brain, and she racked our brains, for a clue. It had to be someone who knew something of her needs and wants—how else could he have decided upon just the thing she needed? She wrote letters here and there, to distant relations, to friends, to people she had not seen for years.

"Must be one of *your* friends," she would say to my father.

"Oh, probably, probably. I've known a lot of decent people in my time."

She was referring—ironically, of course—to the many strangers to whom he had offered tea. He liked nothing better than to stand down at the gates on a fair day or a race day, engaging passersby in conversation and finally bringing someone up to the house for tea and boiled eggs. He had a genius for making friends.

"I'd say that's it," my father said, delighted to take credit for the rug.

In the warm evenings we sat around the fireplace—we'd never

had a fire in that room throughout the whole of my childhood—and around the rug, listening to the radio. And now and then, Mama or Dada would remember someone else from whom the rug might have come. Before a week had passed, she had written to a dozen people—an acquaintance who had moved up to Dublin with a greyhound pup Dada had given him, which greyhound had turned out a winner; an unfrocked priest who had stayed in our house for a week, gathering strength from Mama to travel on home and meet his family; a magician who had stolen Dada's gold watch and never been seen since; a farmer who once sold us a tubercular cow and would not take it back.

Weeks passed. The rug was taken out on Saturdays and shaken well, the new lino polished. Once, coming home early from school, I looked in the window and saw Mama kneeling on the rug saying a prayer. I'd never seen her pray like that, in the middle of the day, before. My father was going into the next county the following day to look at a horse he thought he might get cheap; she was, of course, praying that he would keep his promise and not touch a drink. If he did, he might be off on a wild progress and would not be seen for a week.

He went the next day; he was to stay overnight with relations. While he was away, I slept with Mama, for company, in the big brass bed. I wakened to see a candle flame and Mama hurriedly putting on her cardigan. Dada had come home? No, she said, but she had been lying awake thinking, and there was something she had to tell Hickey or she would not get a wink of sleep. It was not yet twelve; he might be awake. I didn't want to be left in the dark, I said, but she was already hurrying along the landing. I nipped out of bed and followed. The luminous clock said a quarter to twelve. From the first landing, I looked over and saw her turning the knob of Hickey's door.

Why should he open his door to her then, I thought; he never let anyone in at any time, keeping the door locked when he was out on the farm. Once, we climbed in through the window and found things in such a muddle—his good suit laid out flat on the floor, a shirt soaking in a bucket of dirty green water, a milk can in which there was curdled buttermilk, a bicycle chain, a broken Sacred Heart, and several pairs of worn, distorted, cast-off boots—that she resolved never to set foot in it again.

"What the hell is it?" Hickey said. Then there was a thud. He must have knocked something over while he searched for his flashlamp.

"If it's fine tomorrow, we'll cut the turf," Mama said.

Hickey asked if she'd wakened him at that hour to tell him something he already knew—they discussed it at teatime.

"Open the door," she said. "I have a bit of news for you, about the rug."

He opened the door just a fraction. "Who sent it?" he asked.

"That party from Ballinsloe," she said.

"That party" was her phrase for her two visitors who had come to our house years before—a young girl and an older man who wore brown gauntlet gloves. Almost as soon as they'd arrived, my father went out with them in their motorcar. When they returned to our house an hour later, I gathered from the conversation that they had been to see our local doctor, a friend of Dada's. The girl was the sister of a nun who was headmistress at the convent where my sisters were. She had been crying. I guessed then, or maybe later, that her tears had to do with her having a baby and that Dada had taken her to the doctor so that she could find out for certain if she was pregnant and make preparations to get married. It would have been impossible for her to go to a doctor in her own neighborhood, and I had no doubt but that Dada was glad to do a favor for the nun, as he could not always pay the fees for my sisters' education. Mama gave them tea on a tray—not a spread with hand-embroidered cloth and bone-china cups —and shook hands with them coolly when they were leaving. She could not abide sinful people.

"Nice of them to remember," Hickey said, sucking air between his teeth and making bird noises. "How did you find out?"

"I just guessed," Mama told him.

"Oh, Christ!" Hickey said, closing his door with a fearful bang and getting back into bed with such vehemence that I could hear the springs revolt.

Mama carried me up the stairs, because my feet were cold, and said that Hickey had not one ounce of manners.

Next day, when Dada came home sober, she told him the story, and that night she wrote to the nun. In due course, a letter came to us —with holy medals and scapulars enclosed for me—saying that neither the nun nor her married sister had sent a gift. I expect the girl had married the man with the gauntlet gloves.

" 'Twill be one of life's mysteries," Mama said, as she beat the rug against the pier, closed her eyes to escape the dust, and reconciled herself to never knowing.

But a knock came on our back door four weeks later, when we were upstairs changing the sheets on the beds. "Run down and see who it is," she said.

It was a namesake of Dada's from the village, a man who always came to borrow something—a donkey, or a mowing machine, or even a spade.

"Is your mother in?" he asked, and I went halfway up the stairs and called her down.

"I've come for the rug," he said.

"What rug?" Mama said. It was the nearest she ever got to lying. Her breath caught short and she blushed a little.

"I hear you have a new rug here. Well, 'tis our rug, because my wife's sister sent it to us months ago and we never got it."

"What are you talking about?" she said in a very sarcastic voice. He was a cowardly man, and it was said that he was so ineffectual he would call his wife in from the garden to pour him a cup of tea. I suppose my mother hoped that she would frighten him off.

"The rug the postman brought here one morning and handed it to your youngster there." He nodded at me.

"Oh, that," Mama said, a little stunned by the news that the postman had given information about it. Then a ray of hope, or a ray of lunacy, must have struck her, because she asked what color rug he was inquiring about.

"A black sheepskin," he said.

There could be no more doubt about it. Her whole being drooped—shoulders, stomach, voice, everything.

"It's here," she said absently, and she went through the hall into the sitting room.

"Being namesakes and that, the postman got us mixed up," he said stupidly to me.

She had winked at me to stay there and see he did not follow her, because she did not want him to know that we had been using it.

It was rolled and had a piece of cord around the middle when she handed it to him. As she watched him go down the avenue she wept, not so much for the loss—though the loss was enormous—as for her own foolishness in thinking that someone had wanted to do her a kindness at last.

"We live and learn," she said, as she undid her apron strings, out of habit, and then retied them slowly and methodically, making a tighter knot.

Paradise

In the harbor were the four boats. Boats named after a country, a railroad, an emotion, and a girl. She first saw them at sundown. Very beautiful they were, and tranquil, white boats at a distance from each other, cosseting the harbor. On the far side a mountain. Lilac at that moment. It seemed to be made of collapsible substance so insubstantial was it. Between the boats and the mountain a lighthouse, on an island.

Somebody said the light was not nearly so pretty as in the old days when the coast guard lived there and worked it by gas. It was automatic now and much brighter. Between them and the sea were four fields cultivated with fig trees. Dry yellow fields that seemed to be exhaling dust. No grass. She looked again at the four boats, the fields, the fig trees, the suave ocean; she looked at the house behind her and she thought, It can be mine, mine, and her heart gave a little somersault. He recognized her agitation and smiled. The house acted like a spell on all who came. He took her by the hand and led her up the main stairs. Stone stairs with a wobbly banister. The undersides of each step bright blue. "Stop," he said, where it got dark near the top, and before he switched on the light.

A servant had unpacked for her. There were flowers in the room. They smelled of confectionery. In the bathroom a great glass urn filled with talcum powder. She leaned over the rim and inhaled. It caused her to sneeze three times. Ovaries of dark-purple soap had been taken out of their wrapping paper, and for several minutes she held one in either hand. Yes. She had done the right thing in coming. She need not have feared; he needed her, his expression and their clasped hands already confirmed that.

They sat on the terrace drinking a cocktail he had made. It was of rum and lemon and proved to be extremely potent. One of the guests said the angle of light on the mountain was at its most magnificent. He put his fingers to his lips and blew a kiss to the mountain. She counted the peaks, thirteen in all, with a plateau between the first four and the last nine.

The peaks were close to the sky. Farther down on the face of the mountain various juts stuck out, and these made shadows on their neighboring juts. She was told its name. At the same moment she overheard a question being put to a young woman, "Are you interested in Mary Queen of Scots?" The woman, whose skin had a beguiling radiance, answered yes overreadily. It was possible that such radiance was the result of constant supplies of male sperm. The man had a high pale forehead and a look of death.

They drank. They smoked. All twelve smokers tossing the butts onto the tiled roof that sloped toward the farm buildings. Summer lightning started up. It was random and quiet and faintly theatrical. It seemed to be something devised for their amusement. It lit one part of the sky, then another. There were bats flying about also, and their dark shapes and the random fugitive shots of summer lightning were a distraction and gave them something to point to. "If I had a horse I'd call it Summer Lightning," one of the women said, and the man next to her said, How charming. She knew she ought to speak. She wanted to. Both for his sake and for her own. Her mind would give a little leap and be still and would leap again; words were struggling to be set free, to say something, a little amusing something to establish her among them. But her tongue was tied. They would know her predecessors. They would compare her minutely, her appearance, her accent, the way he behaved with her. They would know better than she how important she was to him, if it were serious or just a passing notion. They had all read in the gossip columns how she came to meet him; how he had gone to have an X-ray and met her there, the radiographer in white, committed to a dark room and films showing lungs and pulmonary tracts.

"Am I right in thinking you are to take swimming lessons?" a man asked, choosing the moment when she had leaned back and was staring up at a big pine tree.

"Yes," she said, wishing that he had not been told.

"There's nothing to it, you just get in and swim," he said.

How surprised they all were, surprised and amused. Asked where she had lived and if it was really true.

"Can't imagine anyone not swimming as a child."

"Can't imagine anyone not swimming, period."

"Nothing to it, you just fight, fight."

The sun filtered by the green needles fell and made play on the dense clusters of brown nuts. They never ridicule nature, she thought, they never dare. He came and stood behind her, his hand patting her bare pale shoulder. A man who was not holding a camera pretended to take a photograph of them. How long would she last? It would be uppermost in all their minds.

"We'll take you on the boat tomorrow," he said. They cooed. They all went to such pains, such excesses, to describe the cruiser. They competed with each other to tell her. They were really telling him. She thought, I should be honest, say I do not like the sea, say I am an inland person, that I like rain and roses in a field, thin rain, and through it the roses and the vegetation, and that for me the sea is dark as the shells of mussels, and signifies catastrophe. But she couldn't.

"It must be wonderful" was what she said.

"It's quite, quite something," he said shyly.

At dinner she sat at one end of the egg-shaped table and he at the other. Six white candles in glass sconces separated them. The secretary had arranged the places. A fat woman on his right wore a lot of silver bracelets and was veiled in crepe. They had cold soup to start with. The garnishings were so finely chopped that it was impossible to identify each one except by its flavor. She slipped out of her shoes. A man describing his trip to India dwelt for an unnaturally long time on the disgustingness of the food. He had gone to see the temples.

Another man, who was repeatedly trying to buoy them up, threw the question to the table at large: "Which of the Mediterranean ports is best to dock at?" Everyone had a favorite. Some picked ports where exciting things had happened, some chose ports where the approach was most beguiling, harbor fees were compared as a matter of interest; the man who had asked the question amused them all with an account of a cruise he had made once with his young daughter and of how he was unable to land when they got to Venice because of inebriation. She had to admit that she did not know any ports. They were touched by that confession.

"We're going to try them all," he said from the opposite end of the table, "and keep a logbook." People looked from him to her and smiled knowingly.

That night behind closed shutters they enacted their rite. They were both impatient to get there. Long before the coffee had been brought they had moved away from the table and contrived to be alone, choosing the stone seat that girdled the big pine tree. The seat was smeared all over with the tree's transparent gum. The nuts bobbing together made a dull clatter like castanets. They sat for as long as courtesy required, then they retired. In bed she felt safe again, united to him not only by passion and by pleasure but by some more radical entanglement. She had no name for it, that puzzling emotion that was more than love, or perhaps less, that was not simply sexual, although sex was vital to it and held it together like wires supporting a broken bowl. They both had had many breakages and therefore loved with a wary superstition.

"What you do to me," he said. "How you know me, all my vibrations."

"I think we are connected underneath," she said quietly. She often thought he hated her for implicating him in something too tender. But he was not hating her then.

At length it was necessary to go back to her bedroom, because he had promised to get up early to go spearfishing with the men.

As she kissed him goodbye she caught sight of herself in the chrome surface of the coffee flask which was on his bedside table—eyes emitting satisfaction and chagrin and panic were what stared back at her. Each time as she left him she expected not to see him again; each parting promised to be final.

The men left soon after six; she heard car doors because she had been unable to sleep.

In the morning she had her first swimming lesson. It was arranged that she would take it when the others sat down to breakfast. Her instructor had been brought from England. She asked if he'd slept well. She did not ask where. The servants disappeared from the house late at night and departed toward the settlement of low-roofed buildings. The dog went with them. The instructor told her to go backward down the metal stepladder. There were wasps hovering about and she thought that if she were to get stung she could bypass the lesson. No wasp obliged.

Some children, who had been swimming earlier, had left their plastic toys—a yellow ring that craned into the neck and head of a duck. It was a duck with a thoroughly disgusted expression. There was as well a blue dolphin with a name painted on it, and all kinds of battleships. They were the children of guests. The older ones, who were boys, took no notice of any of the adults and moved about, raucous and meddlesome, taking full advantage of every aspect of the place—at night they watched the lizards patiently and for hours, in the heat of the day they remained in the water, in the early morning they gathered almonds, for which they received from him a harvesting fee. One black flipper lurked on the bottom of the pool. She looked down at it and touched it with her toe. Those were her last unclaimed moments, those moments before the lesson began.

The instructor told her to sit, to sit in it, as if it were a bath. He crouched and slowly she crouched, too. "Now hold your nose and put your head under water," he said. She pulled the bathing cap well over her ears and forehead to protect her hairstyle, and with her nose gripped too tightly she went underneath. "Feel it?" he said excitedly. "Feel the water holding you up?" She felt no such thing. She felt the water engulfing her. He told her to press the water from her eyes. He was gentleness itself. Then he dived in, swam a few strokes, and stood up, shaking the water from his gray hair. He took her hands and walked backward until they were at arm's length. He asked her to lie on her stomach and give herself to it. He promised not to let go of her hands. Each time, on the verge of doing so, she stopped: first her body, then her mind refused. She felt that if she was to take her feet off the ground the unmentionable would happen. "What do I fear?" she asked herself. "Death," she said, and yet, it was not that. It was as if some horrible experience would happen before her actual death. She thought perhaps it might be the fight she would put up.

When she succeeded in stretching out for one desperate minute, he proclaimed with joy. But that first lesson was a failure as far as she was concerned. Walking back to the house, she realized it was a mistake to have allowed an instructor to be brought. It put too much emphasis on it. It would be incumbent upon her to conquer it. They would concern themselves with her progress, not because they cared, but like the summer lightning or the yachts going by, it would be something to talk about. But she could not send the instructor home. He was an old man and he had never been abroad before. Already he was marveling at the scenery. She had to go on with it. Going back to the terrace, she was not sure of her feet on land, she was not sure of land itself; it seemed to sway, and her knees shook uncontrollably.

When she sat down to breakfast she found that a saucer of almonds had been peeled for her. They were sweet and fresh, reinvoking the sweetness and freshness of a country morning. They tasted like hazelnuts. She said so. Nobody agreed. Nobody disagreed. Some were reading papers. Now and then someone read a piece aloud, some amusing piece about some acquaintance of theirs who had done a dizzy, newsworthy thing. The children read the thermometer and argued about the penciled shadow on the sundial. The temperature was already in the eighties. The women were forming a plan to go on the speedboat to get their midriffs brown. She declined. He called her into the conservatory and said she might give some time to supervising the meals because the secretary had rather a lot to do.

Passion-flower leaves were stretched along the roof on lifelines of green cord. Each leaf like the five fingers of a hand. Green and yellow leaves on the same hand. No flowers. Flowers later. Flowers that would live a day. Or so the gardener had said. She said, "I hope we will be here to see one." "If you want, we will," he said, but of course he might take a notion and go. He never knew what he might do; no one knew.

When she entered the vast kitchen, the first thing the servants did was to smile. Women in black, with soft-soled shoes, all smiling, no complicity in any of those smiles. She had brought with her a phrase book, a notebook, and an English cookery book. The kitchen was like a laboratory—various white machines stationed against the walls, refrigerators churtling at different speeds, a fan over each of the electric cookers, the red and green lights on the dials faintly menacing, as if they were about to issue an alarm. There was a huge fish on the table. It had been speared that morning by the men. Its mouth was open; its eyes so close together that they barely missed being one eye; its lower lip gaping pathetically. The fins were black and matted with oil. They all stood and looked at it, she and the seven or eight willing women to whom she must make herself understood. When she sat to copy the recipe from the English book and translate it into their language, they turned on another fan. Already they were chopping for the evening meal. Three young girls chopped onions, tomatoes, and peppers. They seemed to take pleasure in their tasks; they seemed to smile into the mounds of vegetable that they so diligently chopped.

There were eight picnic baskets to be taken on the boat. And armfuls of towels. The children begged to be allowed to carry the towels. He had the zip bag with the wine bottles. He shook the bag so that the bottles rattled in their surrounds of ice. The guests smiled. He had a way of drawing people into his mood without having to say or do much. Conversely he had a way of locking people out. Both things were mesmerizing. They crossed the four fields that led to the sea. The figs were hard and green. The sun played like a blow lamp upon her back and neck. He said that she would have to lather herself in suntan oil. It seemed oddly hostile, his saying it out loud like that, in front of the others. As they got nearer the water she felt her heart race. The water was all shimmer. Some swam out, some got in the rowboat. Trailing her hand in the crinkled surface of the water she thought, It is not cramp, jellyfish, or broken glass that I fear, it is something else. A ladder was dropped down at the side of the boat for the swimmers to climb in from the sea. Sandals had to be kicked off as they stepped inside. The floor was of blond wood and burning hot. Swimmers had to have their feet inspected for tar marks. The boatman stood with a pad of cotton soaked in turpentine ready to rub the marks. The men busied themselves—one helped to get the engine going, a couple put awnings up, others carried out large striped cushions and scattered them under the awnings. Two boys refused to come on board.

"It is pleasant to bash my little brother up under water," a young boy said, his voice at once menacing and melodious.

She smiled and went down steps to where there was a kitchen and sleeping quarters with beds for four. He followed her. He looked, inhaled deeply, and murmured.

"Take it out," she said, "I want it now, now." Timorous and whim mad. How he loved it. How he loved that imperative. He pushed the door and she watched as he struggled to take down his shorts but could not get the cord undone. He was the awkward one now. How he stumbled. She waited for one excruciating moment and made him wait. Then she knelt, and as she began he muttered between clenched teeth. He who could tame animals was defenseless in this. She applied herself to it, sucking, sucking, sucking, with all the hunger that she felt and all the simulated hunger that she liked him to think she felt. Threatening to maim him, she always just grazed with the edges of her fine square teeth. Nobody intruded. It took no more than minutes. She stayed behind for a decent interval. She felt thirsty. On the window ledge there were paperback books and bottles of sun oil. Also a spare pair of shorts that had names of all the likely things in the world printed on them—names of drinks and capital cities and the flags of each nation. The sea through the porthole was a small, harmless globule of blue.

They passed out of the harbor, away from the three other boats and the settlement of pines. Soon there was only sea and rock, no reedy inlets, no towns. Mile after mile of hallucinating sea. The madness of mariners conveyed itself to her, the illusion that it was land and that she could traverse it. A land that led to nowhere. The rocks had been reduced to every shape the eye and the mind could comprehend. Near the water there were openings that had been forced through by the sea—some rapacious, some large enough for a small boat to slink in under, some as small and unsettling as the sockets of eyes. The trees on the sheer faces of these rocks were no more than the struggle to be trees. Birds could not perch there, let alone nest. She tried not to remember the swimming lesson, to postpone remembering until the afternoon, until the next lesson.

She came out and joined them. A young girl sat at the stern, among the cushions, playing a guitar. She wore long silver spatula-shaped earrings. A self-appointed gypsy. The children were playing I Spy but finding it hard to locate new objects. They were confined to the things they could see around them. By standing she found that the wind and the spray from the water kept her cool. The mountains that were far away appeared insubstantial, but those that were near glinted when the sharp stones were pierced by the sun.

"I find it a little unreal," she said to one of the men. "Beautiful but unreal." She had to shout because of the noise of the engine.

"I don't know what you mean by unreal," he said.

Their repertoire was small but effective. In the intonation the sting lay. Dreadfully subtle. Impossible to bridle over. In fact, the unnerving thing about it was the terrible bewilderment it induced. Was it intended or not? She distinctly remembered a sensation of once thinking that her face was laced by a cobweb, but being unable to feel it with the hand and being unable to put a finger on their purulence felt exactly the same. To each other, too, they transmitted small malices and then moved on to the next topic. They mostly talked of places they had been to and the people who were there, and though they talked endlessly, they told nothing about themselves.

They picnicked on a small pink strand. He ate very little, and afterward he walked off. She thought to follow him, then didn't. The children waded out to sea on a long whitened log, and one of the women read everybody's hand. She was promised an illness. When he returned he gave his large yellowish hand reluctantly. He was promised a son. She looked at him for a gratifying sign but got none. At that moment he was telling one of the men about a black sloop that he had loved as a child. She thought, What is it that he sees in me, he who loves sea, sloops, jokes, masquerades, and deferment? What is it that he sees in me who loves none of those things?

Her instructor brought flat white boards. He held one end, she the other. She watched his hands carefully. They were very white from being in water. She lay on her stomach and held the boards and watched his hands in case they should let go of the board. The boards kept bobbing about and adding to her uncertainty. He said a rope would be better.

The big fish had had its bones removed and was then pieced together. A perfect decoy. Its head and its too near eyes were gone. On her advice the housekeeper had taken the lemons out of the refrigerator, so that they were like lemons now rather than bits of frozen sponge. Someone remarked on this and she felt childishly pleased. Because of a south wind a strange night exhilaration arose. They drank a lot. They discussed beautiful evenings. Evenings resurrected in them by the wine and the wind and a transient goodwill. One talked of watching golden cock pheasants strutting in a back yard; one talked of bantams perched on a gate at dusk, their forms like notes of music on a blank bar; no one mentioned love or family, it was scenery or nature or a whippet that left them with the best and most serene memories. She relived a stormy night with an ass braying in a field and a blown bough fallen across a road. After dinner various couples went for walks, or swims, or to listen for children. The three men who were single went to the village to reconnoiter. Women confided the diets they were on, or the face creams that they found most beneficial. A divorcée said to her host, "You've *got* to come to bed with me, you've simply *got* to," and he smiled. It was no more than a pleasantry, another remark in a strange night's proceedings where there were also crickets, tree frogs, and the sounds of clandestine kissing. The single men came back presently and reported that the only bar was full of Germans and that the whiskey was inferior. The one who had been most scornful about her swimming sat at her feet and said how awfully pretty she was. Asked her details about her life, her work, her schooling. Yet this friendliness only reinforced her view of her own solitude, her apartness. She answered each question carefully and seriously. By answering she was subscribing to her longing to fit in. He seemed a little jealous, so she got up and went to him. He was not really one of them, either. He simply stage-managed them for his own amusement. Away from them she almost reached him. It was as if he were bound by a knot that maybe, maybe, she could unravel, for a long stretch, living their own life, cultivating a true emotion, independent of other people. But would they ever be away? She dared not ask. For that kind of discussion she had to substitute with a silence.

She stole into their rooms to find clues to their private selves—to see if they had brought sticking plaster, indigestion pills, face flannels, the ordinary necessities. On a dressing table there was a wig block with blond hair very artfully curled. On the face of the block colored sequins were arranged to represent the features of an ancient Egyptian queen. The divorcée had a baby's pillow in a yellow muslin case. Some had carried up bottles of wine and these though not drunk were not removed. The servants only touched what was thrown on the floor or put in the wastepaper baskets. Clothes for washing were thrown on the floor. It was one of the house rules, like having cocktails on the terrace at evening time. Some had written cards which she read eagerly. These cards told nothing except that it was all super.

His secretary, who was mousy, avoided her. Perhaps she knew too much. Plans he had made for the future.

She wrote to her doctor:

> *I am taking the tranquillizers but I don't feel any more relaxed. Could you send me some others?*

She tore it up.

*

Her hair got tangled by the salt in the sea air. She bought some curling tongs.

One woman, who was pregnant, kept sprinkling baby powder and smoothing it over her stomach throughout the day. They always took tea together. They were friends. She thought, If this woman were not pregnant would she be so amiable? Their kind of thinking was beginning to take root in her.

The instructor put a rope over her head. She brought it down around her middle. They heard a quack-quack. She was certain that the plastic duck had intoned. She laughed as she adjusted the noose. The instructor laughed, too. He held a firm grip of the rope. She threshed through the water and tried not to think of where she was. Sometimes she did it well; sometimes she had to be brought in like an old piece of lumber. She could never tell the outcome of each plunge; she never knew how it was going to be or what thoughts would suddenly obstruct her. But each time he said, "Lovely, lovely," and in his exuberance she found consolation.

A woman called Iris swam out to their yacht. She dangled in the water and with one hand gripped the sides of the boat. Her nail varnish was exquisitely applied and the nails had the glow of a rich imbued pearl. By contrast with the pearl coating, the half-moons were chastely white. Her personality was like that, too—full of glow. For each separate face she had a smile, and a word or two for those she already knew. One of the men asked if she was in love. Love! she riled him. She said her good spirits were due to her breathing. She said life was a question of correct breathing. She had come to invite them for drinks but he declined because they were due back at the house. His lawyer had been invited to lunch. She chided him for being so busy, then swam off toward the shore, where her poodle was yapping and waiting for her. At lunch they all talked of her. There was mention of her past escapades, the rows with her husband, his death, which was thought to be a suicide, and the unpleasant business of his burial, which proved impossible on religious grounds. Finally, his body had to be laid in a small paddock adjoining the public cemetery. Altogether an unsavory story, yet preenng in the water had been this radiant woman with no traces of past harm.

"Yes, Iris has incredible willpower, incredible," he said.

"For what?" she asked, from the opposite end of the table.

"For living," he said tartly.

It was not lost on the others. Her jaw muscle twitched.

Again she spoke to herself, remonstrated with her hurt: "I try, I try, I want to fit, I want to join, be the someone who slips into a crowd of marchers when the march has already begun, but there is something in me that I call sense and it balks at your ways. It would seem as if I am here simply to smart under your strictures." Retreating into dreams and monologue.

She posed for a picture. She posed beside the sculptured lady. She repeated the pose of the lady. Hands placed over each other and laid on the left shoulder, head inclining toward those hands. He took it. Click, click. The marble lady had been the sculptor's wife and had died tragically. The hands with their unnaturally long nails were the best feature of it. Click, click. When she was not looking he took another.

She found the account books in a desk drawer and was surprised at the entries. Things like milk and matches had to be accounted for. She thought, Is he generous at the roots? The housekeeper had left some needlework in the book. She had old-fashioned habits and resisted much of the modern kitchen equipment. She kept the milk in little pots, with muslin spread over the top. She skimmed the cream with her fat fingers, tipped the cream into small jugs for their morning coffee. What would they say to that! In the evenings, when every task was done, the housekeeper sat in the back veranda with her husband, doing the mending. They had laid pine branches on the roof, and these had withered and were tough as wire. Her husband made shapes from soft pieces of new white wood, and then in the dark put his penknife aside and tickled his wife. She heard them when she stole in to get some figs from the refrigerator. It was both poignant and untoward.

The instructor let go of the rope. She panicked and stopped using her arms and legs. The water was rising up over her. The water was in complete control of her. She knew that she was screaming convulsively. He had to jump in, clothes and all. Afterward they sat in the linen room with a blanket each and drank brandy. They vouched to tell no one. The brandy went straight to his head. He said in England it would be raining and people would be queueing for buses, and his eyes twinkled because of his own good fate.

More than one guest was called Teddy. One of the Teddys told her that in the mornings before his wife wakened he read Proust in the dressing room. It enabled him to masturbate. It was no more than if he had told her he missed bacon for breakfast. For breakfast there was fruit and scrambled egg. Bacon was a rarity on the island. She said to the older children that the plastic duck was psychic and had squeaked. They laughed. Their laughing was real, but they kept it up long after the joke had expired. A girl said, "Shall I tell you a rude story?" The boys appeared to want to restrain her. The girl said, "Once upon a time there was a lady, and a blind man came to her door every evening for sixpence, and one day she was in the bath and the doorbell rang and she put on a gown and came down and it was the milkman, and she got back in the bath and the doorbell rang and it was the bread man, and at six o'clock the doorbell rang and she thought, I don't have to put on my gown it is the blind man, and when she opened the door the blind man said, 'Madam, I've come to tell you I got my sight back.'" And the laughter that had never really died down started up again, and the whole mountain was boisterous with it. No insect, no singing bird was heard on that walk. She had to watch the time. The children's evening meal was earlier. They ate on the back veranda and she often went there and stole an anchovy or a piece of bread so as to avoid getting too drunk before dinner. There was no telling how late dinner would be. It depended on him, on whether he was bored or not. Extra guests from neighboring houses came each evening for drinks. They added variety. The talk was about sailing and speeding, or about gardens, or about pools. They all seemed to be intrigued by these topics, even the women. One man who followed the snow knew where the best snow surfaces were for every week of every year. That subject did not bore her as much. At least the snow was nice to think about, crisp and blue like he said, and rasping under the skis. The children could often be heard shrieking, but after cocktail hour they never appeared. She believed that it would be better once they were married and had children. She would be accepted by courtesy of them. It was a swindle really, the fact that small creatures, ridiculously easy to beget, should solidify a relationship, but they would. Everyone hinted how he wanted a son. He was nearing sixty. She had stopped using contraceptives and he had stopped asking. Perhaps that was his way of deciding, of finally accepting her.

Gulls' eggs, already shelled, were brought to table. The yolks a very delicate yellow. "Where are the shells?" the fat lady, veiled in crepe, asked. The shells had to be brought. They were crumbled almost to a powder but were brought anyhow. "Where are the nests?" she asked. It missed. It was something they might have laughed at, had they heard, but a wind had risen and they were all getting up and carrying things indoors. The wind was working up to something. It whipped the geranium flowers from their leaves and crazed the candle flames so that they blew this way and that and cracked the glass sconces. That night their lovemaking had all the sweetness and all the release that earth must feel with the long-awaited rain. He was another man now, with another voice—loving and private and incantatory. His coldness, his dismissal of her hard to believe in. Perhaps if they quarreled, their quarrels, like their lovemaking, would bring them closer. But they never did. He said he'd never had a quarrel with any of his women. She gathered that he left his wives once it got to that point. He did not say so, but she felt that must have been so, because he had once said that all his marriages were happy. He said there had been fights with men but that these were decent. He had more rapport with men; with women he was charming but it was a charm devised to keep them at bay. He had no brothers, and no son. He had had a father who bullied him and held his inheritance back for longer than he should. This she got from one of the men who had known him for forty years. His father had caused him to suffer, badly. She did not know in what way and she was unable to ask him, because it was information she should never have been given a hint of.

After their trip to the Roman caves the children came home ravenous. One child objected because the meal was cold. The servant, sensing a certain levity, told her master, and the story sent shrieks of laughter around the lunch table. It was repeated many times. He called to ask if she had heard. He sometimes singled her out in that way. It was one of the few times the guests could glimpse the bond between them. Yes, she had heard. "Sweet, sweet," she said. The word occurred in her repertoire all the time now. She was learning their language. And fawning. Far from home, from where the cattle grazed. The cattle had fields to roam, and a water tank near the house. The earth around the water tank always churned up, always mucky from their trampling there. They were farming people, had their main meal in the middle of the day, had rows. Her father vanished one night after supper, said he was going to count the cattle, brought a flashlamp, never came back. Others sympathized, but she and her mother were secretly relieved. Maybe he drowned himself in one of the many bog lakes, or changed his name and went to a city. At any rate, he did not hang himself from a tree or do anything ridiculous like that.

She lay on her back as the instructor brought her across the pool, his hand under her spine. The sky above an innocent blightless blue, with streamers where the jets had passed over. She let her head go right back. She thought, If I were to give myself to it totally, it would be a pleasure and an achievement, but she couldn't.

Argoroba hung from the trees like blackened banana skins. The men picked them in the early morning and packed them in sacks for winter fodder. In the barn where these sacks were stored there was a smell of decay. And an old olive press. In the linen room next door a pleasant smell of linen. The servants used too much bleach. Clothes lost their sharpness of color after one wash. She used to sit in one or another of these rooms and read. She went to the library for a book. He was in one of the Regency chairs that was covered with ticking. As on a throne. One chair was real and one a copy, but she could never tell them apart. "I saw you yesterday, and you nearly went under," he said. "I still have several lessons to go," she said, and went as she intended, but without the book that she had come to fetch.

His daughter by his third marriage had an eighteen-inch waist. On her first evening she wore a white trouser suit. She held the legs out, and the small pleats when opened were like a concertina. At table she sat next to her father and gazed at him with appropriate awe. He told a story of a dangerous leopard hunt. They had lobster as a special treat. The lobster tails, curving from one place setting to the next, reached far more cordially than the conversation. She tried to remember something she had read that day. She found that by memorizing things she could amuse them at table.

"The gorilla resorts to eating, drinking, or scratching to bypass anxiety," she said later. They all laughed.

"You don't say," he said, with a sneer. It occurred to her that if she were to become too confident he would not want that, either. Or else he had said it to reassure his daughter.

There were moments when she felt confident. She knew in her mind the movements she was required to make in order to pass through the water. She could not do them, but she knew what she was supposed to do. She worked her hands under the table, trying to make deeper and deeper forays into the atmosphere. No one caught her at it. The word "plankton" would not let go of her. She saw dense masses of it, green and serpentine, enfeebling her fingers. She could almost taste it.

His last wife had stitched a backgammon board in green and red. Very beautiful it was. The fat woman played with him after dinner. They carried on the game from one evening to the next. They played very contentedly. The woman wore a different arrangement of rings at each sitting and he never failed to admire and compliment her on them. To those not endowed with beauty he was particularly charming.

Her curling tongs fused the entire electricity system. People rushed out of their bedrooms to know what had happened. He did not show his anger, but she felt it. Next morning they had to send a telegram to summon an electrician. In the telegram office two men sat, one folding the blue pieces of paper, one applying gum with a narrow brush and laying thin borders of white over the blue and pressing down with his hands. On the white strips the name and address had already been printed. A motorcycle was indoors, to protect the tires from the sun, or in case it might be stolen. The men took turns when a telegram had to be delivered. She saved one or the other of them a journey because a telegram from a departed guest arrived while she was waiting. It simply said "Adored it, Harry." Guests invariably forgot something and in their thank-you letters mentioned what they had forgotten. She presumed that some of the hats stacked into one another and laid on the stone ledge were hats forgotten or thrown away. She had grown quite attached to a green one that had lost its ribbons.

The instructor asked to be brought to the souvenir shop. He bought a glass ornament and a collar for his dog. On the way back a man at the petrol station gave one of the children a bird. They put it in the chapel. Made a nest for it. The servant threw it nest and all into the wastepaper basket. That night at supper the talk was of nothing else. He remembered his fish story and he told it to the new people who had come, how one morning he had to abandon his harpoon because the lines got tangled and next day, when he went back, he found that the shark had retreated into the cave and had two great lumps of rock in his mouth, where obviously he had bitten to free himself. That incident had a profound effect on him.

"Is the boat named after your mother?" she asked of his daughter. Her mother's name was Beth and the boat was called *Miss Beth*. "He never said," the daughter replied. She always disappeared after lunch. It must have been to accommodate them. Despite the heat they made a point of going to his room. And made a point of inventiveness. She tried a strong green stalk, to excite him, marveling at it, comparing him and it. He watched. He could not endure such competition. With her head upside down and close to the tiled floor she saw all the oils and ointments on his bathroom ledge and tried reading their labels backward. Do I like all this lovemaking? she asked herself. She had to admit that possibly she did not, that it went on too long, that it was involvement she sought, involvement and threat.

They swapped dreams. It was her idea. He was first. Everyone was careful to humor him. He said in a dream a dog was lost and his grief was great. He seemed to want to say more but didn't, or couldn't. Repeated the same thing, in fact. When it came to her turn, she told a different dream from the one she had meant to tell. A short, uninvolved little dream.

In the night she heard a guest sob. In the morning the same guest wore a flame dressing gown and praised the marmalade, which she ate sparingly.

She asked for the number of lessons to be increased. She had three a day and she did not go on the boat with the others. Between lessons she would walk along the shore. The pine trunks were white, as if a lathe had been put to them. The winds of winter the lathe. In winter they would move; to catch up with friends, business meetings, art exhibitions, to buy presents, to shop. He hated suitcases, he liked clothes to be waiting wherever he went, and they were. She saw a wardrobe with his winter clothes neatly stacked, she saw his frieze cloak with the black astrakhan collar, and she experienced such a longing for that impossible season, that impossible city, and his bulk inside the cloak as they set out in the cold to go to a theater. Walking along the shore, she did the swimming movements in her head. It had got into all her thinking. Invaded her dreams. Atrocious dreams about her mother, her father, and one where lion cubs surrounded her as she lay on a hammock. The cubs were waiting to pounce the second she moved. The hammock, of course, was unsteady. Each time she wakened from one of those dreams she felt certain that her cries were the repeated cries of infancy, and it was then she helped herself to the figs she had brought up.

He put a handkerchief, folded like a letter, before her plate at table. On opening it she found some sprays of fresh mint, wide-leafed and cold. He had obviously put it in the refrigerator first. She smelled it and passed it around. Then on impulse she got up to kiss him and on her journey back nearly bumped into the servant with a tureen of soup, so excited was she.

Her instructor was her friend. "We're winning, we're winning," he said. He walked from dawn onward, walked the hills and saw the earth with dew on it. He wore a handkerchief on his head that he knotted over the ears, but as he approached the house, he removed this headdress. She met him on one of these morning walks. As it got nearer the time, she could neither sleep nor make love. "We're winning, we're winning." He always said it no matter where they met.

They set out to buy finger bowls. In the glass factory there were thin boys with very white skin who secured pieces of glass with pokers and thrust them into the stoves. The whole place smelled of wood. There was chopped wood in piles, in corners. Circular holes were cut along the top of the wall between the square grated windows. The roof was high and yet the place was a furnace. Five kittens with tails like rats lay bunched immobile in a heap. A boy, having washed himself in one of the available buckets of water, took the kittens one by one and dipped them in. She took it to be an act of kindness. Later he bore a hot blue bubble at the end of a poker and laid it before her. As the flame subsided it became mauve, and as it cooled more, it was almost colorless. It had the shape of a sea serpent and an unnaturally long tail. Its color and its finished appearance were an accident, but the gift was clearly intentioned. There was nothing she could do but smile. As they were leaving she saw him waiting near the motorcar, and as she got in, she waved wanly. That night they had asparagus, which is why they went to the trouble to get finger bowls. These were blue with small bubbles throughout, and though the bubbles may have been a defect, they gave to the thick glass an illusion of frost.

There was a new dog, a mongrel, in whom he took no interest. He said the servants got new dogs simply because he allotted money for that. But as they were not willing to feed more than one animal, the previous year's dog was either murdered or put out on the mountain. All these dogs were of the same breed, part wolf; she wondered if when left on the mountain they reverted to being wolves. He said solemnly to the table at large that he would never allow himself to become attached to another dog. She said to him directly, "Is it possible to know beforehand?" He said, "Yes." She could see that she had irritated him.

He came three times and afterward coughed badly. She sat with him and stroked his back, but when the coughing took command he moved her away. He leaned forward, holding a pillow to his mouth. She saw a film of his lungs, orange shapes with insets of dark that boded ill. She wanted to do some simple domestic thing like give him medicine, but he sent her away. Going back along the terrace, she could hear the birds. The birds were busy with their song. She met the fat woman. "You have been derouted," the woman said, "and so have I." And they bowed mockingly.

An archaeologist had been on a dig where a wooden temple was discovered. "Tell me about your temple," she said.

"I would say it's 400 B.C.," he said, nothing more. Dry, dry.

A boy who called himself Jasper and wore mauve shirts received letters under the name of John. The letters were arranged on the hall table, each person's under a separate stone. Her mother wrote to say they were anxiously awaiting the good news. She said she hoped they would get engaged first but admitted that she was quite prepared to be told that the marriage had actually taken place. She knew how unpredictable he was. Her mother managed a poultry farm in England and was a compulsive eater.

Young people came to ask if Clay Sickle was staying at the house. They were in rags, but it looked as if they were rags worn on purpose and for effect. Their shoes were bits of motor tire held up with string. They all got out of the car, though the question could have been asked by any one of them. He was on his way back from the pool, and after two minutes' conversation he invited them for supper. He throve on new people. That night they were the ones in the limelight—the three unkempt boys and the long-haired girl. The girl had very striking eyes, which she fixed on one man and then another. She was determined to compromise one of them. The boys described their holiday, being broke, the trouble they had with the car, which was owned by a hire purchase firm in London. After dinner an incident occurred. The girl followed one of the men into the bathroom. "Want to see what you've got there," she said, and insisted on watching while the man peed. She said they would do any kind of fucking he wanted. She said he would be a slob not to try. It was too late to send them away, because earlier on they'd been invited to spend the night and beds were put up, down in the linen room. The girl was the last to go over there. She started a song, "All around his cock he wears a tricolored rash-eo," and she went on yelling it as she crossed the courtyard and went down the steps, brandishing a bottle.

In the morning, she determined to swim by herself. It was not that she mistrusted her instructor, but the time was getting closer and she was desperate. As she went to the pool, one of the youths appeared in borrowed white shorts, eating a banana. She greeted him with faltering gaiety. He said it was fun to be out before the others. He had a big head with closely cropped hair, a short neck, and a very large nose.

"Beaches are where I most want to be, where it all began," he said. She thought he was referring to creation, and upon hearing such a thing he laughed profanely. "Let's suppose there's a bunch of kids and you're all horsing around with a ball and all your sensory dimensions are working . . ."

"What?" she said.

"A hard-on . . ."

"Oh . . ."

"Now the ball goes into the sea and I follow and she follows me and takes the ball from my hand and a dense rain of energy, call it love, from me to her and vice versa, reciprocity in other words . . ."

Sentientious idiot. She thought, Why do people like that have to be kept under his roof? Where is his judgment, where? She walked back to the house, furious at having to miss her chance to swim.

Dear Mother: It's not that kind of relationship. Being unmarried installs me as positively as being married, and neither installs me with any certainty. It is a beautiful house, but staying here is quite a strain. You could easily get filleted. Friends do it to friends. The food is good. Others cook it, but I am responsible for each day's menu. Shopping takes hours. The shops have a special smell that is impossible to describe. They are all dark, so that the foodstuffs won't perish. An old woman goes along the street in a cart selling fish. She has a very penetrating cry. It is like the commencement of a song. There are always six or seven little girls with her, they all have pierced ears and wear fine gold sleepers. Flies swarm around the cart even when it is upright in the square. Living off scraps and fish scales, I expect. We do not buy from her, we go to the harbor and buy directly from the fishermen. The guests—all but one woman—eat small portions. You would hate it. All platinum people. They have a canny sense of self-preservation; they know how much to eat, how much to drink, how far to go; you would think they invented somebody like Shakespeare, so proprietary are they about his talent. They are not fools—not by any means. There is a chessboard of ivory and it is so large it stands on the floor. Seats of the right height are stationed around it.

Far back—in my most distant childhood, Mother—I remember your nightly cough; it was a lament really and I hated it. At the time I had no idea that I hated it, which goes to show how unreliable feelings are. We do not know what we feel at the time and that is very perplexing. Forgive me for mentioning the cough, it is simply that I think it is high time we spoke our minds on all matters. But don't worry. You are centuries ahead of the people here. In a nutshell, they brand you as idiot if you are harmless. There are jungle laws which you never taught me; you couldn't, you never knew them. Ah well!

I will bring you a present. Probably something suede. He says the needlework here is appalling and that things fall to pieces, but you can always have it remade. We had some nice china jelly molds when I was young. Whatever happened to them? Love.

Like the letter to the doctor, it was not posted. She didn't tear it up or anything, it just lay in an envelope and she omitted to post it from one day to the next. This new tendency disturbed her. This habit of postponing everything. It was as if something vital had first to be gone through. She blamed the swimming.

The day the pool was emptied she missed her three lessons. She could hear the men scrubbing, and from time to time she walked down and stood over them as if her presence could hurry the proceedings and make the water flow in, in one miracle burst, He saw how she fretted, he said they should have had two pools built. He asked her to come with them on the boat. The books and the suntan oil were as she had last seen them. The cliffs as intriguing as ever. "Hello, cliff, can I fall off you?" She waved merrily. In a small harbor they saw another millionaire with his girl. They were alone, without even a crew. And for some reason it went straight to her heart. At dinner the men took bets as to who the girl was. They commented on her prettiness though they had hardly seen her. The water filling the pool sounded like a stream from a faraway hill. He said it would be full by morning.

Other houses had beautiful objects, but theirs was in the best taste. The thing she liked most was the dull brass chandelier from Portugal. In the evenings when it was lit, the cones of light tapered toward the rafters and she thought of woodsmoke and the wings of birds endlessly fluttering. Votive. To please her he had a fire lit in a far-off room simply to have the smell of woodsmoke in the air.

The watercress soup that was to be a specialty tasted like salt water. Nobody blamed her, but afterward she sat at the table and wondered how it had gone wrong. She felt defeated. On request he brought another bottle of red wine, but asked if she was sure she ought to have more. She thought, He does not understand the workings of my mind. But then, neither did she. She was drunk. She held the glass out. Watching the meniscus, letting it tilt from side to side, she wondered how drunk she would be when she stood up. "Tell me," she said, "what interests you?" It was the first blunt question she had ever put to him.

"Why, everything," he said.

"But deep down," she said.

"Discovery," he said, and walked away.

But not self-discovery, she thought, not that.

A neurologist got drunk and played jazz on the chapel organ. He said he could not resist it, there were so many things to press. The organ was stiff from not being used.

She retired early. Next day she was due to swim for them. She thought he would come to visit her. If he did they would lie in one another's arms and talk. She would knead his poor worn scrotum and ask questions about the world beneath the sea where he delved each day, ask about those depths and if there were flowers of some sort down there, and in the telling he would be bound to tell her about himself. She kept wishing for the organ player to fall asleep. She knew he would not come until each guest had retired, because he was strangely reticent about his loving.

But the playing went on. If anything, the player gathered strength and momentum. When at last he did fall asleep, she opened the shutters. The terrace lights were all on. The night breathlessly still. Across the fields came the lap from the sea and then the sound of a sheep bell, tentative and intercepted. Even a sheep recognized the dead of night. The lighthouse worked faithfully as a heartbeat.

The dog lay in the chair, asleep, but with his ears raised. On other chairs were sweaters and books and towels, the remains of the day's activities. She watched and she waited. He did not come. She lamented that she could not go to him on the night she needed him most.

For the first time she thought about cramp.

In the morning she took three headache pills and swallowed them with hot coffee. They disintegrated in her mouth. Afterward she washed them down with soda water. There was no lesson because the actual swimming performance was to be soon after breakfast. She tried on one bathing suit, then another; then, realizing how senseless this was, she put the first one back on and stayed in her room until it was almost time.

When she came down to the pool they were all there ahead of her. They formed quite an audience: the twenty house guests and the six complaining children who had been obliged to quit the pool. Even the housekeeper stood on the stone seat under the tree, to get a view. Some smiled, some were a trifle embarrassed. The pregnant woman gave her a medal for good luck. It was attached to a pin. So they were friends. Her instructor stood near the front, the rope coiled around his wrist just in case. The children gave to the occasion its only levity. She went down the ladder backward and looked at no face in particular. She crouched until the water covered her shoulders, then she gave a short leap and delivered herself to it. Almost at once she knew that she was going to do it. Her hands, no longer loath to delve deep, scooped the water away, and she kicked with a ferocity she had not known to be possible. She was aware of cheering but it did not matter about that. She swam, as she had promised, across the width of the pool in the shallow end. It was pathetically short, but it was what she had vouched to do. Afterward one of the children said that her face was tortured. The rubber flowers had long since come off her bathing cap, and she pulled it off as she stood up and held on to the ladder. They clapped. They said it called for a celebration. He said nothing, but she could see that he was pleased. Her instructor was the happiest person there.

When planning the party they went to the study, where they could sit and make lists. He said they would order gypsies and flowers and guests and caviar and swans of ice to put the caviar in. None of it would be her duty. They would get people to do it. In all, they wrote out twenty telegrams. He asked how she felt. She admitted that being able to swim bore little relation to not being able. They were two unreconcilable feelings. The true thrill, she said, was the moment when she knew she would master it but had not yet achieved it with her body. He said he looked forward to the day when she went in and out of the water like a knife. He did the movement deftly with his hand. He said next thing she would learn was riding. He would teach her himself or he would have her taught. She remembered the chestnut mare with head raised, nostrils searching the air, and she herself unable to stroke it, unable to stand next to it without exuding fear.

"Are you afraid of nothing?" she asked, too afraid to tell him specifically about the encounter with the mare, which took place in his stable.

"Sure, sure."

"You never reveal it."

"At the time I'm too scared."

"But afterward, afterward . . ." she said.

"You try to live it down," he said, and looked at her and hurriedly took her in his arms. She thought, Probably he is as near to me as he has been to any living person and that is not very near, not very near at all. She knew that if he chose her they would not go in the deep end, the deep end that she dreaded and dreamed of. When it came to matters inside himself, he took no risks.

She was tired. Tired of the life she had elected to go into and disappointed with the man she had put pillars around. The tiredness came from inside, and like a deep breath going out slowly, it tore at her gut. She was sick of her own predilection for tyranny. It seemed to her that she always held people to her ear, the way her mother held eggs, shaking them to guess at their rottenness, but unlike her mother she chose the very ones that she would have been wise to throw away. He seemed to sense her sadness, but he said nothing; he held her and squeezed her from time to time in reassurance.

Her dress—his gift—was laid out on the bed, its wide white sleeves hanging down at either side. It was of openwork and it looked uncannily like a corpse. There was a shawl to go with it, and shoes and a bag. The servant was waiting. Beside the bath her book, an ashtray, cigarettes, and a little book of soft matches that were hard to strike. She lit a cigarette and drew on it heartily. She regretted not having brought up a drink. She felt like a drink at that moment, and in her mind she sampled the drink she might have had. The servant knelt down to put in the stopper. She asked that the bath should not be run just yet. Then she took the biggest towel and put it over her bathing suit and went along the corridor and down by the back stairs. She did not have to turn on the lights; she would have known her way blindfolded to that pool. All the toys were on the water, like farm animals just put to bed. She picked them out one by one and laid them at the side near the pile of empty chlorine bottles. She went down the ladder backward.

She swam in the shallow end and allowed the dreadful thought to surface. She thought, I shall do it or I shall not do it, and the fact that she was of two minds about it seemed to confirm her view of the unimportance of the whole thing. Anyone, even the youngest child, could have persuaded her not to, because her mind was without conviction. It just seemed easier, that was all, easier than the strain and the incomplete loving and the excursions that lay ahead.

"This is what I want, this is where I want to go," she said, restraining that part of herself that might scream. Once she went deep, and she submitted to it, the water gathered all around in a great beautiful bountiful baptism. As she went down to the cold and thrilling region she thought, They will never know, they will never, ever know, for sure.

At some point she began to fight and thresh about, and she cried, though she could not know the extent of those cries.

She came to her senses on the ground at the side of the pool, all muffled up and retching. There was an agonizing pain in her chest, as if a shears were snipping at her guts. The servants were with her and two of the guests and him. The floodlights were on around the pool. She put her hands to her breast to make sure; yes, she was naked under the blanket. They would have ripped her bathing suit off. He had obviously been the one to give respiration, because he was breathing quickly and his sleeves were rolled up. She looked at him. He did not smile. There was the sound of music, loud, ridiculous, and hearty. She remembered first the party, then everything. The nice vagueness quit her and she looked at him with shame. She looked at all of them. What things had she shouted as they brought her back to life? What thoughts had they spoken in those crucial moments? How long did it take? Her immediate concern was that they must not carry her to the house, she must not allow that last episode of indignity. But they did. As she was borne along by him and the gardener, she could see the flowers and the oysters and the jellied dishes and the small roast piglets all along the tables, a feast as in a dream, except that she was dreadfully clearheaded. Once alone in her room she vomited.

For two days she did not appear downstairs. He sent up a pile of books, and when he visited her he always brought someone. He professed a great interest in the novels she had read and asked how the plots were. When she did come down, the guests were polite and offhand and still specious, but along with that they were cautious now and deeply disapproving. Their manner told her that it had been a stupid and ghastly thing to do, and had she succeeded she would have involved all of them in her stupid and ghastly mess. She wished she could go home, without any farewells. The children looked at her and from time to time laughed out loud. One boy told her that his brother had once tried to drown him in the bath. Apart from that and the inevitable letter to the gardener, it was never mentioned. The gardener had been the one to hear her cry and raise the alarm. In their eyes he would be a hero.

People swam less. They made plans to leave. They had readymade excuses—work, the change in the weather, airplane bookings. He told her that they would stay until all the guests had gone and then they would leave immediately. His secretary was traveling with them. He asked each day how she felt, but when they were alone, he either read or played patience. He appeared to be calm except that his eyes blazed as with fever. They were young eyes. The blue seemed to sharpen in color once the anger in him was resurrected. He was snappy with the servants. She knew that when they got back to London there would be separate cars waiting for them at the airport. It was only natural. The house, the warm flagstones, the shimmer of the water would sometimes, no doubt, reoccur to her; but she would forget him and he would live somewhere in the attic of her mind, the place where failure is consigned.

FROM

A Scandalous Woman

1974

A Scandalous Woman

Everyone in our village was unique, and one or two of the girls were beautiful. There were others before and after, but it was with Eily I was connected. Sometimes one finds oneself in the swim, one is wanted, one is favored, one is privy, one is caught up in another's destiny that is far more exciting than one's own.

Hers was the face of a madonna. She had brown hair, a great crop of it, fair skin, and eyes that were as big and as soft and as transparent as ripe gooseberries. She was always a little out of breath and gasped when one approached, then embraced and said, "Darling." That was when we met in secret. In front of her parents and others she was somewhat stubborn and withdrawn, and there was a story that when young she always lived under the table to escape her father's thrashings. For one Advent she thought of being a nun, but that fizzled out and her chief interests became clothes and needlework. She helped on the farm and used not to be let out much in the summer, because of all the extra work. She loved the main road with the cars and the bicycles and the buses, and had no interest at all in the sidecar that her parents used for conveyance. She would work like a horse to get to the main road before dark to see the passersby. She was swift as a colt. My father never stopped praising this quality in her and put it down to muscle. It was well known that Eily and her family hid their shoes in a hedge near the road, so that they would have clean footwear when they went to Mass, or to market, or, later on, in Eily's case, to the dress dance.

The dress dance in aid of the new mosaic altar marked her debut. She wore a georgette dress and court shoes threaded with silver and gold. The dress had come from America long before but had been restyled by Eily, and during the week before the dance she was never to be seen without a bunch of pins in her mouth as she tried out some different fitting. Peter the Master, one of the local tyrants, stood inside the door with two or three of his cronies, both to count the money and to survey the couples and comment on their clumsiness or on their dancing "technique." When Eily arrived in her tweed coat and said, "Evening, gentlemen," no one passed any remark, but the moment she slipped off the coat and the transparency of the georgette plus her naked shoulders were revealed, Peter the Master spat into the palm of his hand and said didn't she strip a fine woman.

The locals were mesmerized. She was not off the floor once, and the more she danced, the more fetching she became, and was saying "ooh" and "aah" as her partners spun her round and round. Eventually one of the ladies in charge of the supper had to take her into the supper room and fan her with a bit of cardboard. I was let to look in the window, admiring the couples and the hanging streamers and the very handsome men in the orchestra with their sideburns and striped suits. Then in the supper room, where I had stolen to, Eily confided to me that something out of this world had taken place. Almost immediately after, she was brought home by her sister, Nuala.

Eily and Nuala always quarreled—issues such as who would milk, or who would separate the milk, or who would draw water from the well, or who would churn, or who would bake bread. Usually Eily got the lighter tasks, because of her breathlessness and her accomplishments with the needle. She was wonderful at knitting and could copy any stitch just from seeing it in a magazine or in a knitting pattern. I used to go over there to play, and though they were older than me, they used to beg me to come and bribe me with empty spools or scraps of cloth for my dolls. Sometimes we played hide-and-seek, sometimes we played families and gave ourselves posh names and posh jobs, and we used to paint each other with the dye from plants or blue bags and treat one another's faces as if they were palettes, and then laugh and marvel at the blues and indigos and pretend to be natives and do hula-hula and eat dock leaves.

Nuala was happiest when someone was upset, and almost always she trumped for playing hospital. She was doctor and Eily was nurse. Nuala liked to operate with a big black carving knife, and long before she commenced, she gloated over the method and over what tumors she was going to remove. She used to say that there would be nothing but a shell by the time she had finished, and that one wouldn't be able to have babies or women's complaints ever. She had names for the female parts of one, Susies for the breasts, Florries for the stomach, and Matilda for lower down. She would sharpen and resharpen the knife on the steps, order Eily to get the hot water, the soap, to sterilize the utensils and to have to hand a big winding sheet.

Eily also had to don an apron, a white apron that formerly she had worn at cookery classes. The kettle always took an age to boil on the open hearth, and very often Nuala threw sugar on it to encourage the flame. The two doors would be wide open, a bucket against one and a stone to the other. Nuala would be sharpening the knife and humming "Waltzing Matilda," the birds would almost always be singing or chirruping, the dogs would be outside on their hindquarters, snapping at flies, and I would be lying on the kitchen table, terrified and in a state of undress. Now and then, when I caught Eily's eye, she would raise hers to heaven as much as to say, "you poor little mite," but she never contradicted Nuala or disobeyed orders. Nuala would don her mask. It was a bright-red papier-mâché mask that had been in the house from the time when some mummers came on the Day of the Wren, got bitten by the dog, and lost some of their regalia, including the mask and a legging. Before she commenced, she let out a few dry, knowing coughs, exactly imitating the doctor's dry, knowing coughs. I shall never stop remembering those last few seconds as she snapped the elastic band around the back of her head and said to Eily, "All set, Nurse?"

For some reason I always looked upward and backward and therefore could see the dresser upside down, and the contents of it. There was a whole row of jugs, mostly white jugs with sepia designs of corn, or cattle, or a couple toiling in the fields. The jugs hung on hooks at the edge of the dresser, and behind them were the plates with ripe pears painted in the center of each one. But most beautiful of all were the little dessert dishes of carnival glass, with their orange tints and their scalloped edges. I used to say goodbye to them, and then it would be time to close eyes before the ordeal.

She never called it an operation, just an "op," the same as the doctor did. I would feel the point of the knife like the point of a compass going around my scarcely formed breasts. My bodice would not be removed, just lifted up. She would comment on what she saw and say, "Interesting," or "Quite," or "Oh, dearie me," as the case may be, and then when she got at the stomach she would always say, "Tut tut tut," and "What nasty business have we got here." She would list the unwholesome things I had been eating, such as sherbet or rainbow toffees, hit my stomach with the flat of the knife, and order two spoons of turpentine and three spoons of castor oil before commencing. These potions had then to be downed. Meanwhile, Eily, as the considerate nurse, would be mopping the doctor's brow and handing extra implements such as sugar tongs, spoon, or fork. The spoon was to flatten the tongue and make the patient say "Aah." Scabs or cuts would be regarded as nasty devils, and elastic marks as a sign of iniquity. I would also have to make a general confession. I used to lie there praying that their mother would come home unexpectedly. It was always a Tuesday, the day their mother went to the market to sell things, to buy commodities, and to draw her husband's pension. I used to wait for a sound from the dogs. They were vicious dogs and bit everyone except their owners, and on my arrival there I used to have to yell for Eily to come out and escort me past them.

All in all, it was a woeful event, but still I went each Tuesday on the way home from school, and by the time their mother returned, all would be over and I would be sitting demurely by the fire, waiting to be offered a shop biscuit, which of course at first I made a great pretense of refusing.

Eily always conveyed me down the first field as far as the white gate, and though the dogs snarled and showed their teeth, they never tried biting once I was leaving. One evening, though it was nearly milking time, she came farther, and I thought it was to gather a few hazel-nuts, because there was a little tree between our boundary and theirs that was laden with them. You had only to shake the tree for the nuts to come tumbling down, and you had only to sit on the nearby wall, take one of the loose stones, and crack away to your heart's content. They were just ripe, and they tasted young and clean, and helped as well to get all fur off the backs of the teeth. So we sat on the wall, but Eily did not reach up and draw a branch and therefore a shower of nuts down. Instead, she asked me what I thought of Romeo. He was a new bank clerk, a Protestant, and to me a right toff in his plus-fours with his white sports bicycle. The bicycle had a dynamo attached, so that he was never without lights. He rode the bicycle with his body hunched forward, so that as she mentioned him I could see his snout and his lock of falling hair coming toward me on the road. He also distinguished himself by riding the bicycle into shops or hallways. In fact, he was scarcely ever off it. It seems he had danced with her the night she wore the green georgette, and next day left a note in the hedge where she and her family kept their shoes. She said it was the grace of God that she had gone there first thing that morning, otherwise the note might have come into someone else's hand. He had made an assignation for the following Sunday, and she did not know how she was going to get out of her house and under what excuse. At least Nuala was gone, back to Technical School, where she was learning to be a domestic-economy instructor, and my sisters had returned to the convent, so that we were able to hatch it without the bother of them eavesdropping on us. I said yes, I would be her accomplice, without knowing what I was letting myself in for. On Sunday I told my parents that I was going with Eily to visit a cousin of theirs in the hospital, and she in turn told her parents that we were visiting a cousin of mine. We met at the white gate and both of us were peppering. She had an old black dirndl skirt which she slipped out of; underneath was her cerise dress with the slits at the side. It was a most compromising garment. She wore a brooch at the bosom. Her mother's brooch, a plain flat gold pin with a little star in the center that shone feverishly. She took out her little gold flap-jack and proceeded to dab powder on. She removed the little muslin cover, made me hold it delicately while she dipped into the powder proper. It was ocher stuff and completely wrecked her complexion. Then she applied lipstick, wet her kiss curl, and made me kneel down in the field and promise never ever to spill.

We went toward the hospital, but instead of going up that dark cedar-lined avenue, we crossed over a field, nearly drowning ourselves in the swamp, and permanently stooping so as not to be sighted. I said we were like soldiers in a war and she said we should have worn green or brown as camouflage. Her shapely bottom, bobbing up and down, could easily have been spotted by anyone going along the road. When we got to the thick of the woods, Romeo was there. He looked very indifferent, his face forward, his head almost as low as the handlebars of the bicycle, and he surveyed us carefully as we approached. Then he let out a couple of whistles to let her know how welcome she was. She stood beside him, and I faced them, and we all remarked what a fine evening it was. I could hardly believe my eyes when I saw his hand go around her waist, and then her dress crumpled as it was being raised up from the back, and though the two of them stood perfectly still, they were both looking at each other intently and making signals with their lips. Her dress was above the back of her knees. Eily began to get very flushed and he studied her face most carefully, asking if it was nice, nice. I was told by him to run along: "Run along, Junior" was what he said. I went and adhered to the bark of a tree, eyes closed, fists closed, and every bit of me in a clinch. Not long after, Eily hollered, and on the way home and walking very smartly, she and I discussed growing pains and she said there were no such things but that it was all rheumatism.

So it continued Sunday after Sunday, with one holy day, Ascension Thursday, thrown in. We got wizard in our excuses—once it was to practice with the school choir, another time it was to teach the younger children how to receive Holy Communion, and once—this was our riskiest ploy—it was to get gooseberries from an old crank called Miss MacNamara. That proved to be dangerous, because both our mothers were hoping for some, either for eating or for stewing, and we had to say that Miss MacNamara was not home, whereupon they said weren't the bushes there anyhow with the gooseberries hanging off. For a moment I imagined that I had actually been there, in the little choked garden, with the bantam hens and the small moldy bushes, weighed down with the big hairy gooseberries that were soft to the touch and that burst when you bit into them. We used to pray on the way home, say prayers and ejaculations, and very often when we leaned against the grass bank while Eily donned her old skirt and her old canvas shoes, we said one or another of the mysteries of the Rosary. She had new shoes that were slippers really and that her mother had not seen. They were olive green and she bought them from a gypsy woman in return for a tablecloth of her mother's that she had stolen. It was a special cloth that had been sent all the way from Australia by a nun. She was a thief as well. One day all these sins would have to be reckoned with. I used to shudder at night when I went over the number of commandments we were both breaking, but I grieved more on her behalf, because she was breaking the worst one of all in those embraces and transactions with him. She never discussed him except to say that his middle name was Jack.

During those weeks my mother used to say I was pale and why wasn't I eating and why did I gargle so often with salt and water. These were forms of atonement to God. Even seeing Eily on Tuesdays was no longer the source of delight that it used to be. I was racked. I used to say, "Is this a dagger which I see before me," and recalled all the queer people around who had visions and suffered from delusions. The same would be our cruel cup. She flared up. "Marry! did I or did I not love her?" Of course I loved her and would hang for her, but she was asking me to do the two hardest things on earth—to disobey God and my own mother. Often she took huff, swore that she would get someone else—usually Una, my greatest rival—to play gooseberry for her and be her dogsbody in her whole secret life. But then she would make up and be waiting for me on the road as I came from school, and we would climb in over the wall that led to their fields, and we would link and discuss the possible excuse for the following Sunday. Once, she suggested wearing the green georgette, and even I, who also lacked restraint in matters of dress, thought it would draw untoward attention to her, since it was a dance dress and since as Peter the Master said, "She looked stripped in it." I said Mrs. Bolan would smell a rat. Mrs. Bolan was one of the many women who were always prowling and turning up at graveyards or in the slate quarry to see if there were courting couples. She always said she was looking for stray turkeys or turkey eggs, but in fact she had no fowl, and was known to tell tales that were caluminious; as a result, one temporary schoolteacher had to leave the neighborhood, do a flit in the night, and did not even have time to get her shoes back from the cobbler's. But Eily said that we would never be found out, that the god Cupid was on our side, and while I was with her I believed it.

I had a surprise a few evenings later. Eily was lying in wait for me on the way home from school. She peeped up over the wall, said "Yoo hoo," and then darted down again. I climbed over. She was wearing nothing under her dress, since it was such a scorching day. We walked for a bit, then we flopped down against a cock of hay, the last one in the field, as the twenty-three other cocks had been brought in the day before. It looked a bit silly and was there only because of an accident: the mare had bolted, broken away from the hay cart, and nearly strangled the driver, who was himself an idiot and whose chin was permanently smeared with spittle. She said to close my eyes, open my hands, and see what God would give me. There are moments in life when the pleasure is more than one can bear, and one descends willy-nilly into a wild tunnel of flounder and vertigo. It happens on swing boats and chairoplanes, it happens maybe at waterfalls, it is said to happen to some when they fall in love, but it happened to me that day, propped against the cock of hay, the sun shining, a breeze commencing, the clouds like cruisers in the heavens on their way to some distant port. I had closed my eyes, and then the cold thing hit the palm of my hand, fitting it exactly, and my fingers came over it to further the hold on it and to guess what it was. I did not dare say in case I should be wrong. It was, of course, a little bottle, with a screw-on cap and a label adhering to one side, but it was too much to hope that it would be my favorite perfume, the one called Mischief. She was urging me to guess. I feared that it might be an empty bottle, though such a gift would not be wholly unwelcome, since the remains of the smell always lingered; or that it might be a cheaper perfume, a less mysterious one named after a carnation or a poppy, a perfume that did not send shivers of joy down my throat and through my swallow to my very heart. At last I opened my eyes, and there it was, my most prized thing, in a little dark-blue bottle with a silverish label and a little rubber stopper, and inside, the precious stuff itself. I unscrewed the cap, lifted off the little rubber top, and a drop of the precious stuff was assigned to the flat of my finger and then conveyed to a particular spot in the hollow behind the left ear. She did exactly the same, and we kissed each other and breathed in the rapturous smell. The smell of hay intervened, so we ran to where there was no hay and kissed again. That moment had an air of mystery and sanctity about it, what with the surprise and our speechlessness, and a realization somewhere in the back of my mind that we were engaged in murky business indeed and that our larking days were over.

If things went well my mother had a saying that it was all too good to be true. It proved prophetic the following Saturday, because as my hair was being washed at the kitchen table, Eily arrived and sat at the end of the table and kept snapping her fingers in my direction. When I looked up from my expanse of suds, I saw that she was on the verge of tears and was blotchy all over. My mother almost scalded me, because in welcoming Eily she had forgotten to add the cold water to the pot of boiling water, and I screamed and leaped about the kitchen shouting hellfire and purgatory. Afterward Eily and I went around to the front of the house and sat on the step, where she told me that all was U.P. She had gone to him, as was her wont, under the bridge, where he did a spot of fishing each Friday, and he told her to make herself scarce. She refused, whereupon he moved downstream, and the moment she followed, he waded into the water. He kept telling her to beat it, beat it. She sat on the little milk stool, where he in fact had been sitting; then he did a terrible thing, which was to cast his rod in her direction and almost remove one of her eyes with the nasty hook. She burst into tears, and I began to plait her hair for comfort's sake. She swore that she would throw herself in the selfsame river before the night was out, then said it was only a lovers' quarrel, then said that he would have to see her, and finally announced that her heart was utterly broken, in smithereens. I had the little bottle of perfume in my pocket, and I held it up to the light to show how sparing I had been with it, but she was interested in nothing, only the ways and means of recovering him, or then again of taking her own life. Apart from drowning, she considered hanging, the intake of a bottle of Jeyes Fluid, or a few of the grains of strychnine that her father had for foxes.

Her father was a very gruff man who never spoke to the family except to order his meals and to tell the girls to mind their books. He himself had never gone to school, but had great acumen in the buying and selling of cattle and sheep, and put that down to the fact that he had met the scholars. He was an old man with an atrocious temper, and once on a fairs day had ripped the clothing off an auctioneer who tried to diddle him over the price of an old Aladdin lamp.

My mother came to sit with us, and this alarmed me, since my mother never took the time to sit, either indoors or outdoors. She began to talk to Eily about knitting, about a new tweedex wool, asking if she secured some would Eily help her knit a three-quarter-length jacket. Eily had knitted lots of things for us, including the dress I was wearing—a salmon pink, with scalloped edges and a border of white angora decorating those edges. At that very second, as I had the angora to my face tickling it, my mother said to Eily that once she had gone to a fortune-teller, had removed her wedding ring as a decoy, and when the fortune-teller asked was she married, she had replied no, whereupon the fortune-teller said, "How come you have four children?" My mother said they were uncanny, those ladies, with their gypsy blood and their clairvoyant powers. I guessed exactly what Eily was thinking: Could we find a fortune-teller or a witch who could predict her future?

There was a witch twenty miles away who ran a public house and who was notorious, but who only took people on a whim. When my mother ran off to see if it was a fox because of the racket in the hen house, I said to Eily that instead of consulting a witch we ought first to resort to other things, such as novenas, putting wedding cake under our pillows, or gathering bottles of dew in the early morning and putting them in a certain fort to make a wish. Anyhow, how could we get to a village twenty miles away, unless it was on foot or by bicycle, and neither of us had a machine. Nevertheless, the following Sunday we were to be found setting off with a bottle of tea, a little puncture kit, and eight shillings, which was all the money we managed to scrape together.

We were not long started when Eily complained of feeling weak, and suddenly the bicycle was wobbling all over the road, and she came a cropper as she tried to slow it down by heading for a grass bank. Her brakes were nonexistent, as indeed were mine. They were borrowed bicycles. I had to use the same method to dismount, and the two of us with our front wheels wedged into the bank and our handlebars askew, caused a passing motorist to call out that we were a right pair of Mohawks and a danger to the county council.

I gave her a sup of tea, and forced on her one of the eggs which we had stolen from various nests and which were intended as a bribe for our witch. Along with the eggs we had a little flitch of home-cured bacon. She cracked it on the handlebars and, with much persuasion from me, swallowed it whole, saying it was worse than castor oil. It being Sunday, she recalled other Sundays and where she would be at that exact moment, and she prayed to St. Anthony to please bring him back. We had heard that he went to Limerick most weekends now, and there was rumor that he was going out with a bacon curer's daughter and that they were getting engaged.

The woman who opened the side door of the pub said that the witch did not live there any longer. She was very cross, had eyebrows that met, and these as well as the hairs in her head were a yellowish gray. She told us to leave her threshold at once, and how dare we intrude upon her Sunday leisure. She closed the door in our faces. I said to Eily, "That's her." And just as we were screwing up our courage to knock again, she reopened the door and said who in the name of Jacob had sent us. I said we'd come a long way, miles and miles; I showed the eggs and the bacon in its dusting of saltpeter, and she said she was extremely busy, seeing as it was her birthday and that sons and daughters and cousins were coming for a high tea. She opened and closed the door numerous times, and through it all we stood our ground, until finally we were brought in, but it was my fortune she wanted to tell. The kitchen was tiny and stuffy, and the same linoleum was on the floor as on the little wobbling table. There was a little wooden armchair for her, a long stool for visitors, and a stove that was smoking. Two rhubarb tarts were cooling on top, and that plus a card were the only indications of a birthday celebration. A small man, her husband, excused himself and wedged sideways through another door. I pleaded with her to take Eily rather than me, and after much dithering, and even going out to the garden to empty tea leaves, she said that maybe she would, but that we were pests, the pair of us. I was sent to join her husband in the little pantry, and was nearly smothered from the puffing of his pipe. There was also a strong smell of flour, and no furniture except a sewing machine with a half-finished garment, a shift, wedged in under the needle. He talked in a whisper, said that Mau Mau would come to Ireland and that St. Columbus would rise from his grave, to make it once again the island of saints and scholars. I was certain that I would suffocate. Yet it was worth it. Eily was jubilant. Things could not have been better. The witch had not only seen his initial, J, but seen it twice in a concoction that she had done with the whites of one of the eggs and some gruel. Yes, things had been bad, very bad, there had been grievous misunderstandings, but all was to be changed, and leaning across the table, she said to Eily, "Ah sure, you'll end your days with him."

Cycling home was a joy; we spun downhill, saying to hell with safety, to hell with brakes, saluted strangers, admired all the little cottages and the outhouses and the milk tanks and the whining mongrels, and had no nerves passing the haunted house. In fact, we would have liked to see an apparition on that most buoyant of days. When we got to the crossroads that led to our own village, Eily had a strong presentiment, as indeed had I, that he would be there waiting for us, contrite, in a hair shirt, on bended knees. But he was not. There was the usual crowd of lads playing pitch and toss. A couple of the younger ones tried to impede us by standing in front of the bikes, and Eily blushed red. She was a favorite with everyone that summer, and she had a different dress for every day of the week. She was called a fashion plate. We said good night and knew that it did not matter, that though he had not been waiting for us, before long he and Eily would be united. She resolved to be patient and be a little haughty and not seek him out.

Three weeks later, on a Saturday night, my mother was soaking her feet in a mixture of warm water and washing soda when a rap came on the scullery window. We both trembled. There was a madman who had taken up residence in a bog hole and we were certain that it must be him. "Call your father," she said. My father had gone to bed in a huff, because she had given him a boiled egg instead of a fry for his tea. I didn't want to leave her alone and unattended, so I yelled up to my father, and at the same time a second assault was delivered on the windowpane. I heard the words "Sir, sir."

It was Eily's father, since he was the only person who called my father sir. When we opened the door to him, the first thing I saw was the slash hook in his hand, and then the condition of his hair, which was upstanding and wild. He said, "I'll hang, draw, and quarter him," and my mother said, "Come in, Mr. Hogan," not knowing whom this graphic fate was intended for. He said he had found his daughter in the lime kiln, with the bank clerk, in the most satanic position, with her belly showing.

My first thought was one of delight at their reunion, and then I felt piqued that Eily hadn't told me but had chosen instead to meet him at night in that disused kiln, which reeked of damp. Better the woods, I thought, and the call of the cuckoo, and myself keeping some kind of watch, though invariably glued to the bark of a tree.

He said he had come to fetch a lantern, to follow them as they had scattered in different directions, and he did not know which of them to kill first. My father, whose good humor was restored by this sudden and unexpected intrusion, said to hold on for a moment, to step inside so that they could consider a plan of campaign. Mr. Hogan left his cap on the step, a thing he always did, and my mother begged him to bring it in, since the new pup ate every article of clothing that it could find. Only that very morning my mother looked out on the field and thought it was flakes of snow, but in fact it was her line of washing, chewed to pieces. He refused to bring in his cap, which to me was a perfect example of how stubborn he was and how awkward things were going to be. At once, my father ordered my mother to make tea, and though still gruff, there was between them now an understanding, because of the worse tragedy that loomed. My mother seemed the most perturbed, made a hopeless cup of tea, cut the bread in agricultural hunks, and did everything wrong, as if she herself had just been found out in some base transaction. After the men had gone out on their search party, she got me to go down on my knees to pray with her; I found it hard to pray, because I was already thinking of the flogging I would get for being implicated. She cross-examined me. Did I know anything about it? Had Eily ever met him? Why had she made herself so much style, especially that slit skirt.

I said no to everything. These no's were much too hastily delivered, and if my mother had not been so busy cogitating and surmising, she would have suspected something for sure. Kneeling there, I saw them trace every movement of ours, get bits of information from this one and that one, the so-called cousins, the woman who had promised us the gooseberries, and Mrs. Bolan. I knew we had no hope. Eily! Her most precious thing was gone, her jewel. The inside of one was like a little watch, and once the jewel or jewels were gone, the outside was nothing but a sham. I saw her die in the cold lime kiln and then again in a sick room, and then stretched out on an operating table, the very way I used to be. She had joined that small sodality of scandalous women who had conceived children without securing fathers and who were damned in body and soul. Had they convened they would have been a band of seven or eight, and might have sent up an unholy wail to their Maker and their covert seducers. The one thing I could not endure was the thought of her stomach protuberant and a baby coming out saying "Ba ba." Had I had the chance to see her, I should have suggested that we run away with gypsies.

Poor Eily, from then on she was kept under lock and key, and allowed out only to Mass, and then so concealed was she, with a mantilla over her face, that she was not even able to make a lip sign to me. Never did she look so beautiful as those subsequent Sundays in chapel, her hair and her face veiled, her pensive eyes peering through. I once sat directly in front of her, and when we stood up for the first Gospel, I stared up into her face and got such a dig in the ribs from my mother that I toppled over.

A mission commenced the following week, and a strange priest with a beautiful accent and a strong sense of rhetoric delivered the sermons each evening. It was better than a theater—the chapel in a state of hush, ladders of candles, all lit, extra flowers on the altar, a medley of smells, the white linen, and the place so packed that we youngsters had to sit on the altar steps and saw everything clearer, including the priest's Adam's apple as it bobbed up and down. Always I could sight Eily, hemmed in by her mother and some other old woman, pale and impassive, and I was certain that she was about to die. On the evening that the sermon centered on the sixth commandment, we youngsters were kept outside until Benediction time. We spent the time wandering through the stalls, looking at the tiers of rosary beads that were as dazzling as necklaces, all hanging side by side and quivering in the breeze, all colors, and of different stones, then of course the bright scapulars, and all kinds of little medals and beautiful crucifixes that were bigger than the girth of one's hand, and even some that had a little cavity within, where a relic was contained, and also beautiful prayer books and missals, some with gold edging, and little holdalls made of filigree.

When we trooped in for the Benediction, Eily slipped me a holy picture. It had Christ on the cross and a verse beneath it: "You have but one soul to save/One God to love and serve/One eternity to prepare for/Death will come soon./Judgment will follow—and then/Heaven or Hell forever." I was musing on it and swallowing back my tears at the very moment that Eily began to retch and was hefted out by four of the men. They bore her aloft as if she were a corpse on a litter. I said to my mother that most likely Eily would die, and my mother said if only such a solution could occur. My mother already knew. The next evening Eily was in our house, in the front room, and though I was not admitted, I listened at the door and ran off only when there was a scream or a blow or a thud. She was being questioned about each and every event, and about the bank clerk and what exactly were her associations with him. She said no, over and over again, and at moments was quite defiant and, as they said, an "upstart." One minute they were asking her kindly, another minute they were heckling, another minute her father swore that it was to the lunatic asylum that she would be sent, and then at once her mother was condemning her for not having milked for two weeks.

They were inconsistency itself. How could she have milked since she was locked in the room off the kitchen, where they stowed the oats and which was teeming with mice. I knew for a fact that her meals—a hunk of bread and a mug of weak tea—were handed into her twice a day, and that she had nothing else to do, only cry and think and sit herself upon the oats and run her fingers through it, and probably have to keep making noises to frighten off the mice. When they were examining her, my mother was the most reasonable, but also the most exacting. My mother would ask such things as "Where did you meet? How long were you together? Were others present?" Eily denied ever having met him and was spry enough to say, "What do you take me for, Mrs. Brady, a hussy?" But that incurred some sort of a belt from her father, because I heard my mother say that there was no need to resort to savagery. I almost swooned when on the glass panel of our hall door I saw a shadow, then knuckles, and through the glass the appearance of a brown habit, such as the missioner wore.

He saw Eily alone; we all waited in the kitchen, the men supping tea, my mother segmenting a grapefruit to offer to the priest. It seemed odd fare to give him in the evening, but she was used to entertaining priests only at breakfast time, when one came every five or ten years to say Mass in the house to rebless it and put paid to the handiwork of the devil. When he was leaving, the missioner shook hands with each of us, then patted my hair. Watching his sallow face and his rimless spectacles, and drinking in his beautiful speaking voice, I thought that if I were Eily I would prefer him to the bank clerk, and would do anything to be in his company.

I had one second with Eily, while they all trooped out to open the gate for the priest and to wave him off. She said for God's sake not to spill on her. Then she was taken upstairs by my mother, and when they reemerged, Eily was wearing one of my mother's mackintoshes, a Mrs. Miniver hat, and a pair of old sunglasses. It was a form of disguise, since they were setting out on a journey. Eily's father wanted to put a halter around her, but my mother said it wasn't the Middle Ages. I was enjoined to wash cups and saucers, to empty the ashtray, and to plump the cushions again, but once they were gone, I was unable to move because of a dreadful pain that gripped the lower part of my back and stomach. I was convinced that I, too, was having a baby and that if I were to move or part my legs, some freakish thing would come tumbling out.

The following morning Eily's father went to the bank, where he broke two glass panels, sent coins flying about the place, assaulted the bank manager, and tried to saw off part of the bank clerk's anatomy. The two customers—the butcher and the undertaker—had to intervene, and the lady clerk, who was in the cloakroom, managed to get to the telephone to call the barracks. When the sergeant came on the scene, Eily's father was being held down, his hands tied with a skipping rope, but he was still trying to aim a kick at the blackguard who had ruined his daughter. Very quickly the sergeant got the gist of things. It was agreed that Jack—that was the culprit's name—would come to their house that evening. Though the whole occasion was to be fraught with misfortune, my mother, upon hearing of it, said some sort of buffet would have to be considered.

It proved to be an arduous day. The oats had to be shoveled out of the room, and the women were left to do it, since my father was busy seeing the solicitor and the priest, and Eily's father remained in the town, boasting about what he would have done to the bugger if only the sergeant hadn't come on the scene.

Eily was silence itself. She didn't even smile at me when I brought the basket of groceries that her mother had sent me to fetch. Her mother kept referring to the fact that they would never provide bricks and mortar for the new house now. For years she and her husband had been skimping and saving, intending to build a house two fields nearer the road. It was to be identical to their own house, that is to say, a cement two-story house, but with the addition of a lavatory and a tiny hall inside the front door, so that, as she said, if company came, they could be vetted there instead of plunging straight into the kitchen. She was a backward woman, and probably because of living in the fields she had no friends and had never stepped inside anyone else's door. She always washed outdoors at the rain barrel, and never called her husband anything but mister. Unpacking the groceries, she said that it was a pity to waste them on him, and the only indulgence she permitted herself was to smell the things, especially the packet of raspberry and custard biscuits. There was black-currant jam, a Scribona Swiss roll, a tin of herring in tomato sauce, a loaf, and a large tin of fruit cocktail.

Eily kept whitening and rewhitening her buckskin shoes. No sooner were they out on the window than she would bring them in and whiten again. The women were in the room putting the oats into sacks. They didn't have much to say. My mother always used to laugh, because when they met, Mrs. Hogan used to say, "Any newses?" and look up at her with that wild stare, opening her mouth to show the big gaps between her front teeth, but the "newses" had at last come to her own door, and though she must have minded dreadfully, she seemed vexed more than ashamed, as if it was inconvenience rather than disgrace that had hit her. But from that day on, she almost stopped calling Eily by her pet name, which was Alannah.

I said to Eily that if she liked we could make toffee, because making toffee always humored her. She pretended not to hear. Even to her mother she refused to speak, and when asked a question she bared her teeth like one of the dogs. She wanted one of the dogs, Spot, to bite me, and led him to me by the ear, but he was more interested in a sheep's head that I had brought from the town. It was an arduous day, what with carting out the oats in cans and buckets, and refilling it into sacks, moving a table in there and tea chests, finding suitable covers for them, laying the table properly, getting rid of all the cobwebs in the corners, sweeping up the soot that had fallen down the chimney, and even running up a little curtain. Eily had to hem it, and as she sat outside the back door, I could see her face and her expression; she looked very stubborn and not nearly so amenable as before. My mother provided a roast chicken, some pickles, and freshly boiled beets. She skinned the hot beets with her hands and said, "Ah, you've made your bed now," but Eily gave no evidence of having heard. She simply washed her face in the aluminum basin, combed her hair severely back, put on her whitened shoes, and then turned around to make sure that the seams of her stockings were straight. Her father came home drunk, and he looked like a younger man, trotting up the fields in his oatmeal-colored socks—he'd lost his shoes. When he saw the sitting room that had up to then been the oats room, he exclaimed, took off his hat to it, and said, "Am I in my own house at all, mister?" My father arrived full of important news which, as he kept saying, he would discuss later. We waited in a ring, seated around the fire, and the odd words said were said only by the men, and then without any point. They discussed a beast that had had some ailment.

The dogs were the first to let us know. We all jumped up and looked through the window. The bank clerk was coming on foot, and my mother said to look at that swagger, and wasn't it the swagger of a hobo. Eily ran to look in the mirror that was fixed to the window ledge. For some extraordinary reason my father went out to meet him and straightaway produced a pack of cigarettes. The two of them came in smoking, and he was shown to the sitting room, which was directly inside the door to the left. There were no drinks on offer, since the women decided that the men might only get obstreperous. Eily's father kept pointing to the glories of the room, and lifted up a bit of cretonne, to make sure that it was a tea chest underneath and not a piece of pricy mahogany. My father said,

"Well, Mr. Jacksie, you'll have to do your duty by her and make an honest woman of her." Eily was standing by the window, looking out at the oncoming dark. The bank clerk said, "Why so?" and whistled in a way that I had heard him whistle in the past. He did not seem put out. I was afraid that on impulse he might rush over and put his hands somewhere on Eily's person. Eily's father mortified us all by saying she had a porker in her, and the bank clerk said so had many a lass, whereupon he got a slap across the face and was told to sit down and behave himself.

From that moment on, he must have realized he was lost. On all other occasions I had seen him wear a khaki jacket and plus-fours, but that evening he wore a brown suit that gave him a certain air of reliability and dullness. He didn't say a word to Eily, or even look in her direction, as she sat on a little stool staring out the window and biting on the little lavaliere that she wore around her neck. My father said he had been pup enough and the only thing to do was to own up to it and marry her. The bank clerk put forward three objections—one, that he had no house; two, that he had no money; and three, that he was not considering marrying. During the supper Eily's mother refused to sit down and stayed in the kitchen, nursing the big tin of fruit cocktail and having feeble jabs at it with the old iron tin opener. She talked aloud to herself about the folks "hither" in the room and what a sorry pass things had come to. As usual, my mother ate only the pope's nose, and served the men the breasts of chicken. Matters changed every other second, they were polite to him, remembering his status as a bank clerk, then they were asking him what kind of crops grew in his part of the country, and then again they would refer to him as if he were not there, saying, "The pup likes his bit of meat." He was told that he would marry her on the Wednesday week, that he was being transferred from the bank, that he would go with his new wife and take rooms in a midland town. He just shrugged, and I was thinking that he would probably vanish on the morrow, but I didn't know that they had alerted everyone and that when he did in fact try to leave at dawn the following morning, three strong men impeded him and brought him up the mountain for a drive in their lorry. For a week after, he was indisposed, and it is said that his black eyes were bulbous. It left a permanent hole in his lower cheek, as if a little pebble of flesh had been tweezed out of him.

Anyhow, they discussed the practicalities of the wedding while they ate their fruit cocktail. It was served in the little carnival dishes, and I thought of the numerous operations that Nuala had done, and how if it was left to Eily and me, things would not be nearly so crucial. I did not want her to have to marry him, and I almost blurted that out. But the plans were going ahead; he was being told that it would cost him ten pounds, that it would be in the sacristy of the Catholic church, since he was a Protestant, and there were to be no guests except those present and Eily's former teacher, a Miss Melody. Even her sister, Nuala, was not going to be told until after the event. They kept asking him was that clear, and he kept saying, "Oh yeah," as if it were a simple matter of whether he would have more fruit cocktail or not. The number of cherries were few and far between, and for some reason had a faint mauve hue to them. I got one and my mother passed me hers. Eily ate well but listlessly, as if she weren't there at all. Toward the end my father sang "Master McGrath," a song about a greyhound, and Mr. Hogan told the ghost story about seeing the headless liveried man at a crossroads when he was a boy.

Going down the field, Eily was told to walk on ahead with her intended, probably so that she could discuss her trousseau or any last-minute things. The stars were bewitching, and the moonlight cast as white a glow as if it were morning and the world was veiled with frost. Eily and he walked in utter silence. At last, she looked up at him and said something, and all he did was to draw away from her; there was such a distance between them that a cart or a car could pass through. She edged a little to the right to get nearer, and as she did, he moved farther away, so that eventually she was on the edge of a path and he was right by the hedge, hitting the bushes with a bit of a stick he had picked up. We followed behind, the grownups discussing whether or not it would rain the next day while I wondered what Eily had tried to say to him.

*

They met twice more before the wedding, once in the sitting room of the hotel, when the traveling solicitor drew up the papers guaranteeing her a dowry of two hundred pounds, and once in the city, when he was sent with her to the jeweler's to buy a wedding ring. It was the same city as where he had been seeing the bacon curer's daughter, and Eily said that in the jeweler's he expressed the wish that she would drop dead. At the wedding breakfast itself there were only sighs and tears, and the teacher, as was her wont, stood in front of the fire and, mindless of the mixed company, hitched up her dress behind, the better to warm the cheeks of her bottom. In his giving-away speech, my father said they had only to make the best of it. Eily sniveled, her mother wept and wept and said, "Oh, Alannah, Alannah," while the groom muttered, "Once bitten, twice shy." The reception was in their new lodgings, and my mother said that she thought it was bad form the way the landlady included herself in the proceedings. My mother also said that their household utensils were pathetic, two forks, two knives, two spoons, an old kettle, an egg saucepan, a primus, and, as she said, not even a nice enamel bin for the bread but a rusted biscuit tin. When they came to leave, Eily tried to dart into the back of the car, tried it more than once, just like an animal trying to get back to its lair.

On returning home my mother let me put on her lipstick and praised me untowardly for being such a good, such a pure little girl, and never did I feel so guilty, because of the leading part I had played in Eily's romance. The only thing that my mother had eaten at the wedding was a jelly made with milk. We tried it the following Sunday, a raspberry-flavored jelly made with equal quantities of milk and water—and then whisked. It was like a beautiful pink tongue, dotted with spittle, and it tasted slippery. I had not been found out, had received no punishment, and life was getting back to normal again. I gargled with salt and water, on Sundays longed for visitors that never came, and on Monday mornings had all my books newly covered so that the teacher would praise me. Ever since the scandal she was enjoining us to go home in pairs, to speak Irish, and not to walk with any sense of provocation.

Yet she herself stood by the fire grate and, after having hitched up her dress, petted herself. When she lost her temper, she threw chalk or implements at us, and used very bad language.

It was a wonderful year for lilac, and the windowsills used to be full of it, first the big moist bunches, with the lovely cool green leaves, and then a wilting display, and following that, the seeds in pools all over the sill and the purple itself much sadder and more dolorous than when first plucked off the trees.

When I daydreamed, which was often, it hinged on Eily. Did she have a friend, did her husband love her, was she homesick, and, above all, was her body swelling up? She wrote to her mother every second week. Her mother used to come with her apron on, and the letter in one of those pockets, and sit on the back step and hesitate before reading it. She never came in, being too shy, but she would sit there while my father fetched her a cup of raspberry cordial. We all had sweet tooths. The letters told next to nothing, only such things as that their chimney had caught fire, or a boy herding goats found an old coin in a field, or could her mother root out some old clothes from a trunk and send them to her as she hadn't got a stitch. "'Tis style enough she has," her mother would say bitterly, and then advise that it was better to cut my hair and not have me go around in ringlets, because, as she said, "Fine feathers make fine birds." Now and then she would cry and then feed the birds the crumbs of the biscuit or shortbread that my mother had given her.

She liked the birds and in secret in her own yard made little perches for them, and if you please hung bits of colored rags and the shaving mirror for them to amuse themselves by. My mother had made a quilt for Eily, and I believe that was the only wedding present she received. They parceled it together. It was a red flannel quilt, lined with white, and had a herringbone stitch around the edge. It was not like the big soft quilt that once occupied the entire window of the draper's, a pink satin on which one's body could bask, then levitate. One day her mother looked right at me and said, "Has she passed any more worms?" I had passed a big tapeworm, and that was a talking point for a week or so after the furor of the wedding had died down. Then she gave me half a crown. It was some way of thanking me for being a friend of Eily's. When her son was born, the family received a wire. He was given the name of Jack, the same as his father, and I thought how the witch had been right when she had seen the initial twice, but how we had misconstrued it and took it to be glad tidings.

Eily began to grow odd, began talking to herself, and then her lovely hair began to fall out in clumps. I would hear her mother tell my mother these things. The news came in snatches, first from a family who had gone up there to rent grazing, and then from a private nurse who had to give Eily pills and potions. Eily's own letters were disconnected and she asked about dead people or people she'd hardly known. Her mother meant to go by bus one day and stay overnight, but she postponed it until her arthritis got too bad and she was not able to go out at all.

Four years later, at Christmastime, Eily, her husband, and their three children paid a visit home, and she kept eyeing everything and asking people to please stop staring at her, and then she went around the house and looked under the beds, for some male spy whom she believed to be there. She was dressed in brown and had brown fur-backed gloves. Her husband was very suave, had let his hair grow long, and during the tea kept pressing his knee against mine and asking me which did I like best, sweet or savory. The only moment of levity was when the three children, clothes and all, got into a pig trough and began to splash in it. Eily laughed her head off as they were being hosed down by her mother. Then they had to be put into the settle bed, alongside the sacks of flour and the brooms and the bric-à-brac, while their clothes were first washed and then put on a little wooden horse to dry before the fire. They were laughing, but their teeth chattered. Eily didn't remember me very clearly and kept asking me if I was the oldest or the middle girl in the family. We heard later that her husband got promoted and was running a little shop and had young girls working as his assistants.

I was pregnant, and walking up a street in a city with my own mother, under not very happy circumstances, when we saw this wild creature coming toward us, talking and debating to herself. Her hair was gray and frizzed, her costume was streelish, and she looked at us, and then peered, as if she was going to pounce on us; then she started to laugh at us, or rather, to sneer, and she stalked away and pounced on some other persons. My mother said, "I think that was Eily," and warned me not to look back. We both walked on, in terror, and then ducked into the porchway of a shop, so that we could follow her with our eyes without ourselves being seen. She was being avoided by all sorts of people, and by now she was shouting something and brandishing her fist and struggling to get heard. I shook, as indeed the child within me was induced to shake, and for one moment I wanted to go down that street to her, but my mother held me back and said that she was dangerous, and that in my condition I must not go. I did not need much in the way of persuading. She moved on; by now several people were laughing and looking after her, and I was unable to move, and all the gladness of our summer day, and a little bottle of Mischief pressed itself into the palm of my hand again, and I saw her lithe and beautiful as she once was, and in the street a great flood of light pillared itself around a little cock of hay while the two of us danced with joy.

I did go in search of her years later. My husband waited up at the cross and I went down the narrow steep road with my son, who was thrilled to be approaching a shop. Eily was behind the counter, her head bent over a pile of bills that she was attaching to a skewer. She looked up and smiled. The same face but much coarser. Her hair was permed and a newly pared pencil protruded from it. She was pleased to see me, and at once reached out and handed my son a fistful of rainbow toffees.

It was the very same as if we'd parted only a little while ago. She didn't shake hands or make any special fuss, she simply said, "Talk of an angel," because she had been thinking of me that very morning. Her children were helping; one was weighing sugar, the little girl was funneling castor oil into four-ounce bottles, and her oldest son was up on a ladder fixing a flex to a ceiling light. He said my name, said it with a sauciness as soon as she introduced me, but she told him to whist. For her own children she had no time, because they were already grown, but for my son she was full of welcome and kept saying he was a cute little fellow. She weighed him on the big meal scales and then let him scoop the grain with a little trowel, and let it slide down the length of his arm and made him gurgle.

People kept coming in and out, and she went on talking to me while serving them. She was complete mistress of her surroundings and said what a pity that her husband was away, off on the lorry, doing the door-to-door orders. He had given up banking, found the business more profitable. She winked each time she hit the cash register, letting me see what an expert she was. Whenever there was a lull, I thought of saying something, but my son's pranks commandeered the occasion. She was very keen to offer me something and ripped the glass paper off a two-pound box of chocolates and laid them before me, slantwise, propped against a can or something. They were eminently inviting, and when I refused, she made some reference to the figure.

"You were always too generous," I said, sounding like my mother or some stiff relation.

"Go on," she said, and biffed me.

It seemed the right moment to broach it, but how?

"How are you?" I said. She said that, as I could see, she was topping, getting on a bit, and the children were great sorts, and the next time I came I'd have to give her notice so that we could have a singsong. I didn't say that my husband was up at the road and by now would be looking at his watch and saying "Damn" and maybe would have got out to polish or do some cosseting to the vintage motorcar that he loved so. I said, and again it was lamentable, "Remember the old days, Eily."

"Not much," she said.

"The good old days," I said.

"They're all much of a muchness," she said.

"Bad," I said.

"No, busy," she said. My first thought was that they must have drugged the feelings out of her, they must have given her strange brews, and along with quelling her madness, they had taken her spark away. To revive a dead friendship is almost always a risk, and we both knew it but tried to be polite.

She kissed me and put a little holy water on my forehead, delving it in deeply, as if I were dough. They waved to us, and my son could not return those waves, encumbered as he was with the various presents that both the children and Eily had showered on him. It was beginning to spot with rain, and what with that and the holy water and the red rowan tree bright and instinct with life, I thought that ours indeed was a land of shame, a land of murder, and a land of strange, throttled, sacrificial women.

Over

Oh my dear I would like to be something else, anything else, an albatross. In short, I wish I never knew you. Or could forget. Or be a bone—you could suck it. Or a stone in the bottom of your pocket, slipped down, if you like, through one of the holes in the lining and wedged into the hem more or less forever, until you threw the coat away or gave it to one of your relations. I never saw you in a coat, only in a sort of jacket, what they call an anorak. A funny word.

The first time you came to see me, you were on the point of leaving as I opened the door. Leaving already. Yes, you were that intrepid. So was I. You asked me where you might put your coat, or rather that anorak thing, and I couldn't think, there being no hall stand. Do you remember the room was too big for us? I remember. Seeing you sitting an ocean away, on a print-covered chair, ill at ease, young, younger than your thirty years, and I thought how I would walk across somehow or even stride across and cradle you. It was too grand: the room, the upright piano, the cut-glass chandelier. I have had notions of grandeur in the past but they are vanishing. Oh, my God, everything is vanishing, except you.

A younger man. I go over our years ahead; jump ahead if you will. I will be gray before you. What a humbling thing. I will dye my tresses, all my tresses. Perhaps I should experiment now with a bottle of brown dye and a little soft brush, experiment even with my hidden hairs. I must forestall you always, always. Leave no loopholes, nothing that will disappoint or disenchant you. What nonsense, when you have already gone. I don't expect to see you again unless we bump into one another. I think I am getting disappointed in you and that is good. Excellent. You told me yourself how you lied to me. You are back from your lecturing and probably thinking of getting in touch with me, probably at this very moment. Your hand on the telephone, debating, all of you debating. Now you've taken your hand away. You've put it off. You know you can, you can put it aside like a treat, a childhood treat.

I did that as a child with a watch. Not a real watch, but still a watch. It was the color of jam, raspberry color, and I left it somewhere, in fact in a vestibule, in order that I could go look at it, in order to see it there, mine, mine.

I did it. I crossed the room, and what you did was to feel my hair over and over again and in different ways, touch it with the palm of your hand, your drink was in your other hand (at first you refused a drink), felt it, strands of hair with your fingers, touched it as if it were cloth, the way a child touches its favorite surfaces such as a doll or a toy.

I keep saying child. It was like that, and you staring, staring, right through me, into me.

No knowing what I surrendered that night, what I gave up. I gave up most people, and gave up the taste for clothes and dinners and anything that could be called frivolous. I even gave up my desire to talk, to intrude, or to make my presence felt. I went right back; that is true, right back to the fields, so to speak, where I grew up. All the features of that place, the simplest things, the sensations repossessed me. Crystal clear. A gate, a hasp, a water trough, the meadows, and the way one can flop down into the corner of a field, a hay field. Dew again. And the image I had was of the wetness that babies and calves and foals have when they are just born and are about to be licked, and yet I was the mother.

Undoubtedly I was the mother when I gave you that soup and peeled a potato for you and cut it in half and mashed it as if you couldn't do it yourself and you said, "I have a poor appetite." You thought I should have been more imposing. Even my kitchen you liked, the untidiness and the laurel leaves in a jug. They last a long time and I am told that they are lucky.

I should have enjoyed that night, that first unplanned meeting. As a matter of fact I did, but it has been overlaid with so much else that it is like something crushed, something smothered, something at the bottom of a cupboard that has been forgotten, its very shape destroyed, its denomination ignored, and yet it is something that will always be there, except that no one will know or care about it, and no one will want to retrieve it, and in the years to come if the cupboard should be cleaned out, if, for instance, the occupants are leaving, it will indeed be found, but it will be so crumpled as to be useless.

I dreamed of you before I met you. That was rash. I dream of you still, quite unedifying dreams where you are embracing me and whispering and we are interrupted the way we are constantly interrupted in life. You once told me that there were only ten minutes left for us because you had to buy a piece of perspex for a painting, make sure of getting it before the shops closed. The painting was a present to you both. It must have been in lieu of a wedding present.

Yes, I believe you are afraid of her. You say it's pity that holds you. But I believe that you are afraid of her and don't know it, and I believe that you love her and don't know it. You don't know very much about yourself, you shirk that. I asked you once, I went down on my knees, I asked you to go away for three days, without her or me or anyone, and you looked at me as if I were sending you to Van Diemen's Land.

And another thing, you told me the same stories, the same escapades. You seem to forget that you have already told me that story when you broke bottles of champagne, stole them, and then broke them. In your youth. And how you pity chambermaids, make the bed with them, that is to say, help them with the tuckings. Another virtue of yours is that you never flirt. You don't trade on your good looks, and really you deserve a beautiful young girl. I don't think you are in your right mind. Neither am I. We should never have met. I do believe it's a tribal thing. When I saw your daughter I thought it was me. No, not quite. I thought, or rather I knew, I was once her. She looked at me like a familiar. That gaze. She didn't make strange. I touched her all over. I had to touch her. I had to tickle her, her toes, her soft knees (like blancmange she was), her little crevices, and she smiled up at me and you said, "Smile for your auntie," and I was glad you called me Auntie, it was so ordinary and so plain and put me on the same footing as you.

Couldn't we all live together, couldn't we try? I used to be so jealous, green with it, as they say, eaten up. I still am, but couldn't we ride that way, the way the waves, the white horses, ride the sea? When I said it to you, the mere suggestion made you panic, which makes me realize, of course, that you are not able for it, you are not up to it, you are only able for lies, you are only able for deceit.

So one day you will disappear forever. Maybe you have. Isn't there some way of letting me know? I had so many wishes concerning us, but I had one in particular, the smallest most harmless one, and it was this: that one day I would come in from the outside and you would be here, already waiting for me, quite at home, maybe the kettle on or a drink poured. Not an outlandish wish. I suppose you wouldn't have wanted to make the journey without the certainty of seeing me. You said that coming up the street you always wondered what I would look like and what I would be wearing. I wear brown now. I suppose it's to be somber.

After your baby smiled you put her on the swivel chair and I watched her and you watched me, and your friend, whom you'd brought as a safety measure, was watching you watching me, and the baby watched over us all. It was a perfect moment. I know that. None of us wanted it to end. Your friend knew. He knew how much I loved you and maybe he knew how much you loved me, but neither you nor I knew it because we didn't dare to and possibly never will.

Possibly and perhaps—your two favorite words. Damn it. You see, I had just got used to the possibility of nobody, a barren life, when you came along. Of course you don't believe that; you think with all my frocks and my bracelets and my platform shoes that I am always gallivanting. The truth is, I used to. I have collected those garments over the years and that parasol you saw was given to me once on my way to a bullfight. About a year ago—I stopped gallivanting. It is not that I want to be good, no. If anything, I want to be bad, because I would like it to end without its being too sickly.

Endings are hideous. Take flowers, for instance; some go putrid, the very sweetest smelling of all go putrid—so does parsley. I would like it just to shrivel away. It mustn't, though.

The strangest thing is, he lost his parents too at a young age. My father, that is. You see, I am mixing you up with everyone, my father, my mother, my former husband, myself. Could you not come, could you not contact me now, so I could tell you about them, their customs and their ways? The whole parish I know. The lady called Josie walking out for three evenings with a man and saying, "I have no story to tell," meaning was he going to propose to her, and next day he sent for a tray of engagement rings. He must have done it out of fright. Later she went mad. People depend on each other so much. Too much. You listen to me all right, in fact you repeat things that I say. My thoughts are like sprouts, like sprouts on the branch of your brain. Why are you so cold, so silent? Your element is mercury.

All sorts of things remind me of you. On a dump today I saw a remains of a gas cooker and a Christmas tree, though we're bang in the middle of the year. Christmas. That will rankle. You will celebrate it with your family as you did last year. Well anyhow, it looked pathetic, out in the rain—a small gas oven and a Christmas tree with a stump of clay around it. I stood and looked at it. I had a feeling that you might come around the corner, swiftly, the way you do. We would not have needed to say anything, you would have understood. That is the worst thing, that at times you understand.

We were seen twice in public. I hated you buying me drinks, but you refused to allow me to. I wanted to slip you a note but couldn't. As a matter of fact, I lost all my confidence and quite a few of my movements. I was ashamed to remove my coat, even though I was sweating. I thought it would make me seem too much at home, and after all, I had asked you there and you hadn't wanted to come, you had resisted even to the extent that you couldn't think of the name of a pub despite the fact that it was your district, and what I had to do was go there and prowl around and find a quiet one and ring you. You allowed me to ring because she was away, staying with her sister. Her sister is an invalid. You seemed to imply that she had harmed herself. Are they a hysterical family, are they musical? Shall we call her Bimba? I can't use her name, that would be too friendly. I dream of her death, in her sleep, in an airplane crash. Anyhow, in the pub you made me promise, take an oath, that I would never ring again. I took an oath. Is that commendable? I was thinking of you even as I sat there and promised; I was thinking of you, in another state altogether, a former state, a state of grace, a you saying, "I'll always come back to you, always, there's nothing else," and I was thinking of the expression attached to that time, the sad eyes and so forth. Your eyes pierce people. You may say it again with your sad true eyes. Anything may happen, anything.

Anyhow, to get back to my father and yours. There are resemblances and there are differences. Yours loved his wife and died soon after her, to rejoin her in the next world. You felt left out maybe, excluded as a child. In the middle of a family, neither the youngest nor the oldest. My father's parents also died within a short space of one another. Pneumonia. Wintertime and snow at the funeral and snow falling in on the coffin, and then the four children divided up among cousins; the method of division was that each child was told to choose which pony and trap it wanted to be in, and in so doing choose its future home. Not a scrap of love had he. Once when he was sick he hid in the harness room, and when he was found, the woman of the house gave him a good thrashing and then a laxative. Not a scrap of love had he.

Maybe you're like him somewhere in the center of you, maybe you're alike. No, you're not. You're as unalike as chalk and cheese. You have nature. He lacks it. Not many people have nature. And not many people have gentleness. Take my next-door neighbors, they shout and go around in dressing gowns, and as their friends arrive they shout even louder, and the hostess puts on a horrible red raincoat when she wants to go and get something from her car and it happens to be raining. I have a dreadful feeling that she's trying to impress me with her shouting and her car and her rainwear.

It's teeming today. Wouldn't you know. I have a feeling, a very definite feeling that it might not cease, might turn into a second flood. We will all be incarcerated wherever we happen to be. Are you indoors, are you addressing a meeting, are you, or rather were you, on your way to a bus stop and obliged to take shelter under a tree. You said you had no knowledge of ever in your life missing anybody. Yes, I think it might rain forever, or at least for forty days and forty nights. That is a form of ever. I will smash these chandeliers bit by bit. It won't be difficult. They break easily; once when we were washing them, a few of the pieces crumbled. The woman who was helping me couldn't understand why I laughed, neither could I.

She gave me a bit of advice, said by loving you I was closing the door to all other suitors.

Maybe you are in bed making love to her, or just caressing, the curtains drawn. Anyhow, your rooms are so small that if you are indoors you are bound to be very close. I can see it, the little room, the sofa, the cushions, and I never told you this but there are three ornaments in that room identical to three ornaments of mine. I shall not tell you now either, as I am leaving you to guess.

If only we had been more exuberant. I went there three times in all, two of them against your will. The last time I was hungry, as it happened. You offered me nothing. Are you by any chance a miserly man? I dearly wanted a keepsake of you, and true enough, on one of these unfortunate visits you gave me a handkerchief to dry my eyes, but it was a new one and had nothing of your person on it. I cried a lot. I wonder who washed it. You wash your own trousers, because when I inquired about the white round stains on them you said it was where you had spattered on the undiluted bleach. I could have told you. I wish I had them. If I could hold them now—would hold them and hug them and press them to me.

It is not right to love so. I suppose there is a sickness of heart as well as a sickness of mind and body. Yes, when you first came I really had reached a point where I had stopped looking and you appeared at my door with a pamphlet and you were leaving again and I liked the look of you and I invited you in. They call it fate. I still see your face in the windowpane, appearing, disappearing, reappearing. Oh, my God, a face.

*

Don't get married, or if you do, tell me, give me warning so that I can get used to it. I won't give you a wedding present. What an ugly thing to say. Yes, it's ugly. This house is upside down, that drawing room that you saw, well, it's a shambles, and there are glasses lying around and the plants haven't been watered, or if they have, it has been reckless, too much water one day so that they brimmed over, then none for days. There are little pools of water on the floor and those that have dried up have left white marks on the parquet not unlike the bleach on your trousers. How long is it now. My God, it is all a matter of how long it is. The days are jumbled. Just now, lying on my bed—another fatal habit—I saw the tree that I always see, the plane tree, its leaves, and would you believe it, it seemed to me that the bits of sky that I saw through the leaves were leaves also, different-colored leaves, serrated at the edges, so I saw tree leaves and cloud leaves. I am losing my reason. The garden is soggy, a wreck. And although it is summer I definitely smell autumn. I keep thinking that by autumn it will have improved a bit. Then again I think that you will have come back as you threatened to, and that we will be together in the darkest light, under covers, talking, touching, the most terrible reconciliations uttered, uttering. Do you know that in your sleep I stroke and stroke you, and when you waken, no matter how late the hour, you always say, "A lovely way to waken," and you always stayed a few minutes longer, defied time, and yes, come to think of it, those were our most valuable moments. You were at your best then and without fear. I stood at the door to see you off and only once did you look back. I expect you hate farewells.

The last fling I had was not like this at all, except that he was actually hitched, married. An odd fellow. A Harry. We spent five days away from his country and mine, though in a country much similar, dark and craggy and with a heavy rainfall. Some interesting excavations there, skeletons intact in peat. We drove a lot. He told me how he loved his wife, always did, always would. Wives do not come out too badly in the human maul. We had the same thing each day for lunch—salt bread and herrings and a small glass of spirit. When we got to our destination, we had a suite, and one set of windows faced the sea and another set faced the dormitory town. We picked stones the first morning. I found a beautiful white stone, nearly pearl. I wanted to give it to you. I gave it to a friend of yours, a man you brought here. I didn't do it to make you jealous but rather to let you know that if all this weight didn't exist between us I would be able to be nice to you, and maybe you in your turn would be nice to me and even funny and even frivolous. Yes, we once made the noise of turkeys, beeping.

As I got to know this man Harry, he decreased in my estimation. He made a point of telling me about other loves of his and there was always a lot of blood in question. One story of his concerned a very beautiful Spanish virgin, all about her beauty and her moisture, etc. On the very last evening, just as he was consulting the menu for dinner, he said he hoped I had money because he hadn't brought very much. You see, I was ashamed of him and that is why I paid. Whereas when we went to a hotel, you, who could scarcely afford it, paid. And you set the clock twenty minutes before we were due to wake up so that we could be together for one of those lovely moments, those lovely series of moments. Even you, who profess to miss nothing, can you tell me you don't miss those? That morning in the hotel was when you first talked of love and made a plan for the future, our future. That morning you lost your head. You must have imagined yourself as someone else or that you could have explained it all to her, ironed it all out. You were quite practical. You said it would take five weeks, but instead of that you were back in a week and I might have known something was amiss, because you came early and you drank heavily and you said could we talk, could we talk. We talked. You said you had had rows with her, two dirty rows, and then at the very end you said you collapsed into one another.

Sweet Jesus, never have I known such a stab. That collapse, I could actually see it and feel it. I saw the hour, it was dawn, and your tiredness and hers and both of you washed out and one or the other of you saying—it matters not which of you—saying, "What am I saying, what am I doing," and then the collapse, lying down, in your clothes, fitting in a bit of sleep until your baby stirred, and one of you went to tend to it while the other prepared two cups of tea. Maybe while you were shaving you called in and said, "Hey, I hope I didn't give you a black eye." Of course it was not all erased, or indeed forgotten, but it was over, it was behind you, and you had accomplished something, shown your ugly colors and got nearer to one another.

I brought you nearer, God help us. Most probably you went out for the day, maybe you went to the library. But no doubt you said roughly what time you would be back and that is the thing. You made it known that you would be back whatever the hour. That was the second bitterest thing, for there is another.

The evening—one of the three occasions when I telephoned and dropped the phone out of shock and then redialed and later saw you in the pub—I asked if I could have a child of yours. You told me point-blank that it was impossible; also, you inferred that I was too old, what with my divorce and my children reared and all that. Then after a few whiskeys you decided to invite me back to your house, and on the way back you allowed me to link you until we got near your street, and then you ran on ahead so as not to be spied upon and I followed, slightly ashamed, and, as I said, like a dog.

Still, inside the house you were different. The moment you discovered that your baby hadn't smothered itself or wasn't kidnapped or wasn't choking, you kissed me fondly, fond kisses, many of them, and you removed my coat, and later as we fell to talking you said that in the morning you had got someone to mind your child and you had gone to market and bought razor blades and white cotton handkerchiefs, one of which you offered me—and then came the second and bitterest blow, because as you were telling me, I realized that you had had free time, that you could have seen me, that you could have contacted me, that for once you were not tied to her, but you didn't, and I realized that it wasn't she who always came between us. Sometimes it was you.

Guessing my thoughts, you said you loved no one and were interested only in your educational work. When you remember that night, that is, if ever you let loose the hogs of memory, if they stalk, do you remember the subsequent time, the goatskin, you, me, us, perfect then. You can't have forgotten it all. Couldn't you have written? Ah yes, you did. A circumspect little letter about how you mustn't get out of your depth, how it mustn't be allowed to blossom. Well, it didn't. Yes, it did. It blossomed, and what's more, it caught fire, a whole forest of fire.

And another thing, you have softened me toward others. I am prepared to nurse my aged father and my aged mother when the time comes and they call on me. Shall I tell you why. I think by your expression and by one or two things that you say that you did want to be by my side, and constantly, but that a sense of duty restrained you, and a comparison. I needed you less than her. It seems to you that I have advantages over her. Which reminds me, I haven't told you about the boy who died. I feel responsible; no, not responsible, but somehow involved.

The day I met you I also met another good-looking young man, a doctor in fact. He was a new doctor that I had gone to and he took a bit of a shine to me. I'd gone about my depression. A thing I didn't want you to know. He saw how it was and he prescribed accordingly. Later that day I met you, having taken the first set of tablets and already believing that magic was at work.

The young doctor visited me in a private capacity, that is, after I had met you. He kissed me, yes. By then I was so enraptured with you that I was nice to everybody. I let him kiss me. I remember our exact conversation, his describing a Caesarean birth, putting his two hands in and lifting the imaginary baby out. He said Caesarean babies had less gumption because they didn't have to push. He was telling me all this, and I was remarking to myself how deftly his nostrils flared in and out, and then he went a bit far demonstrating this Caesarean to me and I jumped off the cushions. That was another thing. He arranged the cushions for us to loll on. You never did that. You sat at a distance. We talked stiffly. After a long time and nearly always as you were about to leave, you asked if you might come and kiss me, and quite often we met halfway across the room like two animals, little animals charging into one another. Only once did you rebuff me altogether, you said did I have to be so demonstrative. I rushed toward you and embraced you, and you threw me off. You even said that if we did make love it would preclude its ever happening again.

Why did you say that? To punish me for going to your house, for pleading with you. And on the way out I said, "Are you angry" and you said no but that maybe I was, a little. Of course I was. Not a little, a lot. Another time you said, did I have to talk so much. The trouble is, I talked to no one else in between. That is the worst of putting all one's eggs in one basket. I loved your smell. You may have heard it from others, but you smell of gardens, not flower gardens, but herb gardens, and grasses and plants and dock and all those rampant things.

Do you use the same words exactly, and exactly the same caresses, the same touch, the same hesitation, the same fingering? Are you as shy with her as with me? If only you had had courage and a braver heart.

I do believe we would have been happy. It is perhaps foolish to say so, but there was nothing in you that I did not like and admire. Even your faults, even your forgetfulness. There was nothing in you that clashed with me. You were startled once by the flowers, very white flowers they were, with very thick blossoms. You admired them. It was as if you had never seen flowers before, or certainly never seen those. You made me feel as if I had cultivated them, as if they were an extension of me.

I heard from that friend you brought that she is more demanding, makes her needs felt. You found a lack in me. You told me I am kind. I did a favor for your friend, but that was only to woo you.

I am not kind, I cut people off as with the shears, and I drop them, like nettles. At this moment there are several people who could do with my company and I withhold it and that poor cat sits day after day on the window ledge or outside the door and when I open it to take in the milk, that poor black cat tries to slink in, but I kick it with my shoe, in fact, with the heel of my shoe. The same black cat as I held on my breast one night when you came and I was lounging. That was a false moment, but I had to vary things because the previous time you said it was unnatural to spend so many hours over a dinner table and I felt that already it was all getting a bit stale, and I wished in my heart that you would invent something, that you would think up some new plan, some diversion, arrange for us to meet elsewhere. Of course you couldn't. There was a matter of secrecy and shortage of money. When I am short of money I borrow, and to tell you the truth, my debts are catching up with me, but when you are short, you go without. I wanted to give a big cushion to your child. You refused. At the same time as you swore me to secrecy I broke that pledge. I told a few of my women friends, and then you introduced me to a few of your men friends. I think you were showing me off. Come to think of it, we were like children. It is just as well it got nowhere.

Yes, there are times when I think the whole thing seems ridiculous. For instance, the night you were to come to dinner, or rather, one of the nights you were to come to dinner, and after waiting for about two hours I got restless and began to walk back and forth, paced, and did little things, hoping that would speed you up—changed my shoes, brushed my hair, thumped the piano, kept opening and shutting the door. It was winter then and I could tell the seconds passing by a lot of ways but most of all by the candle burning down. It was a blue candle. At length I couldn't bear it any longer, so I turned down the stove—I always had food that could be kept hot—and went out without a coat to wait at the bus stop. And do you know something, there was a moment standing there, an absolute moment, when I mistook someone else for you. Yes, I was convinced. I saw him at the top of the bus, wild hair, the anorak, and then I saw him rise and I saw his back as he went down the stairs of the bus and I got myself ready to smile, to kiss, to reach out my hand, and yes, I was shaking and as excited as if it were you.

I wish it had been. That was the second occasion I went to your house. A very cold reception. You kept on the television. I was prepared to end it, and the next day you appeared out of breath and you sat and you talked and you said how it would all improve and everything would be better between us.

Did you believe that then? I must confess I did. That particular evening, the objects—the room getting dark, the end of the blue candle, the two of us thinking that the worst of our troubles were behind us.

You had to go away the next day. Away. Of course there are ruses for passing the time. I didn't see my friends, alas I have abandoned my friends, but what I did do was to go to cafés where it was very full and very noisy. I searched them out, but no matter how full a café is, there is always room for one, usually at someone else's table. The way they argued or looked into one another's eyes. I was having a rest from you. I could tell the lesbians, even though they couldn't tell, and those who would be together forever and those who wouldn't. I had such a way of seeing into them, such clarity. That is another thing. I often see you as an old man and you are in a trench coat, white with the belt hanging down, one of those stiff trench coats with perforations under the arm, and you are recuperating from some illness and you are, yes, a disillusioned man. It will all be behind you then, she and I, and your daughter and your life's work, and how will you remember it, how?

In those restaurants they play waltzes. I loved the first bars of the waltz. I often stood up to dance, with my mind meandering. Yes, that has been my life of late, restaurants, people saying to each other, "Happy?" and people saying what François said and how much of that hair they should cut.

I did something awful. Friends of mine were going away on a boat forever and I didn't see them off. It was my godson going away forever and I didn't see him off. I thought you might ring and I didn't want to be out.

My lovely godson. I sent him a cup and saucer to the cabin, but it is not the same thing. You see, I had a moment with him, unique; I think it was tantamount to a sexual moment. It was this.

I had been in his house once, or rather, in their garden, and there was a party in full swing. A lot of people, a lot of drinking and jabber, and he and I sat far apart from the others, under a tree, asking riddles. There were flies bothering us and we used to blow them away, and he told me about his dreams when he was always winning, and then he said would I like to walk around, to go out of the garden. And we did that; we went out and walked all around the clapboard fence, and met a lady, a sort of serving lady going in with a platter of strawberries, and he held my hand and squeezed it on and off, and when we got back to our starting point and were just about to go in by the lych-gate he pointed to the nearby woods and told me there was a dirty man in there who pulled down his trousers and showed his butt, and then we hurried in. I didn't see him off.

And another thing, I bought fire irons—don't ask me why, because it's summer—and I tried to beat the lady down about the price. I went to her private house, having got the address from the assistant, and when she opened the door I saw that I was confronted by a hunchback, and still I tried to beat her down about the price. It was nothing. A matter of shillings. I stood there waiting for her to concede and she did. We are to be pitied.

Another haunt of mine is cinemas, before they open. Oh, my God, they have to be seen to be believed. Shabby. Quite a long way from Strauss and the waltzes. Usherettes, mostly elderly ladies and people like myself, killing time in the afternoon. I want all my teeth drawn out of me and other teeth, molars, if you will, stuck back into my gums. I want to grind these new teeth, these molars, to a pulp. Perhaps I want to eat you alive. Ah yes, the seat of this love must indeed be a hate. So the sages would tell me. The hate extends to others. Good friends. How boring they have become. They tell me the shape of their new rooms, or the colors of their walls and what they eat in restaurants. Most terrible bilge. I get listless. Then I get angry. I have to leave right in the middle of their conversation. Mostly I don't see them.

I don't work now. Waiting. It gets on one's nerves. I can keep going a little longer, but only a little. One good thing about being out is that I imagine you telephoning. I exist on that little ploy for hours. I even live your disappointment with you. Your phoning once, then again immediately, then asking the operator to get the number, then phoning again in about an hour and another hour, and concluding that I have gone somewhere, abroad, maybe as far as Morocco, when all the time I am in one of those cafés listening to one of those waltzes, thinking of you, or in one of those cinemas waiting for the performance to start, reading a sign that says FRUITS AND ICES, unable to stop thinking of you. It can't be hate. Do you ever imagine me with another man? You offered me one of your friends once, the night we were all together, here, dancing and cavorting and laughing. Laughing we were. "Why don't you have Mike?" you said. But your arms were all around me, and anyhow, we were on the landing, on our way to bed. Believe me, I even wanted you to feed and drink off me. I wanted to waste away in your service. To be a bone.

Am I saying wanted when I actually mean want? It is still my purpose, still my intention. You forbade me the gift of having your child, and I was too honest or else too cowardly to betray you, to dupe you. Maybe you have taken the plunge, maybe you have got married and that is why you are not showing yourself. You told me once that you muttered something about it. You mutterer. That doctor I mentioned got killed in a plane crash along with a hundred others. You may get killed. Do you know what I hate about myself: I have never done a brave thing, I have never risked death. If only I had done something you could have admired me for. If only I'd renounced you. She is by your side. Your guardian angel, perhaps your little helpmate? Not from what I know of her. You told me little but you inferred a lot. We are so hard on ourselves. Ah yes, those waltzes in those restaurants make me cry, and so do mushrooms. If only I could hear your voice for a minute, half a minute, less. You go from place to place. She is by your side, whether you like it or not. I often imagine you in trains sitting opposite each other, saying the odd word, then getting off, the two of you sharing the carrier cot. What bliss.

Tell me, is she pretty, is she soft, your lady, or does she have what is called a whim of iron? I did ask you once if she had blue eyes and you professed not to know. You must know. It is not that I am a lover of blue eyes, the question simply cropped up. You must have seen them in all lights, and at all moments, maybe even in childbirth. On these numerous train journeys, do you ever think of me? I know you do. I am certain of it. I can feel you thinking of me even now. You may carry the thought through. You may contact me. Yes, he died, that young doctor. I am glad that I didn't make love to him. I would not care to have made love to a dead man. Yes, it got killed between us, you and I. Contravened. That is a fact, a bitter fact. It wasn't that it didn't happen, oh, it did. Oh, how it happened. Your face and mine, your voice and mine. Evening. Just like milking time, and the cows lowing as if we were in the byre. Then the moon came up. Our faces shone. I could have touched the stars. One should be thankful for a moment, even grateful, and not be plaintive like this. Yes, it is nothing short of a miracle, the way you met me, more than halfway. The way you came out of your innerness and complexity and came to me, and I told you things, nonsense things. I told you, for instance, about the one wooden sweet which was mixed up with all the other sweets in a carnival assortment. This wooden sweet had bright wrapping like all the others, and more than once I got it and I didn't know whether to be glad or sorry, and neither of us could tell why it was in the box in the first place, whether it was some sort of joke or the like. And you told me about having to undress at the doctor's and having a dirty vest on, and being scolded by your mother. She was ashamed.

It is when I think about you suffering that I cannot bear it. I think of you crying. You cried lest you could never see me again, and I said you always could and that I would always understand and be womanly and be patient. King Lear says women must be kind, or something to that effect. Yes, that is what I must be, kind and womanly. I know what I will do. I will talk to your friend Mike, the friend you brought here. I will tell him some little pleasantry and he will pass it on to you, and you will be touched, regaled. I will do that now.

Oh, God, I have done it. I rang. He told me. You have gone back to your own country, you have fled. Gone with your family. I knew it. It seems she did something silly like her sister, something extreme. Oh, how mad I was to think that she would give you up, that we would all share. Oh, how cracked one's thoughts get. You did the right thing, the only thing. Yes, I will see you when you are old, just as I visualized it, in the off-white mackintosh with the perforations under the armpit, and you will be convalescing. I suppose you're married. And yes; you have no nature. Oh, God, send me some word, some sign, some token. Tell me if you are married, or if you've forgotten, tell me how you are. It has all been disastrous, tell me something, I have to know . . . I will never know, I do not want to know now.

The Creature

She was always referred to as the Creature by the townspeople, the dressmaker for whom she did buttonholing; the sacristan, who used to search for her in the pews on the dark winter evenings before locking up; and even the little girl Sally, for whom she wrote out the words of a famine song. Life had treated her rottenly, yet she never complained but always had a ready smile, so that her face, with its round rosy cheeks, was more like something you could eat or lick; she reminded me of nothing so much as an apple fritter.

I used to encounter her on her way from devotions or from Mass, or having a stroll, and when we passed she smiled, but she never spoke, probably for fear of intruding. I was doing a temporary teaching job in a little town in the west of Ireland and soon came to know that she lived in a tiny house facing a garage that was also used by the town's undertaker. The first time I visited her, we sat in the parlor and looked out on the crooked lettering on the door. There seemed to be no one in attendance at the station. A man helped himself to petrol. Nor was there any little muslin curtain to obscure the world, because, as she kept repeating, she had washed it that very day and what a shame. She gave me a glass of rhubarb wine, and we shared the same chair, which was really a wooden seat with a latticed wooden back that she had got from a rubbish heap and had varnished herself. After varnishing it, she had dragged a nail over the wood to give a sort of mottled effect, and you could see where her hand had shaken, because the lines were wavery.

I had come from another part of the country; in fact, I had come to get over a love affair, and since I must have emanated some sort of sadness, she was very much at home with me and called me dearest when we met and when we were taking leave of one another. After correcting the exercises from school, filling in my diary, and going for a walk, I would knock on her door and then sit with her in the little room almost devoid of furniture—devoid even of a plant or a picture—and oftener than not, I would be given a glass of rhubarb wine and sometimes a slice of porter cake. She lived alone and had done so for seventeen years. She was a widow and had two children. Her daughter was in Canada; the son lived about four miles away. She had not set eyes on him for the seventeen years—not since his wife had slung her out—and the children that she had seen as babies were big now and, as she heard, marvelously handsome. She had a pension and once a year made a journey to the southern end of the country, where her relatives lived in a cottage looking out over the Atlantic.

Her husband had been killed two years after their marriage, shot in the back of a lorry, in an incident that was later described by the British Forces as regrettable. She had had to conceal the fact of his death and the manner of his death from her own mother, since her mother had lost a son about the same time, also in combat; and on the very day of her husband's funeral, when the chapel bells were ringing and reringing, she had to pretend it was for a traveling man, a tinker, who had died suddenly.

She and her husband had lived with her mother. She reared her children in the old farmhouse, eventually told her mother that she, too, was a widow, and as women together they worked and toiled and looked after the stock and milked and churned and kept a sow to whom she gave the name of Bessie. Each year the bonhams would become pets of hers, and follow her along the road toward the chapel or wherever, and to them, too, she gave pretty names. A migrant workman helped in the summer months, and in the autumn he would kill the pig for their winter meat. The killing of the pig always made her sad, and she reckoned she could hear those roars—each successive roar—over the years, and she would dwell on that, and then tell how a particular naughty pig stole into the house one time and lapped up the bowls of cream and then lay down on the floor, snoring and belching like a drunken man. The workman slept downstairs on the settle bed, got drunk on Saturdays, and was the cause of an accident; when he was teaching her son to shoot at targets, the boy shot off three of his own fingers. Otherwise, her life had passed without incident.

When her children came home from school, she cleared half the table for them to do their exercises—she was an untidy woman—then every night she made blancmange for them, before sending them to bed. She used to color it red or brown or green, as the case may be, and she marveled at these coloring essences almost as much as the children themselves did. She knitted two sweaters each year for them—two identical sweaters of bawneen wool—and she was indeed the proud mother when her son was allowed to serve at Mass.

Her finances suffered a dreadful setback when her entire stock contracted foot-and-mouth disease, and to add to her grief, she had to see the animals that she so loved die and be buried around the farm, wherever they happened to stagger down. Her lands were disinfected and empty for over a year, and yet she scraped enough to send her son to boarding school and felt lucky in that she got a reduction of the fees because of her reduced circumstances. The parish priest had intervened on her behalf. He admired her and used to joke her on account of the novelettes she so cravenly read. Her children left, her mother died, and she went through a phase of not wanting to see anyone—not even a neighbor—and she reckoned that was her Garden of Gethsemane. She contracted shingles, and one night, dipping into the well for a bucket of water, she looked first at the stars, then down at the water, and thought how much simpler it would be if she were to drown. Then she remembered being put into the well for sport one time by her brother, and another time having a bucket of water douched over her by a jealous sister, and the memory of the shock of these two experiences and a plea to God made her draw back from the well and hurry up through the nettle garden to the kitchen, where the dog and the fire, at least, awaited her. She went down on her knees and prayed for the strength to press on.

Imagine her joy when, after years of wandering, her son returned from the city, and announced that he would become a farmer and that he was getting engaged to a local girl who worked in the city as a chiropodist. Her gift to them was a patchwork quilt and a special border of cornflowers she planted outside the window, because the bride-to-be was more than proud of her violet-blue eyes and referred to them in one way or another whenever she got the chance. The Creature thought how nice it would be to have a border of complementary flowers outside the window, and how fitting, even though *she* preferred wallflowers, both for their smell and their softness. When the young couple came home from the honeymoon, she was down on her knees weeding the bed of flowers, and looking up at the young bride in her veiled hat, she thought an oil painting was no lovelier or no more sumptuous. In secret, she hoped that her daughter-in-law might pare her corns after they had become intimate friends.

Soon, she took to going out to the cowshed to let the young couple be alone, because even by going upstairs she could overhear. It was a small house, and the bedrooms were directly above the kitchen. They quarreled constantly. The first time she heard angry words she prayed that it be just a lovers' quarrel, but such spiteful things were said that she shuddered and remembered her own dead partner and how they had never exchanged a cross word between them. That night she dreamed she was looking for him, and though others knew of his whereabouts, they would not guide her. It was not long before she realized that her daughter-in-law was cursed with a sour and grudging nature. A woman who automatically bickered over everything—the price of eggs, the best potato plants to put down, even the fields that should be pasture and those that should be reserved for tillage. The women got on well enough during the day, but rows were inevitable at night when the son came in and, as always, the Creature went out to the cowshed or down the road while things transpired. Up in her bedroom, she put little swabs of cotton wool in her ears to hide whatever sounds might be forthcoming. The birth of their first child did everything to exacerbate the young woman's nerves, and after three days the milk went dry in her breasts. The son called his mother out to the shed, lit a cigarette for himself, and told her that unless she signed the farm and the house over to him he would have no peace from his young barging wife.

This the Creature did soon after, and within three months she was packing her few belongings and walking away from the house where she had lived for fifty-eight of her sixty years. All she took was her clothing, her Aladdin lamp, and a tapestry denoting ships on a hemp-colored sea. It was an heirloom. She found lodgings in the town and was the subject of much curiosity, then ridicule, because of having given her farm over to her son and daughter-in-law. Her son defected on the weekly payments he was supposed to make, but though she took the matter to her solicitor, on the appointed day she did not appear in court and as it happened spent the entire night in the chapel, hiding in the confessional.

Hearing the tale over the months, and how the Creature had settled down and made a soup most days, was saving for an electric blanket, and much preferred winter to summer, I decided to make the acquaintance of her son, unbeknownst to his wife. One evening I followed him to the field, where he was driving a tractor. I found a sullen, middle-aged man, who did not condescend to look at me but proceeded to roll his own cigarette. I recognized him chiefly by the three missing fingers and wondered pointlessly what they had done with them on that dreadful day. He was in the long field where she used to go twice daily with buckets of separated milk, to feed the suckling calves. The house was to be seen behind some trees, and because of either secrecy or nervousness he got off the tractor, crossed over, and stood beneath a tree, his back balanced against the knobbled trunk. It was a little hawthorn, and somewhat superstitious, I hesitated to stand under it. Its flowers gave a certain dreaminess to the otherwise forlorn place. There is something gruesome about plowed earth, maybe because it suggests the grave.

He seemed to know me, and he looked, I thought, distastefully at my patent boots and my tweed cape. He said there was nothing he could do, that the past was the past, and that his mother had made her own life in the town. You would think she had prospered or remarried, his tone was so caustic when he spoke of "her own life." Perhaps he had relied on her to die. I said how dearly she still held him in her thoughts, and he said that she always had a soft heart and, if there was one thing in life he hated, it was the sodden handkerchief.

With much hedging, he agreed to visit her, and we arranged an afternoon at the end of that week. He called after me to keep it to myself, and I realized that he did not want his wife to know. All I knew about his wife was that she had grown withdrawn, that she had had improvements made on the place—larger windows and a bathroom installed—and that they were never seen together, not even on Christmas morning at chapel.

By the time I called on the Creature that eventful day, it was long after school, and as usual, she had left the key in the front door for me. I found her dozing in the armchair, very near the stove, her book still in one hand and the fingers of the other hand fidgeting as if she were engaged in some work. Her beautiful embroidered shawl was in a heap on the floor, and the first thing she did when she wakened was to retrieve it and dust it down. I could see that she had come out in some sort of heat rash, and her face resembled nothing so much as a frog's, with her little raisin eyes submerged between pink swollen lids.

At first she was speechless; she just kept shaking her head. But eventually she said that life was a crucible, life was a crucible. I tried consoling her, not knowing what exactly I had to console her about. She pointed to the back door and said things were kiboshed from the very moment he stepped over that threshold. It seems he came up the back garden and found her putting the finishing touches to her hair. Taken by surprise, she reverted to her long-lost state of excitement and could say nothing that made sense. "I thought it was a thief," she said to me, still staring at the back door, with her cane hanging from a nail there.

When she realized who he was, without giving him time to catch breath, she plied both food and drink on him, and I could see that he had eaten nothing, because the ox tongue in its mold of jelly was still on the table, untouched. A little whiskey bottle lay on its side, empty. She told me how he'd aged and that when she put her hand up to his gray hairs he backed away from her as if she'd given him an electric shock. He who hated the soft heart and the sodden handkerchief must have hated that touch. She asked for photos of his family, but he had brought none. All he told her was that his daughter was learning to be a mannequin, and she put her foot in it further by saying there was no need to gild the lily. He had newspapers in the soles of his shoes to keep out the damp, and she took off those damp shoes and tried polishing them. I could see how it all had been, with her jumping up and down trying to please him but in fact just making him edgy. "They were drying on the range," she said, "when he picked them up and put them on." He was gone before she could put a shine on them, and the worst thing was that he had made no promise concerning the future. When she asked, "Will I see you?" he had said, "Perhaps," and she told me that if there was one word in the English vocabulary that scalded her, it was the word "perhaps."

"I did the wrong thing," I said, and though she didn't nod, I knew that she also was thinking it—that secretly she would consider me from then on a meddler. All at once I remembered the little hawthorn tree, the bare plowed field, his heart as black and unawakened as the man I had come away to forget, and there was released in me, too, a gigantic and useless sorrow. Whereas for twenty years she had lived on that last high tightrope of hope, it had been taken away from her, leaving her without anyone, without anything, and I wished that I had never punished myself by applying to be a sub in that stagnant, godforsaken little place.

The House of My Dreams

She hurried home from the neighbor's house to have a few spare moments to herself. The rooms were stripped, the windows bare, the dust and the disrepair of the ledges totally revealed, everything gone except for the few things she insisted on taking herself—a geranium, a ewer, and a few little china coffee cups that miraculously had escaped being broken. There was a broom against the wall—a soft green twig that scarcely grazed the floor or penetrated to the rubble adhering there. Neighbors were good the day one moved house. No, that was not fair. She had had good neighbors, and a variety of them. She had spent nights with them, got drunk with some of them, slept with one of them and later regretted it, quarreled with one of them, and with another had made a definite plan to have a walk in the country once a week, but excuses always intervened, hers and the woman's.

She went to the children's room and hollered, "Hey, around the corner, po-po, waiting for Henry Lee." This was the room where, nightly, her children used to squabble over who would have the top bunk, and where she brought cups of hot milk, thick with honey, for the colds and congestions they did not have, and where her older son used to enjoy looking up at the skylight, listening to the rain go pitter-patter, hoping for the snow to fall, listening (though one cannot hear it) to the sun coming up and lighting the pane of glass, watching the gradual change from dark sheet to transparent sheet, and then to a resemblance of something dipped in a quick wash of bright morning gold. Her son had dreamed that there were pink flamingos in a glass, a glass that he was drinking from, and that they were there because of a special bacteria in the water. That pink, or rather those multiples of feathered pink, layer upon layer, could compare with no color that he had ever seen. He feasted on it.

The room was empty except for the marks of casters, the initial J daubed on the wall, and the various stains. When she repeated, "Hey, around the corner, po-po," there was not the slightest hint of an echo. Ah yes! The children had ritually buried a coin under one of the loose floorboards, and no doubt it was down there somewhere; in its hole, covered in dust and maybe smeared with cobwebs.

The night she had served their father with a custody writ, she had gone all around the house and lifted off the telephone receivers and watched them where they lay, somehow like numbed animals, black things or white things, or a red thing, that had gone temporarily dead. In the middle of the night her husband came and slipped the threatening letter in under the hall door (she had nailed down the letter box), and she was there cowering and waiting for it, the letter saying, "They are mine, they are not yours, you are going to be a nervous corpse if you take this to court, you gain nothing except your gross humiliation, you are bound to lose, I cannot show you any mercy, I am really determined to do everything within the law to get custody of those children, no holds barred." She had read it and reread it and wrung her hands and wondered how she could have married such a man.

Another time she had waited in the hall, being too shy to stand at the window, and at intervals had pushed the letter box open to peep out into space. She was waiting for a man who did not appear. They happened to have the same birthday, and that factor, along with his smile, made her think somehow he would come, and listening for the car or the taxi, she had found herself in a particular stance, a stance repeated from long ago, waiting behind a window in a flannel nightgown for a man, her father, who anyhow might thrash her to death. It was as if all those past states only begged to be repeated, to be relived, to go on forever and ever, amen. Those things were like shackles that bound her.

•

The house had been her fortress. And yet there were snags. The time when a total stranger knocked, a tall thin man, asking if he could have a word with her, stepping inside onto the rubber mat and telling her that he had no intention of leaving her alone. It happened to be late spring, and he was framed by the hawthorn tree, and looking at it, and the soft nearly emergent petals, she thought, If I pretend not to be in the least bit afraid, he will go away. That was what she did—stared at the tree, giving the impression that someone else was in the house, that she was not petrified, that she was not stranded, not alone. He repeated his intention, then she dismissed him, saying, "We will see about that," and she closed the door very quietly. But back in the house she began to tremble and was too incapacitated even to lift the telephone to call anyone; then when she heard his footsteps go away, she lay down on the floor and wondered why it was that she could not have talked to him, but she knew why it was, because she was petrified of such people. They were usually fanatical, they had a funny stare, and they laughed at things that were no laughingstock. The first such person she had ever come across had been a woman, a tall streelish creature whose mania gave her a wild energy, made her stalk fields, roads, byroads, lanes, made her rap on people's doors at all hours of the day and night, insult them about their jobs, their self-importance, their furniture, and everything that they had taken to be enhancing. She could not have appeared casual for fear he might strangle her, or misbehave, treat the floor as a lavatory, or, worse, split her head. She had the glass changed, so that she was enabled to see out but no caller could see in. He came a few times but was told to scarper by a builder who was in her employment.

It had been a nice lunch, delicate—poached eggs and leaf spinach. When she sat down the neighbor handed her a linen napkin and said, "There you are, pet." They drank wine, they clinked glasses, they recalled Christmases, numerous parties, the Scottish boy whom they both fancied and deceived each other over. At the time it had rankled. She herself had met him on the road one morning, by the merest chance, and he had the temerity to tell her he had been looking for a hardware shop, although it was a street solely of private houses. But that was well behind her. The garden would go on blooming. The Virginia creeper would attach itself to everything and finally encumber everything. She had put down three trees, numerous creepers, herbs, and wonderful bright shrubs that defied the nourishless London soil. She would recall the garden in times to come, the evenings sitting out on the low wall, looking at the river, or again at the blocks of flats on the opposite side, feeling the vibrations of the distant tube train go right through her stomach and her bowels, admiring the flowers, and sometimes getting down to stake up a rose that had straggled and bowed along the ground. It had been a home. "No place like home," her parents used to say whenever they went away from their ramshackle farm, to be ill, or to shop for a day, or, in the case of her father, to go on binges.

She went up to her bedroom. Nothing left of its character but the wallpaper. Beige wallpaper with bosses of red roses, each rose like an embryo bud, and all intricately joined by stems that were as thin as thread and on the point of raveling. Not many people had seen her bedroom, but those who had were still in it, like ghosts, specters, frozen in the positions that they had once unthinkingly occupied. There was a boy, blond, freckled, who had never made love to her but had harbored some true feelings for her. He always used to arrive with a group, but almost always got too drunk to go home, and once, though not drunk, felt disinclined to go home and took off his boots by the fire, and held the soles of his feet toward it, asking if by any chance seers read feet, if feet had lines of destiny just like hands. She thought that maybe shyness had deterred him, or maybe distaste. He used to talk in the early morning, the very early morning, touching the stems of the roses with his forefinger, watching the careens of the birds through the window and the course of the river beyond. People used to envy her that view of the river. Yes, it was a shame to leave. At night because of the aspect of the water and its lap, it often seemed as if it were another city altogether, and now just as the trees were beginning to grow she was leaving it all behind. She ought to desecrate it, do some misdeed, such as at school when they got holidays and used to throw compasses and chalk about, used to chant, "Kick up tables, kick up chairs, kick Sister So-and-so down the stairs, no more Latin, no more French, no more sitting on a hard old bench." But those were the carefree days, or seemed to be.

I am loath to leave, she thought, and dragged the broom over the bare wood floor. Dust rose out of nowhere, so she filled a coffee cup with water and spattered it over the floor to keep the motes down. Once, during a very special party, she thought that the freckled boy must not be coming, and then just as her hopes were dashed, he arrived with a new girl, a girl not unlike herself, but younger, tougher, and more self-assured. The girl had asked for cigars immediately, and strode around the room smoking a cigar, telling all the men that she knew they lusted after her. She was both clever and revolting. At the end of the night there were only the three of them left and they sat in a little huddle. He was right in the throes of a sentence, when all of a sudden he fell fast asleep, the way children do, leaving the two of them to watch over him, which they did like vultures. Together they removed his high boots, his suede jacket, and his outer sweater. When at last the girl fell asleep, she herself went around her own house, stacking glasses, thinking it had been a good party, primarily because he was there. And occasionally, even in those very early days, things would suddenly become otherwise, and her heart would predict a disaster. She would forget a name, even her own name, or a cigarette butt in a glass would be enlarged a hundredfold, and once, the violets came out of a brooch and it seemed to her they were exuding either sweat or tears. The cheeky girl rang her mother the moment she wakened and asked how Kafka, her dog, was. Then she borrowed money and, walking away from him with a strut, said, "Isn't he chubby," his function in her life now completed.

The children used to have parties too, birthday parties, where all the glasses of diluted orange would be lined up on the tray, and the piles of paper hats towered into a cone; and later meringue crumbs would be sent flying about the place and some children would be found crying because they had not gone to the lavatory. It was worst when they left to go away to boarding school—empty rooms, empty beds, and two bicycles just lying there in the shed. They would come home for holidays and there would be the usual bustle again, various garments left on the various steps of the stairs, but it was always as if they were visitors, and gradually the house began to have something of the chilliness of a tomb.

But she met the holy man, and having talked to him at length, and hearing his creed, she asked him to join her, to come under her roof. The very first evening, however, she had a premonition, because when he arrived at the appointed hour, and with his rucksack, she saw that he had a black scarf draped over his head, and when she caught sight of him in the doorway he looked like nothing so much as a harlot, his Asiatic features sharply defined, his eyes like darts and full of expectation. They sat by the fire; she served the casserole, bringing a little table close for him to balance his plate on. He even drank some wine. He told her of his daydream to go by boat down the French canals, throughout the length of a summer. When the time came to retire it seemed to her that he let out some sort of whimper.

Once in her bedroom, she locked her door and began to tremble. She had just embarked on another catastrophe. On his way to bed he coughed loudly, and it seemed to her that he lingered on the landing, just outside her door. She was inside, cringing, listening. She seemed to be always listening, cringing, in some bed, or under some bed, or behind some pile of furniture, or behind a door that was weighed down with overcoats and trench coats. She seemed to be always the culprit, although in truth the other person was the killer.

In the morning the holy man slipped a note under her bedroom door to say she was to join him the moment she wakened, as they did not want to lose a moment of their precious time together. She greeted him coldly in the kitchen, but already she could see that he was hanging on her words, on her looks, and on her every gesture. After three days it was intolerable. His sighs filled the house, and the rooms that were tolerably cheerful with flowers and pretty objects, these too began to accumulate a sadness. She found herself hiding, anywhere, in the lavatory, in the garden shed, in the park, even though it was bitter cold. He would rush with a towel and slippers whenever she came in and had some mush ready, which he insisted she eat. He called her "Angel" and used this endearment at every possible moment. The neighbors said he would have to go. She knew he would have to go.

The day she told him, he said it was his greatest fear realized, that of becoming happy at long last—his wife had died ten years before—only to be robbed of it. He broke down, said how he had dreamed of bringing her up the French canals, of buoying her with cushions so that she could see the countryside, loving her and caring for her and lulling her to sleep.

On the day of his departure he wrote a note saying that he would stay in his room, his "hole," as he called it, and not bother her, and not require any food, and leave quietly at four as arranged. At lunchtime she called him to partake of a soup she had made. He was in his saffron robe, all neat and groomed, like a man about to set out on a journey. But he was shivering, and his eyes had a veil over them, a heavy veil of tears. He sat and dragged the spoon through the thick potato soup, and at first she thought that it must be some way of cooling it, but as the time went by she saw that it was merely a ploy to fiddle with it, like a child.

He did not say a word. She clapped her hands and, much too raucously, said, "Hey diddle diddle, the cat and the fiddle, the cow jumped over the moon; the little dog laughed to see such sport, and the dish ran away with the spoon." He looked at her as if she had gone mad. She said, "Please don't take it so badly." He said she was the second person he had ever loved, said how his wife had been a European, too, sired in a dark wet country, a lover of rain and a lover of music. He loved nothing Asiatic, nothing related to his own land, not even the sunshine or the bright colors or the smells that pervaded the air of Bombay. His destiny was his dead wife, and now her.

Anger overtook her so that she wanted to beat him with the spoon, grind his face into the mush of soup, she wanted to humiliate him. When she was clearing away the dishes, he said again that he would stay in his "hole" and leave quietly at four. But when the clock struck she waited for his footsteps on the stairs, and then along the hall, but she waited in vain. She prayed to God that he would go.

At five she decided that he must have killed himself; before going up, she took the precaution to call in the neighbor. Together they climbed the stairs, smoking vigorously, manifesting a display of courage. He was sitting in the middle of the floor with his rucksack on, his head lowered. He appeared to be praying. He said "Angel" and how he must have lost track of time. Then he said that it was too late to go and that he would postpone his departure until the morrow.

Eventually she had to call the police; upon leaving he handed her a note which said that he would never get in touch with her, never ever, but telling her where he would be at each and every given hour. He was taking employment as cook, and he wrote his employer's number, stressing that he would be there at all hours, except when he intended to travel by bus, two afternoons a week, to take guitar lessons. Then he gave her the various possible numbers of the guitarist, who had no fixed abode. Next morning another letter was slipped under the door, and so each morning faithfully until he died seven days later. She refused to admit her guilt.

Soon after, she decided to have the renovations done—kitchen and living room made into one, a big picture window, to afford a grander view of the river, and a stained-glass window in which a medley of colors could interact as they did in the church windows seen long ago. The cubes and the circles and the slithers of light that had fascinated her in childhood were still able to repossess her at a moment's flounder. Like the knots, and the waits, and the various sets of chattering teeth. Other things, too—shouts, murmurs, screams, an elderly drunk falling down a stair, his corpse later laid out in an off-white monkish habit, on a wrought-iron bed, and she herself being told that he had died of pneumonia, that he had not died of a fall.

So many puzzling things were said, things that contradicted one another. They congratulated you for singing, then told you never to open your gob again as long as you lived. Your tongue was not your friend, it was too thick and unwieldy, it doubled back in your throat, it parched, it longed for lozenges. Yes, rows, and the prefaces to rows, and thumpings and beatings and the rash actions of your sister, the flighty one, going out at night, winter night, with blue satin knickers on, which she had stolen, going to a certain gateway, to cavort with a traveling creamery manager, coming in long after midnight and trying desperately not to be heard, but being heard and thrashed fiercely.

For some curious reason creaks are more pronounced in the dark, and her sister was always heard and always badly punished, so that there were cries after midnight and don't, don't, don't. Her sister bled on that stair; then soon after her mother, her father, a clergyman, and two other important men interrogated her about her private life. Her sister denied everything, just stayed there, glued to the damp area of the stairs. Then the next day, her mother, her sister, and she walked along a hedged road, and every minute her sister was cross-examined, and every minute she denied the accusations and said she was a virgin. They were on their way to another doctor, a doctor who did not know them. When they passed an orchard, the little apples were already formed on the trees and they were desperately bright, but hard and inedible. Her sister had been found to have lied—had tried to abort herself, was sent to the Magdalen laundry for the five remaining months, and had her bitter confinement there.

But there had been consoling things, too—treats. On Sundays a trifle left to set on the other side of the stained-glass panel, a trifle in a big pudding bowl, left down on tiles to cool. She would go down the stairs in her nightdress, creep, go through the glass door, squat on those tiles, and scoop out some of the lovely cold jollop with her hands, and swallow it. It was cakey. Later it would be covered over with a layer of whipped cream, then sprinkled with hundreds and thousands—sparklets which would shine away as they were being swallowed. She never got a walloping for that misdemeanor, because in her mother's eyes she was a little mite. On the other hand, her father punished her for everything, particularly for sleeping in her mother's bed. When her father got in, she tried not to look, not to listen, not to see, not to hear, and not to be. She moved over to the wall, smelled the damp of the paper, and could even smell the mortar behind the paper. There were mice in that room. They scuttled. Shame, shame, shame. Always for one second, a dreadful swoon used to overwhelm her, too. Her bones and every bit of her dissolved. Then she contracted and steadied herself.

After her father went back to his own bed, she and her mother ate the chocolate sweets, little brown buttons. They used to melt on the tongue, like Holy Communion. They were so soothing and so satisfying after the onslaught. Then the worst was over for a week or so, until it happened again.

On one side of the bed was a lattice, and when a finger was put through, it was like a finger being dispatched into space. Fingers alone could do nothing, but fingers seamed to knuckles, belonging to palms, to wrists and to arms, could stir cakes or pound potatoes, or shake the living daylights out of someone, out of one's own self. One's lights were in there, residing, not as an illumination, but as offal. Lights that were given to dogs, to curs, and did not show the way as did a lamp or a lantern.

Saturday mornings were languor time. Her mother brought her tea and fingers of toast. The sun would be streaming through the blind, making shapes and gestures, warming the weeping, historied walls, the dark linoleum would be lit up, the dust rambling all over it, the dust an amusement in itself, while out on the landing the sun beamed through a stained-glass window, resulting in a different pattern altogether. Happily she munched on those fingers of toast. Even the stone hot-water bottle that had gone cold became a source of pleasure as she pressed on it with her feet and pushed it right down to the rungs of the brass bed and threatened to eject it. When her father threatened her with the slash hook, her nostrils went out like angel's wings, and she sped with prodigal speed over three marsh fields to a neighbor's house, to one of the cottagers who was stirring damson jam, while at the same time giving her husband a bath in the aluminum tub. They laughed at her because of the way she shook and asked if perhaps she had seen the banshee.

"No, pet, no one can help you, you can only help yourself," the neighbor had said. Was that true? Would that always be true?

She went into her empty bathroom. The woodwork was as new and blond as in a showroom, and the bar of almond-shaped soap hanging from the tap asked to be used. She whispered things. She looked at the shower, its beautiful blue trough and the glass-fronted door. They had taken a shower together, she and a new man, a hulky fellow. She hung his shirt over the glass door to serve as a sort of screen. She came and came. He was so good-looking, and so heavy, and so warm, and so urgent as he pressed upon her that she thought she might burst, like fruit. It was such a pity that he turned out to be crass. "Let's get married," he said at once.

She brought him to Paris, and in the hotel room he made himself at home, threw his belongings about, started to swagger, ordered the most expensive champagne, and booked two long-distance telephone calls. Her children were in the adjoining suite. They had not wanted him to come, but remembering the pleasure in the shower, that full knob of flesh inside her, truer, more persuasive than words or deeds, the scalding half happiness, she had let him accompany them, knowing she could not afford it, knowing that he would cadge. The moment he used her toothbrush she knew. She went out to the chemist to buy another, and he said what a pity that she hadn't bought him some after-shave.

She could not sleep with him again. She went down and reserved another room for him, a cheaper room. They quarreled disgracefully. He picked up the telephone and asked the telephonist would she like him to come down and fuck her. He said he was "bad news" but that bad news traveled like wildfire. He moved to the other room but would not leave them alone. He followed them wherever they went, and hence the visit was ruined. He rang her saying he was a health officer and had to look at her cunt. He ordered the costliest wines from the cellars, and she was certain he would steal furniture or linen. It was a beautiful hotel with circular rooms, and little separated balconies on each landing, affording a view into the well of the hall. The bathroom was like a sitting room, with even a chaise for lying on, and the walls were a lovely warm pink. It was a dry paint, like a powder, and the walls were warm to nestle against. She sat on the chaise and very formally cursed him.

In the maid's room she stood over the washbasin. That was one room she had neglected. The washbasin was an eyesore. Would the new people have it mended or have it removed? The new owner was a doctor, and there would be a sign chalked up on the pavement saying DOCTOR—IN CONSTANT USE. The Spanish maid had been a nice girl but a slut. She used to do old-fashioned things like plait her hair at night, or press her clothes by putting them under the mattress. They used to talk a lot, were chatterboxes. The first day the maid arrived was in January, and the children were playing snowballs and had just acquired a new dog. The new dog left little piddles all over the floor, tiny yellow piddles, no bigger than a capsule, and the dinner was especially special because of the new girl, and the children were as bright as cherries, what with the exercise and having been pasted with snowballs and the excitement of a new dog.

The girl had had a mad father who broke clocks, and a mother who pampered her. She came from a small town in the north of Spain, where there was nothing to do in the evenings except go for a walk with other girls. The girl ironed her hair to straighten it, and took camomile tisane for her headaches. They exchanged dreams. In the mornings she used to go to the girl's room, sit at the foot of the bed, and take a long time deciding what she should wear that day.

The girl began to dream in English, dreamed of cats, shoals of cats, coming through the window, miaowing, and of herself trying to get the latch closed, trying to push them back. The girl got spoiled, stayed in bed three or four certain days of each month, left banana skins under her pillow, neglected her laundry, and never took the hairs out of her brush or comb. Eventually she had to go. Another parting. So also the little dog, because although house-trained, he developed a nervous disease which made him whine all the time, even in sleep, and made him grit his little teeth and grind them, and grind most things.

It was not long after that something began to go awry. She got the first sniff of it, like a foretaste, and it was a sniff as of blood freshly drawn. Yet it was nothing. There was a space where the small bay window had been. The builder had hung a strip of sacking there, but she was certain something would come through, not simply a burglar, or wind, or rain, but some catastrophe, some unknown, a beast of prey. Whenever she entered that room she felt that something had just vacated it. A wolf, she thought. It made people laugh. "A wolf," they said, "the proverbial big bad wolf." She rummaged through her old books for a copy of *Red Riding Hood* but could not find it. She could remember it. It was a cloth book with serrated edges. The edges were cut carefully, so that the book did not ravel. She saw the little specks of cloth that had been ripped out, in a heap on the floor, colored like confetti.

When the big new window was delivered, that hall door had to be taken off its hinges. Six men carried it through, each one bossing the other, telling the other to get a move on, to move on, for Christ's sake, to do this, to do that, to watch it, watch it. She saw it break into smithereens a hundred times over, but in fact it wasn't until it was in, and well puttied, that she realized what a risk they had taken. She opened a bottle of whiskey, and they drank, looking out at the river, which happened on that day to have the sheen and consistency of liquid paraffin. It was like a bright skin over the brown water. She imagined spoons of it being donated to loads of constipated tourists who went by on the pleasure boats.

Naturally, there was a party to christen the room. Would that have been the time that he brought the insolent girl, who had a dog called Kafka, or was that another time? They were all jumbled together, those parties, those times, like the dishes stacked on the long refectory table, or the bottles of wine, or the damp gold champagne labels, or the beautiful entrées. Perfection and waste.

She placed two men together, whereupon one took offense, thinking he was assumed to be a homosexual. She had to bring him out into the garden and in the moonlight solemnly tell him that she had not been sensitive, that she was careless, a bad hostess. He was full of umbrage. He said he should not have come. She knew that he would never be invited again. A foreign woman stayed on, and they drank a bit and picked at the food and drank more, and lay down on the mat by the dying fire. Even the embers were gray. She puffed on it, and slowly one coal came to life, then another. Without thinking about it, she began to caress the woman and soon realized that she was well on the way to seducing her.

It was a strange sensation, as if touching gauze, or some substance that was about to vanish into thin air. Like the clocks of dandelions that were and then were not, fugitive dandelions vanishing, running away, everything running away, everything escaping its former state.

The woman asked her to go on, to please go on. She thought of other loves, other touches, and it was as if all these things were getting added together in her, like numbers being totted up in a vast cash register, poor numbers that would never be able to be separated.

She did go on, and then her own eyes swam in her head, and for no reason she recalled the transparent paper that her mother used to apply to the lower halves of windowpanes, paper with patterns of butterflies and the consistency of water when dampened. They were both wet. Her fingers inside the woman would leave a telltale for all time.

They didn't know what to say. The woman spoke about her chap, what a regular maniac he was. Then the woman told her some facts about her sordid childhood in Cairo, about being a little girl, constantly raped by uncles and cousins, and great-uncles, and great-great-uncles, and with each similar revelation she would say, "Horrible eh, horrible eh."

The woman had lived through wars, had half starved, had eaten cactus root, had been bruised and beaten by soldiers, and hideous though these events were, they had not made her deep or brave, they had not penetrated to her. She was like any other woman at the tail end of a party, a little drunk, a little fatigued, soured about her fate.

The little dog bared his eyeteeth at them. He knew he was being put down before it happened, hence bit doors, wainscotting, and the legs of chairs, bit avidly in anticipation of his fate. She hadn't told the children until it was over. They cried. Then they forgot.

But did they forget? They, too, had brimming hearts. Children's hearts broke, but they did not know that for a long time. One day they discovered it, and then it was as if some part of them had been removed unthinkingly, on a ritual operating table.

Soon after that she caught the illness, or rather, it descended on her, an escalating fever. It centered in the throat, the nose, and behind the eyes, and everything about her felt raw. The neighbor used to come to see her, bring Bovril in a thermos, and the doctor came twice a day. But when they were gone it used to possess her again, that hound of terror. Would her heart be plucked out of her body, would the roof fall in, would a rat come out of its hiding? She often saw one, on the head of the bed, on the bedknob, poised, bristling.

A girl she'd known had had a rat in her bedroom that got killed by a cat, after hours and hours of play, and had witnessed the last screeching tussle, the leaps, then described the remains—a little heart of dry triangular flesh and a string which was the tail. The girl had found a nice bloke and moved with him into his barge. The very day the girl saw him she wrote him a note saying no person, animal, insect, or thing had sniffed about her sex for almost a year and asked were there any offers. They clicked.

At the height of the fever, small flying creatures assembled and performed a medieval drama. They flew from the ceiling, perched on the various big brass curtain rings, hid in the dusty hollow space above the wardrobe, and hissed at one another: hiss-hiss. They chattered in a rich and barbarous language. She could comprehend it, though she could not speak it. They stripped her bare. They worked in pairs, sometimes like angels, sometimes like little imps. They, too, had tails. They worked quickly, everything was quick and preordained.

She lay prostrate. Her nipples were like two aching mouths, unable to beseech. The Leader, half man, half woman, lay upon her, and in that unfamiliar, mocking, rocking copulation, all strength seemed to be sucked out of her. Her nipples had nothing left to give. After milk came blood, and after blood, lymph. Her seducer, though light as a proverbial feather, had one long black curved whisker jutting from his left nostril, and there was no part of her body that did not come under the impact of its maddening trail. The others kept up some kind of screeching chorus. She was wrung dry.

She came to on the floor. She saw the pictures, and her oval, silver-backed mirror, as if she had been away on a long long journey, and she resaluted them. In the silence there was a heaviness, as of something snoring, and various hairs had got into the glass of orange juice beside the bed.

The next day, when her temperature had abated somewhat, she decided to get a grip on herself, to find the use of her legs again, and to walk around. There was even a walking stick that someone had left behind. She opened a door that led into a room, a little vacant room, as it happened, but it was no longer empty; she saw numbers of coffins throughout the room, lifting and flying about, and she heard a saw cutting through wood, slowly and obstinately.

Good God, I am dying, she thought, as the coffins careened about, and then she closed the door and then opened it again, and the room was as it should be, with a single bed, covered in an orange counterpane, a lamp with a white globe, a buckled dressing table, and a painting that represented a purring heart.

That was the first time. Not long after, the washbasin in the maid's room did a little dance, and the enamel was like a meal inside her mouth, crushing her teeth. They said it was bad to be alone. It was.

She lost interest in cooking and housekeeping, wagged her finger at her own self, and pronounced a ridiculous verdict, "You are slipping, slipping." Very often she caught sight of a bright sixpence concealed inside a wad of dough, and she thought that if she could get it and keep it in her purse, it would be a good augury for the future. Yes, she was slipping. Her hardworking mother would not approve. Her mother had been a good cook, superb at puddings, blood puddings, suet puddings, and, of course, the doyen of all, the inimitable queen of puddings.

The neighbors suggested she take driving lessons, and she did.

On the second lesson, she headed straight for a pond, escaped only because the instructor grabbed the steering wheel. All she could hear was "The pond, the pond." She saw it, with its fine fuzz of green scum, looking exceedingly calm and undangerous. The instructor drove home.

She went to a boy called Pierre to have streaks and highlighting. Consequently, her hair at night suggested the lights of an Aladdin's cave. She should have streetwalked. She got a new outfit. She got new boots. They were the color of hessian and thickly crusted with threaded flowers. In the shop, the male assistant told her that their consultant psychiatrist could tell any woman's character from the footwear she chose. For that she smirked.

There was only one tune in her head, and it was that London Bridge was falling down, falling down. She would sit far back in a chair and try to keep still. But very often it would come, this mutiny, and there was no knowing what blood battles, what carnivals, what mad eyes and bulbous eyeballs would swim before her. Get thee to a nunnery, she said to them in vain. The bills poured in. Nevertheless, she bought unnecessary things, an ivory inlaid occasional table, a prayer chair.

The chair had to stay in the shop window for three days, until a dexterous man came to haul it out. She used to go up to the shop and look at it, observe the word SOLD in bold red letters and her name just beneath it. She envisaged sitting on it, kneeling on it. She never did, because it had to go back to the shop, still with its corrugated wrapping on, since the check had bounced.

She had stopped work supposedly for a month, but by then it was several months. She had been replaced by a younger girl, and the column that used to carry her name and her oval-faced likeness each Tuesday morning now had a cute little photograph of a blond lady who used the pseudonym of Sappho. Her former editor wrote and said if he could ever do anything for her, he would be only too glad to help. It was both touching and useless.

As time went on, she was selling instead of buying. Her dresses, both chiffon affairs, in beautiful airy designs, were in a shop window not far away, and her fox cape had been snatched up two minutes after she had deposited it in the secondhand market. She saw the new owner go out in it, strutting, and she wanted to stab her. The new owner wore red platform shoes, and she herself made a note to procure a pair when her ship came home.

The children guessed but never said. They got little presents for her—usually nice notebooks and Biros to try and coax her back to work. From school they wrote insouciant notes—how they were out of socks, they were almost out of underwear, they wondered if she'd had the leak fixed. A man whom she'd met in the park, another nutter, drew her a graph of her waning sexuality and presented her with a sealed letter. He wrote:

> *It appears you do not appreciate a mature person, such as myself, you know many cultured children, some you worship and some you ridicule, but, dear friend, you say you are very occupied, so are the Pope, the United Nations, the Brotherhood of Workers, the Black Militants, the White Pacifists; all playing similar games.*
>
> *Fellow puppet of nature, from outside, stationed in my space, time, and tranquillity, I observe the stardust drifting and pulsating through the Milky Way. Goodbye. It is not the end of me.*

Then he told her to beware. All because she stood him up one day on a park bench, where he was going anyhow, after his afternoon ration of fresh air.

She let the bills come and then dropped them into the boiler. She was glad she had not converted to oil, otherwise there would have been no boiler, and no ashes, and no ash pan, with its lovely big surreal clinkers. The house was silent, and yet in those silences she could hear a little gong summoning her to something, to prayer perhaps, and then the voices, real and imagined, were like packing needles, being dispatched in one ear and out the other, through the brawn of her head. Yet no one had died, not even her parents, so that there was no excuse for those ridiculous coffins.

Still, morning was morning. She would creep down into the garden, quietly, so that she did not even disturb the pigeons out of their roost, and at once she would be possessed of such a nice feeling, a safeness—talking amicably to the sweetness of nature about her. There were still such things, the milky air, the camellias in their trembling backdrop of shining foliage, which she would smell and touch and inhale, and thank for being there. Symbols of another world, a former world, a beautiful world. What world? Where, when, and why had she gone wrong?

It was inside that things were worst. If she sat, or lingered too long in any room, it seemed as if the books, the encyclopedias might commence to talk, the pages might fly open and reveal something dire. At intervals the walls purred. She was several sizes, tiny and shrinking, holding a doll's stomach, pressing, making it say "Ma-ma, ba-ba," she was beating nettles with a stick, she was squatting under the trees, she was a freak being hoisted up on stilts, she was flying, not flying, fixed frozen. She began to lock the door on one room after another, and she would listen outside these doors and peer through their keyholes, but not go in. She locked every room in that house, had a camp bed down in the hall, and was ready to fly at the slightest hint of irregularity. In the end she rented a room in a small hotel and came home only for a change of clothing or to collect the mail.

"Knock-knock." He was there. She went out smiling and he helped her with the few things that she was carrying. He hesitated before pulling on the choke. In the back seat were two cardboard boxes, full of empty milk bottles, and the moment they started up, two or three of the bottles rolled off.

"Any regrets?" Yes, plenty of regrets. She was going to a place named after a lake, and she and others would be under supervision. He said she would be all right, that there were plenty of others in the same boat. Her hackles did not rise.

Ah, never did the house look so lovely as just then, the sheltering eaves from which the birds were darting in and out, the multicolored brick with its hues of violet and crimson, the paintwork, which with a bit of effort could be renewed. She had thrown it all away, she had let it go. Her lungs burst for a moment with regret, and she thought of the alternative, of how blissful it would be, to be going in there and starting all over again, with wooden spoons and a kitchen table, and a primus or a stove; a few belongings. Then she checked herself. It was no use wishing. She saw the living death and the demons behind her, she saw the sad world that she had invented for herself, but of the future she saw nothing, not even one little godsend.

FROM

A Rose in the Heart

1978

Number 10

Everything began to be better for Mrs. Reinhardt from the moment she started to sleepwalk. Every night her journey yielded a fresh surprise. First it was that she saw sheep—not sheep as one sees them in life, a bit sooty and bleating away, but sheep as one sees them in a dream. She saw myriads of white fleece on a hilltop, surrounded by little lambs frisking and suckling to their heart's content.

Then she saw pictures such as she had not seen in life. Her husband owned an art gallery and Mrs. Reinhardt had the opportunity to see many pictures, yet the ones she saw at night were much more satisfying. For one thing, she was inside them. She was not an outsider looking in, making idiotic remarks, she was part of the picture: an arm or a lily or the gray mane of a horse. She did not have to compete, did not have to say anything. All her movements were preordained. She was simply aware of her own breath, a soft, steady, sustaining breath.

In the mornings her husband would say she looked a bit frayed or a bit intense, and she would say, "Nonsense," because in twenty years of marriage she had never felt better. Her sleeping life suited her, and of course, she never knew what to expect. Her daily life had a pattern to it. Weekday mornings she spent at home, helping or supervising Fatima, the Spanish maid. She gave two afternoons a week to teaching autistic children, two afternoons were devoted to an exercise class, and on Fridays she shopped in Harrods and got all the groceries for the weekend. Mr. Reinhardt had bought a farm two years before, and weekends they spent in the country, in their newly renovated cottage. In the country she did not sleepwalk, and Mrs.

Reinhardt wondered if it might be that she was inhibited by the barbed-wire fence that skirted their garden. But there are gates, she thought, and I should open them. She was a little vexed with herself for not being more venturesome.

Then one May night, back in her house in London, she had an incredible dream. She walked over a field with her son—in real life he was at university—and all of a sudden, and in unison, the two of them knelt down and began scraping the earth up with their bare hands. It was a rich red earth and easy to crumble. They were so eager because they knew that treasure was about to be theirs. Sure enough, they found bits of gold, tiny specks of it which they put in a handkerchief, and then, to crown her happiness, Mrs. Reinhardt found the loveliest little gold key and held it up to the light while her son laughed and in a baby voice said, "Mama."

Soon after this dream Mrs. Reinhardt embarked on a bit of spring cleaning. Curtains and carpets for the dry cleaner's, drawers depleted of all the old useless odds and ends that had been piling up. Her husband's clothing, too, she must put in order. A little rift had sprung up between them and was widening day by day. He was moody. He got home later than usual, and though he did not say so, she knew that he had stopped at the corner and had a few drinks. Once that spring he had pulled her down beside him on the living-room sofa and stroked her thighs and started to undress her within hearing distance of Fatima, who was in the kitchen chopping and singing. Always chopping and singing or humming. For the most part, though, Mr. Reinhardt went straight to the liquor cabinet and gave them both a gin, pouring himself a bigger one because, as he said, all her bloody fasting made Mrs. Reinhardt lightheaded.

She was sorting Mr. Reinhardt's shirts—T-shirts, summer sweaters, thick crew-neck sweaters—and putting them each in a neat pile, when out of his seersucker jacket there tumbled a little gold key that caused her to let out a cry. The first thing she felt was a jet of fear. Then she bent down and picked it up. It was exactly like the one in her sleepwalk. She held it in her hand, promising herself never to let it go. What fools we are to pursue in daylight what we should leave for nighttime.

Her next sleepwalking brought Mrs. Reinhardt out of her house into a waiting taxi and, some distance away, to a mews house. Outside the mews house was a black-and-white tub filled with pretty flowers. She simply put her hand under a bit of foliage and there was the latchkey. Inside was a little nest. The wallpaper in the hall was the very one she had always wanted for their house, a pale gold with the tiniest white flowers—mere suggestions of flowers, like those of the wild strawberry. The kitchen was immaculate. On the landing upstairs was a little fretwork bench. The cushions in the sitting room were stiff and stately, and so was the upholstery, but the bedroom—ah, the bedroom.

It was everything she had ever wanted their own to be. In fact, the bedroom was the very room she had envisaged over and over again and had described to her husband down to the last detail. Here it was—a brass bed with a little lace canopy above it, the entire opposite wall a dark metallic mirror in which dark shadows seemed to swim around, a light-blue velvet chaise longue, a hanging plant with shining leaves, and a floor lamp with an amber shade that gave off the softest of light.

She sat on the edge of the bed, marveling, and saw the other things that she had always wanted. She saw, for instance, the photo of a little girl in First Communion attire; she saw the paperweight that when shaken yielded a miniature snowstorm; she saw the mother-of-pearl tray with the two champagne glasses—and all of a sudden she began to cry, because her happiness was so immense. Perhaps, she thought, he will come to me here, he will visit, and it will be like the old days and he won't be irritable and he won't be tapping with his fingers or fiddling with the lever of his fountain pen. He will smother me with hugs and kisses and we will tumble about on the big bed.

She sat there in the bedroom and she touched nothing, not even the two white irises in the tall glass vase. The little key was in her hand and she knew it was for the wardrobe and that she had only to open it to find there a nightdress with a pleated top, a voile dance dress, a silver-fox cape, and a pair of sling-back shoes. But she did not open it. She wanted to leave something a secret. She crept away and was home in her own bed without her husband being aware of her absence. He had complained on other occasions about her cold feet as she got back into bed, and asked in Christ's name what was she doing—making tea or what? That morning her happiness was so great that she leaned over, unknotted his pajamas, and made love to him very sweetly, very slowly, and to his apparent delight. Yet when he wakened he was angry, as if a wrong had been done him.

Naturally, Mrs. Reinhardt now went to the mews house night after night, and her heart would light up as she saw the pillar of the house with its number, 10, lettered in gold edged with black. Sometimes she slipped into the brass bed, knowing it was only a question of time before Mr. Reinhardt followed her there.

One night as she lay in the bed, a little breathless, he came in very softly, closed the door, removed his dressing gown, and took possession of her with such force that afterward she suspected she had a broken rib. They used words that they had not used for years. She was young and wild. A lovely fever took hold of her. She was saucy while he kept imploring her to please marry him, to please give up her independence, to please be his—adding that even if she said no, he was going to whisk her off. Then to prove his point he took possession of her again. She almost died, so deep and so thorough was her pleasure, and each time, as she came back to her senses, she saw some little object or trinket that was intended to add to her pleasure—once it was a mobile in which silver horses chased one another around, once it was a sound as of a running stream. He gave her some champagne and they drank in utter silence.

But when she wakened from this idyll she was in fact in her own bed and so was he. She felt mortified. Had she cried out in her sleep? Had she moaned? There was no rib broken. She reached for the hand mirror and saw no sign of wantonness on her face, no tossed hair, and the buttons of her nightdress were neatly done up to the throat.

He was a solid mass of sleep. He opened his eyes. She said something to him, something anxious, but he did not reply. She got out of bed and went down to the sitting room to think. Where would it all lead to? Should she tell him? She thought not. All morning she tried the key in different locks, but it was too small. In fact, once she nearly lost it because it slipped into a lock and she had to tease it out with the prong of a fork. Of course, she did not let Fatima, the maid, see what she was doing.

It was Friday, their day to go to the country, and she was feeling reluctant about it. She knew that when they arrived they would rush around their garden and look at their plants to see if they'd thrived, and look at the rose leaves to make sure there was no green fly. Then, staring out across the fields to where the cows were, they would tell each other how lucky they were to have such a nice place, and how clever. The magnolia flowers would be fully out, and she would stand and stare at the tree as if by staring at it she could imbue her body with something of its whiteness.

The magnolias were out when they arrived—like little white china eggcups, each bloom lifted to the heavens. Two of the elms definitely had the blight, Mr. Reinhardt said, as the leaves were withering away. The elms would have to be chopped, and Mr. Reinhardt estimated that there would be enough firewood for two winters. He would speak to the farm manager, who lived down the road, about this. They carried in the shopping, raised the blinds, and switched on the central heating. The little kitchen was just as they had left it, except that the primroses in the jar had faded and were like bits of yellow skin. She unpacked the food they had brought, put some things in the fridge, and began to peel the carrots and potatoes for the evening meal. Mr. Reinhardt hammered four picture hangers into the wall for the new prints that he had brought down. From time to time he would call her to ask what order he should put them in, and she would go in, her hands covered with flour, and rather absently suggest a grouping.

She had the little key with her in her purse and would open the purse from time to time to make sure that it was there. Then she would blush.

At dusk she went out to get a branch of apple wood for the fire, in order to engender a lovely smell. A bird chirped from a tree. It was more sound than song. She could not tell what bird it was. The magnolia tree was a mass of white in the surrounding darkness. The dew was falling and she bent for a moment to touch the wet grass. She wished it were Sunday, so that they could be going home. In London the evenings seemed to pass more quickly and they each had more chores to do. She felt in some way she was deceiving him.

They drank some red wine as they sat by the fire. Mr. Reinhardt was fidgety but at the very same time accused her of being fidgety. He was being adamant about the Common Market. Why did he expound on the logistics of it when she was not even contradicting him? He got carried away, made gestures, said he loved England, loved it passionately, that England was going to the dogs. When she got up to push in a log that had fallen from the grate, he asked her for God's sake to pay attention.

She sat down at once, and hoped that there was not going to be one of those terrible, unexpected, meaningless rows. But blessedly they were distracted. She heard him say "Crikey!" and then she looked up and saw what he had just seen. There was a herd of cattle staring in at them. She jumped up. Mr. Reinhardt rushed to the phone to call the farm manager, since he himself knew nothing about country life, certainly not how to drive away cattle.

She grabbed a walking stick and went outside to prevent the cows from falling in the swimming pool. It was cold outdoors and the wind rustled in all the trees. The cows looked at her, suspicious. Their ears pricked. She made tentative movements with the stick, and at that moment four of them leaped over the barbed wire and back into the adjoining field. The remaining cow began to race around. From the field the four cows began to bawl. The fifth cow was butting against the paling. Mrs. Reinhardt thought, I know what you are feeling—you are feeling lost and muddled, and you have gone astray.

Her husband came out in a frenzy, because when he had rung the farm manager no one was there. "Bloody never there!" he said. His loud voice so frightened the poor cow that she made a leap for it and got stuck in the barbed wire. Mrs. Reinhardt could see the barb in her huge udder and thought, What a place for it to have landed. They must rescue her. Very cautiously they both approached the animal; the intention was that Mr. Reinhardt would hold the cow while Mrs. Reinhardt freed the flesh. She tried to be gentle. The cow's smell was milky and soft compared with her roar, which was beseeching. Mr. Reinhardt caught hold of the hindquarters and told his wife to hurry up. The cow was bucking. As Mrs. Reinhardt lifted the bleeding flesh away, the cow took a high jump and was over the fence and down the field, where she hurried to the river to drink.

The others followed her, and suddenly the whole meadow was the scene of bawling and mad commotion. Mr. Reinhardt rubbed his hands and let out a sigh of relief. He suggested that they open a bottle of champagne. Mrs. Reinhardt was delighted. Of late he had become very thrifty and did not permit her any extravagances. In fact, he had been saying that they would soon have to give up wine because of the state of the country. As they went indoors he put an arm around her. And back in the room she sat and felt like a mistress as she drank the champagne, smiled at him, and felt the stuff coursing through her body. The champagne put them in a nice mood and they linked as they went up the narrow stairs to bed. Nevertheless, Mrs. Reinhardt did not feel like any intimacy; she wanted it reserved for the hidden room.

They returned to London on Sunday evening, and that night Mrs. Reinhardt did not sleep. Consequently she walked nowhere in her dreams. In the morning she felt fidgety. She looked in the mirror. She was getting old. After breakfast, as Mr. Reinhardt was hurrying out of the house, she held up the little key.

"What is it?" she said.

"How would I know?" he said. He looked livid.

She called and made an appointment at the hairdresser's. She addressed herself. She must not get old. Later when her hair was set she would surprise him—she would drop in at his gallery and ask him to take her to a nice pub. On the way she would buy a new scarf and knot it at the neck and she would be youthful.

When she got to the gallery, Mr. Reinhardt was not there. Hans, his assistant, was busy with a client from the Middle East. She said she would wait. The new secretary went off to make some tea. Mrs. Reinhardt sat at her husband's desk, brooding, and then idly she began to flick through his desk diary, just to pass the time. Lunch with this one and that one. A reminder to buy her a present for their anniversary—which he had done. He had bought her a beautiful ring with a sphinx on it.

Then she saw it—the address that she went to night after night. Number 10. The digits danced before her eyes as they had danced when she drove up in the taxi the very first time. All her movements became hurried and mechanical. She gulped her tea, she gave a distracted handshake to the Arab gentleman, she ate the ginger biscuit and gnashed her teeth, so violently did she chew. She paced the floor, she went back to the diary. The same address—three, four, or five times a week. She flicked back to see how long it had been going on. It was no use. She simply had to go there.

At the mews, she found the key in the flower tub. In the kitchen were eggshells and a pan in which an omelet had been cooked. There were two brown eggshells and one white. She dipped her finger in the fat; it was still warm. Her heart went ahead of her up the stairs. It was like a pellet in her body. She had her hand on the bedroom doorknob, when all of a sudden she stopped in her tracks and became motionless. She crept away from the door and went back to the landing seat.

She would not intrude, no. It was perfectly clear why Mr. Reinhardt went there. He went by day to keep his tryst with her, be unfaithful with her, just as she went by night. One day or one night, if they were very lucky, they might meet and share their secret, but until then Mrs. Reinhardt was content to leave everything just as it was. She tiptoed down the stairs and was pleased that she had not acted rashly, that she had not broken the spell.

Baby Blue

Three short quick death knocks resounded in her bedroom the night before they met. He said not to give it a thought, not to fret. He asked if she would like a kiss later on and she nodded. They were alike in everything and they talked with their heads lolled against the back of the armchairs so that to any spectators it was their throats that would be readily visible. The others had gone. He had been brought in unexpectedly by a friend, and as she said, somewhat frankly, it wasn't every day that one met an eligible man. He for his part said that if he had seen her in a restaurant he would have knocked over tables to get to her. Her hand was on the serge of his knee, his hand on the velvet of hers, and they were telling each other that there was no hurry at all, that their bodies were as perfectly placed as neighboring plants.

She escorted him to the corner to get a taxi, and on the way they found a pack of cards on the wet road, cut them there and then, and cut identically. Next day he would be making the short flight across the Channel to his home, which sounded stately, with its beech trees, its peach houses, its asparagus bed, and Corinthian pillars supporting the front porch. In time she would be acquainted with the rooms, she would ask him to describe them one by one—library, kitchen, drawing room, and last, but very last of all, bedroom. It was his wife's house. His wife was her coloring and also five foot seven and somewhat assertive. His children were adorable. He had thought of suicide the previous summer, but that was over, meeting her had changed all that. It was like Aladdin, magical; his hair would begin to grow again and he would trim his black beard, so that by the next weekend his lips would feel and imprint hers. He worked as a designer and had to come back each week to continue plans for a little theater that was being built as part of a modern complex. It was the first thing he had done in years.

The card he sent her was a historic building going up in flames and she thought, Ominous, but because of the greetings on it she was in an ecstasy.

He would arrive on Fridays, telephone from the airport, and in the hallway, with his black mohair bag still in his hand, he would kiss her while she bit at his beard and got to the secrecy of his lips. Then he would hold her at a distance from him and tilt her head until she became flawless. There she would be, white-skinned, agog, and all of a blush, and there he would be, trying not to palpitate so hard. His smell was dearer to her than any she could remember and yet it was redolent of some deep, buried memory. Her mother, she feared. Something of the same creaminess and the same mildness united them as if poised for life's knife. He plaited her hair around his finger, they constantly swapped plates, glasses, knives, forks, and were unable to eat, what with all the jumping up and down and swapping of these things. He took her hands to his face, and she said all the little pouches of tension would get pressed away, and not long after this, and during one of those infinite infinities, he cried and she drank in two huge drops of very salty tears. He confessed to her that when he was little and got his first bicycle he had to ride around and around the same bit of safe suburban street so that his mother would not worry about his getting run over on a main road. She said that fused them together, that made him known to her throughout, and again she thought of slaughter and of some lamb waiting for life's knife.

"Will it last, Eleanor?" he said.

"It will last," she said.

She never was so sure of anything in her life. In the bedroom she drew the pink curtains, and he peeled the layers of her clothing off, and talked to her skin, then bones beneath it, then to her blood, then their bloods raced together.

*

"I can't stop my wife coming to London to shop," he said, getting out of bed, dressing, and then undressing again. He scarcely knew what he wanted to do. He had a migraine and asked if she ever suffered from that. She said go, please go. They had known each other for six weekends and he intended to get her a ring. Her mascara was badly crusted on her lashes and had smeared onto her lids.

This was no way to be. She had left her earrings on and knew that the crystal would have made a semblance of a gash on each side of her neck. They had gone to bed drunk, and were drunk oftener than they need be. He used to intend to go early to the family he was supposed to be staying with, but always his resolution broke and he stayed with her until breakfast time, or later.

"Go, please go," she said it again.

His smile was like a cowl placed over a very wretched face.

The next weekend it didn't work out too badly. It was a question of him running back and forth to her, and from her, helping his wife with shopping, getting his daughter a diary, getting his son some toy motors, once having to fail her by not showing up at all, and then in a panic ringing her from the flat in the middle of the night—presumably his wife was asleep—saying, "I have to talk to you, I will see you tomorrow at ten; if you are not there I will wait, I will see you tomorrow at ten, I have to talk to you, if you are not there I will wait..."

At ten he arrived and his complexion was that of an old gray sock.

"What is it?" she said sympathetically, and still relatively in control of herself. If only she had crystal-gazed.

"I dread looking into my wife's eyes and telling her that I am in love with another woman."

"Then don't," she said.

"Do you love me anymore?" he asked.

"Yes," she said, and they sat in the dining room, on a carved chair, looking out at the winter trees in the winter sky, feeling sad for each other, and for themselves, and remembering to the future when the trees would be in leaf, and they would walk in the gardens together and there and then, a bit teary, unslept, and grave beyond belief, they started to build.

Christmas comes but once a year, and when it does it brings families together. He went home and, as the friend who had introduced them said, was probably busy, dressing the tree, going to parties, pulling crackers, and, as she silently added, looking into his wife's eyes, or his old cat's eyes, putting drops into his cat's eyes, doing his duty. He used to tell her how he sat on the stairs, talking to his cat as if it were her, and then biting one of his whiskers. No letter. She didn't know it but the huge gilt mirror in their hall fell, broke, and just missed his wife by inches; she did not know it then, but that miss was relevant. New Year's Eve saw her drunk again and maudlinly recalling dead friends, those in the grave and those who were still walking around. She would not leave the restaurant but sat all night at the corner table until the waiter brought her coffee and a little jug of warm milk in the morning. He found her curled up in her fox cape.

"Gigo, am I old . . . ?" she said.

"No . . . not old, well-looking," he said.

He knew her well and had often helped her out with her parties. He knew her as a woman who worked for a public relations firm, and brought them nice customers and did lots of entertaining. They sat and talked of towns in Italy—Siena, Pisa, Padua, Fuerti di Marmi, Spoleto. At the mention of each town he kissed the air. On the twelfth day—little Christmas—he wrote to say, "Only that I love you more and miss you desperately, I am in a spruce wood and it is growing dark." It was. She saw that but she refused to comprehend.

When she saw his wife she thought that yes she would have known her and felt that the scalded expression and marmalade hair would make an incision inside her brain. "I will dream of this person," she said warningly to herself as they shook hands. Then she handed him the bottle of white wine but kept the little parcel of quails' eggs, because they looked too intimate and would be a revelation in their little nest of chaff, speckled, freshly boiled an hour before, blue-green with spots of brown, eggs as fresh as their sex. It was at his hospital bedside, and there beside him were these two women and above him a little screen denoting the waver of his heart. It was all a bit unreal to Eleanor. No two people looked more unsuited, what with his shyness and his wife's blatancy, his dark coloring and hers, which had the ire of desert sand. For a moment she felt there was some mistake, it was perhaps his wife's sister, but no, she was busying herself doing a wife's things, touching the lapel of his pajamas, putting a saucer over the jug of water, acknowledging the flowers. The lilies of the valley that Eleanor had sent him were in a tumbler, the twenty sprays dispatched from Ascot. Asked by his wife where they had come from, he said an "admirer" and smiled. He smiled quite a lot as he nestled back against the pillows, seeming like a man with nothing on his mind except the happy guarantee that there would be hot milk at ten, two sleeping pills, and oblivion. She kept eying his wife, and the feeling she got was of a body, tanklike, filled with some kind of explosive. His wife suddenly told them that she was something of a seer and he asked politely if he would recover. The wine she brought they drank from cups. Exquisite, chilled white wine, such as she and he had often drunk, and such as he had drunk with his wife in the very first stages of their courtship. He was a man to whom the same thing was happening twice. The nurses were beginning to busy themselves and bade good night overloudly to one lame visitor who was getting up to leave. The man in the next bed begged if he could have his clothes in order to go home to his own house, whereupon the night sister gave him a little peck on the cheek.

"I must go," Eleanor said, and looked at him as if there were some means of becoming invisible and staying.

"So must I," his wife said, and it was apparent that she wanted them to go together, to have a chinwag perhaps. Eleanor touched the counterpane beneath where his feet were and left hurriedly, as if she were walking on springs instead of high-heeled patent shoes. No chinwag, no nothing with this self-claimed seer. Yet something in her wanted to tell it, to have it known there and then, to have each person speak their mind. She ran down the stairs, crossed the road, and stood trembling in the porchway of the pub, dividing her glance between the darkness of the hospital doorway and the welcoming soft pink light inside the pub itself. When she saw the woman, the wife, emerge in a black coat with a little travel bag, she felt momentarily sorry for her, felt her defeat or perhaps her intuition in the way she walked down the street. She watched her and thought that if they had been at school together or were not torn between the same unfortunate man, they might have some crumb of friendship to toss at one another.

Back at his bedside making the most of the two minutes the sister had allowed her, she looked at him and said, "Well."

"What did you think?" he said.

"She talks a lot," she said.

"Now you see," he said, and then he held her and she knew that there was something that she did not see, something that existed but was hidden from her. Some betrayal that would one day come out.

"I am not jealous," she said.

"How could you be?" he said, and they sobbed and kissed and rocked back and forth, as if they were in their own room.

"I would like you to have a baby," he said.

"I'll have twins," she said.

"My wife says if it was anyone but you."

"But me," she said, and she could feel herself boiling.

His wife had gone on a short holiday in order to recoup her strength so that they could finalize the marriage. Eleanor had flown over to see him and was staying in a hotel a few miles from where he lived.

"She won't let me see the children," he said.

"That's what everyone says, that's standard."

"I had to lie about your key."

"How did she find it?"

"In my pocket," he said, then asked if he should demonstrate it.

"No," she said, "don't."

The question escaped out of her: "Do you sleep together?"

"Once . . ." he said. "I thought it was honorable."

"Don't," she said.

"It's a big bed, it's almost as big as this room."

Although she meant to hold her tears at all costs, they accrued, dropped onto the toasted sandwich and into the champagne that he had bought her and onto the orange-colored napkin. They were like rain softening the paper napkin. He squeezed her hand and led her back to the hotel room; there he undressed her, washed her, powdered her, and put her to dry in a big towel, then told her he loved her, that he would always love her, and she lay inside the towel listening to the crows cawing, then the rain pelting off the roof, and the old trees with their old branches groaning, then the spatters against the windowpane, and she thought of the daffodils getting soaked as he clasped her through the warm towel and begged of her to let him in, always to let him in. Later that evening when she caught the plane back he simply said, "Soon, soon." All through the journey, talking to a juggernaut who sat next to her, she kept thinking, Soon, and yet there was one little niggle that bothered her, his saying that he would have to tax the car next day, because his wife liked everything to be kept in order.

The night his wife returned he phoned her from a booth and said he was never in all his life so incensed. He said he had no idea what he might do next. She did not know it then but he had a black eye caused by a punch from a ringed finger, and wounds around the thighs where he was ridiculed for being a cunt. She said he ought to leave at once, but he was too drunk to understand. The next day when he phoned he said everything was going to be more protracted but that he would phone when he could, and that she was to be well, be well. He was with her within twenty-four hours, sitting on the swivel chair, pale, bruised, and so disheveled that she realized he had known more ordeal in a day than in the sum of his life. He kissed her, asked her to please, please, never pull his hair by the roots, because he minded that more than anything. They made love, and on and off throughout the day and in his short sleeps he kept threshing about and muttering things. He dreamed of a dog, a dog at their gate lodge, and when he told her she felt inadequate. She would have to replace wife, children, animals, a sixteen-room house, the garden, cloches, the river, and the countryside with its ranges of blue-black mountains. As if he guessed her thoughts, he said sadly that he owned nothing, and the little stone he once gave her would be the only gift he could afford for a while. The theater design was complete, but no other offers of work loomed. That was the other thing that galled. He had busied himself in craven domesticity and let his work slide. He had beggared himself.

He would telephone her when he was out and say he was on his way "home, so to speak." He was seeing various friends and, though she did not know it, getting communiqués from his wife to come back, to come back. The evening he broke it to her, he first asked if she had seen a rainbow in the sky and described how he saw it when standing in a bus shelter. Then he coughed and said, "I rang my wife," and she gulped.

"My wife isn't like you, she never cries, but she cried, she sounded ill, very ill," he said.

"She's a maneuvering liar," she said.

"I have to be there," he said.

"Go now," she said, not wanting the ritual of a wake, and in fact he had forestalled her in that, because his wife was flying at the very moment and they had arranged to meet in a friend's house, empty, as it happened.

Then followed their first dirty quarrel, because he had told her so many hideous things that his wife had said about her, so many outrageous untruths.

"She's mad," she said. "It's a madhouse."

"I'll tell you what a madhouse it is," he said, and proceeded to describe how as a farewell barter his wife had induced him to make love to her and was now in the process of looking for an abortionist.

"You mean you did," she said.

"In the morning I'm always, a man is always . . ."

"You went in."

"I didn't ejaculate."

"She stinks."

"It stinks," he said, and as he left she clung to his sleeve, which must have been clung to a few mornings earlier, and she saw his hair so soft, so jet, his eyes bright hazel and overalive, and then she let go without as much as a murmur.

"I'll always love you," he said.

She walked with him in imagination up the road, to the house where his wife waited, to their embrace, or their quarrel, or their whatever, and all night she kept vigil, expecting one or the other of them to come back to her, to consult her, to include her, to console her, but no one came.

The Sunday he was due to arrive back, she went into the country, both to escape the dread of waiting and to pick flowers. She picked the loveliest wildflowers, put them all around the house, then put the side of salmon in a copper pan, peeled cucumber, sliced it thin as wafers, proceeded to make a sauce, and was whipping, stopping every other minute for the sound of the telephone, when in fact the doorbell rang. He was in a sweat, carrying a bag of hers that he had once borrowed. Yes, his wife had insisted on coming with him and was in the friend's house a mile away, making the same threats about writs, about custody, about children, about his whoring. They drank and kissed and ate dinner, and it was the very same as in the first wayward weeks when he kept kneeling by her, asking for special favors, telling her how much more he loved her. Around midnight he said he had no intention of going back to the house where his wife was, and falling half asleep and still engaged in the tangle of love, he thanked her from the bottom of his heart and said this was only the beginning. Next day when he telephoned, his wife demanded to see him within the hour, but he decided not to go, said, "Let it stew."

They were invited by friends of Eleanor's to the country, and he chose what she should wear, he himself having only the clothes that were on his back, his suitcase being in his wife's possession. It was a beautiful house and he had some trepidation about going.

"Look, black swans," she said, pointing to the artificial lake as they drove up to the avenue and stepped out onto the very white gravel, her shoes making a grating sound. The butler took their bags, and straightaway, with their hostess, they set out for a walk. The lawn was scattered with duck droppings and swan droppings and fallen acacia petals. It was a soft misty day, and the black swans were as coordinated and elegant as if they were performing a pageant. It was perfect. A few last acacia flowers still clung to the bushes and made a little show of pink. In the grotto one of the guests was identifying the hundreds of varieties of rock there. Had they stayed outside they could have watched a plane go by. He loved planes, and for some reason to do with portent, she kept count of them for him. When she entered the dark and caught him by surprise, their two faces rubbed together and their breaths met. That night in a different bed, a four-poster, they made love differently, and he told her as he tore at the beautiful lingerie that she had bought for the occasion that never had he loved her so much as earlier in the dark grotto, with her big eyes and her winged nose looming over him. The torn silk garments fell away from her and she felt at last that they had truly met, they had truly come into their own.

He went back, but in his own time. Each night when he phoned he said there was no question now of their losing each other, because he was recovering his self-esteem. Then he returned sooner than she expected, in fact unannounced. She was hemming curtains, lovely cream lace curtains that she had bought with him in mind. They went to the kitchen and he said yes, that his wife had come again and was making the same contradictory threats, one minute telling him to get out, the next minute begging him to stay, showing him her scarred stomach, scars incurred from all her operations. He was wearing a striped seersucker jacket, and it was the first time that she saw him as his wife's property, dressed expensively but brashly. He was restless, and without knowing it, she kept waiting for the crisis.

"I can't phone you in the future," he said.

"You can," she said, coaxing him.

"They listen at the exchange," he said.

"I insist," she said, and began in jest to hit him. All of a sudden he told her how he had thrown his wife out of a room the night before and how he realized he wanted to kill her.

"And?" she said.

"She came back to say she was bleeding from the inner ear."

"And?" she said.

"Good, I said."

There was a dreadful silence. They sat down to eat a bit of bread and cheese, but the jesting was over. Next day he went to inquire about work, and when he came home in the evening, everything was friendly but something needed to be said. He was going to be incommunicado, he said, thus making it impossible for his wife to find him. Next night they went to a party and she made certain not to cling to him, not to make him feel hemmed in. Yet they had to rush to the little cloakroom to kiss. He lifted her dress and touched her lingeringly, and she said wasn't he the philanderer, then. On the way home she expressed the wish to be in Paris, so they could have breakfast and dawdle all day. What she really wished was not Paris but a place where they could be free. It was a midsummer night, and they decided to go into the square and sit under a tree where the pigeons were mildly cogitating. He gave her a borough council rose and said would she keep it forever, even when it crumpled. He said there was no doubt about it but that she was psychic, that his wife, who always wore girdles, was now buying the same panties as her. He had seen them in a case—white, brown, and cream, with the maker's name and little borders of lace. She asked a question. He said no, there had not been a reunion, but that he went into the bedroom to get his book from the bedside table and there they were on the top of the opened suitcase.

"I would like to be there, just once, invisible," she said.

He shook his head and said all she would see would be himself at a table trying to draw something, his wife in her cashmere dressing gown, coming in, snatching it out of his hand, saying, "You cunt, don't forget that, you louse," then going on about *her* worth, *her* intelligence, the sacrifice she had made for him, leaving the room to down another glass of wine, coming back to start all over again with fresh reinforcements, to get into her stride.

"Are you hiding something, Jay?" she said.

"Only that I love you passionately," he said, and together they held the rose, which was dark red and vibrant as blood.

A few days later he was remote, refused to eat or drink, and was always just short of frowning when she entered the room. He sat and watched cricket on television, and sometimes would get up and mime the movement of the batsman, or would point to one of the fielders who were running and say how miraculous it was. A few times he went upstairs to kiss her, kisses of reassurance, but each time when she commenced to talk, he was gone again. Young love, outings to the country, a holiday, all those things seemed improbable, a figment. They were too racked by everything. She was glad that there was a guest for dinner, because he became his old self again, warm and friendly; then he sang and in the course of singing put one lock of her hair behind his ear, which made him look like a girl. They met each other's glance and smiled and it was all like before. The friend said no two people were so well matched and they drank to it. In bed he tossed and turned, said it would have been better if he stayed in a hotel, so as not to disturb her sleep, said all in all he was a very spoiled person and that he would have to get a steady job. He said he had to admit that his wife was now nothing, no one, although he had dreamed of her the previous night, and that he was hoping that she would go far away and, like a Santa Claus, send back some of her money. Yes, it was like that. All his past life was over, finished; then he doubled over with pain and she massaged him gently, but it gave no relief; he said the pain went right through to the fillings of his teeth.

"You have something to tell me?" she asked.

"Yes." He said it so quietly that the whole room was taut with expectation. The room where eight months previously she had heard the unfathomable death knocks, the room to which they climbed at all hours, drinking one another in, the room where the sun coming through the gauze curtains played on the brass rungs of the bed and seemed to reveal and scatter imaginary petals, the room where he gave her one drop of his precious blood instead of a gold wedding ring. What he had to tell her was that he was giving it all up, her, his wife, his family, his beautiful house, the huge spider's web that he had got himself into. For a moment she panicked. He once told her that he would like to go to a hotel room and write to the people concerned—herself, his children, his wife—and, as he implied, put an end to himself. She thought not that, not that, no matter what, and for a second rehearsed a conciliatory conversation with his wife where they would both do everything to help him. He could not be allowed to.

"I'll leave here tomorrow," he said.

"Where will you go?" she asked.

"I'll go home to say goodbye." And in those few words she knew that he would go home not to say goodbye but to say "Hello, I'm back." She prayed that by the morrow he would change his mind and feel less conclusive about things.

I am not dead, she thought, and clutched at objects as if they could assure her of the fact. Then she did rash things, went outdoors, but had to be indoors at once, and barely inside was she than suffocation strangled her again, and yet out in the street the concrete slabs were marshy and the spiked railings threatening to brain her. It was the very same finality as if someone had died and she could see, without looking, his returned latchkey, its yellow-green metal reflected in the co-green of her ring stone. The ring she had taken off the previous night in order for her fingers to be completely at one with his fingers. It was not long after that he said it, and it seemed to her that she must have precipitated it in some mysterious way, and that maybe she had made him feel lacking in something and that it need never have happened, but that it had happened and he had suddenly announced that there was no room for her in his life, that she was not someone he wished to spend his life with, that it was over. Instantly she was off the cliff again. The night and the morning were getting crushed together: the night, when he told her, and the morning, when he had packed every stitch while she was having a shower and had his bag down in the hall and was whistling like a merry traveler.

"I can't," she kept saying, "can't, can't," and then she would refer to his hair, his brown tweed jacket, and the beautiful somberness of him, and then again she would remember the words, the fatal words, his Adam's apple moving, juggling, and the way she bit at it out of love, out of need, and in the morning—yes, it was morning—when she folded his two legs together and kissed as much of him as protruded, and he asked would she do that when he was very old and very infirm and in an institution, and for a moment they both cried. He left. She knew in her bones that it was final, that he had deceived her, that all those promises, the reams of love letters, the daily pledge, "You, I hold fast," were no longer true, and she thought with wizard hatred that perhaps they never had been true, and she thought uselessly but continuously of his house with the fawn blinds drawn down, his getting home after dark, putting his bag on a chair, throwing down the gauntlet at last, saying he was back for good and all, had sown his wild oats. That would not be for a few hours yet, because he was still traveling, but that is what would happen. To get through until dark, she asked of God, as if dark itself had some sort of solution to the problem. Two women held her pressed to a chair, and said commiseratingly to each other that it was impossible to help someone. Judging by their startled faces and by the words that flowed out of her mouth, she knew that she was experiencing the real madness that follows upon loss.

"We're here, we're here," her friend would say.

"Where is he, where is he?" she said, rising, stampeding.

The swivel chair was like a corpse in the room and she threw the paperweight at it. What had once been a dandelion clock inside pale-green glass was now pale-green splinters and smithereens. If he had had a garden, or rather, if he had tended their own garden, he would only cultivate green-and-white flowers, such things as snowdrops and Christmas roses. Between her tears she tried to tell them that, so they would have some inkling of what he was like, and what had gone on between them, and for a moment she saw those Christmas roses, a sea of them, pale and unassuming in a damp incline from the opposite side, and he eerily still.

She went to a friend's house to write it, being too afraid to do it in her own house, in case he might telephone. She used a friend's foolscap paper and over that hour filled three full pages. It was the most furious letter she had ever written, and she wished that she had a black-edged envelope in which to post it. There was no tab on the postbox telling the time of the next collection, so she went into a nearby shop to ask if it was reliable. It was a lighting shop. Long glass shades hung down like crystals, like domes, like translucent mushrooms, reminding her of some nonexistent time in the future when she would entertain him. After posting the letter she went back to the friend's house to finish her tea, and as she was being conveyed up the street, they saw an elderly woman with a big sheepdog in her arms, holding it upright, like a baby, and she wanted to run across and embrace both of them.

"That woman saw her father being run over when she was fourteen and hasn't been the same since," her friend said.

"And we think we're badly off," she said.

She felt curiously elated and began to count, first in hours, then in minutes, then in seconds, the length of time before he received the epistle.

He was sleeping in his wife's bedroom again. That was part of the pact, that, and a vow that he would never travel abroad without her, that he would pay attention to her at parties, appreciate her more than he had been doing. He said yes to all her demands and thought that somehow they would not be exacted once she was over her fit. He slept badly. He talked, shouted in his sleep, and in the morning while being rebuked about it, he never inquired in case he might have said the other woman's name. Her photo, the small snapshot of her that he had kissed and licked so many times, was in the woodshed along with the one letter that he had brought away out of the pile that he had left in her study for safety. It was the night of his thirty-fifth birthday, and they had been parted but a week. He stood over his son's bed telling himself that what he had done was the right thing. The little boy had one finger in his mouth and the other hand was splayed out like a doll's. "It's the hands that kill you, isn't it?" said his wife, who had crept in to enjoy the moment of domesticity.

He kept going to the front door long before the visitors were due to arrive, and he was even in two minds about nipping the lead off to the master telephone, because he was in dread of its ringing. At the party he sang the same songs as he had sung to her, in fact, his repertoire. His wife drank his health, and the old nanny, who had been in the habit of hearing and seeing the most frightful things and had seen bottles flying, thought how changeable a thing human nature can be. Even staggering to bed he thought he heard footsteps. His wife dared him to fuck her, but it was a drunken dare and drunkenly dismissed; in fact, it made them laugh. She didn't sleep well, what with her thirst, his tossing and turning, and those son-of-a-bitch snores. She was downstairs sipping black coffee, putting a touch of varnish on her nails, when the footsteps came over the gravel.

Early Monday, she thought, and went out to open the door for the postman, who always said the same dumb thing—"Fine day, ma'am," regardless of the weather. Now more than ever his letters concerned her, and her own letter from her sister in Florida took mere second place as she looked at the two business envelopes and then the large envelope with its deceiving blue-ribboned type. She decided to read it outdoors.

"Drivel," she said, starting in on the first stupid nostalgic bits, and then in her element as she saw words she knew, words that could have been her own, the accusation of his being a crooked cunt, the reference to his wife's dandruffy womb, to his own idle, truthless, working-class stinking heart, and she knew that she had won.

"What's that?" she said, and snatched the letter from him. She read it with a speed that made him think for a minute she had written it herself. He saw her eyes get narrower and narrower, and she was as compressed now as a peach stone. She pursed her lips the way she did when entering a party. She got to the bits referring to herself, read them aloud, cursed, and then jubilantly tore it up and tossed the pieces in the air as if they were old raffle tickets. She danced, and said what whoopee, and said "kiss-kiss," and said he'd be a good boy now. He got out of bed and said he had to go to the hotel, have a drink, and not to forget that they were going to a party that night and not to get "drunkies" early in the day, as there were plenty of parties for the summer vacation. As he left she was phoning to ask the girl in the boutique to send up some dresses, a few, and then she started discussing colors.

"Wait a minute . . . hey . . ." He turned around in order to be asked if pale blue and baby blue were one and the same thing.

"Just asking my beau," she said to the girl on the telephone, but he was unable to give any reply.

In the driveway he tried to remember the letter from start to finish, tried to remember how the sentences led from one to another, but all that he could remember were single vicious words that flew up into the air; it was the very same as if the black crows had turned into great black razors and were inside his head, cutting, cutting away. He would stay in the hotel for as long as possible, all day, all night maybe, and he would go back tomorrow and the next day, and maybe one day he would take a room and do the thing he wanted to do, maybe one day.

They were simply little slabs of stone laid into and just beneath the level of the grass, about a hundred of them almost begging for feet to dance, or play hopscotch. Here and there was a vase or mug filled with flowers, mostly roses. She asked one of the gardeners what the slabs signified and he said each one covered someone's ashes. "There's two boxes in some, where was a husband and wife, but most of 'em there's one," he said. The words went straight to her heart. Not long after, she found a tomb with Jay's name on it and nearby was his daughter's name. These names swam before her eyes. She wished that her name were there, too, and began to search. She went around and around the main graveyard, then to that part where the meadowsweet was so high, the tomb and the stone effigies were all covered over, and she could not read a thing. Some French children, on a conducted tour, were running back and forth, amused at what they saw and even more amused when they went in under the redstone ruin that had a big sign saying DANGEROUS STRUCTURE. A few hundred yards away they were setting up wagons for the weekend's amusement fair, and men in vests with big muscles were laying aluminum tracks for the Dodg'em cars. Graveyard and pleasure green were side by side, with a tennis court and a miniature golf course at the northern end. The caravans had arrived, the women were getting out their artificial flowers, their china plates, and their bits of net curtain, to set up yet again their temporary dwellings. She tried to hold on to life, to see what she was seeing, these people setting up house for a day or two or three, muscles, burial places, schoolchildren with no thought of death. It was a windy day, and the roses in the containers kept falling over and girls kept bullying each other to come on or not come on. In the Church of St. Nicholas she looked at the altar, at the one little slit of light from the aperture above, under half of which was stained and half was clear. Then she looked at oddments in a glass case, bits of tiling, and one tiny bit of bone as perfect as a pillar that had been found by a schoolchild whose statement it bore. Outside, the lawn mowers were full on, and those plus the shrieks of the visiting children tried to claim her head; she hoped that they would, thereby banishing forever the thought of all that had gone before. The sun came in fits and starts, the tiers of yellow bulbs were all bunched up, waiting to be lit, the haunted caravan with its black skull and its blooded talons looked a little ridiculous, since no wicked ogre lurked within. She had come on a train journey to consult a faith healer but was much too early. All was still, and only the bright garish daubs of paint suggested that by Saturday all would be in motion, and for better or worse people would go and get on the Dodg'ems and the mad merry-go-round.

What would she have not given to see him for a moment, to clasp him utterly silent, no longer trusting to speech.

It will pass, she thought, going from grave to grave, and unconsciously and almost mundanely she prayed for the living, prayed for the dead, then prayed for the living again, went back to find the tomb where his name was, and prayed for all those who were in boxes alone or together above or below ground, all those unable to escape their afflicted selves.

The Small-Town Lovers

It is a narrow country road in Ireland, tarred very blue and hedged in by ditches on either side. Growing along the ditches and fighting for place are hawthorns, fuchsias, elderberry trees, nettles, honeysuckle, and foxgloves, so that there is almost always a smell of flowers carried by the breeze from the water—the Shannon is only two fields away from the road. In the mild summer evenings, lovers cross the fields down to the water to lie or sit among the lush bamboos. In the morning, the priest reads his prayers there, and when tinkers come around to these parts they park a caravan in a disused gateway leading off that road.

It was not the road I traveled to school, but I often went out there to convey a friend or collect day-old chicks from the Protestant woman who had the incubator. Always, either coming or going, I encountered the Donnellys—Jack and Hilda, the town lovers. They had met in America twenty or thirty years before, two lonely immigrants working in an asylum, and they had married and returned to Ireland, where they opened a little grocery and pub. They lived in the back of the shop, using some of the rooms as storerooms. It amazed me how anyone could love Hilda. She was fat, stolid, uninspiring. They passed me on the road but did not salute me, being too busy with one another.

"Hilda, love, are we walking too fast?" Jack would say.

"No, darling Jack."

"Just say so if we're going too fast," he would say, speaking lovingly to her powdered gooseflesh neck.

"I'll be all right."

Puffing, she would link him, and it seemed as if her entire weight rested on his arm. He was an insignificant little man in a gray flannel suit and black patent-leather shoes.

When they reached that part of the road where there was a gap in the ditch, Hilda carefully edged sideways through the gap and Jack held briars aloft so that she did not scratch herself. Then he stepped in after her and they crossed the potato field toward the lake, hands joined, looking into one another's face.

It astonished everyone how they had not got bored with one another, especially as they had had no children. They were the laugh of the village—Hilda Love and Jack Darling. Each afternoon, they drew down the patched blue blind over the shop window, bolted the shop door, and set out for their walk. Their "bye-byes," Hilda called it. Winter and summer, she wore a blue silk dress that had a flared skirt and a discreet V neck. It must have been the style of dress that was in fashion the year she fell in love, or else she thought it disguised her fat. In the V of the neck she had insertions of lace that she crocheted herself as she sat behind the counter waiting for customers. Waiting for customers that never came, that is, except for the few children who wanted a pennyworth of licorice sweets, or some old woman who would pretend that she was going in to buy groceries and so stop by just to have a chat with Hilda. The local fellows did not drink there, because there was no comfort in it—no fire in the big black grate, no free drinks at Christmastime, no cups of tea on a winter's night, no generosity. Visitors to the house were never offered more than a drink of water, and that is why I feel so privileged to have been given tea in the kitchen.

It was all due to my father. Once, when he was on a batter, Hilda let him have half a bottle of whiskey. Mama had hidden his wallet and he was so desperate for drink that he promised Hilda free grazing for her cow in exchange for the whiskey. He was true to his word, and the cow was driven over to our front field the next afternoon.

On the following Sunday, Hilda rushed to greet my mother as we came out from Mass. Hilda beamed behind her gold-rimmed spectacles, but Mama looked away toward the horizon and said to us children that it looked like rain. Hilda was affronted. After all, Jack and she were a model couple, known to love one another, not to eat meat on Friday, to pay more than enough for their church dues, and, in fact, to be so generous as once to have gone bail for a local insurance collector who was in jail for embezzling money—though, of course, they got the insurance man to paint their house during the period of the bail and did not pay him for it.

"How dare she, and only th'other day I read in the paper that they got another legacy!" Mama said as we walked home over the weary dusty road. Two mornings later, along with the ordinary mail, the postman brought a letter marked BY HAND. It was from Hilda. The letter was an invitation for my sister, my brother, and me to come to tea the following Sunday. Cunningly, she had not invited Mama, knowing, I suppose, that Mama was likely to get confidential and tell her that we could not really afford the free grazing, what with our own debts and everything.

"They better go, Mama," my father said, thinking it a great compliment that we were asked at all.

Sunday came, and we set out in our best clothes and with clean hankies. It was exciting to go around to the hall door at the side of the house, tap the rusty knocker, and in a moment be greeted by Hilda, who was smelling of lavender water as she kissed us. She wore a clean brown dress and a lovely gold pendant, and I envied her the circumstances of her life—mistress of that large house, with money and perfume, and a piano at her convenience. One Sunday evening, the thin sound of piano music had wandered out into the street as we passed down the chapel road to devotions.

Hilda led us across the tiled hallway and into the front parlor, where it was shaded, as the blind was drawn. She let it up halfway and we saw a large room with several armchairs, which were covered with loose pieces of frayed linen sheets. She lifted off one piece of sheet, and a cloud of dust rose up and swirled gently in the air as it approached the yellowed ceiling. The room smelled stale, and there was about the place a lingering smell of whiskey or porter.

"Do any of you children play?" she asked, and very courteously my brother, who was thirteen, said that he played a little. She drew out the piano stool, and ceremoniously he sat down. We sat on high-backed chairs around the big mahogany table, and with my index finger I made patterns on the dusty surface. The table was old and stained, and it was also covered with circles of brown directly at the place where I sat—hundreds of circles running into one another. Being bored with the piano music, I put my hand underneath the table to see if there was anything hidden on the shelf that supported the top. Mama kept bars of chocolate hidden under our dining-room table. I felt splinters, cobwebs, then something cold made of metal. It felt like—I almost screamed. It was a gun. At that instant, my brother began to play loudly, and in keeping with the sentiments of the song (it was "Clare's Dragoons") he moved his head about frantically, so that his red hair fell down onto his forehead and he looked like a genius. None of us saw or heard the movement of the doorknob as it was turned; when we saw Jack, he was already standing in the room, in his shirt sleeves, livid.

"Hilda!" he said in a cross voice.

My brother stopped playing and I took my arms off the table, where they had left a pretty crescent on the surface. Jack stared at us but never said "You're welcome," or "Hello," or anything. Hilda pushed him out of the room and went with him, closing the door behind her. We could not hear what they were saying, but we could feel the anger and rumpus in the hallway. We all felt it.

"They're having a row," my sister said. We were used to rows. My mother and father had plenty.

"Sh-h-h, sh-h-h," my brother said. "That's nothing to say," and he made us talk about something else. Within a few minutes, Hilda came back, smiling, but her ears and neck were blazing.

"Poor Jack is trying to get a snooze, the creature. We mustn't make noise," she said in a whisper, and wagged her finger at each of us in turn.

"Poor Jack, he was awake all night attending to me because I had a dose of heartburn," and with her white, fat hand she touched her chest around about where her heart must have been beating. Then she suggested that we go down to the kitchen, as the bedroom was directly over the parlor and Jack was likely to be disturbed further if we stayed there. Very quietly, my brother let down the top of the piano, Hilda drew the blind, and we left the room as ghostly as we had found it, with dust on everything and dead moths clinging to the globe of the brass lamp that stood on the sideboard.

In the kitchen, the table was already laid for tea—white china cups with a thin gold scroll on them, two plates of sandwiches, rock buns, and marietta biscuits.

"She didn't break her heart with preparations," my sister said to me when Hilda was out in the scullery filling the kettle.

We all sat around, and Hilda said, "Have a tomato sandwich, children."

We did. They were not real tomato sandwiches at all. Hilda had just smeared the slices of bread with tomato ketchup. I laughed, but was nudged by my brother, who began talking to Hilda about the distillation of alcohol. He always talked about lofty things.

"Have one of these," my sister said as she passed me the second plate of sandwiches.

The filling was a curious red-brown color; I took a bite and for a minute could not identify the flavor. And then it came to me. Rhubarb sandwiches! I was choking with laughter by now, and my brother said, "Perhaps you'd like to share the joke." However, he ate nothing himself except one rock bun, and he left the shreds of lemon peel on his plate. My sister ate like a horse; she was eleven at that time and reckoned that she had to eat a lot so that she would grow very tall. She longed to be a policewoman and heard that one had to be tall for that.

Hilda was uneasy—you could see by the way she sat on the edge of the chair with her ear cocked—and she asked us no questions. Normally, she tapped the window with her knitting needle and called us in on the way from school to ask about my mother and father and if there were any parcels from America and if Mama had got anything new. But that evening she said very little, and we left immediately after we had done the washing up. At home, we kept our parents laughing for an hour as we told them about the house and the food. Mama was very inquisitive to know what the furniture was like and if there were pretty knickknacks in the parlor. "Not as nice as ours?" she said, pleased that at least we had a large house furnished in the style and period of the twenties.

After our visit, Hilda began to call on us when Jack and she came each evening to milk the cow. Tina No-Nose milked in the mornings. (Tina was a flat-nosed girl who got fits.) While Jack was milking, Hilda came around to the back door to have a chat with Mama. "Am I making a nuisance of myself?" she asked the first evening, and Mama was very cold with her. But after some weeks Mama accepted the fact that the cow was there to stay and she talked to Hilda as she would to a friend. She may even have been glad of Hilda's company, because our house was in the middle of a field and our nearest neighbors were a mile away. It was summertime when Hilda first came, and I recall them as they sat on the stone step of the back kitchen, Hilda with a glass of milk or homemade wine in her hand and Mama's cheeks flushed with the excitement of talking about their gay days in America, because she also had worked there when she was young. They talked of Coney Island on Sundays, of a boy they had both known in Brooklyn—the lost curly-headed phantoms of their girlhood. And sooner or later Hilda would mention the terrible thunderstorms in New York. I can see her as she sipped the wine greedily—a clean, fat, pampered woman in a blue silk dress, with thick ankles that were brimming over the edges of her black leather shoes. It was my job to watch for Jack as he came out of the cowshed and went down the avenue toward the road. One evening, I missed him as I was gargling my throat, around the side of the house near the rain barrel.

"Your husband is gone, Mrs. Donnelly," I said.

"Oh, I'll be killed!" she said, and she ran after him, her great body flopping in her blue flared dress.

"Darling huh-huh!" she called as she ran, but he did not wait for her.

I grew up and went to boarding school with my sister; still Hilda came. I would see her at holiday time and note that she was getting breathless and gray. Each Christmas, she gave Mama a bottle of cooking sherry; they had become closer, and Mama was heard to say, "Hilda isn't the worst, you know." With the annual bottle of sherry, Hilda had found a way to Mama's heart—not that Mama drank, but she liked getting something.

"Darling huh-huh!" Hilda always seemed to be calling when I was home on holiday.

"I don't know what she sees in him; he's a dry fish," Mama said as we watched the two of them go out the gate one evening. "She hasn't it all sunshine, either," she added, showing a sly pleasure at the fact that someone else's marriage was unhappy also.

Not that Hilda ever said anything openly. But once she hinted that she hoped life would be better in the next world, and quite often her eyelids were swollen from crying. When she sent to Dublin for her special corsets, she had to have them posted to our house and later she collected them there.

"What they don't know doesn't trouble them," she said to Mama in her slow, false voice. Her voice is the thing I remember best—slow, unctuous, oversweet, like golden syrup.

The years passed. One Christmas morning, Hickey, our hired help, said to my mother, "Did you hear the news, missus?"

"No," she said in a piercing voice. She was angry with Hickey, because he had come home drunk on Christmas Eve and had wakened us trying to get in through the back kitchen window, being too drunk to find the doorkey in its usual place under the soap dish on the window ledge.

"Hilda Donnelly is dead," he said.

"Dead!" my mother said.

"Dead," he repeated.

"My God!" Mama exclaimed, and let the straining cloth fall into the can of milk.

"How could she be dead?" Mama said.

Hilda had been over the previous evening with the bottle of sherry. We had all had tea together in our breakfast room, and Mama had given Hilda a little tray cloth.

"She's dead, that's all I know," Hickey said. "Found her dead when he came down this morning. I heard it over at the creamery."

"Who found her dead?"

Hickey raised his eyes to the ceiling to indicate to me that Mama was stupid.

"Jack Darlin', of course—who else? She was dead for hours."

She was found at the foot of the stairs, her face gashed and the lamp in pieces beside her. The thought of a dead woman, a broken globe, a lamp in smithereens, and a face running with blood was gruesome and just like a scene from a melodrama. My mother said it was lucky the house hadn't burned down, and where was Jack Darling?

"Blankets town tram," Hickey said, and imitated being asleep.

"And how did he sleep through the night and not miss her out of the bed—was he blind or something?" Mama said.

"You're asking me?" Hickey shrugged. He was a workman, and as a workman he never said anything disrespectful about his superiors.

"She was at the foot of the stairs, stone dead, and the lamp in pieces beside her."

"Lucky she wasn't burned," Mama said again.

"It wouldn't have mattered once she was dead," Hickey said, quite without pity.

My father came in from feeding the calves and Mama said to him, "Did you hear that, Father?"

"Hear what?"

She told him word for word, as Hickey had told it to her. "Poor aul creature, I always liked her," my father said proudly, as if his affection could bring Hilda back to life.

Our Christmas dinner was spoiled, because Mama talked of Hilda all the time.

"Well, for all we know now, this could be our last meal on earth. Little did Hilda think, this time yesterday," she said in a voice that was close to crying. Eventually, my father asked her to shut up moaning and let us enjoy our turkey. When we were washing up, she said to me, "You never know the hour or the minute. You always want to be prepared, because when the Lord wants us, He just calls us . . ."

And we both looked through the misted window at the rain and the desolate black winter branches outside.

"And my little tray cloth," Mama said regretfully.

After tea, we went to Hilda's wake. As we set out, it was a bright frosty night with a vast tranquil sky made silver by so many stars—a beautiful, hushed night with white frost on the holly leaves and the ground frozen under our feet. I would rather have sat at home with my brother and sister and listened to the wireless, but Mama said, "You must come; Hilda was always fond of you." To be honest, I hadn't noticed that Hilda was fond of any children. When we got there, the side door was held open with the back of a chair, and we went in the hallway and up the stairs, toward a room where voices murmured softly. The dead room. People, women mostly, sat on the chairs, whispering, and two or three knelt beside the bed on which Hilda was laid out—Hilda, solemn and immaculate in a brown habit, younger-looking than when I had ever known her, with an amber rosary twined between her fingers. The flame of the candle threw crocus shadows on her face, and she looked almost beautiful. There was no gash to be seen on her face unless it was near the temple. Her snow-white hair was draped in curls all around her. It was odd hair, almost like angora. People remarked on her youthfulness. After we had prayed for her soul, we got up and looked around to sympathize with Jack, but he was not there. Dada concluded that he was downstairs, giving the men drinks in the kitchen, so he went down, and I shared the chair with Jack Holland.

"Was it a stroke, or what?" I heard one woman say.

"She always had an unhealthy flush," another woman said, and then a third asked, "Where is himself tonight?"

"Uncle Jack is having to lie down because of the shock," said Hilda's niece, a flashy girl who was passing around glasses of port wine. She was a buttermaker in the next town.

"Oh," somebody said knowingly.

The room smelled of damp, candle grease, and port wine. It was bitterly cold, as there was no fire at all, and you could see by the stains on the wallpaper that it had been a damp room all winter. Mama leaned over and whispered to me that I ought to go downstairs and see if Dada was all right. Then, out loud, she said to me, "You could make a cup of tea for the ladies."

The niece told me where to get the cups and things, and I set off on tiptoe. Down in the kitchen, the men helped themselves to pints of porter, which they filled from the big barrel that rested on a stool. There was a cheerful fire, and they sat around talking.

By mistake, Jim Tuohey began to sing. He was nicknamed the Ferret, because he kept a ferret and hunted with it for foxes on Sundays. He sang, "If I were a blackbird I'd whistle and sing and I'd follow the ship that my true love sails in," and my father shut him up with, "Bloody fool, have you no respect for the dead?"

The Ferret got very embarrassed and went out in the yard—and was sick.

"I'm making a cup of tea," I said to my father.

"Good girl," he said. I was thankful to him because he hadn't touched a drink; I could tell by his eyes. Always when he drank his eyes got wild.

I carried a candle up to the parlor to get cups out of the sideboard. It was the room where we had sat so many years before. I could see Hilda as she was then, breathing heavily under her clean dress, and I was suddenly nervous in case she should appear to me. Quickly I opened the door of the sideboard to get the good cups. As I piled them on the tray, a thought came to me, but I put it aside. It went on bothering me like a stone in the shoe, and finally I could not stop myself. I put my hand under the table to see if the gun was there. I could not find it, so I shone the candlelight under the table and saw nothing but dust and a green bankbook. I felt certain that Jack had shot his wife and had hidden the gun somewhere. Should I run and tell my mother or someone? I ran out of the room with the tray in my hands and almost crashed into Hickey, who was in the hallway.

"God's sake, will you look where you're going!" he said angrily.

"What are you up to?" I asked.

"Mind your own business." He was stealing a bottle of whiskey from the crate of drink under the stairs. "Jack Darlin' won't want it all," he said, as he wrapped a piece of sacking around it.

I couldn't tell Hickey; he would only laugh. He laughed at most things except riddles.

"Where is Jack?" I asked.

"Blotto," Hickey said.

"Does he drink?" I asked. I had never seen him drunk.

"Can a duck swim?" Hickey said. He tiptoed up the hallway and went outside to hide the whiskey in some convenient spot where he could collect it when he was going home. I made the tea, gave my father a cup, and carried a tray upstairs.

"What time is High Mass in the morning?" I heard Mama ask.

"There isn't a High Mass," said the niece. "We couldn't arrange it in time," she added hurriedly.

"Not High Mass!" A sigh of indignation traveled around the room, and we looked at Hilda's calm face as if to apologize to her.

On the way home, Mama said to my father, "Not a very nice house, John."

"Oh, I was very disappointed in it," he said.

"Not as nice as ours," she said, knowing what his answer would be.

"Not a patch on ours," he said proudly, and sniffed.

I could not tell them now about the gun, because in the clean air my suspicions seemed foolish and sordid.

"Poor man was drunk, it seems."

"What did I always tell you? He never came to milk but there was a smell of whiskey off him."

Mama sighed and said that Hilda ought to go straight to heaven, because she had earned it. Next morning, we went over to the low Mass. The remains had been brought from the house to the church, and Mass was offered for Hilda's soul. As we knelt down, I nudged Mama and whispered, "There's Jack up front there." He was kneeling, with his head lowered and a black diamond of cloth stitched onto the arm of his raincoat, which the niece must have seen to. We were relieved to see him, because there was a lot of gossip about why he hadn't appeared at the wake. After Mass, while we waited for the coffin to be put in the hearse and for people to get into their cars and pony traps, we went to sympathize with Jack. He looked stupefied and his nose was more purple than ever. Other people came and shook his hand, but he wore the same baffled expression and simply thanked them for coming.

Then the funeral procession began to move. The car following the hearse was the family car, in which sat the niece and her parents. There was a place for Jack, but he didn't get in. He walked beside the hearse, and we all said, "Ah, the poor man," thinking that he wanted to be close to her by walking the whole three-mile journey to the graveyard—the same road they had traversed each afternoon. My parents thought it a lovely sentiment and accused themselves of having misjudged him the previous evening.

When the hearse drove by the shop, Jack stepped out of line and went indoors. We gaped through the car window, and someone said that he must have felt faint and gone in for a drink or something. We were sure he would follow in another car. At the graveside, we looked for him; we could see the niece looking around anxiously, but like us, she did not find him. The coffin was lowered and we heard the eerie thud of the first sods as they were thrown in, but Jack had not come. He did not come at all. The mystery was solved, or partly solved, the following week, when the parish priest called on Jack. "I had enough of her," Jack said, or so the priest's housekeeper told us.

My father and the men in the village said it was a scandal and that they'd give Jack a good hammering to teach him a lesson. They were waiting for him to come out. A week passed, and still the blinds were drawn and the shutters remained on the shop window. The can of milk left by Tina No-Nose each morning had not been collected. People got worried and said that he must be dead. Tim Hayes decided to break in the side door one Monday morning. He burst it in with the aid of a sledgehammer and went in the hallway, shouting Jack's name. He opened the various doors and found Jack asleep in an armchair in the parlor. There were rum bottles all around him and he had a rug over his shoulders.

"What has got into you?" Hayes asked.

Jack poured himself a tumbler of rum from the half-filled bottle on the mantelpiece and then looked at Hayes and began to laugh.

"The whole town is talking about you. Pull yourself together, man," Hayes said. "The way your missus died and you didn't even go to her funeral . . ."

Jack stopped laughing quite suddenly, and he rummaged behind the cushion of his chair to look for something. His gun. He held it in his hand, showing it to Hayes, and Hayes, who had deserted from the army for cowardice, ran for his life, up the hallway and into the street, telling everyone that Jack was "blind drunk." After that, children and cats and mongrel dogs came to look in at the mysterious hallway, where Hilda's gray coat and walking stick lay on the old-fashioned hall stand. Hearing them, Jack staggered to the doorway and shouted, "Be off!" whereupon they scattered like mice down the street. One day, he propped the door back in place, and from the inside he put furniture against it, to keep it from falling down. There were no more callers, except the niece, who cycled over on her half day to do some cleaning and to buy tea and sugar and things. Her visit coincided with the delivery day of the brewery people, and she opened one half of the shop door and took in whatever drink Jack had ordered her to. That was the time when Mama asked the niece if there was any chance of recovering the little tray cloth she had given Hilda; just for sentiment's sake, Mama said, she would like to have it back. The niece gave it to us, along with a few dresses and some table linen. Herself, she took Hilda's jewelry, as Jack had told her that he was going to burn "the whole damn lot." True enough, we saw a bonfire in their garden one spring night, and the fire smoldered for close to two days.

Gradually, the house came to look deserted; the paintwork peeled on the outside window frames, and the gutters leaked. A statue that stood on the landing upstairs got knocked down and remained in broken pieces behind the lace curtain. The curtain itself was gray and fraying. Some days the can of milk left by Tina No-Nose would be taken in; other times it stayed, for the dogs and the flies. She swears he came to the door once and invited her inside, and he hadn't a stitch on. She ran down the street yelling, and telling of the incident, but people thought she was having one of her fits and disregarded it.

I was waiting very early one morning for a lift on a creamery car to take me to some cousins. There was not a soul about. Suddenly Jack called from the upstairs window, said, "Missy, missy."

I could not tell if he knew me, but I suppose to him I was a young girl, just waiting there, a little on the plump side, but ripe and ready for entanglement. Indeed, the visit I was taking was primarily to see a young man whom I did not know but whose looks—black hair and very dark sallow skin—had lured me. Soon indeed I was startled, because a tennis ball fell at my feet. It was grazed and somewhat greenish. I looked to the doorway and saw that Jack was beckoning me urgently. I went across, thinking he might want the priest or the doctor, and already I was afraid. That fear that makes the whole body quake, like a wind conductor. He was quite drunk and his eyes were vacant. He asked if I was yet clicking, and I said "No," a rapid puritanical no.

"Can't you come in?" he said.

"I'm in a hurry," I said, and took a few steps backward.

"I have nice wine," he said.

"I took the pledge," I said, and he sniggered at that.

"C'mon, can't you?" he said, and he grasped my arm.

It was summer and I was wearing a flowery dress that I was most proud of. It had elasticized sleeves and he let his finger go under the elastic, then let it snap, then repeated it. I said that I was waiting for a lift on the creamery car, and he said the driver was notorious and that I would not be safe in the lorry with him. That did not cheer me one bit.

"He's a prime boy," he said, and his face came very close to mine. His chin was full of gray bristling old-age stubble. A beard would have been better. The thought that I might have to kiss him made me inwardly curdle.

"I'll give you half a crown," he said.

"For what?" I rashly asked.

"Just lift your dress," he said, and a small trickle of spittle flowed from the corner of his lip. His nose and lips were full of cold sores. I thought of saints being boiled in oil, of other saints enduring all sorts of beatings and lacerations, and I would have swapped any of these punishments for the ordeal that I felt was imminent.

"Just a sensation," he said, and he was dragging me in despite my hefty screams. I was stronger than he, but it was not put to the test, because at that moment, and without yet seeing it, we could hear the sound of the lorry. The tankards on the back always made a terrible din. I ran to the driver in a gasp and asked him to take me in. It was high and he had to haul me up. He said had I seen a ghost or what, but I said no, that I was anemic. I dared not tell him lest the same fegary occurred to him, and in truth I was quivering. It struck me as odd and not uncomical that I was yet going forty miles to meet a man and risk the very proceedings that I was dreading with any other. I told the driver nothing but dreary stories so that his hand would not come onto my knee. The dress was short and I kept pulling it down, down, down so that he did not see flesh. I discussed my mother's corns, my father's lumbago, and a workman who had shingles. Once he stopped the lorry and asked me did I want to get out and that was an awful moment, but I braved it and said I wasn't well. "Flag day," he said, and I nodded, giving him the impression that I had my period and was undesirable and untouchable.

Jack died in December, alone in the downstairs room, with only dust and shadows to succor him. The niece found him beside the dead ashes, in the armchair with his clothes on. Nearby on the table was an unfinished game of patience, and of course, the rum bottles were all around. She found a letter he had scrawled, requesting that his body be cremated. But the parish priest and the locals said that the man was mad and not aware of what he was saying, so they ignored his wishes and buried him alongside Hilda.

I still believe he killed her, just as I believe it was clear what he wanted from me that dewy morning, but not being certain of these things, I told no one; yet as the years go by, the certainty of them plagues me. Indeed, it has become a ghost, and the trouble with ghosts is that no one but oneself knows how zealously they stalk the everyday air.

Christmas Roses

Miss Hawkins had seen it all. At least she told people that she had seen it all. She told her few friends about her cabaret life, when she had toured all Europe and was the toast of the richest man in Baghdad. According to her she had had lovers of all nationalities, endless proposals of marriage, champagne in every known vessel, not forgetting the slipper. Yet Miss Hawkins had always had a soft spot for gardening and in Beirut she had planted roses, hers becoming the first English rose garden in that far-off spicy land. She told how she watered them at dawn as she returned accompanied, or unaccompanied, from one of her sallies.

But time passes, and when Miss Hawkins was fifty-five she was no longer in gold-meshed suits dashing from one capital to the next. She taught private dancing to supplement her income and eventually she worked in a municipal garden. As time went by, the gardening was more dear to her than ever her cabaret had been. How she fretted over it, over the health of the soil, over the flowers and the plants, over the overall design and what the residents thought of it. Her success with it became more and more engrossing. She introduced things that had not been there before, and her greatest pride was that the silly old black railing was now smothered with sweet-smelling honeysuckle and other climbing things. She kept busy in all the four seasons, busy and bright. In the autumn she not only raked all the leaves but got down on her knees and picked every stray fallen leaf out of the flower beds, where they tended to lodge under rosebushes. She burned them then. Indeed, there was not a day throughout all of autumn when there was not a bonfire in Miss

Hawkins's municipal garden. And not a month without some blooms. At Christmas was she not proud of her Christmas roses and the Mexican firebush with berries as bright as the decoration on a woman's hat?

In her spare time she visited other municipal gardens and found to her satisfaction that hers was far better, far brighter, more daring, while also well-kempt and cheerful. Her pruning was better, her beds were tidier, her peat was darker, her shrubs sturdier, and the very branches of her rosebushes were red with a sort of inner energy. Of course, the short winter days drove Miss Hawkins into her flat and there she became churlish. She did have her little dog, Clara, but understandably Clara, too, preferred the outdoors. How they barked at each other and squabbled, one blaming the other for being bad-tempered, for baring teeth. The dog was white, with a little crown of orange at the top of her head, and Miss Hawkins favored orange, too, when she tinted her hair. Her hair was long and she dried it by laying it along the length of an ironing board and pressing it with a warm iron.

The flat was a nest of souvenirs, souvenirs from her dancing days—a gauze fan, several pairs of ballet shoes, gloves, photographs, a magnifying glass, programs. All these items were arranged carefully along the bureau and were reflected in the long mirror which Miss Hawkins had acquired so that she could continue to do her exercising. Miss Hawkins danced every night for thirty minutes. That was before she had her Ovaltine. Her figure was still trim, and on the odd occasion when Miss Hawkins got into her black costume and her stiff-necked white blouse, rouged her cheeks, pointed her insteps, and donned her black patent court shoes, she knew that she could pass for forty.

She dressed up when going to see the town councillor about the budget and plans for the garden, and she dressed in her lamé when one of her ex-dancing pupils invited her to a cocktail party. She dressed up no more than three times a year. But Miss Hawkins herself said that she did not need outings. She was quite content to go into her room at nightfall, heat up the previous day's dinner, or else poach eggs, get into bed, cuddle her little dog, look at television, and drop off to sleep. She retired early so that she could be in her garden while the rest of London was surfacing. Her boast was that she was often up starting her day while the stars were still in the heavens and that she moved about like a spirit so as not to disturb neighbors.

It was on such a morning and at such an unearthly hour that Miss Hawkins got a terrible shock concerning her garden. She looked through her window and saw a blue tent, a triangle of utter impertinence, in her terrain. She stormed out, vowing to her little dog and to herself that within minutes it would be a thing of the past. In fact, she found herself closing and reclosing her right fist as if squashing an egg. She was livid.

As she came up to it Miss Hawkins was expecting to find a truant schoolchild. But not at all. There was a grown boy of twenty or perhaps twenty-one on a mattress, asleep. Miss Hawkins was fuming. She noticed at once that he had soft brown hair, white angelic skin, and thick sensual lips. To make matters worse, he was asleep, and as she wakened him, he threw his hands up and remonstrated like a child. Then he blinked, and as soon as he got his bearings, he smiled at her. Miss Hawkins had to tell him that he was breaking the law. He was the soul of obligingness. He said, "Oh, sorry," and explained how he had come from Kenya, how he had arrived late at night, had not been able to find a hostel, had walked around London, and eventually had climbed in over her railing. Miss Hawkins was unable to say the furious things that she had intended to say; indeed, his good manners had made her almost speechless. He asked her what time it was. She could see that he wanted a conversation, but she realized that it was out of keeping with her original mission, and so she turned away.

Miss Hawkins was beneath a tree putting some crocus bulbs in when the young visitor left. She knew it by the clang of the gate. She had left the gate on its latch so that he could go out without having to be conducted by her. As she patted the earth around the little crocuses she thought, What a pity that there couldn't be laws for some and not for others! His smile, his enthusiasm, and his good manners had stirred her. And after all, what harm was he doing?

Yet, thought Miss Hawkins, bylaws are bylaws, and she hit the ground with her little trowel.

As with most winter days there were scarcely any visitors to the square and the time dragged. There were the few residents who brought their dogs in, there was the lady who knitted, and there were the lunchtime stragglers who had keys, although Miss Hawkins knew that they were not residents in the square. Interlopers. All in all, she was dispirited. She even reverted to a bit of debating. What harm had he been doing? Why had she sent him away? Why had she not discussed Africa and the game preserves and the wilds? Oh, how Miss Hawkins wished she had known those legendary spaces.

That evening, as she crossed the road to her house, she stood under the lamplight and looked up the street to where there was the red neon glow from the public house. She had a very definite and foolish longing to be going into the lounge bar with a young escort and demurring as to whether to have a gin-and-tonic or a gin-and-pink. Presently she found that she had slapped herself. The rule was never to go into public houses, since it was vulgar, and never to drink, since it was the road that led to ruin. She ran on home. Her little dog, Clara, and she had an argument, bared their teeth at each other, turned away from each other, and flounced off. The upshot was that Miss Hawkins nicked her thumb with the jagged metal of a tin she was opening, and in a moment of uncustomary self-pity rang one of her dancing pupils and launched into a tirade about hawkers, circulars, and the appalling state of the country. This was unusual for Miss Hawkins, as she had vowed never to submit to self-pity and as she had pinned to her very wall a philosophy that she had meant to adhere to. She read it, but it seemed pretty irrelevant:

I will know who I am
I will keep my mouth shut
I will learn from everything
I will train every day.

She would have ripped it off, except that the effort was too much. Yet as she was able to say next day, the darkest hours are before the dawn.

As she stepped out of her house in her warm trouser suit, with the brown muffler around her neck, she found herself raising her hand in an airy, almost coquettish hello. There he was. He was actually waiting for her by the garden gate, and he was as solemn as a fledgling altar boy. He said that he had come to apologize, that after twenty-four hours in England he was a little more cognizant of rules and regulations, and that he had come to ask her to forgive him. She said certainly. She said he could come in if he wished, and when she walked toward the toolshed, he followed and helped her out with the implements. Miss Hawkins instructed him what to do: he was to dig a patch into which she would put her summer blooms. She told him the Latin names of all these flowers, their appearance, and their characteristics. He was amazed at the way she could rattle off all these items while digging or pruning or even overseeing what he was doing. And so it went on. He would work for an hour or so and then tootle off, and once when it was very cold and they had to fetch watering cans of warm water to thaw out a certain flower bed, she weakened and offered him a coffee. The result was that he arrived the next day with biscuits. He said that he had been given a present of two tickets for the theater and was she by the merest tiniest chance free and would she be so kind as to come with him. Miss Hawkins hesitated, but of course her heart had yielded. She frowned and said could he not ask someone younger, someone in his own age group, to which he said no. Dash it, she thought, theater was theater and her very first calling, and without doubt she would go. The play was *Othello*. Oh, how she loved it, understood it, and was above it all! The jealous Moor, the telltale handkerchief, confessions, counterconfessions, the poor sweet wretched Desdemona. Miss Hawkins raised her hands, sighed for a moment, and said, "The poor dear girl caught in a jealous paradox."

As an escort he was utter perfection. When she arrived breathlessly in the foyer, he was there, beaming. He admired how she looked, he helped remove her shawl, he had already bought a box of chocolate truffles and was discreetly steering her to the bar to have a drink. It was while she was in the bar savoring the glass of gin-and-it that Miss Hawkins conceded what a beauty he was. She called his name and said what a pretty name it was, what an awfully pretty name. His hands caught her attention. Hands, lovely shining nails, a gleam of health on them, and his face framed by the stiff white old-fashioned collar, held in place with a gold stud. His hair was like a girl's. He radiated happiness. Miss Hawkins pinched herself three times in order not to give in to any sentiment. Yet all through the play—riveted though she was—she would glance from the side of her eye at his lovely, untroubled, and perfect profile. In fact, the socket of that eye hurt, so frequently and so lengthily did Miss Hawkins gaze. Miss Hawkins took issue with the costumes and said it should be period and who wanted to see those drab everyday brown things. She also thought poorly of Iago's enunciation. She almost made a scene, so positive was she in her criticism. But of course the play itself was divine, simply divine. At the supper afterward they discussed jealousy, and Miss Hawkins was able to assure him that she no longer suffered from that ghastly complaint. He did. He was a positive pickle of jealousy. "Teach me not to be," he said. He almost touched her when she drew back alarmed, and offended, apparently, by the indiscretion. He retrieved things by offering to pick up her plastic lighter and light her cigarette. Miss Hawkins was enjoying herself. She ate a lot, smoked a lot, drank a lot, but at no time did she lose her composure. In fact, she was mirth personified, and after he had dropped her at her front door, she sauntered down the steps to her basement, then waved her beaded purse at him and said, as English workmen say, "Mind how you go."

But indoors Miss Hawkins dropped her mask. She waltzed about her room, using her shawl as partner, did ooh-la-las and oh-lay-lays such as she had not done since she hit the boards at twenty.

"Sweet boy, utterly sweet, utterly well bred," Miss Hawkins assured herself and Clara, who was peeved from neglect but eventually had to succumb to this carnival and had to dance and lap in accordance with Miss Hawkins's ribald humor. God knows what time they retired.

Naturally things took a turn for the better. She and he now had a topic to discuss and it was theater. It, too, was his ambition; he had come to England to study theater. So, in between pruning or digging or manuring, Miss Hawkins was giving her sage opinion of things, or endeavoring to improve his projection by making him say certain key sentences. She even made him sing. She begged him to concentrate on his alto notes and to do it comfortably and in utter freedom. Miss Hawkins made "no no no" sounds when he slipped into tenor or, as she put it, sank totally into his chest. He was told to pull his voice up again. "Up up up, from the chest," Miss Hawkins would say, conducting him with her thin wrist and dangling hand, and it is true that the lunchtime strollers in the garden came to the conclusion that Miss Hawkins had lost her head. "No, thank you very much" was her unvoiced reply to those snooping people, these spinsters, these divorcées, et cetera. She had not lost her head or any other part of her anatomy, either, and what is more, she was not going to. The only concession she made to him was that she rouged her cheeks, since she herself admitted that her skin was a trifle yellow. All that sunshine in Baghdad long ago and the hepatitis that she had had. As time went by, she did a bit of mending for him, put leather patches on his sleeves, and tried unsuccessfully to interest him in a macrobiotic diet. About this he teased her, and as he dug up a worm or came across a snail in its slow dewy mysterious course, he would ask Miss Hawkins if that was a yin or a yang item, and she would do one of her little involuntary shrugs, toss her gray hair, and say, "D'you mind!" He seemed to like that and would provoke her into situations where she would have to do these little haughty tosses and ask, "D'you mind!"

It was on St. Valentine's Day that he told Miss Hawkins he had to quit the flat he was lodging in.

"I'm not surprised," she said, evincing great relief, and then she went a step further and muttered something about those sort of people. He was staying with some young people in Notting Hill Gate, and from what Miss Hawkins could gather, they hadn't got a clue! They slept all hours, they ate at all hours, they drew national assistance and spent their time—the country's time—strumming music on their various hideous tom-toms and broken guitars. Miss Hawkins had been against his staying there from the start and indeed had fretted about their influence over him. He defended them as best he could, said they were idealists and that one did the crossword puzzles and the other worked in a health-juice bar, but Miss Hawkins just tipped something off the end of the shovel the very same as if she were tipping them off her consciousness. She deliberated, then said he must move in with her. He was aghast with relief. He asked did she mean it. He stressed what a quiet lodger he would be, and how it would only be a matter of weeks until he found another place.

"Stay as long as you like," Miss Hawkins said, and all through this encounter she was brusque in order not to let things slide into a bath of sentiment. But inside, Miss Hawkins was rippling.

That evening she went to a supermarket so as to stock up with things. She now took her rightful place alongside other housewives, alongside women who shopped and cared for their men. She would pick up a tin, muse over it, look at the price, and then drop it with a certain disdain. He would have yin and yang, he would have brown rice, and he would have curry dishes. She did, however, choose a mild curry. The color was so pretty, being ocher, that she thought it would be very becoming on the eyelids, that is if it did not sting. Miss Hawkins was becoming more beauty conscious and plucked her eyebrows again. At the cash register she asked for free recipes and made a somewhat idiotic to-do when they said they were out of them. In fact, she flounced off murmuring about people's bad manners, bad tempers, and abominable breeding.

That night Miss Hawkins got tipsy. She danced as she might dance for him one night. It was all being exquisitely planned. He was arriving on the morrow at five. It would not be quite dark, but it would be dusk, and therefore dim, so that he need not be daunted by her little room. His new nest. Before he arrived she would have switched on the lamps, put a scarf over one; she would have a nice display of forsythia in the tall china jug, she would have the table laid for supper, and she would announce that since it was his first night they would have a bit of a celebration. She ferreted through her six cookery books (those from her married days) before deciding on the recipe she wanted. Naturally she could not afford anything too extravagant, and yet she would not want it to be miserly. It must, it simply must, have "bouquet." She had definitely decided on baked eggs with a sprinkling of cheese, and kidneys cooked in red wine, and button mushrooms. In fact, the wine had been bought for the recipe and Miss Hawkins was busily chiding herself for having drunk too much of it. It was a Spanish wine and rather heady. Then after dinner, as she envisaged it, she would toss a salad. There and then Miss Hawkins picked up her wooden spoon and fork and began to wave them in the air and thought how nice it was to feel jolly and thought ahead to the attention that awaited him. He would be in a comfortable room, he would be the recipient of intelligent theatrical conversation, he could loll in an armchair and think, rather than be subjected to the strumming of some stupid guitar. He had suggested that he would bring some wine, and she had already got out the cut glasses, washed them, and shone them so that their little wedges were a sea of instant and changeable rainbows. He had not been told the sleeping arrangements, but the plan was that he would sleep on a divan and that the Victorian folding screen would be placed the length of the room when either of them wished to retire. Unfortunately, Miss Hawkins would have to pass through his half of the room to get to the bathroom, but as she said, a woman who has danced naked in Baghdad has no hesitation passing through a gentleman's room in her robe. She realized that there would be little debacles, perhaps misunderstandings, but the difficulties could be worked out. She had no doubt that they would achieve a harmony. She sat at the little round supper table and passed things politely. She was practicing. Miss Hawkins had not passed an entrée dish for years. She decided to use the linen napkins and got out two of her mother's bone napkin holders. They smelled of vanilla. "Nice man coming," she would tell her little dog, as she tripped about tidying her drawers, dusting her dressing table, and debating the most subtle position for a photograph of her, from her cabaret days.

At length and without fully undressing, Miss Hawkins flopped onto her bed with her little dog beside her. Miss Hawkins had such dratted nightmares, stupid rigmaroles in which she was incarcerated, or ones in which she had to carry furniture or cater on nothing for a host of people. Indeed, an unsavory one, in which a cowpat became confused with a fried egg. Oh, was she vexed! She blamed the wine and she thanked the gods that she had not touched the little plum pudding which she had bought as a surprise for the Sunday meal. Her hands trembled and she was definitely on edge.

In the garden Miss Hawkins kept looking toward her own door lest he arrive early, lest she miss him. Her heart was in a dither. She thought, Supposing he changes his mind, or supposing he brings his horrid friends, or supposing he stays out all night; each new crop of supposing made Miss Hawkins more bad-tempered. Supposing he did not arrive. Unfortunately, it brought to mind those earlier occasions in Miss Hawkins's life when she had been disappointed, nay jilted. The day when she had packed to go abroad with her diamond-smuggling lover, who never came, and when somehow, out of shock, she had remained fully dressed, even with her lace gloves on, in her rocking chair for two days until her cleaning woman came. She also remembered that a man proposed to her, gave her an engagement ring, and was in fact already married. A bigamist. But, as he had the gall to tell her, he did not feel emotionally married, and then, to make matters worse, took photos of his children, twins, out of his wallet. Other losses came back to her, and she remembered bitterly her last tour in the provinces, when people laughed and guffawed at her and even threw eggs.

By lunchtime Miss Hawkins was quite distraught, and she wished that she had a best friend. She even wished that there was some telephone service by which she could ring up an intelligent person, preferably a woman, and tell her the whole saga and have her fears dismissed.

By three o'clock Miss Hawkins was pacing her floor. The real trouble had been admitted. She was afraid. Afraid of the obvious. She might become attached, she might fall a fraction in love, she might cross the room, or shyly, he might cross the room and a wonderful surprise embrace might ensue, and Then. It was that Then that horrified her. She shuddered, she let out an involuntary "No." She could not bear to see him leave, even leave amicably. She dreaded suitcases, packing, goodbyes, stoicism, chin-up, her empty hand, the whole unbearable lodestone of it. She could not have him there. Quickly she penned the note; then she got her coat, her handbag, and her little dog in its basket and flounced out.

The note was on the top step under a milk bottle. It was addressed to him. The message said:

YOU MUST NEVER EVER UNDER ANY CIRCUMSTANCES COME HERE AGAIN.

Miss Hawkins took a taxi to Victoria and thence a train to Brighton. She had an invalid friend there to whom she owed a visit. In the train, as she looked out at the sooty suburbs, Miss Hawkins was willing to concede that she had done a very stupid thing indeed, but that it had to be admitted that it was not the most stupid thing she could have done. The most stupid thing would have been to welcome him in.

Ways

A narrow road and the first tentative fall of snow. A light fall that is merely preparatory and does not as yet make life cumbersome for the people of the herds. Around each clapboard house a belt of trees, and around the younger trees wooden V's to protect the boughs from the heavier snow. The air is crisp, and it is as if the countryside is suddenly, miraculously revealed—each hill, each hedgerow, each tiny declivity more pronounced in the mantle of snow. Autumn dreaminess is over and winter is being ushered in.

The road could be anywhere. The little birches, the sound of a river, the humped steel bridge, the herds of cattle, the silo sheds, and the little ill-defined tracks suggest the backwardness of Ireland or Scotland or Wales. But in fact it is Vermont. Together they are braving the elements—two women in their thirties who have met for a day. Jane has lent Nell, her visitor, a cape, snow boots, and fuzzy socks. They pass a house where three chained guard dogs rear up in the air and bark so fiercely it seems as if they might break their fetters and come and devour the passersby. Jane is a little ashamed; it is, after all, her neighborhood, her Vermont, and she wants things to be perfect for Nell. She is glad of the snow and points proudly to the little pouches of it, like doves' feathers, on a tree. She apologizes for the dogs by saying that the poor man has a wife who has been mentally ill for twenty years and has no help in the house.

"In there?" Nell says.

"Yes, she's in there somewhere," Jane says, and together they look at a little turret window with its second frame of fresh snow and a plate glass with a tint of blue in it. Together they say, "Jane Eyre," and think how eerie to be telepathic, having only just met.

"You were wonderful last night," Jane says.

"I was nervous," Nell says.

"Ironing your dress, I guess I was, too. It was so delicate, I was so afraid."

"Afraid?"

"That it might just disappear."

Nell remembers the evening before—arriving from New York, going up to a cold bedroom, and taking out a sheaf of poems she was going to read to the English Department of the university where Jane and her husband teach. Scrambling through her notes in the guest bedroom, searching anxiously for a spare refill for her pen, she was once again envisaging a terrible scene in which her head would be hacked off and would go rolling down the aisle between rows of patient people, while her obedient mouth would go on uttering the lines she had prepared. Always, before she appeared in public, these nervous fits assailed her, and more than anything she longed for a kind hand on her brow, a voice saying "There, there."

Jane had ironed the dress Nell had chosen to wear and brought it up, moving on tiptoe. She asked if Nell wanted to wash and had given her a towel that was halfway between a hand towel and a bath towel. Nell said that she might like a drink to steady her nerves—only one—and shortly afterward, on a tiny little gallery tray, there was a glass of sweet sherry and some oatmeal biscuits. As she changed into the dress, taking her time to fasten the little buttons along the cuffs, the bells from three different churches pealed out, and she said an impromptu prayer and felt dismally alone. As if guessing, her hostess reentered, carrying an electric heater and a patchwork bedcover. They stood listening to the last peal of the last bell, and Nell thought how Jane was kindness itself in opening her house to a stranger. Not only that, but Jane had gone to the trouble of typing out a list of people at the university whom Nell would meet, adding little dossiers as to their function and what they were like.

"And what do you do apart from teaching?" Nell asked.

"I like to give my time to my family," Jane said.

"Social life?"

"No, we keep to ourselves," Jane said, following this with a little smile, a smile with which she punctuated most of her remarks.

Jane took her on a tour of the house then, and Nell saw it all—the three bedrooms, the guest room with the patchwork quilt, the pink shells on the little girl's bureau, the teddy bear with most of its fur sucked bare, four easy chairs in the living room, and the seven new kittens around the kitchen stove, curled up and as motionless as muffs in a shop window. Jane explained how two kittens were already booked, three would be taken on loan, and the remaining two would stay with the mother and be part of their family. Pinned to the wall in the kitchen was a list of possible Christmas gifts, and when Nell read them she felt some sort of twinge:

Make skirt for Sarah
Grape jelly for Anne
Secondhand book for Josh
Little bottles of bath essence

The house and its order made such an impression on her that she thought she would like to live in it and be part of its solidity. Then two things happened. A kitten detached itself from the fur mass, stood on its hind legs, and nibbled one of Jane's slippers, which was lying there. Then it shadow-boxed, expecting the slipper also to move. Next thing, the hall door opened, someone came in, went through to the parlor, another door was heard to bang, and almost at once Mozart was being played on a fiddle. It was Jane's husband. Jane went to see him, to inquire if he wanted anything, and to tell him that the new guest had come and was very content and had brought a wonderful present—a cut-glass decanter, no less. He seemed not to reply. The fiddle playing went on, and to Nell there was something desperate in it.

Soon after, the two women left for the reading and Jane kept a beautiful silence in the car, allowing Nell to do her deep breathing and memorize her poems. Afterward, they went to a party, and during the party Nell went into the bathroom, watched herself in someone's cracked mirror, and asked herself why it was that everyone was married, or coupled—that everyone had a husband to go home to, a husband to get a drink for, a husband to humor, a husband to deceive—but not she. She wondered if there was some basic attribute missing in her that made her unwifely or unlovable, and concluded that it must be so. She then had an unbearable longing to be at home in her own house in Ireland, having a solitary drink by the open fire as she looked out at the river Blackwater.

"What does your husband look like?" she asks of Jane now as they trudge along the road. It is colder than when they set out, and the snow is pelting against their faces. They have to step aside to let a snowplow pass them on the road, and Jane is smiling as she envisages her answer. It is as if she enjoys the prospect of describing her husband, of doing him justice.

"You two girls in trouble?" asks the driver of the snowplow, and they both say they are simply taking a walk. He shakes his head and seems to think that they are a little mad, then he smiles. His smile reaches them in a haze of snow. They wave him on.

The branches of the birches teeter like swaying children. The icicles are just formed and wet; they look enticing and as if they might melt. With her thumbnail Jane flicks open a round locket that hangs from a fine chain about her neck, and there in cameo is a man—gaunt and pensive, very much the type that Nell is drawn toward. At once she feels in herself some premonition of a betrayal.

"He's lovely," she says, but offhandedly.

" 'I don't want you lovely' was what he told me," Jane says.

"Not one of King Arthur's knights," Nell says, gobbling a few flakes of snow.

"It wasn't a romantic thing," Jane says.

"What was it?" Nell says, nettled.

"It was me being very adoring," Jane says. "I have a theory it's better that way."

"I don't believe you," Nell says, and stands still, causing Jane to stand also, so that she can look into Jane's eyes. They are gray and not particularly fetching, but they are without guile.

"You're prying," Jane says.

"You're hiding," Nell says, and they laugh. They are bickering now. They look again at his likeness. The snow has smeared the features, and with her gloved thumb Jane wipes them. Then she snaps the locket closed and drops it down inside her turtleneck sweater—to warm him, she says.

"How did you catch him?" Nell says, putting her arm around Jane and tickling her lightly below her ribs.

"Unfortunately, I was one of those exceptional women who get pregnant even when they take precautions," Jane says, shaking her head.

"Was he livid?" Nell says, putting herself in the man's shoes.

"No; he said, 'I guess I'll have to marry you, Sarah Jane,' and we did."

It is the "we" that Nell envies. It has assurance, despite the other woman's nonassertiveness.

"I was married in gray," Jane says. "I simply had a prayer book and spring flowers. Dan's mother was so upset about it all that she left during the breakfast. Then we went back to the college, and he read a paper to the students on Mary Shelley."

"Poor Mary Shelley," Nell says, feeling a chill all of a sudden, a knife-edged chill that she cannot account for.

"You'd like him," Jane says, worried by the sudden silence.

"Why would I like him?" Nell says, picturing the face of the man that stared out of the locket. All of a sudden Nell has a longing not to leave as planned, at six o'clock, for New York, but to stay and meet him.

"Why don't I stay till tomorrow?" she says as casually as she can.

"But that would be wonderful," Jane says, and without hesitation turns sharply around so that they can hurry home to get the Jerusalem artichokes out of the pit before it has snowed over. She discusses a menu, says Dan will play his favorite pieces for them on the phonograph—adding that he never lets anybody else touch the machine, only himself.

Nell's thought is "a prison"—a prison such as she had once been in, where the precious objects belonged to the man, and the dusters and brooms belonged to her, the woman.

"He's good to you?" Nell says.

"He's quite good to me," Jane says.

Men are hunting deer up in the hills, and the noise of the shots volleys across the field with far greater clarity because of the soundlessness created by the snow. Again, on their way back, they pass the snarling dogs, and they literally run down a hill and across a stubbled field to take a shortcut home. The menu is decided—artichoke soup, roast pork, fried potatoes, and pecan pie. They both profess to be starving. They pass through a village on the way home and Nell stays behind to buy wine and other treats. She lingers outside the one general store, imagining what it would be like to live in such a place—to be wife, widow, or spinster. She thinks again of her own stone house, the scene of occasional parties and gatherings, when her friends come and she and Biddy, a helper from the village, cook for days; then the aftermath, when they clean up.

The three village churches are white and enveloped in snow; the garage is offering a discount on snow tires, and an elderly woman is pushing in the door to the general store, bringing back three circulating-library novels. In the shop window are two hand-printed signs:

> WE ARE A FAMILY OF THREE SISTERS LOOKING FOR A HOUSE TO RENT. WE CAN AFFORD UP TO $300.
>
> LOST: HARVEST TABLE, WEATHERED.

She goes inside and buys rashly. Yes, she is curious. Something in Dan's expression makes her tremble with pleasure. Already she has decided on her wardrobe for tonight, and resolves to be timid, in her best sky-blue georgette dress. She buys a gourd filled with sweets for the little girl and a storm lamp for the little boy.

The children are in the kitchen when she gets back, and how excited they are at receiving these presents. They gabble outrageously about their school lunch, and how gooey it was; then they sing a carol out of harmony; then the little girl admits in a whisper that she loves Nell and gives her a present of a composition she has just written about King Arthur. Nell reads it aloud; it is about King Arthur looking for a magic harp for his bride, Guinevere. The little boy says it is soppy and his sister whacks him with his new lamp. What can she do to help? Nell asks. Jane says she can do nothing.

After the ordeal of the night before, and the fitful sleep because of the boiler going on and off, she must be tired and should nap. Jane tells the children that they must be like little mice and do their homework and not squabble.

There is a harness bell attached to the back door, and it trembles a second before it actually rings, and by then he is in. He is like someone out of Nell's fantasy—an ascetic man in a long leather coat turned up about the neck, and he wears gauntlet gloves, which he immediately begins to remove. His children run to him; he kisses his wife; and, upon being introduced to Nell, he nods. There is something in that nod that is significant. It is too offhand. Nell sees him look at her with his lids lowered, and she sees him stiffen when his wife says that their guest will stay overnight and then points to the wine. He says, "Fancy," as he looks at the labels with approval, and the children ask if they can make butter sauce for the pecan pie.

Nell is having to tell them, the children, the size of her house in Ireland, the kind of ceiling, the cornices, the different wallpapers in the bedrooms, the orchard, the long tree-lined drive, the white gate, the lych-gate, the supposed ghost, and everything else pertaining to the place. They say they will visit her when they come to Europe. He does not comment but keeps moving about the kitchen. He looks at the thermometer, pushes the kittens to one side with a toe of his shoe, rakes the stove, and then very slowly begins to open the wine. He smells the corks and very carefully attaches them to the sides of the bottles, using the metallic paper as a cord.

Jane is recalling London—springtime there, a hotel in Bayswater, a trip she had made as a girl with a blind aunt—and remarking to Nell how she saw everything so much more clearly simply by having had to describe it to her aunt. She speaks of the picture galleries, the parks, the little squares, the muffins they were served for breakfast, and the high anthracite-colored wire mesh around the London Zoo.

"I like being an escort," she says shyly.

Suddenly Nell has to excuse herself, saying that she must take a last-minute nap, that her eyes feel scorched.

"I can't," she says later as she lies coiled on her bed, trying to eat back her own tears. All she wants is for the man to come up and nuzzle her and hold her and temporarily squeeze all the solitude out of her. All she wants is a kiss. But that is vicious. She foresees the evening, a replica of other evenings—a look, then ignoring him, then a longer look, a signal, an intuition, a hand maybe, pouring wine, brushing lightly against a wrist, the hair on his knuckles, her chaste cuffs, innocent chatter stoked with something else. She imagines the night—lying awake, creaks, desire fulfilled or unfulfilled. She sees it all. She bites the bedcover; she makes a face. Every tiny eye muscle is squeezed together. The chill that she felt up on the road is upon her again. She might clench the bedpost, but it is made of brass and is unwelcoming.

"I'm afraid I can't," she says, bursting into the bathroom where Jane has taken a shower. She knows it is Jane because of the shadow through the glass-paneled door.

"Oh, my dear," Jane says, pushing the door open and stepping out.

"I just realized it isn't possible," Nell says, not able to make any excuse except that she has packed and that she must make her plane for New York. Jane says she understands and reaches for a towel to dry herself. Nell begins to help.

"I'm tiny up top," Jane says, apologizing for her little nipples and flat chest. She drags on a thick sweater, slacks, her husband's socks, and then she reaches to a china soap dish and picks up a cluster of hairpins, putting them quickly in her long damp hair.

Dan is in the toolshed, and the two women holler goodbye. The children say, "No, no, no," and to make up for this sudden disappointment, Jane and Nell carry them to the car in their slippers and put them under a blanket on the back seat. They will come for the drive. In the car, Jane says that maybe next year, when the attic room is ready, Nell will come back and stay up there and write her poetry. Jane's face is faintly Technicolor because of the lights from the dashboard, and her hair is gradually starting to fall down because of the careless way she has put in the hairpins. She looks almost rakish. She says what a shame that Nell has not seen one maple tree in full leaf, to which Nell says yes, that she might come back one day—but she knows that she is just saying this.

Does Jane know? Nell wonders. Does Jane guess? Behind that

lovely exterior is Jane a woman who knows all the ways, all the wiles, all the heart's crooked actions?

"Are you jealous, or do you ever have occasion?" Nell asks.

"I have had occasion," Jane says.

"And what did you do?" Nell asks.

"Well, the first time I made a scene—a bad scene. I threw dishes," she says, lowering her voice.

"Christ," Nell says, but is unable to visualize it, is unable to connect the violence with Jane's restraint.

"The second time, I started to teach. I kept busy," Jane says.

They are driving very slowly, and Nell wonders if, in the back, the children are listening as they pretend to sleep under the blanket. Nell looks out of the window at rows of tombstones covered in snow and evenly spaced. The cemetery is on a hill and, being just on the outskirts of the town, seems to command it. It seems integral to the town, as if the living and the dead are wedded to one another.

"And now?" Nell says.

"I guess Dan and I have had to do some growing up," Jane says.

"Who's growing up—Daddy?" asks the little girl from under the blanket.

Her mother says, "Yes, Daddy," and then adds that his feet are getting bigger.

All four of them laugh.

"He liked you," Jane says, and gives Nell a little glance.

"I doubt it," Nell says.

"He sure did," Jane tells her, convinced.

Nell knows then that Jane has perceived it all and has been willing to let the night and its drama occur. She feels such a tenderness, a current not unlike love, but she does not say a word.

In the airport, they have only minutes to check in the luggage and have Nell's ticket endorsed. The children become exhilarated and pretend to want to place their slippered feet on the conveyor belt so as to get whisked away. The flight is called.

"I think you're very fine," Nell says at the turnstile by the passenger area.

"Not as fine as you," Jane says.

Something is waiting to get said. It hangs in the air and Nell recalls the newly formed icicles that they had seen on their walk the day before. More than anything she wants to turn back, to sit in that house, beside the stove, to exchange stories and become a friend of this woman. Politeness drives her forward. Her sleeve catches in the metal pike of the turnstile and Jane picks it out, in the nick of time.

"Clumsy," Nell says, holding up a cuff with one thread raveled.

"We're all clumsy," Jane says.

They exchange a look, and realizing that they are on the point of either laughing or crying, they say goodbye hurriedly. Ahead of her Nell sees a long slope of cork-covered floor and for a minute she's afraid that her legs will not see her safely along it, but they do. Walking down, she smiles and thanks the small voice of instinct that has sent her away without doing the slightest damage to one who meets life's little treacheries with a smile and dissembles them simply by pretending that they are not meant.

A Rose in the Heart of New York

December night. Jack Frost in scales along the outside of the windows giving to the various rooms a white filtered light. The ice like bits of mirror beveling the puddles of the potholes. The rooms were cold inside, and for the most part identically furnished. The room with no furniture at all—save for the apples gathered in the autumn—was called the Vacant Room. The apples were all over the place. Their smell was heady, many of them having begun to rot. Rooms into which no one had stepped for days, and yet these rooms and their belongings would become part of the remembered story. A solemn house, set in its own grounds, away from the lazy bustle of the village. A lonesome house, it would prove to be, and with a strange lifelikeness, as if it were not a house at all but a person observing and breathing, a presence amid a cluster of trees and sturdy wind-shorn hedges.

The overweight midwife hurried up the drive, her serge cape blowing behind her. She was puffing. She carried her barrel-shaped leather bag in which were disinfectant, gauze, forceps, instruments, and a small bottle of holy water lest the new child should prove to be in danger of death. More infants died around Christmastime than in any other month of the year. When she passed the little sycamore tree that was halfway up, she began to hear the roaring and beseeching to God. Poor mother, she thought, poor poor mother. She was not too early, had come more or less at the correct time, even though she was summoned hours before by Donal, the serving boy who worked on the farm. She had brought most of the children of that parish into the world, yet had neither kith nor kin of her own. Coming in the back door, she took off her bonnet and then attached it to the knob by means of its elastic string.

It was a blue room—walls of dark wet morose blue, furniture made of walnut, including the bed on which the event was taking place. Fronting the fireplace was a huge lid of a chocolate box with the representation of a saucy-looking lady. The tassel of the blind kept bobbing against the frosted windowpane. There was a washstand, a basin and ewer of off-white, with big roses splashed throughout the china itself, and a huge lumbering beast of a wardrobe. The midwife recalled once going to a house up the mountain, and finding that the child had been smothered by the time she arrived, the fatherless child had been stuffed in a drawer. The moans filled that room and went beyond the distempered walls out into the cold hall outside, where the black felt doggie with the amber eyes stood sentinel on a tall varnished whatnot. At intervals the woman apologized to the midwife for the untoward commotion, said sorry in a gasping whisper, and then was seized again by a pain that at different times she described as being a knife, a dagger, a hell on earth. It was her fourth labor. The previous child had died two days after being born. An earlier child, also a daughter, had died of whooping cough. Her womb was sick unto death. Why be a woman. Oh, cruel life; oh, merciless fate; oh, heartless man, she sobbed. Gripping the coverlet and remembering that between those selfsame, much-patched sheets, she had been prized apart, again and again, with not a word to her, not a little endearment, only rammed through and told to open up. When she married she had escaped the life of a serving girl, the possible experience of living in some grim institution, but as time went on and the bottom drawer was emptied of its gifts, she saw that she was made to serve in an altogether other way. When she wasn't screaming she was grinding her head into the pillow and praying for it to be all over. She dreaded the eventual bloodshed long before they saw any. The midwife made her ease up as she put an old sheet under her and over that a bit of oilcloth. The midwife said it was no joke and repeated the hypothesis that if men had to give birth there would not be a child born in the whole wide world. The husband was downstairs getting paralytic. Earlier when his wife had announced that she would have to go upstairs because of her labor, he said, looking for the slightest pretext for a celebration, that if there was any homemade wine or altar wine stacked away, to get it out, to produce it, and also the cut glasses. She said there was none and well he knew it, since they could hardly afford tea and sugar. He started to root and to rummage, to empty cupboards of their contents of rags, garments, and provisions, even to put his hand inside the bolster case, to delve into pillows; on he went, rampaging until he found a bottle in the wardrobe, in the very room into which she delivered her moans and exhortations. She begged of him not to, but all he did was to wield the amber-colored bottle in her direction, and then put it to his head so that the spirit started to go glug-glug. It was intoxicating stuff. By a wicked coincidence a crony of his had come to sell them another stove, most likely another crock, a thing that would have to be coaxed alight with constant attention and puffing to create a draft. The other child was with a neighbor, the dead ones in a graveyard six or seven miles away, among strangers and distant relatives, without their names being carved on the crooked rain-soaked tomb.

"O Jesus," she cried out as he came back to ask for a knitting needle to skewer out the bit of broken cork.

"Blazes," he said to her as she coiled into a knot and felt the big urgent ball—that would be the head—as it pressed on the base of her bowels and battered at her insides.

Curses and prayers combined to issue out of her mouth, and as time went on, they became most pitiful and were interrupted with screams. The midwife put a facecloth on her forehead and told her to push, in the name of the Lord to push. She said she had no strength left, but the midwife went on enjoining her and simulating a hefty breath. It took over an hour. The little head showing its tonsure would recoil, would reshow itself, each time a fraction more, although, in between, it was seeming to shrink from the world that it was hurtling toward. She said to the nurse that she was being burst apart, and that she no longer cared if she died, or if they drank themselves to death. In the kitchen they were sparring over who had the best greyhound, who had the successor to Mick the Miller. The crucifix that had been in her hand had fallen out, and her hands themselves felt bony and skinned because of the way they wrenched one another.

"In the name of God, push, missus."

She would have pushed everything out of herself, her guts, her womb, her craw, her lights, and her liver, but the center of her body was holding on and this center seemed to be the governor of her. She wished to be nothing, a shell, devoid of everything and everyone, and she was announcing that, and roaring and raving, when the child came hurtling out, slowly at first, as if its neck could not wring its way through, then the shoulder—that was the worst bit—carving a straight course, then the hideous turnabout, and a scream other than her own, and an urgent presage of things, as the great gouts of blood and lymph followed upon the mewling creature itself. Her last bit of easiness was then torn from her, and she was without hope. It had come into the world lopsided, and the first announcement from the midwife was a fatality, was that it had clubbed feet. Its little feet, she ventured to say, were like two stumps adhering to one another, and the blasted cord was bound around its neck. The result was a mewling piece of screwed-up, inert, dark-purple misery. The men subsided a little when the announcement was shouted down and they came to say congrats. The father waved a strip of pink flesh on a fork that he was carrying and remarked on its being unappetizing. They were cooking a goose downstairs and he said in future he would insist on turkey, as goose was only for gobs and goms. The mother felt green and disgusted, asked them to leave her alone. The salesman said was it a boy or a child, although he had just been told that it was a daughter. The mother could feel the blood gushing out of her, like water at a weir. The midwife told them to go down and behave like gentlemen.

Then she got three back numbers of the weekly paper, and a shoe box with a lid, and into it she stuffed the mess and the unnecessaries. She hummed as she prepared to do the stitching down the line of torn flesh that was gaping and coated with blood. The mother roared again and said this indeed was her vinegar and gall. She bit into the crucifix and dented it further. She could feel her mouth and her eyelids being stitched, too; she was no longer a lovely body, she was a vehicle for pain and for insult. The child was so quiet it scarcely breathed. The afterbirth was placed on the stove, where the dog, Shep, sniffed at it through its layers of paper and for his curiosity got a kick in the tail. The stove had been quenched, and the midwife said to the men that it was a crying shame to leave a good goose like that, neither cooked nor uncooked. The men had torn off bits of the breast so that the goose looked wounded, like the woman upstairs, who was then tightening her heart and soul, tightening inside the array of catgut stitches, and regarding her whole life as a vast disappointment. The midwife carried the big bundle up to the cellar, put an oil rag to it, set a match to it, and knew that she would have to be off soon to do the same task elsewhere. She would have liked to stay and swaddle the infant, and comfort the woman, and drink hot sweet tea, but there was not enough time. There was never enough time, and she hadn't even cleaned out the ashes or the cinders in her grate that morning.

The child was in a corner of the room in a brown cot with slats that rattled because of the racket they had received from the previous children. The mother was not proud, far from it. She fed the child its first bottle, looked down at its wizened face, and thought, Where have you come from and why? She had no choice of a name. In fact, she said to her first visitor, a lieutenant from the army, not to tell her a pack of lies, because this child had the ugliest face that had ever seen the light of day. That Christmas the drinking and sparring went on, the odd neighbor called, the mother got up on the third day and staggered down to do something about the unruly kitchen. Each evening at nightfall she got a bit of a candle to have handy and re-oiled the Sacred Heart lamp for when the child cried. They both contracted bronchitis and the child was impounded in masses of flannel and flannelette.

Things changed. The mother came to idolize the child, because it was so quiet, never bawling, never asking for anything, just weirdly still in its pram, the dog watching over it, its eyes staring out at whatever happened to loom in. Its very ugliness disappeared. It seemed to drink them in with its huge, contemplating, slightly hazed-over, navy eyes. They shone at whatever they saw. The mother would look in the direction of the pram and say a little prayer for it, or smile, and often at night she held the candle shielded by her hand to see the face, to say pet or tush, to say nonsense to it. It ate whatever it was given, but as time went on, it knew what it liked and had a sweet tooth. The food was what united them, eating off the same plate, using the same spoon, watching one another's chews, feeling the food as it went down the other's neck. The child was slow to crawl and slower still to walk, but it knew everything, it perceived everything. When it ate blancmange or junket, it was eating part of the lovely substance of its mother.

They were together, always together. If its mother went to the post office, the child stood in the middle of the drive praying until its mother returned safely. The child cut the ridges of four fingers along the edge of a razor blade that had been wedged upright in the wood of the dresser, and seeing these four deep, horizontal identical slits the mother took the poor fingers into her own mouth and sucked them, to lessen the pain, and licked them to abolish the blood, and kept saying soft things until the child was stilled again.

Her mother's knuckles were her knuckles, her mother's veins were her veins, her mother's lap was a second heaven, her mother's forehead a copybook onto which she traced A B C D, her mother's body was a recess that she would wander inside forever and ever, a sepulcher growing deeper and deeper. When she saw other people, especially her pretty sister, she would simply wave from that safe place, she would not budge, would not be lured out. Her father took a hatchet to her mother and threatened that he would split open the head of her. The child watched through the kitchen window, because this debacle took place outdoors on a hillock under the three beech trees where the clothesline stretched, then sagged. The mother had been hanging out the four sheets washed that morning, two off each bed. The child was engaged in twisting her hair, looping it around bits of white rag, to form ringlets, decking herself in the kitchen mirror, and then every other minute running across to the window to reconnoiter, wondering what she ought to do, jumping up and down as if she had a pain, not knowing what to do, running back to the mirror, hoping that the terrible scene would pass, that the ground would open up and swallow her father, that the hatchet would turn into a magic wand, that her mother would come through the kitchen door and say "Fear not," that travail would all be over. Later she heard a verbatim account of what had happened. Her father demanded money, her mother refused same on the grounds that she had none, but added that if she had it she would hang sooner than give it to him. That did it. It was then he really got bucking, gritted his teeth and his muscles, said that he would split the head of her, and the mother said that if he did so there was a place for him. That place was the lunatic asylum. It was twenty or thirty miles away, a big gray edifice, men and women lumped in together, some in strait-jackets, some in padded cells, some blindfolded because of having sacks thrown over their heads, some strapped across the chest to quell and impede them. Those who did not want to go there were dragged by relatives, or by means of rope, some being tied on to the end of a plow or a harrow and brought in on all fours, like beasts of the earth. Then when they were not so mad, not so rampaging, they were let home again, where they were very peculiar and given to smiling and to chattering to themselves, and in no time they were ripe to go off again or to be dragged off. March was the worst month, when everything went askew, even the wind, even the March hares. Her father did not go there. He went off on a batter and then went to a monastery, and then was brought home and shook in the bed chair for five days, eating bread and milk and asking who would convey him over the fields, until he saw his yearlings, and when no one volunteered to, it fell to her because she was the youngest. Over in the fields he patted the yearlings and said soppy things that he'd never say indoors, or to a human, and he cried and said he'd never touch a drop again, and there was a dribble on his pewter-brown mustache that was the remains of the mush he had been eating, and the yearling herself became fidgety and fretful as if she might bolt or stamp the ground to smithereens.

The girl and her mother took walks on Sundays—strolls, picked blackberries, consulted them for worms, made preserve, and slept side by side, entwined like twigs of trees or the ends of the sugar tongs. When she wakened and found that her mother had got up and was already mixing meals for the hens or stirabout for the young pigs, she hurried down, carrying her clothes under her arm, and dressed in whatever spot she could feast on the sight of her mother most. Always an egg for breakfast. An egg a day and she would grow strong. Her mother never ate an egg but topped the girl's egg and fed her it off the tarnished eggy spoon and gave her little sups of tea with which to wash it down. She had her own mug, red enamel and with not a chip. The girl kept looking back as she went down the drive for school, and as time went on, she mastered the knack of walking backward to be able to look all the longer, look at the aproned figure waving or holding up a potato pounder or a colander, or whatever happened to be in her hand.

The girl came home once and the mother was missing. Her mother had actually fulfilled her promise of going away one day and going to a spot where she would not be found. That threatened spot was the bottom of the lake. But in fact her mother had gone back to her own family, because the father had taken a shotgun to her and had shot her but was not a good aim like William Tell, had missed, had instead made a hole in the Blue Room wall. What were they doing upstairs in the middle of the day, an ascent they never made except the mother alone to dress the two beds. She could guess. She slept in a neighbor's house, slept in a bed with two old people who reeked of eucalyptus. She kept most of her clothes on and shriveled into herself, not wanting to touch or be touched by these two old people buried in their various layers of skin and hair and winceyette. Outside the window was a climbing rose with three or four red flowers along the bow of it, and looking at the flowers and thinking of the wormy clay, she would try to shut out what these two old people were saying, in order that she could remember the mother whom she despaired of ever seeing again. Not far away was their own house, with the back door wide open so that any stranger or tinker could come in or out. The dog was probably lonely and bloodied from hunting rabbits, the hens were forgotten about and were probably in their coops, hysterical, picking at one another's feathers because of their nerves. Eggs would rot. If she stood on the low whitewashed wall that fronted the cottage, she could see over the high limestone wall that boundaried their fields and then look to the driveway that led to the abandoned house itself. To her it was like a kind of castle where strange things had happened and would go on happening. She loved it and she feared it. The sky behind and above gave it mystery, sometimes made it broody, and gave it a kind of splendor when the red streaks in the heavens were like torches that betokened the performance of a gory play. All of a sudden, standing there, with a bit of grass between her front teeth, looking at her home and imagining this future drama, she heard the nearby lych-gate open and then shut with a clang, and saw her father appear, and jumped so clumsily she thought she had broken everything, particularly her ribs. She felt she was in pieces. She would be like Humpty-Dumpty, and all the king's horses and all the king's men would not be able to put her together again. Dismemberment did happen, a long time before, the time when her neck swelled out into a big fleshed balloon. She could only move her neck on one side, because the other side was like a ball and full of fluid and made gluggles when she touched it with her fingers. They were going to lance it. They placed her on a kitchen chair. Her mother boiled a saucepan of water. Her mother stood on another chair and reached far into the rear of a cupboard and hauled out a new towel. Everything was in that cupboard, sugar and tea and round biscuits and white flour and linen and must and mice. First one man, then another, then another man, then a last man who was mending the chimney, and then last of all her father each took hold of her—an arm, another arm, a shoulder, a waist, and her two flying legs that were doing everything possible not to be there. The lady doctor said nice things and cut into the big football of her neck, and it was like a pig's bladder bursting all over, the waters flowing out, and then it was not like that at all; it was like a sword on the bone of her neck sawing, cutting into the flesh, deeper and deeper, the men pressing upon her with all their might, saying that she was a demon, and the knife went into her swallow or where she thought of forever more as her swallow, and the lady doctor said, "Drat it," because she had done the wrong thing—had cut too deep and had to start scraping now, and her older sister danced a jig out on the flagstones so that neighbors going down the road would not get the impression that someone was being murdered. Long afterward she came back to the world of voices, muffled voices, and their reassurances, and a little something sweet to help her get over it all, and the lady doctor putting on her brown fur coat and hurrying to her next important work of mercy.

When she slept with the neighbors the old man asked the old woman were they ever going to be rid of her, were they going to have this dunce off their hands, were they saddled with her for the rest of their blooming lives. She declined the milk they gave her because it was goat's milk and too yellow and there was dust in it. She would answer them in single syllables, just yes or no, mostly no. She was learning to frown, so that she, too, would have A B C's. Her mother's forehead and hers would meet in heaven, salute, and all their lines would coincide. She refused food. She pined. In all, it was about a week.

The day her mother returned home—it was still January—the water pipes had burst, and when she got to the neighbors' and was told she could go on up home, she ran with all her might and resolution, so that her windpipe ached and then stopped aching when she found her mother down on her knees dealing with pools of water that had gushed from the red pipes. The brown rag was wet every other second and had to be wrung out and squeezed in the big chipped basin, the one she was first bathed in. The lodges of water were everywhere, lapping back and forth, threatening to expand, to discolor the tiles, and it was of this hazard they talked and fretted over rather than the mother's disappearance, or the dire cause of it, or the reason for her return. They went indoors and got the ingredients and the utensils and the sieve so as to make an orange cake with orange filling and orange icing. She never tasted anything so wonderful in all her life. She ate three big hunks, and her mother put her hand around her and said if she ate any more she would have a little corporation.

The father came home from the hospital, cried again, said that sure he wouldn't hurt a fly, and predicted that he would never break his pledge or go outside the gate again, only to Mass, never leave his own sweet acres. As before, the girl slept with her mother, recited the Rosary with her, and shared the small cubes of dark raisin-filled chocolate, then trembled while her mother went along to her father's bedroom for a tick, to stop him bucking. The consequences of those visits were deterred by the bits of tissue paper, a protection between herself and any emission. No other child got conceived, and there was no further use for the baggy napkins, the bottle, and the dark-brown mottled teat. The cot itself was sawn up and used to back two chairs, and they constituted something of the furniture in the big upstairs landing, where the felt dog still lorded over it but now had an eye missing because a visiting child had poked wire at it. The chairs were painted oxblood red and had the sharp end of a nail dragged along the varnish to give a wavering effect. Also on the landing was a bowl with a bit of wire inside to hold a profusion of artificial tea roses. These tea roses were a two-toned color, were red and yellow plastic, and the point of each petal was seared like the point of a thorn. Cloth flowers were softer. She had seen some once, very pale pink and purple, made of voile, in another house, in a big jug, tumbling over a lady's bureau. In the landing at home, too, was the speared head of Christ, which looked down on all the proceedings with endless patience, endless commiseration. Underneath Christ was a pussy cat of black papier-mâché which originally had sweets stuffed into its middle, sweets the exact image of strawberries and even with a little leaf at the base, a leaf made of green-glazed angelica. They liked the same things—applesauce and beetroot and tomato sausages and angelica. They cleaned the windows, one the inside, the other the outside, they sang duets, they put newspapers over the newly washed dark-red tiles so as to keep them safe from the muck and trampalations of the men. About everything they agreed, or almost everything.

In the dark nights the wind used to sweep through the window and out on the landing and into the other rooms, and into the Blue Room, by now uninhabited. The wardrobe door would open of its own accord, or the ewer would rattle, or the lovely buxom Our Lady of Limerick picture would fall onto the marble washstand and there was a rumpus followed by prognostications of bad luck for seven years. When the other child came back from boarding school, the girl was at first excited, prepared lovingly for her, made cakes, and, soon after, was plunged into a state of wretchedness. Her mother was being taken away from her, or, worse, was gladly giving her speech, her attention, her hands, and all of her gaze to this intruder. Her mother and her older sister would go upstairs, where her mother would have some little treat for her, a hanky or a hanky sachet, and once a remnant that had been got at the mill at reduced price, due to a fire there. Beautiful, a flecked salmon pink.

Downstairs *she* had to stack dishes onto the tray. She banged the cups, she put a butter knife into the two-pound pot of black-currant jam and hauled out a big helping, then stuck the greasy plates one on top of the other, whereas normally she would have put a fork in between to protect the undersides. She dreamed that her mother and her rival sister were going for a walk and she asked to go too, but they sneaked off. She followed on a bicycle, but once outside the main gate could not decide whether to go to the left or the right, and then, having decided, made the wrong choice and stumbled on a herd of bullocks, all butting one another and endeavoring to get up into one another's backside. She turned back, and there they were strolling up the drive, like two sedate ladies linking and laughing, and the salmon-flecked remnant was already a garment, a beautiful swagger coat which her sister wore with a dash.

"I wanted to be with you," she said, and one said to the other, "She wanted to be with us," and then no matter what she said, no matter what the appeal, they repeated it as if she weren't there. In the end she knew that she would have to turn away from them, because she was not wanted, she was in their way. As a result of that dream, or rather the commotion that she made in her sleep, it was decided that she had worms, and the following morning they gave her a dose of turpentine and castor oil, the same as they gave the horses.

When her sister went back to the city, happiness was restored again. Her mother consulted her about the design on a leather bag which she was making. Her mother wanted a very old design, something concerning the history of their country. She said there would have to be battles and then peace and wonderful scenes from nature. Her mother said that there must be a lot of back history to a land and that education was a very fine thing. Preferable to the bog, her mother said. The girl said when she grew up that she would get a very good job and bring her mother to America. Her mother mentioned the street in Brooklyn where she had lodged and said that it had adjoined a park. They would go there one day. Her mother said maybe.

The growing girl began to say the word "backside" to herself and knew that her mother would be appalled. The girl laughed at bullocks and the sport they had. Then she went one further and jumped up and down and said "Jumping Jack," as if some devil were inside her, touching and tickling the lining of her. It was creepy. It was done outdoors, far from the house, out in the fields, in a grove, or under a canopy of rhododendrons. The buds of the rhododendrons were sticky and oozed with life, and everything along with herself was soaking wet, and she was given to wandering flushes and then fits of untoward laughter, so that she had to scold herself into some state of normality and this she did by slapping both cheeks vehemently. As a dire punishment she took cups of Glauber's salts three times a day, choosing to drink it when it was lukewarm and at its most nauseating. She would be told by her father to get out, to stop hatching, to get out from under her mother's apron strings, and he would send her for a spin on the woeful brakeless bicycle. She would go to the chapel, finding it empty of all but herself and the lady sacristan, who spent her life in there polishing and rearranging the artificial flowers; or she would go down into a bog and make certain unattainable wishes, but always at the end of every day, and at the end of every thought, and at the beginning of sleep and the precise moment of wakening, it was of her mother and for her mother she existed, and her prayers and her good deeds and her ringlets and the ire on her legs—created by the serge of her gym frock—were for her mother's intention, and on and on. Only death could part them, and not even that, because she resolved that she would take her own life if some disease or some calamity snatched her mother away. Her mother's three-quarter-length jacket she would don, sink her hands into the deep pockets, and say the name "Delia," her mother's, say it in different tones of voice, over and over again, always in a whisper and with a note of conspiracy.

A lovely thing happened. Her mother and father went on a journey by hire car to do a transaction whereby they could get some credit on his lands, and her father did not get drunk but ordered a nice pot of tea, and then sat back gripping his braces and gave her mother a few bob, with which her mother procured a most beautiful lipstick in a ridged gold case. It was like fresh fruit, so moist was it, and coral red. Her mother and she tried it on over and over again, were comical with it, trying it on, then wiping it off, trying it on again, making cupids so that her mother expostulated and said what scatterbrains they were, and even the father joined in the hilarity and daubed down the mother's cheek and said Fanny Anny, and the mother said that was enough, as the lipstick was liable to get broken. With her thumbnail she pressed on the little catch, pushing the lipstick down into its case, into its bed. As the years went on, it dried out and developed a peculiar shape, and they read somewhere that a lady's character could be told by that particular shape, and they wished that they could discover whether the mother was the extrovert or the shy violet.

The girl had no friends, she didn't need any. Her cup was full. Her mother was the cup, the cupboard, the sideboard with all the things in it, the tabernacle with God in it, the lake with the legends in it, the bog with the wishing well in it, the sea with the oysters and the corpses in it, her mother a gigantic sponge, a habitation in which she longed to sink and disappear forever and ever. Yet she was afraid to sink, caught in that hideous trap between fear of sinking and fear of swimming, she moved like a flounderer through this and that; through school, through inoculation, through a man who put his white handkerchief between naked her and naked him, and against a galvanized outhouse door came, gruntling and disgruntling like a tethered beast upon her; through a best friend, a girl friend who tried to clip the hairs of her vagina with a shears. The hairs of her vagina were mahogany-colored, and her best friend said that that denoted mortal sin. She agonized over it. Then came a dreadful blow. Two nuns called and her mother and her father said that she was to stay outside in the kitchen and see that the kettle boiled and then lift it off so that water would not boil over. She went on tiptoe through the hall and listened at the door of the room. She got it in snatches. She was being discussed. She was being sent away to school. A fee was being discussed and her mother was asking if they could make a reduction. She ran out of the house in a dreadful state. She ran to the chicken run and went inside to cry and to go berserk. The floor was full of damp and gray-green mottled droppings. The nests were full of sour sops of hay. She thought she was going out of her mind. When they found her later, her father said to cut out the "bull," but her mother tried to comfort her by saying they had a prospectus and that she would have to get a whole lot of new clothes in navy blue. But where would the money come from?

In the convent to which they sent her she eventually found solace. A nun became her new idol. A nun with a dreadfully pale face and a master's degree in science. This nun and she worked out codes with the eyelids, and the flutter of the lashes, so they always knew each other's moods and feelings, so that the slightest hurt imposed by one was spotted by the other and responded to with a glance. The nun gave another girl more marks at the mid-term examination, and did it solely to hurt her, to wound her pride; the nun addressed her briskly in front of the whole class, said her full name and asked her a theological conundrum that was impossible to answer. In turn, she let one of the nun's holy pictures fall on the chapel floor, where of course it was found by the cleaning nun, who gave it back to the nun, who gave it to her with a "This seems to have got mislaid." They exchanged Christmas presents and notes that contained blissful innuendos. She had given chocolates with a kingfisher on the cover, and she had received a prayer book with gilt edging and it was as tiny as her little finger. She could not read the print but she held it to herself like a talisman, like a secret scroll in which love was mentioned.

Home on holiday it was a different story. Now *she* did the avoiding, the shunning. All the little treats and the carrageen soufflé that her mother had prepared were not gloated over. Then the pink crepe-de-Chine apron that her mother had made from an old dance dress did not receive the acclamation that the mother expected. It was fitted on and at once taken off and flung over the back of a chair with no praise except to remark on the braiding, which was cleverly done.

"These things are not to be sniffed at," her mother said, passing the plate of scones for the third or fourth time. The love of the nun dominated all her thoughts, and the nun's pale face got between her and the visible world that she was supposed to be seeing. At times she could taste it. It interfered with her studies, her other friendships, it got known about. She was called to see the Reverend Mother. The nun and she never had a tête-à-tête again and never swapped holy pictures. The day she was leaving forever they made an illicit date to meet in the summerhouse, out in the grounds, but neither of them turned up. They each sent a message with an apology, and it was, in fact, the messengers who met, a junior girl and a postulant carrying the same sentence on separate lips—"So-and-so is sorry—she wishes to say she can't . . ." They might have broken down or done anything, they might have kissed.

Out of school, away from the spell of nuns and gods and flower gardens and acts of contrition, away from the chapel with its incense and its brimstone sermons, away from surveillance, she met a bakery man who was also a notable hurley player and they started up that kind of courtship common to their sort—a date at Nelson's pillar two evenings a week, then to a café to have coffee and cream cakes, to hold hands under the table, to take a bus to her digs, to kiss against a railing and devour each other's face, as earlier they had devoured the mock cream and the sugar-dusted sponge cakes. But these orgies only increased her hunger, made it into something that could not be appeased. She would recall her mother from the very long ago, in the three-quarter-length jacket of salmon tweed, the brooch on the lapel, the smell of face powder, the lipstick hurriedly put on so that a little of it always smudged on the upper or the lower lip and appeared like some kind of birthmark. Recall that they even had the same mole on the back of the left hand, a mole that did not alter winter or summer and was made to seem paler when the fist was clenched. But she was recalling someone whom she wanted to banish. The bakery man got fed up, wanted more than a cuddle, hopped it. Then there was no one, just a long stretch, doing novenas, working in the library, and her mother's letters arriving, saying the usual things, how life was hard, how inclement the weather, how she'd send a cake that day or the next day, as soon as there were enough eggs to make it with. The parcels arrived once a fortnight, bound in layers of newspaper, and then a strong outer layer of brown paper, all held with hideous assortments of twines—binding twine, very white twine, and colored plastic string from the stools that she had taken to making; then great spatters of sealing wax adorning it. Always a registered parcel, always a cake, a pound of butter, and a chicken that had to be cooked at once, because of its being nearly putrid from the four-day journey. It was not difficult to imagine the kitchen table, the bucket full of feathers, the moled hand picking away at the pin feathers, the other hand plunging in and drawing out all the undesirables, tremulous, making sure not to break a certain little pouch, since its tobacco-colored fluid could ruin the taste of the bird. Phew. Always the same implications in each letter, the same cry—

"Who knows what life brings. Your father is not hard-boiled despite his failings. It makes me sad to think of the little things that I used to be able to do for you." She hated those parcels, despite the fact that they were most welcome.

She married. Married in haste. Her mother said from the outset that he was as odd as two left shoes. He worked on an encyclopedia and was a mine of information on certain subjects. His specialty was vegetation in pond life. They lived to themselves. She learned to do chores, to bottle and preserve, to comply, to be a wife, to undress neatly at night, to fold her clothes, to put them on a cane chair, making sure to put her corset and her underthings respectfully under her dress or her skirt. It was like being at school again. The mother did not visit, being at odds with the censuring husband. Mother and daughter would meet in a market town midway between each of their rural homes, and when they met they sat in some hotel lounge, ordered tea, and discussed things that can easily be discussed—

recipes, patterns for knitting, her sister, items of furniture that they envisaged buying. Her mother was getting older, had developed a slight stoop, and held up her hands to show the rheumatism in her joints. Then all of a sudden, as if she had just remembered it, she spoke about the cataracts, and her journey to the specialist, and how the specialist had asked her if she remembered anything about her eyes and how she had to tell him that she had lost her sight for five or six minutes one morning and that then it came back. He had told her how lucky it was, because in some instances it does not come back at all. She said yes, the shades of life were closing in on her. The daughter knew that her marriage would not last, but she dared not say so. Things were happening such as that they had separate meals, that he did not speak for weeks on end, and yet she defended him, talked of the open pine dresser he had made, and her mother rued the fact that she never had a handyman to do odd things for her. She said the window had broken in a storm and that there was still a bit of cardboard in it. She said she had her heart on two armchairs, armchairs with damask covers. The daughter longed to give them to her and thought that she might steal from her husband when he was asleep, steal the deposit, that is, and pay for them on hire purchase. But they said none of the things that they should have said.

"You didn't get any new style," the mother said, restating her particular dislike for a sheepskin coat.

"I don't want it," the girl said tersely.

"You were always a softie," the mother said, and inherent in this was disapproval for a man who allowed his wife to be dowdy. Perhaps she thought that her daughter's marriage might have amended for her own.

When her marriage did end, the girl wrote and said that it was all over, and the mother wrote posthaste, exacting two dire promises —the girl must write back on her oath and promise her that she would never touch an alcoholic drink as long as she lived and she would never again have to do with any man in body or soul. High commands. At the time the girl was walking the streets in a daze and stopping strangers to tell of her plight. One day in a park she met a man who was very sympathetic, a sort of tramp. She told him her story, and then all of a sudden he told her this terrible dream. He had wakened up and he was swimming in water and the water kept changing color, it was blue and red and green, and these changing colors terrified him. She saw that he was not all there and invented an excuse to go somewhere. In time she sold her bicycle and pawned a gold bracelet and a gold watch and chain. She fled to England. She wanted to go somewhere where she knew no one. She was trying to start afresh, to wipe out the previous life. She was staggered by the assaults of memory—a bowl with her mother's menstrual cloth soaking in it and her sacrilegious idea that if lit it could resemble the heart of Christ, the conical wick of the Aladdin lamp being lit too high and disappearing into a jet of black; the roses, the five freakish winter roses that were in bloom when the pipes burst; the mice that came out of the shoes, then out of the shoe closet itself, onto the floor where the newspapers had been laid to prevent the muck and manure of the trampling men; the little box of rouge that almost asked to be licked, so dry and rosy was it; the black range whose temperature could be tested by just spitting on it and watching the immediate jig and trepidation of the spit; the pancakes on Shrove Tuesday (if there wasn't a row); the flitches of bacon hanging to smoke; the forgotten jam jars with inevitably the bit of moldy jam in the bottom; and always, like an overseeing spirit, the figure of the mother, who was responsible for each and every one of these facets, and always the pending doom in which the mother would perhaps be struck with the rim of a bucket, or a sledgehammer, or some improvised weapon; struck by the near-crazed father. It would be something as slight as that the mother had a splinter under her nail and the girl felt her own nail being lifted up, felt hurt to the quick, or felt her mother's sputum, could taste it like a dish. She was possessed by these thoughts in the library where she worked day in and day out, filing and cataloguing and handing over books. They were more than thoughts, they were the presence of this woman whom she resolved to kill. Yes, she would have to kill. She would have to take up arms and commit a murder. She thought of choking or drowning. Certainly the method had to do with suffocation, and she foresaw herself holding big suffocating pillows or a bolster, in the secrecy of the Blue Room, where it had all begun. Her mother turned into the bursting red pipes, into the brown dishcloths, into swamps of black-brown blooded water. Her mother turned into a streetwalker and paraded. Her mother was taking down her knickers in public, squatting to do awful things, left little piddles, small as puppies' piddles, her mother was drifting down a well in a big bucket, crying for help, but no help was forthcoming. The oddest dream came along. Her mother was on her deathbed, having just given birth to her—the little tonsured head jutted above the sheet—and had a neck rash, and was busy trying to catch a little insect, trying to cup it in the palms of her hands, and was saying that in the end "all there is, is yourself and this little insect that you're trying to kill." The word "kill" was everywhere, on the hoardings, in the evening air, on the tip of her thoughts. But life goes on. She bought a yellow two-piece worsted, and wrote home and said, "I must be getting cheerful, I wear less black." Her mother wrote, "I have only one wish now and it is that we will be buried together." The more she tried to kill, the more clinging the advances became. Her mother was taking out all the old souvenirs, the brown scapulars salvaged from the hurtful night in December, a mug, with their similar initial on it, a tablecloth that the girl had sent from her first earnings when she qualified as a librarian. The mother's letters began to show signs of wandering. They broke off in midsentence; one was written on blotting paper and almost indecipherable; they contained snatches of information such as "So-and-so died, there was a big turnout at the funeral," "I could do with a copper bracelet for rheumatism," "You know life gets lonelier."

She dreaded the summer holidays, but still she went. The geese and the gander would be trailing by the riverbank, the cows would gape at her as if an alien had entered their terrain. It was only the horses she avoided—always on the nervy side, as if ready to bolt. The fields themselves as beguiling as ever, fields full of herbage and meadowsweet, fields adorned with spangles of gold as the buttercups caught the shafts of intermittent sunshine. If only she could pick them up and carry them away. They sat indoors. A dog had a deep cut in his paw and it was thought that a fox did it, that the dog and the fox had tussled one night. As a result of this, he was admitted to the house. The mother and the dog spoke, although not a word passed between them. The father asked pointed questions, such as would it rain or was it teatime. For a pastime they then discussed all the dogs that they had had. The mother especially remembered Monkey and said that he was a queer one, that he'd know what you were thinking of. The father and daughter remembered further back to Shep, the big collie, who guarded the child's pram and drove thoroughbred horses off the drive, causing risk to his own person. Then there were the several pairs of dogs, all of whom sparred and quarreled throughout their lives, yet all of whom died within a week of one another, the surviving dog dying of grief for his pal. No matter how they avoided it, death crept into the conversation. The mother said unconvincingly how lucky they were never to have been crippled, to have enjoyed good health and enough to eat. The curtains behind her chair were a warm red velveteen and gave a glow to her face. A glow that was reminiscent of her lost beauty.

She decided on a celebration. She owed it to her mother. They would meet somewhere else, away from that house, and its skeletons and its old cunning tug at the heartstrings. She planned it a year in advance, a holiday in a hotel, set in beautiful woodland surroundings on the verge of the Atlantic Ocean. Their first hours were happily and most joyfully passed as they looked at the rooms, the view, the various tapestries, found where things were located, looked at the games room and then at the display cabinets, where there were cut-glass and marble souvenirs on sale. The mother said that everything was "poison, dear." They took a walk by the seashore and remarked one to the other on the different stripes of color on the water, how definite they were, each color claiming its surface of sea, just like oats or grass or a plowed land. The brown plaits of seaweed slapped and slathered over rocks, long-legged birds let out their lonesome shrieks, and the mountains that loomed beyond seemed to hold the specter of continents inside them so vast were they, so old. They dined early. Afterward there was a singsong and the mother whispered that money wasn't everything; to look at the hard-boiled faces. Something snapped inside her, and forgetting that this was her errand of mercy, she thought instead how this mother had a whole series of grudges, bitter grudges concerning love, happiness, and her hard impecunious fate. The angora jumpers, the court shoes, the brown and the fawn garments, the milk complexion, the auburn tresses, the little breathlessnesses, the hands worn by toil, the sore feet, these were but the trimmings, behind them lay the real person, who demanded her pound of flesh from life. They sat on a sofa. The mother sipped tea and she her whiskey. They said, "Cheers." The girl tried to get the conversation back to before she was born, or before other children were born, to the dances and the annual race day and the courtship that preempted the marriage. The mother refused to speak, balked, had no story to tell, said that even if she had a story she would not tell it. Said she hated raking up the past. The girl tweezed it out of her in scraps. The mother said yes, that as a young girl she was bold and obstinate and she did have fancy dreams but soon learned to toe the line. Then she burst out laughing and said she climbed up a ladder once into the chapel, and into the confessional, so as to be the first person there to have her confession heard by the missioner. The missioner nearly lost his life because he didn't know how anyone could possibly have got in, since the door was bolted and he had simply come to sit in the confessional to compose himself, when there she was, spouting sins. What sins?

The mother said, "Oh, I forget, love. I forget everything now."

The girl said, "No, you don't."

They said night-night and arranged to meet in the dining room the following morning.

The mother didn't sleep a wink, complained that her eyes and her nose were itchy, and she feared she was catching a cold. She drank tea noisily, slugged it down. They walked by the sea, which was now the color of gunmetal, and the mountains were no longer a talking point. They visited a ruined monastery where the nettles, the sorrel, the clover, and the seedy dock grew high in a rectangle. Powder shed from walls that were built of solid stone. The mother said that probably it was a chapel, or a chancery, a seat of sanctity down through the centuries, and she genuflected. To the girl it was just a ruin, unhallowed, full of weeds and buzzing with wasps and insects. Outside, there was a flock of noisy starlings. She could feel the trouble brewing. She said that there was a lovely smell, that it was most likely some wild herb, and she got down on her knees to locate it. Peering with eyes and fingers among the low grass, she came upon a nest of ants that were crawling over a tiny bit of ground with an amazing amount of energy and will. She felt barely in control.

They trailed back in time for coffee. The mother said hotel life was demoralizing as she bit into an iced biscuit. The porter fetched the paper. Two strange little puppies lapped at the mother's feet, and the porter said they would have to be drowned if they were not claimed before dusk. The mother said what a shame and recalled her own little pups, who didn't eat clothes on the line during the day but when night came got down to work on them.

"You'd be fit to kill them, but of course you couldn't," she said lamely. She was speaking of puppies from ten or fifteen years back.

He asked if she was enjoying it, and the mother said, "I quote the saying 'See Naples and die,' the same applies to this."

The daughter knew that the mother wanted to go home there and then, but they had booked for four days and it would be an admission of failure to cut it short. She asked the porter to arrange a boat trip to the island inhabited by seabirds, then a car drive to the Lakes of Killarney and another to see the home of the liberator Daniel O'Connell, the man who had asked to have his dead heart sent to Rome, to the Holy See. The porter said certainly and made a great to-do about accepting the tip she gave him. It was he who told them where Daniel O'Connell's heart lay, and the mother said it was the most rending thing she had ever heard, and the most devout. Then she said yes, that a holiday was an uplift, but that it came too late, as she wasn't used to the spoiling. The girl did not like that. To change the conversation the girl produced a postcard that she used as a bookmark. It was a photograph of a gouged torso and she told the porter that was how she felt, that was the state of her mind. The mother said later she didn't think the girl should have said such a thing and wasn't it a bit extreme. Then the mother wrote a six-page letter to her friend Molly and the girl conspired to be the one to post it so that she could read it and find some clue to the chasm that stretched between them. As it happened, she could not bring herself to read it, because the mother gave it to her unsealed, as if she had guessed those thoughts, and the girl bit her lower lip and said, "How's Molly doing?"

The mother became very sentimental and said, "Poor creature, blind as a bat," but added that people were kind and how when they saw her with the white cane, they knew. The letter would be read to her by a daughter who was married and overweight and who suffered with her nerves. The girl recalled an autograph book, the mother's, with its confectionery-colored pages and its likewise rhymes and ditties. The mother recalled ice creams that she had eaten in Brooklyn long before. The mother remembered the embroidery she had done, making the statement in stitches that there was a rose in the heart of New York. The girl said stitches played such an important role in life and said, "A stitch in time saves nine." They tittered. They were getting nearer. The girl delicately inquired into the name and occupation of the mother's previous lover, in short, the father's rival. The mother would not divulge, except to say that he loved his mother, loved his sister, was most thoughtful, and that was that. Another long silence. Then the mother stirred in her chair, coughed, confided, said that in fact she and this thoughtful man, fearing, somehow sensing, that they would not be man and wife, had made each other a solemn pact one Sunday afternoon in Coney Island over an ice. They swore that they would get in touch with each other toward the end of their days. Lo and behold, after fifty-five years the mother wrote that letter! The girl's heart quickened, and her blood danced to the news of this tryst, this long-sustained clandestine passion. She felt that something momentous was about to get uttered. They could be true at last, they need not hide from one another's gaze. Her mother would own up. Her own life would not be one of curtained shame. She thought of the married man who was waiting for her in London, the one who took her for delicious weekends, and she shivered. The mother said that her letter had been returned; probably his sister had returned it, always being jealous. The girl begged to know the contents of the letter. The mother said it was harmless. The girl said go on. She tried to revive the spark, but the mother's mind was made up. The mother said that there was no such thing as love between the sexes and that it was all bull. She reaffirmed that there was only one kind of love and that was a mother's love for her child. There passed between them then such a moment, not a moment of sweetness, not a moment of reaffirmation, but a moment dense with hate—one hating and the other receiving it like rays, and then it was glossed over by the mother's remark about the grandeur of the ceiling. The girl gritted her teeth and resolved that they would not be buried in the same grave, and vehemently lit a cigarette, although they had hardly tasted the first course.

"I think you're very unsettled," her mother said.

"I didn't get that from the ground," the daughter said.

The mother bridled, stood up to leave, but was impeded by a waiter who was carrying a big chafing dish, over which a bright blue flame riotously spread. She sat down as if pushed down and said that that remark was the essence of cruelty. The girl said sorry. The mother said she had done all she could and that without maid or car or checkbook or any of life's luxuries. Life's dainties had not dropped on her path, she had to knit her own sweaters, cut and sew her own skirts, be her own hairdresser. The girl said for God's sake to let them enjoy it. The mother said that at seventy-eight one had time to think.

"And at thirty-eight," the girl said.

She wished then that her mother's life had been happier and had not exacted so much from her, and she felt she was being milked emotionally. With all her heart she pitied this woman, pitied her for having her dreams pulped and for betrothing herself to a life of suffering. But also she blamed her. They were both wild with emotion. They were speaking out of turn and eating carelessly; the very food seemed to taunt them. The mother wished that one of those white-coated waiters would tactfully take her plate of dinner away and replace it with a nice warm pot of tea, or better still, that she could be home in her own house by her own fireside, and furthermore she wished that her daughter had never grown into the cruel feelingless hussy that she was.

"What else could I have done?" the mother said.

"A lot," the girl said, and gulped at once.

The mother excused herself.

"When I pass on, I won't be sorry," she said.

Up in the room she locked and bolted the door, and lay curled up on the bed, knotted as a foetus, with a clump of paper handkerchiefs in front of her mouth. Downstairs she left behind her a grown girl, remembering a woman she most bottomlessly loved, then unloved, and cut off from herself in the middle of a large dining room while confronting a plate of undercooked lamb strewn with mint.

Death in its way comes just as much of a surprise as birth. We know we will die, just as the mother knows that she is primed to deliver around such and such a time, yet there is a fierce inner exclamation from her at the first onset of labor, and when the water breaks she is already a shocked woman. So it was. The reconciliation that she had hoped for, and indeed intended to instigate, never came. She was abroad at a conference when her mother died, and when she arrived through her own front door, the phone was ringing with the news of her mother's death. The message though clear to her ears was incredible to her. How had her mother died and why? In a hospital in Dublin as a result of a heart attack. Her mother had gone there to do shopping and was taken ill in the street. How fearful that must have been. Straightaway she set back for the airport, hoping to get a seat on a late-night flight.

Her sister would not be going, as she lived now in Australia, lived on a big farm miles from anywhere. Her letters were always pleas for news, for gossip, for books, for magazines. She had mellowed with the years, had grown fat, and was no longer the daffodil beauty. To her it was like seeing pages of life slip away, and she did not bend down to pick them up. They were carried away in the stream of life itself. And yet something tugged. The last plane had gone, but she decided to sit there until dawn and thought to herself that she might be sitting up at her mother's wake. The tube lighting drained the color from all the other waiting faces, and though she could not cry, she longed to tell someone that something incalculable had happened to her. They seemed as tired and as inert as she did.

Coffee, bread, whiskey, all tasted the same, tasted of nothing, or at best of blotting paper. There was no man in her life at the moment, no one to ring up and tell the news to. Even if there was, she thought that lovers never know the full story of one another, only know the bit they meet, never know the iceberg of hurts that have gone before, and therefore are always strangers, or semi-strangers, even in the folds of love. She could not cry. She asked herself if perhaps her heart had turned to lead. Yet she dreaded that on impulse she might break down and that an attendant might have to lead her away.

When she arrived at the hospital next day, the remains had been removed and were now on their way through the center of Ireland. Through Joyce's Ireland, as she always called it, and thought of the great central plain open to the elements, the teeming rain, the drifting snow, the winds that gave chapped faces to farmers and cattle dealers and croup to the young calves. She passed the big towns and the lesser towns, recited snatches of recitation that she remembered, and hoped that no one could consider her disrespectful because the hire car was a bright ketchup red. When she got to her own part of the world, the sight of the mountains moved her, as they had always done—solemn, beautiful, unchanging except for different ranges of color. Solid and timeless. She tried to speak to her mother, but found the words artificial. She had bought a sandwich at the airport and now removed the glacé paper with her teeth and bit into it. The two days ahead would be awful. There would be her father's wild grief, there would be her aunt's grief, there would be cousins and friends, and strays and workmen; there would be a grave wide open and as they walked to it they would walk over other graves, under hawthorn, stamping the nettles as they went. She knew the graveyard very well, since childhood. She knew the tombs, the headstones, and the hidden vaults. She used to play there alone and both challenge and cower from ghosts. The inside of the grave was always a rich broody brown, and the gravedigger would probably lace it with a trellis of ivy or convolvulus leaf.

At that very moment she found that she had just caught up with the funeral cortege, but she could hardly believe that it would be her mother's. Too much of a coincidence. They drove at a great pace and without too much respect for the dead. She kept up with them. The light was fading, the bushes were like blurs, the air bat-black; the birds had ceased, and the mountains were dark bulks. If the file of cars took a right from the main road toward the lake town, then it must certainly be her mother's. It did. The thought of catching up with it was what made her cry. She cried with such delight, cried like a child who has done something good and is being praised for it and yet cannot bear the weight of emotion. She cried the whole way through the lakeside town and sobbed as they crossed the old bridge toward the lovely dark leafy country road that led toward home. She cried like a homing bird. She was therefore seen as a daughter deeply distressed when she walked past the file of mourners outside the chapel gate, and when she shook the hands or touched the sleeves of those who had come forward to meet her. Earlier a friend had left flowers at the car-hire desk and she carried them as if she had specially chosen them. She thought, They think it is grief, but it is not the grief they think it is. It is emptiness more than grief. It is a grief at not being able to be wholehearted again. It is not a false grief, but it is unyielding, it is blood from a stone.

Inside the chapel she found her father howling, and in the first rows closest to the altar and to the coffin the chief mourners, both men and women, were sobbing, or, having just sobbed, were drying their eyes. As she shook hands with each one of them, she heard the same condolence—"Sorry for your trouble, sorry for your trouble, sorry for your trouble."

That night in her father's house people supped and ate and reminisced. As if in mourning a huge bough of a nearby tree had fallen down. Its roots were like a hand stuck up in the air. The house already reeked of neglect. She kept seeing her mother's figure coming through the door with a large tray, laden down with things. The undertaker called her out. He said since she had not seen the remains he would bring her to the chapel and unscrew the lid. She shrank from it, but she went, because to say no would have brought her disgrace. The chapel was cold, the wood creaked, and even the flowers at night seemed to have departed from themselves, like ghost flowers. Just as he lifted the lid he asked her to please step away, and she thought, Something fateful has happened, the skin has turned black or a finger moves or, the worst, she is not dead, she has merely visited the other world. Then he called her and she walked solemnly over and she almost screamed. The mouth was trying to speak. She was sure of it. One eyelid was not fully shut. It was unfinished. She kissed the face and felt a terrible pity. "O soul," she said, "where are you, on your voyaging, and O soul, are you immortal."

Suddenly she was afraid of her mother's fate and afraid for the fact that one day she, too, would have to make it. She longed to hold the face and utter consolations to it, but she was unable. She thought of the holiday that had been such a fiasco and the love that she had first so cravenly and so rampantly given and the love that she had so callously and so pointedly taken back. She thought why did she have to withdraw, why do people have to withdraw, why?

After the funeral she went around the house tidying and searching, as if for some secret. In the Blue Room damp had seeped through the walls, and there were little burrs of fungus that clung like bobbins on a hat veiling. In drawers she found bits of her mother's life. Emblems. Wishes. Dreams contained in such things as an exotic gauze rose of the darkest drenchingest red. Perfume bottles, dance shoes, boxes of handkerchiefs, and the returned letter. It was to the man called Vincent, the man her mother had intended to marry but whom she had forsaken when she left New York and came back to Ireland, back to her destiny. For the most part it was a practical letter outlining the size of her farm, the crops they grew, asking about mutual friends, his circumstances, and so forth. It seems he worked in a meat factory. There was only one little leak—"I think of you, you would not believe how often." In an instinctive gesture she crumpled the letter up as if it had been her own. The envelope had marked on the outside—*Return to sender*. The words seemed brazen, as if he himself had written them. There were so many hats, with flowers and veiling, all of light color, hats for summer outings, for rainless climes. Ah, the garden parties she must have conceived. Never having had the money for real style, her mother had invested in imitation things—an imitation crocodile handbag and an imitation fur bolero. It felt light, as if made of hair.

There were, too, pink embroidered corsets, long bloomers, and three unworn cardigans.

For some reason she put her hand above the mantelpiece to the place where they hid shillings when she was young. There wrapped in cobweb was an envelope addressed to her in her mother's handwriting. It sent shivers through her, and she prayed that it did not bristle with accusations. Inside, there were some trinkets, a gold sovereign, and some money. The notes were dirty, crumpled, and folded many times. How long had the envelope lain there? How had her mother managed to save? There was no letter, yet in her mind she concocted little tendernesses that her mother might have written—words such as "Buy yourself a jacket," or "Have a night out," or "Don't spend this on Masses." She wanted something, some communiqué. But there was no such thing.

A new wall had arisen, stronger and sturdier than before. Their life together and all those exchanges were like so many spilt feelings, and she looked to see some sign or hear some murmur. Instead, a silence filled the room, and there was a vaster silence beyond, as if the house itself had died or had been carefully put down to sleep.

Mrs. Reinhardt

Mrs. Reinhardt had her routes worked out. Blue ink for the main roads, red when she would want to turn off. A system, and a vow. She must enjoy herself, she must rest, she must recuperate, she must put on weight, and perhaps blossom the merest bit. She must get over it. After all, the world was a green, a sunny, an enchanting place. The hay was being gathered, the spotted cows so sleek they looked like Dalmatians and their movements so lazy in the meadows that they could be somnambulists. The men and women working the fields seemed to be devoid of fret or haste. It was June in Brittany, just before the throngs of visitors arrived, and the roads were relatively clear. The weather was blustery, but as she drove along, the occasional patches of sunlight illumined the trees, the lush grass, and the marshes. Seeds and pollen on the surface of the marshes were a bright mustard yellow. Bits of flowering broom divided the roadside, and at intervals an emergency telephone kiosk in bright orange caught her attention. She did not like that. She did not like emergency and she did not like the telephone. To be avoided.

While driving, Mrs. Reinhardt was occupied and her heart was relatively serene One would not know that recently she had been through so much and that presently much more was to follow. A lull. Observe the roadside, the daisies in the fields, the red and the pink poppies, and the lupins so dozy like the cows; observe the road signs and think in sympathy of the English dead in the last war whose specters floated somewhere in these environments, the English dead of whom some photograph, some relic, or some crushed thought was felt at that moment in some English semidetached home. Think of food, think of shellfish, think of the French or blueberries, think of anything, so long as the mind keeps itself occupied.

It promised to be a beautiful hotel. She had seen photos of it, a dovecote on the edge of a lake, the very essence of stillness, beauty, sequesteredness. A place to remeet the god of peace. On either side of the road the pines were young and spindly, but the cows were pendulous, their udders shockingly large and full. It occurred to her that it was still morning and that they had been only recently milked, so what would they feel like at sundown! What a nuisance that it was those cows' udders that brought the forbidden thought to her mind. Once, in their country cottage, a cow had got caught in the barbed-wire fence and both she and Mr. Reinhardt had a time of it trying to get help, and then trying to release the creature, causing a commotion among the cow community. Afterward they had drunk champagne, intending to celebrate something. Or was it to hide something? Mr. Reinhardt had said that they must not grow apart and yet had quarreled with her about the Common Market and removed her glasses while she was reading a story by Flaubert sitting up in bed. The beginning of the end, as she now knew, as she then knew, or did she, or do we, or is there such a thing, or is it another beginning to another ending, and on and on.

"Damnation," Mrs. Reinhardt said, and speeded just as she came to where there were a variety of signs with thick arrows and names in navy blue. She had lost her bearings. She took a right and realized at once that she had gone to the east town rather than the main town. So much for distraction. Let him go. The worst was already over. She could see the town cathedral as she glanced behind, and already was looking for a way in which to turn right.

The worst was over, the worst being when the other woman, the girl really, was allowed to wear Mrs. Reinhardt's nightdress and necklace. For fun. "She is young," he had said. It seemed she was, this rival, or rather, this replacement. So young that she shouted out of car windows at other motorists, that she carried a big bright umbrella, that she ate chips or cough lozenges on the way to one of these expensive restaurants where Mr. Reinhardt took her. All in all, she was a gamine.

Mrs. Reinhardt drove around a walled city and swore at a system of signs that did not carry the name of the mill town she was looking for. There were other things, like a clock and a bakery and a few strollers, and when she pulled into the tree-lined square, there was a young man naked to the waist in front of an easel, obviously sketching the cathedral. She spread the map over her knees and opened the door to get a puff of air. He looked at her. She smiled at him. She had to smile at someone. All of a sudden she had an irrational wish to have a son, a son who was with her now, to comfort her, to give her confidence, to take her part. Of course, she had a son, but he was grown up and had gone to America and knew none of this and must not know any of this.

The man told her that she need never have gone into the cathedral town, but as she said herself, she had seen it, she had seen the young man painting, she had given a little smile and he had smiled back and that was something. For the rest of the journey she remained alert, she saw trees, gabled houses, a few windmills, she saw dandelions, she passed little towns, she saw washing on the line, and she knew that she was going in the right direction.

Her arrival was tended with magic. Trees, the sound of running water, flowers, wildflowers, and a sense of being in a place that it would take time to know, take time to discover. To make it even more mysterious, the apartments were stone chalets scattered at a distance throughout the grounds. It was a complex, really, but one in which nature dominated. She went down some steps to where it said RECEPTION and, having introduced herself, was asked at once to hurry so as to be served lunch. Finding the dining room was an expedition in itself—up steps, down more steps, and then into a little outer salon where there were round tables covered with lace cloths and on each table a vase of wildflowers. She bent down and smelled some pansies. A pure sweet silken smell, with the texture of childhood. She felt grateful. Her husband was paying for all this, and what a pity that like her he was not now going down more steps, past a satin screen, to a table laid for two by an open window, to the accompaniment of running water. She had a half bottle of champagne, duck pâté, and a flat white grilled fish on a bed of thin strips of boiled leek. The hollandaise sauce was perfect and yellower than usual because they had added mustard. She was alone except for the serving girl and an older couple at a table a few yards away. She could not hear what they said. The man was drinking Calvados. The serving girl had a pretty face and brown curly hair tied back with a ribbon. One curl had been brought onto her forehead for effect. She radiated innocence and a dream. Mrs. Reinhardt could not avoid looking at her for long and thought, She has probably never been to Paris, never even been to Nantes, but she hopes to go and will go one day. That story was in her eyes, in the curls of her hair, in everything she did. That thirst.

After lunch Mrs. Reinhardt was escorted to her room. It was down a dusty road with ferns and dock on either side. Wild roses of the palest pink tumbled over the arch of the door, and when she stood in her bedroom and looked through one of the narrow turret windows, it was these roses and grassland that she saw, while from the other side she could hear the rush of the water; the two images reminded her of herself and of everybody else that she had known. One was green and hushed and quiet and the other was torrential. Did they have to conflict with each other? She undressed, she unpacked, she opened the little refrigerator to see what delights were there. There was beer and champagne and miniatures of whiskey and Vichy water and red cordial. It was like being a child again and looking into one's little toy house. She had a little weep. For what did Mrs. Reinhardt weep—for beauty, for ugliness, for herself, for her son in America, for Mr. Reinhardt, who had lost his reason. So badly did Mr. Reinhardt love this new girl, Rita, that he had made her take him to meet all her friends so that he could ask them how Rita looked at sixteen, and seventeen, what Rita wore, what Rita was like as a debutante, and why Rita stopped going to art school, and had made notes of these things. Had made an utter fool of himself. Yes, she cried for that, and as she cried, it seemed to her the tears were like the strata of this earth, had many levels and many layers, and that those layers differed, and that now she was crying for more than one thing at the same time, that her tears were all mixed up. She was also crying about age, about two gray ribs in her pubic hair, crying for not having tried harder on certain occasions, as when Mr. Reinhardt came home expecting excitement or repose and getting instead a typical story about the nonarrival of the gas man. She had let herself be drawn into the weary and hypnotizing whirl of domesticity. With her the magazines had to be neat, the dust had to be dusted, all her perfectionism had got thrown into that instead of something larger, or instead of Mr. Reinhardt. Where do we go wrong? Is that not what guardian angels are meant to do, to lead us back by the hand?

She cried, too, because of the night she had thrown a platter at him, and he sat there mortified, and said that he knew he was wrecking her life and his, but that he could not stop it, said maybe it was madness or the male menopause or anything she wanted to call it, but that it was what it was, what it was. He had even appealed to her. He told her a story, he told her that very day when he had gone to an auction to buy some pictures for the gallery, he had brought Rita with him, and as they drove along the motorway, he had hoped that they would crash, so terrible for him was his predicament and so impossible for him was it to be parted from this girl, who he admitted had made him delirious, but Happy, but Happy, as he kept insisting.

It was this helplessness of human beings that made her cry most of all, and when long after, which is to say at sunset, Mrs. Reinhardt had dried her eyes and had put on her oyster dress and her Chinese necklace, she was still repeating to herself this matter of helplessness. At the same time she was reminding herself that there lay ahead a life, adventure, that she had not finished; she had merely changed direction and the new road was unknown to her.

She sat down to dinner. She was at a different table. This time she looked out on a lake that was a tableau of prettiness—trees on either side, overhanging branches, green leaves with silver undersides, and a fallen bough where ducks perched. The residents were mostly elderly, except for one woman with orange hair and studded sunglasses. This woman scanned a magazine throughout the dinner and did not address a word to her escort.

Mrs. Reinhardt would look at the view, have a sip of wine, chew a crust of the bread that was so aerated it was like a communion wafer. Suddenly she looked to one side and there in a tank with bubbles of water within were several lobsters. They were so beautiful that at first she thought they were mannequin lobsters, ornaments. Their shells had beautiful blue tints, the blue of lapis lazuli, and though their movements had at first unnerved her, she began to engross herself in their motion and to forget what was going on around her. They moved beautifully and to such purpose. They moved to touch each other, at least some did, and others waited, were the recipients, so to speak, of this reach, this touch. Their movements had all the grandeur of speech without the folly. But there was no mistaking their intention. So caught up was she in this that she did not hear the pretty girl call her out to the phone, and in fact she had to be touched on the bare arm, which of course made her jump. Naturally she went out somewhat flustered, missed her step, and turned but did not wrench her ankle. It was her weak ankle, the one she always fell on. Going into the little booth, she mettled herself. Perhaps he was contrite or drunk, or else there had been an accident, or else their son was getting married. At any rate, it was crucial. She said her hello calmly but pertly. She repeated it. It was a strange voice altogether, a man asking for Rachel. She said who is Rachel. There were a few moments of heated irritation and then complete disappointment as Mrs. Reinhardt made her way back to her table trembling. Stupid girl to have called her! Only the lobsters saved the occasion.

Now she gave them her full attention. Now she forgot the mistake of the phone and observed the drama that was going on. A great long lobster seemed to be lord of the tank. His claws were covered with black elastic bands, but that did not prevent him from proudly stalking through the water, having frontal battles with some, but chiefly trying to arouse another: a sleeping lobster who was obviously his heart's desire. His appeals to her were mesmerizing. He would tickle her with his antennae, he would put claws over her, then edge a claw under her so that he levered her up a fraction, and then he would leave her be for an instant, only to return with a stronger, with a more telling, assault. Of course there were moments when he had to desist, to ward off others who were coming in her region, and this he did with the same determination, facing them with eyes that were vicious yet immobile as beads. He would lunge through the water and drive them back or drive them elsewhere, and then he would return as if to his love and to his oracle. There were secondary movements in the tank, of course, but it was at the main drama Mrs. Reinhardt looked. She presumed it was a him and gave him the name of Napoleon. At times so great was his sexual plight that he would lower a long antenna under his rear and touch the little dun bibs of membrane and obviously excite himself so that he could start afresh on his sleeping lady. Because he was in no doubt but that she would succumb. Mrs. Reinhardt christened her the Japanese Lady, because of her languor, her refusal to be roused, by him, or by any of them, and Mrs. Reinhardt thought, Oh, what a sight it will be when she does rise up and give herself to his embraces; oh, what a wedding that will be! Mrs. Reinhardt also thought that it was very likely that they would only be in this tank for a short number of hours and that in those hours they must act the play of their lives. Looking at them, with her hands pressed together, she hoped, the way children hope, for a happy ending to this courtship.

She had to leave the dining room while it was still going on, but in some way, she felt, with the lights out and visitors gone, the protagonists, safe in their tank, secured by air bubbles, secretly would find each other. She had drunk a little too much, and she swayed slightly as she went down the dusty road to her chalet. She felt elated. She had seen something that moved her. She had seen instinct, she had seen the grope, and she had seen the will that refuses to be refused. She had seen tenderness.

In her bedroom she put the necklace into the heart-shaped wicker box and hid it under the bolster of the second bed. She had robbed her husband of it—this beautiful choker of jade. It had been his mother's. It was worth ten thousand pounds. It was her going-away present. She had extracted it from him. Before closing it in the box she bit on the beads as if they were fruit.

"If you give me the necklace I will go away." That was what

she had said, and she knew that in some corner she was thereby murdering his heart. It was his family necklace and it was the one thing in which he believed his luck was invested. Also, he was born under the sign of Cancer and if he clung, he clung. It was the thing they shared, and by taking it she was telling him that she was going away forever, and that she was taking some of him, his most important talisman, relic of his mother, relic of their life together. She had now become so involved with this piece of jewelry that when she wore it she touched her throat constantly to make sure that it was there, and when she took it off, she kissed it, and at night she dreamed of it, and one night she dreamed that she had tucked it into her vagina for safety and hidden it there. At other times she thought how she would go to the casino and gamble it away, his luck and hers. There was a casino nearby and on Saturday there was to be a cycling tournament, and she thought that one night, maybe on Saturday, she would go out, and maybe she would gamble and maybe she would win. Soon she fell asleep.

On the third day Mrs. Reinhardt went driving. She needed a change of scene. She needed sea air and crag. She needed invigoration. The little nest was cloying. The quack-quack of the ducks, the running water were all very well, but they were beginning to echo her own cravings and she did not like that. So after breakfast she read the seventeenth-century Nun's Prayer, the one which asked the Lord to release one from excessive speech, to make one thoughtful but not moody, to give one a few friends and to keep one reasonably sweet. She thought of Rita. Rita's bright-blue eyes, sapphire eyes, and the little studs in her ears that matched. Rita was ungainly, like a colt. Rita would be the kind of girl who could stay up all night, swim at dawn, and then sleep like a baby all through the day, even in an unshaded room. Youth. Yet it so happened that Mrs. Reinhardt had found an admirer. The Monsieur who owned the hotel had paid her more than passing attention. In fact, she hardly had to turn a corner but he was there, and he could find some distraction to delay her for a moment, so as he could gaze upon her. First it was a hare running through the undergrowth, then it was his dog following some ducks, then it was the electricity van coming to mend the telephone cable. The dreaded telephone. She was pleased that it was out of order. She was also pleased that she was still striking, and there was no denying but that Mrs. Reinhardt could bewitch people.

It was when judging a young persons' art exhibition that he met Rita. Rita's work was the worst, and realizing this, she had torn it up in a tantrum. He came home and told Mrs. Reinhardt and said how sorry he had felt for her but how plucky she had been. It was February the twenty-second. The following day two things happened—he bought several silk shirts and he proposed they go to Paris for a weekend.

"If only I could turn the key on it and close the door and come back when I am an old woman, if only I could do that." So Mrs. Reinhardt said to herself as she drove away from the green nest, from the singing birds and the hovering midges, from the rich hollandaise sauces and the quilted bed, from the overwhelming comfort of it all. Indeed, she thought she might have suffocated her husband in the very same way. For though Mrs. Reinhardt was cold to others, distant in her relationships with men and women, this was not her true nature; this was something she had built up, a screen of reserve to shelter her fear. She was sentimental at home and used to do a million things for Mr. Reinhardt to please him, and to pander to him. She used to warm his side of the bed while he was still undressing, or looking at a drawing he had just bought, or even pacing the room. The pacing had grown more acute. When she knit his socks in cable stitch she always knit a third sock in case one got torn or ruined. While he was fishing or when he hunted in Scotland in August, she went just to be near him, though she dreaded these forays. They were too public. House parties of people thrown in upon each other for a hectic and sociable week. There was no privacy. Some of the women would go as beaters, while some would sit in one of the drawing rooms swapping recipes or discussing face lifts, good clothes, or domestic service bureaus. The landscape and the grouse were the same wonderful color—that of rusted metal. The shot birds often seemed as if they had just lain down in jest, so undead did they seem. Even the few drops of blood seemed unreal, theatrical. She loved the moors, the rusted color of farm and brushwood. She loved the dogs and the excitement, but she balked at the sound of the shots. A sudden violence in those untouched moors and then the glee as the hunters went in search of their kill. He might wink at her once or pass her a cup of bouillon when they sat down, but he didn't include her in conversation. He didn't have to. She often thought that the real secret of their love was that she kept the inside of herself permanently warm for him, like someone keeping an egg under a nest of straw. When she loved, she loved completely, rather like a spaniel. Her eyes were the same yellow-brown. As a young girl she was using a sewing machine one day and by accident put the needle through her index finger, but she did not call out to her parents, who were in the other room, she waited until her mother came through. Upon seeing this casualty her mother let out a scream. Within an instant her father was by her side, and with a jerk of the lever he lifted the thing out and gave her such a look, such a loving look. Mrs. Reinhardt was merely Tilly then, an only daughter, and full of trust. She believed that you loved your mother and father, that you loved your brother, that eventually you loved your husband, and then, most of all, that you loved your children. Her parents had spoiled her, had brought her to the Ritz for birthdays, had left gold trinkets on her pillow on Christmas Eve, had comforted her when she wept. When she was twenty-one, they had an expensive portrait done of her and hung it on the wall in a prominent position so that as guests entered they would say "Who is that! Who is that!" and a rash of compliments would follow.

When she turned thirty, her husband had her portrait painted; it was in their sitting room at that very moment, watching him and Rita, unless he had turned it around, or unless Rita had splashed house paint over it. Rita was unruly, it seemed. Rita's jealousy was more drastic than the occasional submarines of jealousy Mrs. Reinhardt had experienced in their seventeen years of marriage—then it was over women roughly her own age, women with poise, women with husbands, women with guile, women who made a career of straying but were back in their homes by six o'clock. Being jealous of Rita was a more abstract thing—they had met only once and that was on the steps of a theater. Rita had followed him there, run up the steps, handed him a note, and run off again. Being jealous of Rita was being jealous of youth, of freedom, and of spontaneity. Rita did not want marriage or an engagement ring. She wanted to go to Florence, she wanted to go to a ball, to go to the park on roller skates. Rita had a temper. Once at one of her father's soirées she threw twenty gold chairs out the window. If they had had a daughter, things might now be different. And if their son lived at home, things might now be different. Four people might have sat down at a white table, under a red umbrella, looked out at a brown lake, whose color was dimmed by the cluster of trees and saplings. There might be four glasses, one with Coca-Cola, one or maybe two with whiskey, and hers with white wine and soda water. A young voice might say, "What is that?" pointing to a misshapen straw basket on a wooden plinth in the middle of the lake, and as she turned her attention to discern what it was, and as she decided that it was a nest for either swans or ducks, the question would be repeated with a touch of impatience—"Mam, what is that?" and Mrs. Reinhardt might be answering. Oh my, yes, the family tableau smote her.

So transported back was she, to the hotel and a united family, that Mrs. Reinhardt was like a sleepwalker traversing the rocks that were covered with moss and then the wet sand between the rocks. She was making her way toward the distant crags. On the sand there lay caps of seaweed so green, and so shaped like the back of a head, that they were like theatrical wigs. She looked down at one, she bent to pore over its greenness, and when she looked up, he was there. A man in his mid-twenties in a blue shirt with lips parted seemed to be saying something pleasant to her, though perhaps it was only hello, or hi there. He had an American accent. Had they met in a cocktail bar or at an airport lounge, it is doubtful that they would have spoken, but here the situation called for it. One or the other had to express or confirm admiration for the sea, the boats, the white houses on the far side, the whiteness of the light, the vista; and then quite spontaneously he had to grip her wrist and said, "Look, look," as a bird dived down into the water, swooped up again, redived until he came up with a fish.

"A predator," Mrs. Reinhardt said, his hand still on her wrist, casually. They argued about the bird; she said it was a gannet and he said it was some sort of hawk. She said sweetly that she knew more about wildlife than he did. He conceded. He said if you came from Main Street, Iowa, you knew nothing, you were a hick. They laughed.

As they walked back along the shore, he told her how he had been staying farther up with friends and had decided to move on because one never discovers anything except when alone. He'd spend a night or two and then move on, and eventually he would get to Turkey. He wasn't doing a grand tour or a gastronomic tour, he was just seeing the wild parts of Brittany and had found a hotel on the other side that was hidden from everybody. "The savage side," he said.

By the time she had agreed to have a crepe with him, they had exchanged those standard bits of information. He confessed that he didn't speak much French. She confessed that she'd taken a crammer course and was even thinking of spending three months in Paris to do a cookery course. When they went indoors she removed her head-scarf and he was caught at once by the beauty of her brown pile of hair. Some hidden urge of vanity made her toss it as they looked for a table.

"Tell me something," he said, "are you married or not?"

"Yes and no . . ." She had removed her wedding ring and put it in the small leather box that snapped when one shut it.

He found her reply intriguing. Quickly she explained that she had been but was about not to be. He reached out but did not touch her, and she thought that there was something exquisite in that, that delicate indication of sympathy. He said quietly how he had missed out on marriage and on kids. She felt that he meant it. He said he had been a wildcat, and whenever he had met a nice girl he had cheated on her and lost her. He could never settle down.

"I'm bad news," he said, and laughed, and there was something so impish about him that Mrs. Reinhardt was being won over.

On closer acquaintance she had to admit that his looks were

indeed flawless. So perhaps his character was not as terrible as he had made out. She pressed him to tell her things, boyish things like his first holiday in Greece, or his first girl, or his first guitar, and gradually she realized she was becoming interested in these things although in them there was nothing new. It was the warmth really and the way he delighted in telling her these things that made Mrs. Reinhardt ask for more stories. She was like someone who has been on a voyage and upon return wants to hear everything that has happened on land. He told her that he had made a short film that he would love her to see. He would fly home for it that night if only he could! It was a film about motorcycling and he had made it long before anyone else had made a film about it, or written a book about it. He told her some of the stories. Scenes at dusk in a deserted place when a man gets a puncture and says, "What the hell does it matter . . ." as he sits down to take a smoke. She sensed a purity in him alongside everything else. He loved the desert, he loved the prairie, but yes, he had lived on women and he had drunk a lot and he had slept rough and he had smoked every kind of weed under the sun, and he wished he had known Aldous Huxley, that Aldous Huxley had been his dad.

"Still searching," he said.

"It's the fashion now," she said a little dryly.

"Hey, let's get married," he said, and they clapped hands and both pretended it was for real. Both acted a little play; it was the same as if someone had come into the room and said, "Do it for real, kids." In jest, their cheeks met; in jest, their fingers interlocked; in jest, their knuckles mashed one another's; and in jest, they stood up, moved onto the small dance area, and danced as closely as Siamese twins might to the music from the jukebox. In jest, or perhaps not, Mrs. Reinhardt felt through the beautiful folds of her oyster dress the press of his sexuality, and round and round and round they danced, the two jesting betrothed people, who were far from home and who had got each other into such a spin of excitement. How thrilling it was and how rejuvenating to dance round and round and feel the strength and the need of this man pushing closer and closer to her while still keeping her reserve. On her face the most beautiful ecstatic smile. She was smiling for herself. He did slide his other hand on her buttock, but Mrs. Reinhardt just shrugged it off. The moment the dancing stopped they parted.

Soon after they sat down, she looked at her tiny wristwatch, peered at it, and at once he flicked on his blue plastic lighter so that she could read the tiny black insectlike hands. Then he held the lighter in front of her face to admire her, to admire the eyes, the long nose, the sensual mouth, the necklace.

"Real," he said, picking up the green beads that she herself had become so involved with and had been so intimate with.

"Think so," she said, and regretted it instantly. After all, the world did abound in thieves and rogues, and ten thousand pounds was no joke to be carrying around. She had read of women such as she, who took up with men, younger men or older men, only to be robbed, stripped of their possessions, bled. She curdled within and suddenly invented for herself a telephone call back at the hotel. When she excused herself, he rose chivalrously, escorted her through the door, down the steps, and across the gravel path to the car park. They did not kiss good night.

In the morning the world was clean and bright. There had been rain and everything got washed, the water mills, the ducks, the roses, the trees, the lupins, and the little winding paths. The little winding paths, of course, were strewn with white, pink, and pale-blue blossoms. The effect was as of seeing snow when she opened the windows, leaned out, and broke a rose that was still damp and whose full smell had not been restored yet. Its smell was smothered by the smell of rain, and that, too, was beautiful. And so were her bare breasts resting on the window ledge. And so was life, physical well-being, one's own body, roses, encounter, promise, the dance. She drew back quickly when she saw that there Monsieur was, down below, idly hammering a few nails into a wall. He seemed to be doing this to make a trellis for the roses, but he was in no hurry as he looked in her direction. He had a knack of finding her no matter where she was. The night before, as she drove back late, he was in the car park to say that they had kept her a table for dinner. He had brought a spare menu in his pocket. The big black dog looked up, too. Somehow her own whiteness and the milklikeness of her breasts contrasted with the blackness of the dog, and she saw them detached, yet grouped together in a very beautiful painting, opposites, one that was long and black with a snout, and one that was white and like the globe of a lamp. She liked that picture and would add it to the pictures that she had seen during the years she sleepwalked. She sleepwalked no longer. Life was like that, you dreamed a lot, or you cried a lot, or you itched a lot, and then it disappeared and something else came in its place.

Mrs. Reinhardt dawdled. She put on one dress, then another; she lifted a plate ashtray and found a swarm of little ants underneath; she took sparkling mineral water from the refrigerator, drank it, took two of her iron tablets, and by a process of association pulled her lower eyelid down to see if she was still anemic. She realized something wonderful. For whatever number of minutes it had been, she had not given a thought to Mr. Reinhardt, and this was the beginning of recovery. That was how it happened, one forgot for two minutes and remembered for twenty. One forgot for three minutes and remembered for fifteen, but as with a pendulum the states of remembering and the states of forgetting were gradually equalized, and then one great day the pendulum had gone over and the states of forgetting had gained a victory. What more did a woman want? Mrs. Reinhardt danced around the room, leaped over her bed, threw a pillow in the air, and felt as alive and gay as the day she got engaged and knew she would live happily ever after. What more did a woman want? She wanted this American, although he might be a bounder. He might not. She would have him, but in her own time and to suit her own requirements. She would not let him move into her hotel apartment because the privacy of it was sacred. In fact, she was beginning to enjoy herself. Think of it, she could have coffee at noon instead of nine-thirty, she could eat an éclair, she could pluck her eyebrows, she could sing high notes and low notes, she could wander.

"Freedom!" Mrs. Reinhardt told the lovely supple woman in the flowered dressing gown who smiled into the long mirror while the other Mrs. Reinhardt told the lovely woman that the mirabelle she had drunk the night before was still swishing through her brain.

After breakfast she walked in the woods. Crossing a little plaited bridge, she took off her sandals and tiptoed so as not to disturb the sounds and activities of nature. It was the darkest wood she had ever entered. All the trees twined overhead, so that it was a vault with layer upon layer of green. Ferns grew in wizard abundance, and between the ferns other things strove to be seen, while all about were the butterflies and the insects. Mushrooms and toadstools flourished at the base of every tree, and she knelt down to smell them. She loved their dank smell. The air was pierced with birdsong of every note and every variety as the birds darted across the ground or swooped up into the air. This fecundity of nature, this chorus of birds and the distant cooing of the doves from the dovecote, thrilled her and presently something else quickened her desires. The low, suggestive, all-desiring whistle of a male reached her ears. She had almost walked over him. He could see her bare legs under her dress. She drew back. He was lying down with his shirt open. He did not rise to greet her.

"You," she said.

He put up his foot in salutation. She stood over him, trying to decide whether his presence was welcome or an intrusion.

"Amazing," he said, and held his hands out, acceding to the abundance of nature about him. He apologized for his presence but said that he had cycled over to see her just to say hello, he had brought her some croissants hot from the oven, but upon hearing she was sleeping, he decided to have a ramble in the woods. He had fed the croissants to the birds. He used some French words to impress her and she laughed and soon her petulance was washed away. After all, they were not her woods, and he had not knocked on her bedroom door, and she would have been disappointed if he had cycled off without seeing her. She spread her dress like a cushion underneath her and sat, folding her legs to the other side. It was then they talked. They talked for a long time. They talked of courage, the different courage of men and women. The courage when a horse bolts or the car in front of one crashes, the draining courage of every day. She said men were never able to say "*finito*." "Damn right," he said, and the jargon struck her as comic compared with the peace and majesty of the woods.

"You smell good," he would sometimes say, and that, too, belonged to another environment, but for the most part he impressed her with his sincerity and with the way he took his time to say the thing he wanted to say. Before the week was out she would lead him to her bed. It would be stark and it would be unexpected, an invitation tossed at the very last minute, as when someone takes a flower or a handkerchief, and throws it into the bullring. She would be unabashed, as she had not been for years. They stayed for about an hour, talking, and at times one or the other would get up, walk or run toward the little bridge, and pretend to take a photograph. Eventually they got up together and went to find his bicycle. He insisted that she cycle. After the first few wobbles she rode down the path and could hear him clapping. Then she got off, turned around, and rode back toward him. He said that next time she would have to stay on the bicycle while turning around, and she biffed him and said she had not ridden for years. Her face was flushed and bicycle oil had got on her skirt. For fun he sat her on the bar of the bicycle, put his leg across, and they set off down the avenue at a dizzying speed, singing, "Daisy, Daisy, give me your answer, do. I'm half crazy, all for the love of you . . ."

He would not stop, even though she swore that she was going to fall off any minute.

"You're O.K. . . ." he'd say as he turned the next corner. In a while she stopped screaming and enjoyed the queasiness in her stomach.

Mrs. Reinhardt stood in the narrow shower, the disk of green soap held under one armpit, when she saw a rose branch being waved into the room. As in a mirage the petals randomly fell. Which of them was it? Him or Monsieur? She was feeling decidedly amorous. He climbed in through the window and came directly to her. He did not speak. He gripped her roughly, his own clothing still on, and he was so busy taking possession of her that he did not realize that he was getting drenched. The shower was full on, yet neither of them bothered to turn it off. The zipper of his trousers hurt her, but he was mindless of that. The thing is, he had desired her from the very first, and now he was pumping all his arrogance and all his cockatooing into her and she was taking it gladly, also gluttonously. She was recovering her pride as a woman, and much more, as a desirable woman. It was this she had sorely missed in the last ten months. Yet she was surprised by herself, surprised by her savage need to get even with life, or was it to get healed? She leaned against the shower wall, wet and slippery all over, and lolled so that every bit of her was partaking of him. She did not worry about him, though he did seem in quite a frenzy both to prove himself and to please her, and he kept uttering the vilest of words, calling her sow and dog and bitch, and so forth. She even thought that she might conceive, so radical was it, and the only other thought that came to her was of the lobsters and the lady lobster lying so still while all the others sought her.

When he came, she refused to claim to be satisfied and with a few rough strokes insisted he fill her again and search for her every crevice. This all happened without speech except for the names he muttered as she squeezed from him the juices he did not have left to give. She was certainly getting her own back.

Afterward she washed, and as he lay on the bathroom floor out of breath, she stepped over him and went to her room to rest. She felt like a queen, and lying on her bed, her whole body was like a ship decked out with beauty. A victory! She had locked the bedroom door. Let him wait, let him sweat. She would join him for dinner. She had told him so in French, knowing it would doubly confound him. She went to sleep, ordering herself pleasant dreams, colored dreams, the colors of sunlight and of lightning, yellow sun and saffron lightning.

He kept the dinner appointment. Mrs. Reinhardt saw him from a landing, down in the little salon, where there were lace-covered tables and vases of wildflowers. She remembered it from her first day. He was drinking a Pernod. It was almost dark down there except for the light from the table candles. It was a somewhat somber place. The drawings on the wall were all of monks or ascetics, and nailed to a cross of wood was a bird; it seemed to be a dead pheasant. He was wearing green, a green silk dinner jacket—had she not seen it somewhere? Yes, it had been on display in the little hotel showcase where they also sold jewelry and beachwear.

The moment she went to his table she perceived the change in him. The good-natured truant boy had given way to the slightly testy seducer, and he did not move a chair or a muscle as she sat down. He called to Michele, the girl with the curly hair, to bring another Pernod, in fact, to bring two. Mrs. Reinhardt thought that it was just a ruse and that he was proving to her what a man of the world he was. She said she had slept well.

"Where's your loot?" he said, looking at her neck. She had left it in her room and was wearing pearls instead. She did not answer but merely held up the paperback book to show that she had been reading.

"You read that?" he said. It was D. H. Lawrence.

"I haven't read that stuff since I was twelve," he said. He was drunk. It augured badly. She wondered if she should dismiss him there and then, but as on previous occasions when things got very bad, Mrs. Reinhardt became very stupid, became inept. He gave the waitress a wink and gripped her left hand, where she was wearing a bracelet. She moved off as languidly as always.

"You're a doll," he said.

"She doesn't speak English," Mrs. Reinhardt said.

"She speaks my kind of English," he said.

It was thus in a state of anger, pique, and agitation that they went in to dinner. As he studied the four menus, he decided on the costliest one and said it was a damn good thing that she was a rich bitch.

"Rich bitch," he said, and laughed.

She let it pass. He said how about taking him to Pamplona for the bullfights and then went into a rhapsody about past fights and past bullfighters.

"Oh, you read it in Ernest Hemingway," she said, unable to resist a sting.

"Oh, we've got a hot and cold lady," he said as he held the

velvet-covered wine list in front of him. The lobster tank was gapingly empty. There were only three lobsters in there and those lay absolutely still. Perhaps they were shocked from the raid and were lying low, not making a stir, so as not to be seen. She was on the verge of tears. He ordered a classic bottle of wine. It meant the girl getting Monsieur, who then had to get his key and go to the cellar and ceremoniously bring it back and show the label and open it and decant it and wait. The waitress had changed clothes because she was going to the cycle tournament. Her black pinafore was changed for a blue dress with colors in the box pleats. She looked enchanting. Ready for showers of kisses and admiration.

"How would you like me to fuck you?" he said to the young girl, who watched the pouring of the wine.

"You have gone too far," Mrs. Reinhardt said, and perhaps fearing that she might make a scene, he leaned over to her and said: "Don't worry, I'll handle you."

She excused herself, more for the waitress than for him, and hurried out. Never in all her life had Mrs. Reinhardt been so angry. She sat on the hammock in the garden and asked the stars and the lovely hexagonal lamps and the sleeping ducks to please succor her in this nightmare. She thought of the bill and the jacket, which she realized would also be on her bill, and she cried like a very angry child who is unable to tell anyone what happened. Her disgrace was extreme. She swung back and forth in the hammock, cursing and swearing, then praying for patience. The important thing was never to have to see him again. She was shivering and in a state of shock by the time she went to her room. She really went to put on a cardigan and to order a sandwich or soup. There he was in her dressing gown. He had quit dinner, he said, being as she so rudely walked away. He, too, was about to order a sandwich. The fridge door was open, and as she entered he clicked it closed. Obviously he had drunk different things, and she could see that he was wild. He was not giving this up, this luxury, this laissez-faire. He rose and staggered.

"Round one," he said, and caught her.

"Get out of here," she said.

"Not me, I'm in for the licks."

Mrs. Reinhardt knew with complete conviction that she was about to be the witness of, and a participant in, the most sordid kind of embroilment. Alacrity took hold of her, and she thought, Coax him, seem mature, laugh, divert him. But seeing the craze in his eyes, instinct made her resort to stronger measures, and the scream she let out was astounding even to her own ears. It was no more than seconds until Monsieur was in the room grappling with him. She realized that he had been watching all along and that he had been prepared for this in a way that she was not. Monsieur was telling him in French to get dressed and to get lost. It had some elements of farce.

"O.K., O.K.," he was saying. "Just let me get dressed, just let me get out of this asshole."

She was glad of the language barrier. Then an ugly thing happened; the moment Monsieur let go of him, he used a dirty trick. He picked up the empty champagne bottle and wielded it at his opponent's head. Suddenly the two of them were in a clinch. Mrs. Reinhardt searched her mind for what was best to do. She picked up a chair, but her action was like someone in slow motion, because while they were each forcing each other onto the ground, she was holding the chair and not doing anything with it. It was the breaking bottle she dreaded most of all. By then her hand had been on the emergency bell, and as they both fell to the floor, the assistant chef came in with a knife. He must have dashed from the kitchen. The two men were, of course, able to master the situation, and when he got up, he was shaking his head like a boxer who has been badly punched.

Monsieur suggested that she leave and go over to Reception and wait there. As she left the room, he gave her his jacket. Walking down the little road, her body shook like jelly. The jacket kept slipping off. She was conscious of having just escaped indescribable horror. Horror such as one reads of. She realized how sheltered her life had been, but this was no help. What she really wanted was to sit with someone and talk about anything. The hotel lounge was propriety itself. Another young girl, also with a rose in her hair, was slowly preparing a tray of drinks. A party of Dutch people sat in a corner, the dog snapped at some flies, and from the other room came the strains of music, as there was a wedding in progress. Mrs. Reinhardt sat in a deep leather chair and let all those pleasant things lap over her. She could hear speeches and clapping and then the sweet and lovely strains of the accordion, and though she could not explain to herself why these sounds made her feel enormously safe, made her feel as if perhaps she were getting married, she realized that that was the nice aftermath of shock.

The principal excitement next morning was the birth of seven baby ducks. The little creatures had been plunged into the brown rushing water while a delighted audience looked on. Other ducks sat curled up on stones, sulking, perhaps since they were so ignored in favor of a proud mother and these little daft naked creatures. The doves, too, fanned their tails in utter annoyance, while everyone looked toward the water and away from them. She sat and sipped coffee. Monsieur sat a little away from her, dividing his admiration between her and the baby ducks. He flaked bread between his hands, then opened the sliding door and pitched it out. Then he would look at her and smile. Speech was beyond him. He had fallen in love with her, or was infatuated, or was pretending to be infatuated. One of these things. Maybe he was just salvaging her pride. Yet the look was genuinely soft, even adoring. His swallow was affected, his cheeks were as red as the red poppies, and he did little things like wind his watch or rearrange the tops of his socks all for her benefit. Once he put his hand on her shoulder to alert her to some new minutiae of the ducks' behavior and he pressed achingly on her flesh.

If Madame were to find out! she thought, and her being shuddered at the prospect of any further unpleasantness. She did not ask about the bounder, but she did ask later for a glance at her bill and there indeed was the *veston*, the gentleman's *veston*, for sixteen hundred francs. After breakfast she sat out on the lawn and observed the behavior of the other ducks. They pass their time very amiably, she thought; they doze a lot, then scratch or clean themselves, then doze again, then have a little waddle, and perhaps stretch themselves, but she doubted that a duck walked more than a furlong throughout its whole life. Then on beautiful crested hotel notepaper she wrote to her son. She deliberately wrote a blithe letter, a letter about ducks, trees, and nature. Two glasses with the sucked crescent of an orange in each one were laid in an alcove in the wall and she described this to him and thought that soon she would be indulgent and order a champagne cocktail. She did not say, "Your father and I have separated." She would say it later when the pain was not quite so acute, and when it did not matter so much. When would that be? Mrs. Reinhardt looked down at the cushion she was sitting on, and saw that it was a hundred percent Fibranne, and as far as she was concerned, that was the only thing in the world she could be absolutely sure of.

Going back to her room before lunch, she decided to put on a georgette dress and her beads. She owed it to Monsieur. She ought to look nice, even if she could not smile. She ought to pretend to, and by pretending she might become that person. All the burning thoughts and all the recent wounds might just lie low in her and she could appear to be as calm and unperturbed as a summer lake with its water-lily leaves and its starry flowers. Beneath the surface the carp that no one would cast down for. Monsieur's tenderness meant a lot to her, it meant she was still a person on whom another person lavished attention, even love.

Poor lobsters, she thought, and remembered those beseeching moves. When she opened the heart-shaped box in which the beads were hidden, Mrs. Reinhardt let out a shriek. Gone. Gone. Her talisman, her life insurance, her last link with her husband, Harold, gone. Their one chance of being reunited. Gone. She ran back the road to Reception. She was wild. Madame was most annoyed at being told that such a valuable thing had been so carelessly left lying around. As for theft, she did not want to hear of such a thing. It was a vulgarity, was for a different kind of premises altogether, not for her beautiful three-star establishment. She ran a perfect premises, which was her pride and joy and which was a bower against the outside world. How dare the outside world come into her province.

Monsieur's face dissolved in deeper and deeper shades of red and a most wretched expression. He did not say a word. Madame said, of course, it was the visitor, the American gentleman, and there was no knowing what else he had taken. As far as Madame was concerned, the scum of the earth had come into her nest, and though it was a small movement, it was a telling one, when she picked up a vase of flowers, put them down in another place, and put them down so that the water splashed out of them and stained the account she was preparing. This led to a greater vexation. It was a moment of utter terseness, and poor Monsieur could help neither of them. He pulled the dog's ear. Mrs. Reinhardt must ring her husband. She had to. There in full view of them, while Madame scratched figures onto the page and Monsieur pulled the dog's ear, Mrs. Reinhardt said to her husband, Harold, in England that her beads had been stolen, that his beads had been stolen, that their beads had been stolen, and she began to cry. He was no help at all. He asked if they could be traced and she said she doubted it.

"A case of hit-and-run," she said, hoping he would know what she meant. Perhaps he did, because his next remark was that she seemed to be having an eventful time. She said she was in a bad way, and she prayed to God that he would say, "Come home." He didn't. He said he would get in touch with the insurance people.

"Oh, fuck the insurance people," Mrs. Reinhardt said, and slammed the phone down. Monsieur turned away. She walked out the door. She had not a friend in the world.

Mrs. Reinhardt experienced one of those spells that can unsettle one forever. The world became black. A blackness permeated her heart. It was like rats scraping at her brain. It was pitiless. Phrases such as "how are you," or "I love you," or "dear one" were mockery incarnate. The few faces of the strange people around her assumed the masks of animals. The world she stood up in, and was about to fall down in, was green and pretty, but in a second it would be replaced by a bottomless pit into which Mrs. Reinhardt was about to fall for eternity. She fainted.

They must have attended to her, because when she came to, her court shoes were removed, the buttons of her blouse were undone, and there was a warm cup of *tisane* on a stool beside her. A presence had just vanished. Or a ghost. Had just slipped away. She thought it was a woman, and perhaps it was her mother anointing her with ashes, and she thought it was Ash Wednesday. "Because I do not hope to live again," she then said, but fortunately no one seemed to understand. She sat up, sipped the hot tea, apologized about the necklace and about the scene she had made. She was uncertain how far she had gone. King Lear's touching of the robe of Cordelia sprang to mind and she asked God if the dead could in fact live again; if she could witness the miracle that the three apostles witnessed when they came and saw the stone rolled away from Christ's grave. "Come back," she whispered, and it was as if she were taking her own hand and leading herself back to life. The one that led was her present self and the one that was being led was a small child who loved God, loved her parents, loved the trees and the countryside, and had never wanted anything to change. Her two selves stood in the middle, teetering. These were extreme moments for Mrs. Reinhardt, and had she surrendered to them she would have toppled indeed. She asked for water. The tumbler she was holding went soft beneath her grip, and the frightened child in her felt a memory as of shedding flesh, but the woman in her smiled and assured everyone that the crisis had passed, which indeed it had. She lay back for a while and listened to the running water as it lashed and lashed against the jet-black millstone, and she resolved that by afternoon she would go away and bid goodbye to this episode that had had in it enchantment, revenge, shame, and the tenderness of Monsieur.

As she drove away, Monsieur came from behind the tree house bearing a small bunch of fresh pansies. They were multicolored, but the two predominant colors were yellow and maroon. They smelled like young skin and had that same delicacy. Mrs. Reinhardt thanked him and cherished the moment. It was like an assuage. She smiled into his face, their eyes met; for him, too, it was a moment of real happiness, fleeting but real, a moment of good.

The new hotel was on a harbor, and for the second time in four days she walked over boulders that were caked with moss. At her feet the bright crops of seaweed that again looked like theater wigs, but this time she saw who was before and behind her. She was fully in control. What maddened her was that women did as she did all the time and that their pride was not stripped from them, nor their jewelry. Or perhaps they kept it a secret. One had to be so cunning, so concealed.

Looking out along the bay at the boats, the masts, and the occasional double sails, she realized that now indeed her new life had begun, a life of adjustment and change. Life with a question mark. Your ideal of human life is? she asked herself. The answer was none. It had always been her husband, their relationship, his art gallery, their cottage in the country, and plans. One thing above all others came to her mind; it was the thousands of flower petals under the hall carpet which she had put there for pressing. Those pressed flowers were the moments of their life, and what would happen to them—they would lie there for years, or else they would be swept away. She could see them there, thousands of sweet bright petals, mementos of their hours. Before her walk she had been reading Ruskin, reading of the necessary connection between beauty and morality, but it had not touched her. She wanted someone to love. As far as she was concerned, Ruskin's theories were fine sermons, but that is not what the heart wants. She must go home soon and get a job. She must try. Mrs. Reinhardt ran, got out of breath, stood to look at the harbor, ran again, and by an effort of will managed to extricate herself from the rather melancholy state she was in.

During dinner the headwaiter came, between each of the beautiful courses, and asked how she liked them. One was a fish terrine, its colors summery white, pink, green, the colors of flowers. She would love to learn how to make it. Then she had dressed crab, and even the broken-off claws had been dusted with flour and baked for a moment, so that the effect was the same as of smelling warm bread. Everything was right and everything was bright. The little potted plant on the table was a bright cherry pink, robins darted in and out of the dark trees, and the ornamental plates in a glass cupboard had patterns of flowers and trelliswork.

"A gentleman to see you," the younger waiter said. Mrs. Reinhardt froze: the bounder was back. Like a woman ready for battle, she put down her squashed napkin and stalked out of the room. She had to turn a corner to enter the main hall, and there sitting on one of the high-backed Spanish-type chairs was her husband, Mr. Reinhardt. He stood up at once and they shook hands formally, like an attorney and his client at an auspicious meeting. He has come to sue me, she thought, because of the necklace. She did not say, "Why have you come?" He looked tired. Mrs. Reinhardt flinched when she heard that he had taken a private plane. He had been to the other hotel and had motored over. He refused a drink and would not look at her. He was mulling over his attack. She was convinced that she was about to be shot when he put his hand in his pocket and drew the thing out. She did not mind being shot but thought irrationally of the mess on the beautiful Spanish furniture.

"They found it," he said, as he produced the necklace and laid it on the table between them. It lay like a snake in a painting, coiled in order to spring. Yet the sight of it filled her with tears, and she blubbered out about the bounder and how she had met him and how he had used her, and suddenly she realized that she was telling him something that he had no inkling of.

"The maid took them," he said, and she saw the little maid with the brown curly hair dressed for the tournament, and now she could have plucked her tongue out for having precipitated the tale of the bounder.

"Was she sacked?" she asked.

He did not know. He thought not.

"Fine place they have," he said, referring to the lake and the windmills.

"This also is lovely," she said, and went on to talk about the view from the dining room and the light which was so telling, so white, so unavoidable. Just like their predicament. In a minute he would get up and go. If only she had not told him about the bounder. If only she had let him say why he had come. She had closed the last door.

"How have you been?" he said.

"Well," she said, but the nerve in her lower jaw would not keep still, and without intending it and without in any way wanting it to happen, Mrs. Reinhardt burst into tears, much to the astonishment of the young waiter, who was waiting to take an order, as he thought, for a drink.

"He tried to blackmail me," she said, and then immediately denied it.

Her husband was looking at her very quietly, and she was not sure if there was any sympathy left in him. She thought, If he walks out now, it will be catastrophic, and again she thought of the few lobsters who were left in the tank, and who were motionless with grief.

"There is us and there are people like him," Mr. Reinhardt said, and though she had not told the whole story, he sensed the gravity of it. He said that if she did not mind he would stay, and that since he was hungry and since it was late, might they not go in to dinner. She looked at him and her eyes were probably drenched.

"Us and people like him!" she said.

Mr. Reinhardt nodded.

"And Rita?" Mrs. Reinhardt said.

He waited. He looked about. He was by no means at ease.

"She is one of us," he said, and then qualified it. "Or she could be, if she meets the right man."

His expression warned Mrs. Reinhardt to pry no further. She linked him as they went in to dinner.

The wind rustled through the chimney and some soot fell on a bouquet of flowers. She saw that. She heard that. She squeezed his arm. They sat opposite. When the wind roars, when the iron catches rattle, when the very windowpanes seem to shiver, then wind and sea combine, then dogs begin to howl and the oncoming storm has a whiff of the supernatural. What does one do, what then does a Mrs. Reinhardt do? One reaches out to the face that is opposite, that one loves, that one hates, that one fears, that one has been betrayed by, that one half knows, that one longs to touch and be reunited with, at least for the duration of a windy night. And by morning who knows? Who knows anything, anyhow.

Quartet

Uncollected Stories,
1979–1981

Violets

In an hour he is due. In that hour I have tasks to perform and they, of course, revolve around him. I shall lay the fire. I shall lay it as I learned to as a child. I shall put on twists of paper, small pieces of coal, and, last of all, a few dry logs. The kindling is a pale wooden chip basket delivered from the vegetable shop. It was full of Clementines, and their smell lingers in it like a presence. Christmas is but a month gone. Then I did not know him; then I thought of myself as having passed those seesaw states, subject to a man, maybe loving a man, on tenterhooks because of a man.

Christmas I spent with my grown-up children and several old friends in a Tudor house in the North of England. We pulled crackers, put on ridiculous paper hats, and marveled at how happy one can be ripping open packages or finding one's name crusted with a bit of silly gold glitter. My younger son received a Russian sword and went about the room lashing the uncomplaining air. We clapped and summoned up adversaries for him, and he delighted in the game. Next day it snowed and I thought, as I watched the swirl for an entire afternoon, that I could watch forever, because I had reached a plateau. It was quite mesmerizing to see all those flakes coming vertically through the hemisphere, then tilting sideways, and finally giving a beautiful suede sheen to the graveled earth, or to see them forming like small white stones on the rhododendron bushes, and feathery plumes on the branches of the fir trees.

That was only Christmas, and then came the meeting, and now he is due to arrive. My next task is to plump cushions. A man I know said that of all housewifely chores it is the most boring, the most monotonous, but still we do it, and the pink satin or the plum velvet or the patchwork cushion sits there inflated, ridiculously waiting. Next thing is to get more coal into the scuttle, to give the scuttle a bit of Brasso, to sweep up the grains of coal that will have been spilled, and, if possible, tighten the legs of the tongs so that they do not wobble and disgorge the lumps of coal before they get to the fire.

You would think I have not had visitors for years, but I have—in fact, they flock in all the time. But it is as if I see everything with a ruthless clarity. It is the opposite of that vigil when I watched the snow getting thicker and thicker, and saw the icicles extend from the roof, until after some days they were like walking sticks or beautiful javelins that one wanted to play with. I would paint a panel of this sitting room in this one hour if I had time and a pot of emulsion. The walls are apricot-colored, and in lamplight they are most pleasing because so quietly they emit a glow. Sometimes I think of the yolk of a gull's egg when I look at those walls, and the thought ushers me on to the month of June, which for some reason I connect with happy and graceful events. In England people give their annual ball, girls wear myrtle in their hair, there are the races at Ascot, and even the most unsumptuous garden has a display of tea roses or briar roses or rambling roses, and if you stay in one of those lovely country houses there is a vase of them on your bedside table, bright and wide open like the eyes of watchful children.

But this is daylight and winter, and even the myriad bits of fluff on the new Edith Piaf record have caught my eye, as they will undoubtedly catch his. So it's dusting time. I would make it night if I were setting the appointment. Married men are lunchtime callers. I know that. I know so much—albeit so little—about married men. I know how divided they must be, and how cursory, and how mentally they must brush off either her or her kiss as they step off the escalator to reach the Underground, or as they step into their motorcars, or as they glide through their own hallways, whistling or humming a familiar, guarded tune. They deny. They could be called Judas.

I know the mistake I am making. I see the exits in life. It will be six months or the proverbial nine months before it ends, and yet the foreknowledge is as clear as the first meeting. It is just like lifting a latch and seeing into the blazing fire at the far end of the room, with the passage in between, its carpet, its white rug, its chaise longue, its birdcage, and its many secular delights. One day I will come to the other end and I will perhaps get scorched. I was brought up to believe in Hell and I was brought up to believe that men are masterful and fickle. I could, of course, have said no, but I didn't. I demurred and then I succumbed. Nevertheless, I am planning something new for myself. I am putting my room in order. The smell of furniture wax, the incenselike smell, will fill the air and complement the beautiful heady innocent smell of the hyacinths that I have cultivated in a big bowl. Their tubers are just visible above the clay, and they are the dreamiest white, the palest blue, and a pink that looks artificial in color, like a cake icing. They are like crests on the round table, and as I pass to do this or that, I want to bury my face in them, but there is no time, and also, specks of pollen would stain the tip of my nose. There are only thirty minutes left.

The soup that is supposed to be simmering on the kitchen stove is, alas, boiling. I cry out, add cream, and beg all those little curds to disappear as I stir it more and more in a circular motion. Then I cannot find the embroidered cloth that I bought in Spain. Damn it. It is a cream cloth with red appliqués stitched over it. It is both chaste and gay. A stranger sitting down to eat might not only be surprised by it but might in jest say, "Get me the castanets." I am resolved to be gay, to show little of my inner self—no old sores or tragic portraits. The cloth is not in the cupboard, and with no time to spare, I ring up the laundry. The laundry building is eight miles away, and one hundred and thirty people are employed there, yet I am rash enough to think that my Spanish cloth will be located and even delivered before one o'clock.

It is in the middle of my conversation with an insolent girl at the laundry that I realize that the soup is on the boil again. I run to turn the gas off and en route catch my knitted sleeve on the loose nail of the cane chair. Things are getting bungled. These last minutes are the worst. Hurry, hurry.

But when I get out the cut-glass goblets, I remember my dead mother. She gave them to me. Some are thickly cut with raised wedges of glass, some have harps that seem to float inside the walls of the glass itself, and three—the other three in the set got broken—have beautiful indentations to fit exactly the print of a thumb or a finger. I shall use them. I shall lay places for three. That will confuse him. I intend to confuse him. I intend to be someone else. The preparations are going against me—I have cut the bread too thick and the smoked salmon is in slithers. The shop has rooked me. I have met him, this caller, only once, and that was at a Christmas party, and our conversation was pure banter. Then, when he rang, he was crispness itself, and said such things as "Well, are we going to meet? Not that I think we should." I said that we need not meet, and indeed, I meant it. But my stepping back from him whetted his interest. He invited himself to this lunch. "I shall come and lift lunch off you" was what he said. So English. So arch. I have made a cucumber salad. I pressed it all morning between two platters. Each disk of cucumber is softness itself, and even the green has been drained out of it. I sprinkle the salad with parsley. Soon I shall have to take off the cardigan, because I am wearing a new black dress. It fits me as if I were poured into it, as if I were molded to it.

Busy men often cancel at the last minute. Maybe he won't come; maybe he will ring and cancel. He is a company director, he is married, he has a chauffeur, and I gather that his wife and he made it from scratch. He probably got a scholarship and went to Oxford or Cambridge. Now he has two houses and a croft in Scotland. I expect he is used to servants; maybe they have a cook . . . Good God! I left the phone off the hook when I ran from it to save the soup. He may have tried to ring and decided that the phone is out of order, so that he need not ring again to account for his non-appearance. And here all this food, the lovely wine, pellucid, like liquid sun, into which who knows how many precious grapes have gone. The fruits of the earth. I have on black mesh stockings and lace garters that I found in my mother's drawer after she had died. They were wrapped up in a bolster case along with other things—necklaces, veiling, and some velvet flowers. They shocked me, and yet I said, "They will come in handy one day," and put them in my suitcase.

Opening the wine, I gauge my strength by pulling the cork out.

My strength is monumental. He will see me as some monster, devouring. I leave the ladle near the stove and turn the gas down until it shudders and shows signs of extinguishment. The clock has not chimed, but it is about to. It is in the next room, but I know that it has entered that spate of hesitancy that prevails just before it strikes. It broke once, but I had a man in from the city to repair it. He was actually called Mr. Goldsmith. I am superstitious about it and pray that it will not ever again expire.

My God, there is the doorbell. I know that I must answer it, but I cannot. I am unable to move. I am upstairs. I cannot descend. I read something last night when I was unable to sleep. It has affected me. I read that the only paradise is the paradise lost. Proust. I read it years ago, but I had not absorbed it, and last night, after rereading it, I tossed and turned in my wide bed and thought of my caller and how I would seduce him. I saw our little drama as if on a picture postcard: a naked couple oblivious of the serpent that lies between them. And I thought that I could think of him to my heart's delight, and that he need never know, that he must never know, that I could paint postcard after postcard and give to skin the tints and the textures that I love, and give to speech and action all that I ever desire. I could ordain it regardless of him, and of course I thought how futile that would be in the end.

His finger is on the bell. He certainly is not timid—not as timid as I would be entering a paramour's house and not quite knowing what to expect. For God's sake, I must do something. I can't just stand here. After all, I have an intercom. I can pick it up and say, "Go away," or "She's not here," or "Just a minute." But I do not pick it up. I lean against the wall. I am wobbling. I go down the stairs to let him in. He is just leaving. He seems surly. We do not kiss in the hall. I take his tweed coat and very formally lay it sideways on the prayer chair. As he comes into the sitting room, I see his evident pleasure as he takes stock of things.

"Nice room you've got," he says.

"We like it," I say.

"We?"

"Yes, we are a we."

*

I have set the course. I shall lie. I shall invent a lover, a mysterious one who comes at night rather than at noon, a privileged one who is allowed to share the secrets of my soul, as this one must never be. Perhaps in this way I shall have my little Paradise Lost; yet I wonder if one has to enter it in order to find it, in order to lose it.

"Do you always dress like this?" he asks. The question bristles with attraction and reproof.

"If I feel like it."

I am pouring the wine. He says that he does not drink but that he will drink with me. I say there is apple juice, and point to it, on the beautiful gallery tray. He accepts the wine. He puts his tongue out in an involuntary gesture to taste whatever there is to taste.

"You don't know how lucky you are," he tells me.

"Why?" I ask.

"Because I like black stockings and black satin, for some odd reason."

"In that case, you are the lucky one."

His eyes are like violets, but his skin is bleached. There is something frozen about him. Life, too, has left its cold claws on his shoulder. But I will never know. No more than he will ever know about me. He is about to kiss me. I wonder if one has to enter the gates of paradise, even the tiniest adulterous little paradise, in order to find it, in order to lose it, in order to refind it, in perpetuity. And, wondering, I float into the first bewildered kiss.

The Call

She would be, or so she thought, over it—over the need and over the hope and over the certainty of that invisible bond that linked them—when suddenly it would come back. It was like a storm. She would start to shake. One morning, this frenzy made her almost blind, so that she could hardly see the design on the teacup she was washing, and even the simple suds in the aluminum sink seemed to enclose a vast pool of woe. When she saw two pigeons in the plane tree outside, it smote her heart, because they were cooing and because they were close. Then her telephone rang in the other room. Going to answer it, with the tea cloth in her hand, she prayed, "Oh, God, let it be him," and in a sense her prayers were answered, though she could not be sure, because by the time she got to it, whoever it was had rung off. She waited, trembling. It—he—would ring again.

There was sun on the trees in the garden outside, and the varying greenness of each tree was singled out and emphasized in the brightness. There was a dark green, which emitted a gloom that seemed to come from its very interior; there was a pale green, which spoke of happiness and limes; and there was the holly leaf so shiny it might have just been polished. There was the lilac, shedding and rusted because of the recent heavy rain, and the hanging mauve blooms gave the effect of having dropsy. And all of these greens seemed to tell her of her condition—of how it varied, of how sometimes she was not rallying and then again sometimes she would pass to another state, a relatively bright and buoyant state, and sometimes, indeed, she had dropsy. Yet he was not ringing back. But why? Ah, yes. She knew why. He did not care to lose face, and by ringing immediately it would be evident that it had been him. So she busied herself with little chores. She drained the dishes and then dried them thoroughly. Her face on their shining surfaces looked distorted. Just as well he was not coming! She took the loose fallen petals of sweet pea from a vase on the window ledge and squeezed them as if to squeeze the last bit of color and juice out of them. After twenty minutes of devoting herself to pointless trivia, to errands into which she read talismanic import, she decided that he was not going to ring, and so to put herself out of her misery, she must ring him. He had lately given her the number. He had repeated it twice and when last leaving he had said it again. For six months he had kept it a secret. It was his work number. He would not, of course, give his home number, since it was also his wife's. So why not ring? Why not? Because she found herself shaking before even attempting to dial. She foresaw how she would speak rapidly and hurriedly and ask him to lunch, and suppose he said no. She would wait for half an hour and then she would ring.

In that half hour, her whole body seemed to lose its poise and its strength. She felt sick and ashamed, as if she had done some terrible wrong—some childish wrong like wetting or soiling her bed—and she sought to find the root of this pointless notion of wrongdoing that was connected with an excruciating wait. She thought of previous times when she had been spurned by others and tried to marshal in herself the pride, the fury, the common sense that would cause her not to lay herself at his feet. She thought of the day when she would learn to get by—maybe learn to swim—and for an instant she saw herself thrashing through a pool and kicking and conquering. She said, "If I ring, does it not make me the stronger one?" Her words were hollow to herself. The sun shone, yet her house had a coldness—the coldness of a vault, the coldness when you press yourself on the tiled floor of an empty dark country chapel and beg your Maker to help you in these straits—and for no reason there crowded in on her mind images of a wedding, a slow procession down the aisle, a baptismal font with a rim of rust on its marble base, religious booklets about keeping company, and in the chapel porch an umbrella with one spoke protruding. In imagination she went out the graveled path under the yew trees and smelled their solemn, permeating perfume. She thought, Yesterday I could do without him, today I can't. And then she remonstrated, You can.

She was going on a train that afternoon, to the country, and once on the train, no matter how great her unhappiness, she could not succumb to a frenzy. She thought, too, that if she rang him once she might ring him at all hours, she might make a habit of it. If only he would sit opposite her, take her hand, and tell her that he had no interest in her, then she believed that she would be free to let him go . . . Or was he going? Was she herself becoming narked? She saw him once a fortnight, but that was not enough. These clandestine visits were the crumbs of the marriage table. The making do with nearly nothing. Where was the bounty of it? Where the abandon?

"You are what you are," she said. But did others have to suffer so? Did others lie down and almost expire under such longing? No. Others swam; others went far out to sea, others dived, others put oxygen flagons on their backs and went down into the depths of the ocean and saw the life there—the teeming, impersonal life—and detached themselves from the life up above. She feared that her love of nature—her love of woodland, her love of sun on hillside and meadow, her love of wildflowers and dog roses and cow parsley, her love of the tangled hedgerows—was only an excuse, a solace. Mortal love was what she craved.

She imagined how he would come and pass by her in the hall, being too shy to shake hands, and walk around the room inhaling her while also trying to observe by the jug of fresh flowers or the letters on her desk who had been here recently, and if perhaps she had found a lover. He had commanded her to, and had also commanded her not to. Always, when he lay above her, about to possess her, he seemed to be surveying his pasture, to sniff like a bloodhound, making sure that no other would pass through to his burrow, making sure that she would be secret and sweet, and solely for him.

Ah, would that they were out on a hillside, or in the orchards of her youth, away from telephone calls or no telephone calls, away from suspicions, where he believed she wore perfume deliberately so his wife would guess his guilty secret. She was watching the face of her telephone, following with her eye the circle of congealed dust about the digits, where fingernail never reached nor duster ever strove; watching and praying. She heard a letter being pushed through her box and she ran to get it. Any errand was a mercy, a distraction, a slender way of postponing what she would do but must not do.

The letter was from a stranger. It bore a scape of a blue sea, a high craggy cliff, and a flying bird. The message said, "I thought this to be the bluebird of happiness but fear it might only be a common pigeon." It wished her happiness and to be well. It was signed, "A WELL-WISHER, MALE." She thought, Oh, Christ, the whole world knows of my stew, and she wondered calmly if this union she craved was something that others, wiser ones, had forgone—had left behind at their mothers' breast, never to be retasted—and she thought of her dead mother with her hair tautly pinned up and of the wall of unvoiced but palpable hostility that had grown between them. She hoped then that she would be the same toward her man one day, withdrawn, cut off from him. Her mother's visage brought tears to her eyes. They were different tears from the ones she had been shedding earlier. They were a hot burst of uncontrolled grief that within minutes had sluiced her face and streamed over into her temples and wet her hair.

The half hour had passed in which she promised herself that she would ring him, and now she was talking to herself as to an addict, saying could she not wait a bit longer, could her longing not be diverted by work or a walk, could she not assuage the lump inside her throat by swallowing warmed honey on it, so that the syrup would slide down and soothe her. The needless pain there seemed to be intensified, as if a sharp current were passing through her. Could she not put it off until the morrow?

There is no stopping a galloping horse.

She went toward the telephone, and as she did, it began to ring. It rang loudly. It rang like some tutelary ogre, telling her to pick it up quickly, telling her that it was the master of her fate, of her every moment, of the privacy of her room, of the tangle of her thoughts, of the weight of her desire, and of the enormity of her hope. She did not answer it. She did not know why she did not answer it. She simply knew that she could not answer it, and that she waited for its ringing to die down the way one waits for the ambulance siren to move out of one's hearing, to pass to the next street.

"Is this love?" she asked herself, admitting that she had wanted so much to answer it. The longing to see him, communicate with him, clasp her fingers in his, feed him, humor him, and watch him while he ran a comb through his hair was as strong and as candescent as it had ever been.

"You had better go out now," she said aloud, and quickly, but with a certain ceremony, she put an embroidered shawl over the phone, to muffle its sound.

It would be three days before she came back, and she saw a strip of water that would get wider and wider. Green and turbulent it was, and in time, she knew, it would swell into a vast sea, impassable and with no shore in sight. Time would sever them, but as yet it was love, and hard to banish.

The Plan

It is morning. What is more, it is a beautiful morning. There is a sparkle on everything and even the dullest things are shot with radiance. From my back window, the bedroom window, I see that the cats—those wise barometers—are already stretched out on the tiled roofs, taking the sun through their thick fur. From the front window, if I were to walk to the next room, I would no doubt see girls and women going off to work in their sleeveless dresses, the women carrying their cardigans just in case. And I would probably note that the pensioners are out that bit early in search of a shady seat in Dovehouse Green. It is amazing what a steady sunshine does for these blanched English souls.

Just now I put powder on, and the translucency that the shop assistant guaranteed showed up for the first time. It is like seeing specks of mica on a road. I am reminded suddenly of those traveling actresses who came to our little village in Ireland long ago and made such an impression on me. They were quite bedraggled and unhappy when in the daytime they pushed prams down the seedy street that was called Main Street, but at night they were creatures endowed with glitter—glitter on their faces, glitter on their bodices, glitter in their eyes, possibly owing to nerves or maybe fever. They were transformed beings. I loved watching them. I luxuriated in their pain as they strode about the stage, or halted, or flung themselves onto some velvet-covered sofa. Their characters were invariably ones that had to endure pain. There was the young flighty mother who abandoned her little son in order to elope with a rake, and of course, when she repented her wild impulse and tried to come back to her own home, her upright husband had married her rival, who was naturally a woman of steel. The mother was forced to return disguised as a maid, and nurse her little son but behave with distance, as if they were not of the same blood—as if she had not once intrepidly carried him within her. There was another, in direct contrast, who chose the vows of chastity, and was kneeling on a little dais, haloed in white, taking those final and irreversible vows, when her errant scoundrel came to claim her and found that he was too late!

Yes, those ladies come to mind when I pat the powder on and look in my long wardrobe mirror and see that the effect is indeed cheering. Why am I putting the powder on so early, when in fact I have household chores to do and when I know that it is best to leave my skin untampered with through the day, to let it breathe, while no one is seeing me? Ah, to be seen is the big nourishment, the sop of content. If only we could go to each other's house and show ourselves to other women's husbands, or valets, or sons, or employers, then we could display ourselves, come home, and feel justified. We could feel that the effort we put into sereneness, into smiling, into pursing, into deportment, was not completely in vain. I think of all the women in all the houses in London at this moment for whom a visit would change everything, even fleetingly, and I think that if I had organizing abilities I would do something about it. For some reason, I see a young woman, an Eastern woman of sallow complexion, with her baby, and they are placed in an English garden. There are poppies sprouting red in the high yellow unmown grass, and I realize that her baby tugging at her breast defers the emptiness that she might otherwise feel, and yet she is being emptied, and one day her breasts will be like discarded shells. But there is no need for pessimism. This is a special day. It is marked in my diary with a little asterisk and it says "*pour dîner*." I have already laid my outfit on the bed. It is a lace blouse that would not go amiss as an altar cloth. The disks of thick cream lace are stitched loosely together, so that the skin can be seen through the webbing. The skirt is also cream, with spatters of red and violet, just as if one took a marking pen and childishly indented these colored points.

It is probable that we will eat outdoors. There will be several tables covered in white cloth, and the crystal goblets will be like sentinels at each place setting. There will be roses in special glass bowls. The bowls are high, like cake stands, and the roses will be cut close to their petals and laid in there like confectionery; if they are pink, as indeed they may be, they will be like those iced sweets that I loved in childhood, and it will not be hard to recapture that beautiful synthetic almond taste. The lights will be concealed in the foliage, and the smell will be a blend of roses, honeysuckle, and various expensive perfumes. There will perhaps be a summerhouse or a little gazebo where a couple will wander, apparently to study some facet of its design, but really to make an assignation. That will not be him and me. If he gives me five minutes of his time without taking a tweezers to my nervous system, I shall consider myself lucky. To be fair to myself, I did not plan this meeting. The opposite. Two days ago, when I heard of it from my hostess, I flinched. She had come here to discuss her dilemma with her lover and her impatience with her paunchy husband. Just as she was leaving, I asked who were the other guests. As soon as she told me, I tried to get out of going. She said my name sharply. She said, "Anna," and I could feel the inevitable rebuke. She said, "Finding a woman at the last minute is almost as difficult as finding a man." Her nails, her eyes, and the heels of her lizard shoes were all very pointed, and I was afraid to cross her. But my heart did start to gallop.

I am envisioning each group, with the new arrivals like extras waiting for their moment to be received, to be introduced, to find excitement or shock in some unexpected face. The men will all be wearing black tie, and I pray that at least two of them will be personable. I will need all the discipline that I have got. My lover is going to be there. My lover's wife is going to be there. I have never met her. That is not quite true; I once saw her, and so I will recognize her. My eyes will land on her, and rest on her, so that she will know that I am not flinching, and not turning away. She is dark. She is dark, like the raven. At least that is how I remember her. It may have been the lighting, in which green was impregnated with blackness. It was in a marquee at a wedding and there was a great storm outside, so that the event was marked by a kind of menace that I took to be talismanic. Among the guests I saw a dark woman in a cape, but I did not know then to whom she was attached. He and I had just met and we were eating canapés on which there was a single sprig of limp tinned asparagus. I refused a second one, to which he said, "You don't look as if you need to diet," and then announced that he was not as thin as he looked, that the hollows in his face made him seem thinner than he actually was. His face reminds me of those stone effigies that decorate the ceilings or columns of a monastery or a chapel. It is a graven face. In contrast, our conversation was merry and stirring.

"And you don't know how lovely you are," he said, half joking. The marquee was freezing, as there was only one gas heater at the far end, around which the older people had converged. It being spring, the bride and groom naturally had anticipated a warmer day. After all, the daffodils were out; but the wind was blowing their wrinkled flutes. Seeing in the distance the blue coronet of the gas fire, I thought of baby chicks curled up next to each other under a lamp, and I had a sudden unaccountable longing to nestle nearer to him, when I saw that already he had come a few steps closer. Between us was only a fraction of space, in which I could feel a shudder. It was getting to be the moment when the bride's father was to make his speech, and I realized who the dark woman was. She came toward us and said to the man, "Having a good time?" And at once I moved away.

Of course, it could have been that she trusted him so utterly, that they lived in such an understanding, that they even liked to share people such as me, so as to talk about us afterward. At any rate, on that first occasion I could not find words, or the words I could find would have sounded caustic or maybe even brazen. My future lover saw me move, and came and touched my elbow so lightly and so gracefully that I felt as if a ghost had taken charge of his body and brushed against mine, and I thought, Oh, Christ, I am falling in love with a ghost, just as always, and I saw in him shades of others—saw his disappearing tricks, his appearing tricks, his inability to give love, along with his restless pursuit of it. When he touched me, it was as if we had met before, as if we knew each other in some hidden way and the time had now come for us to cross that barrier and to savor each other, to cease to be strangers. Though of course we would always be strangers. Is that not the essence, the requisite, of love?

So I can say—because now I am better acquainted with him—that my instinct was flawless and that I could have predicted almost everything that would happen, that has happened, and that is yet to happen. Even as he is asking to see me, he is asking not to see me; when I am distant, he loves me like a clinging schoolboy, and when I reveal my feelings, he looks at his watch and says he has a meeting at four. Only my near-absence guarantees his near-presence, and it is an exhausting game to play. Yet I feel that if I could reach him things would be different. I believe that he does not know himself, and that if I could lead him to himself he would dispense with all artifice, he would welcome this rapture, he would not shirk it. When he is trying to shrug me off, he eats hurriedly. He throws the cherries into his mouth and gulps them down. He did that the last time he was here to lunch, and in his haste one fell onto his white shirt, which was still open. "Damn," he said, as he looked for it. It had slipped into his belly button, and fitted there like the stone of a ring, a ruby. It had burst. He picked it out. It left a red stain on his shirt. He began to suck the white fabric. He sucked it with such determination. I hated him then. I thought, He is sucking it clean, so that when he goes home he will not be asked, "How did that get there?" I saw his ruthlessness and I saw his fear. In myself I saw stirrings of pain, a dip into that fount of sorrow, a reintroduction to a loss that I thought I had finished with. Perhaps it was then I hatched my revenge.

Sensing a coolness, he reached out for me and drew me onto his knee, and he said, "Do you fantasize about me?" and I said, "Yes," but I was too shy to say how. I asked if he fantasized about me, and he said yes, in the car, when on his way to see me, and then he said that I fantasized too much and that it was unhealthy. I was about to say that so did he, when I realized with staggering clarity that he was right and that I was misled. He only fantasizes when he is on his way to see me, when he is assured of the sight of me and all that I can give, whereas I spin fantasies as the hours go by, as the sprinkler in the garden makes a damp circle around the base of every rosebush, as the shadow on the sundial moves lower, and as the floor that I have polished gleams and has the magic of a ballroom waiting for its waltzers—him and me.

Tonight, I fear that he will snub me. In fact, I know that he is in danger of snubbing me unless I am cunning, unless I preempt him by giving him a glacial look. That will unnerve him, make him doubt the certainty of next week's luncheon date. I will look past him at the moment of being introduced to him, and then I will hurry to some other man, and I know that unwisely but impulsively he will follow me and mutter, "You're very aloof tonight and very beautiful." His flattery is always undisguised, and for that reason it never fails to thrill me. Perhaps I see the transparency of it, and flagrant reason for it, the truth and the untruth of it. Tonight I shall guard myself, so that I can carry out my little scheme. I shall join the group that his wife is in. I know that she will want to talk to me. I know that she will detach herself from the others and veer toward me, that she will talk about everything under the sun—her twins, summer holidays, their garden, her busyness—deferring what she most wants to know, and presently I will unnerve her. She will not be sure whether her little jabs of inner dread are validated or not. What I have decided to do is to listen to her, to admire her dress or her blouse or her jewelry, to admire anything that can be admired without my being obsequious. I am going to be as soft and as patient as a wet nurse. When she needs a drink, I will be the one to signal the waiter, and I will down mine more quickly so that our glasses can be filled, then clinked together. Even if she thinks that I am overfriendly, she will not think it by the time I am finished, because of my trump card. Naturally, others will come over and interrupt this tête-à-tête; others will delay my strategy. Her husband, fearing the worst, may come over and say, "What are you two nattering about?" or our hostess may not allow two lovely women to slink into a corner and while away that half hour when they should be mixing with and delighting the men.

I have no doubt but that we will be alone, because we both want it. I shall whisper. I may even touch her elbow or her wrist. I shall ask if by any chance she has smelling salts or a tranquillizer in her bag, and once she has appraised the question, and felt my shiver, she will ask me why. I shall tell her in all truth that I doubt if I can get through the dinner. Again she will ask me why. She will look at me, and when I say, "The usual," she will know that my trouble is man trouble. I can already see her eyes—dark eyes becoming potent with curiosity—and her blood will quicken, and it will not be long before she asks me who he is, what he does, and I will tell her so much and yet so little. I will describe to her her own husband and any other woman's husband, because do they, do they, differ so radically, those men in dark suits, white shirts, and tasteful silk ties, who want peace in their nests and excitement on their forays? I will say that he gives me pleasure, that he gives me pain, that I never know when to expect him and when not, and that I mean to give him up but I lack the necessary strength, the determination. Then comes my coup. I will ask her to have lunch with me in my favorite restaurant. I will tell her that I long to talk to someone whom I don't know—someone who can help—and with every word I say suspicion will redound in her womb. She may hesitate, but she will not refuse me. I will pin her to a day, and the sooner the better. Nor will he be able to force her to cancel, since that would show him to be implicated, show his culpability. I can hardly wait for tonight to be over, so that I can get on with the proceedings. Their unknown world will gradually unfold to me. I may even meet their twins. She and I may become friends, or getting to know him through her, I may be cured of this passion or together we may overthrow him and send him out into the world stripped of his duplicity. I scarcely know what will happen. All I know is that I cannot endure it alone, and as they have become part of my life I shall become part of theirs; our lives, you see, are intertwined, and if they destroy me they cannot hope to be spared.

The Return

The light is stunning, being of the palest filtered gold, and the clouds are like vast confections made of spun sugar, ruminative orbs that seem to stand in the air, to dally, as if they were being held and willed by some invisible puppeteer. Streams of sunshine issue over the fields and the earth far below—fields that have been mown, others that have been harvested, and still others exuding a ravishing, life-giving, ocher color. Sometimes a range of mountains comes into view and the peaks covered with last year's snow shine with an awesome silver-white brightness. The little houses, the winding rivers, and the ordered fields seem detached from the currents of everyday life, like objects planted in an unpeopled world. All is suspended, and I think how harmonious a life can be. "I do not want to land," I say, and wonder if the force and fierceness of the airliner as it mows through the air has the same impact as the plow piercing the earth and slicing a passage through it. As I wend my way home, all sorts of thoughts come to mind, idle and drifting like thistledown. For no reason I think of a peculiar and timid woman who featured in my childhood and who used to sit at her piano and sing whenever visitors descended on her. Though they complained about her screeching voice, they were glad that she performed for them, that she allowed for no gaps in the conversation, and that she gave them something to mock. One year she acquired a pair of peacocks, of whom she was absurdly proud, even boastful. The female contracted an ailment by which she kept her eggs embedded inside her, and though wanting to, she could not give lay. The mistress was childless, too, and this caused her to cry when she saw the girls decked out in their gauzy veils and the boys, like little men in new suits, in the chapel at their First Holy Communion. Suddenly I think of a peacock's feather and in its center an eye so blue, so riveting, that I am reminded of those china eyes that they sold on my holiday island, supposed to keep evil away. This blue is metallic and belongs to a zone in the bowels of the sea, where the spirits of the Nereids are said to dwell. The sea by which I sat and lulled myself on my holiday did not seem at all ominous. It was always inviting, and in the scorching town it was as soothing and beneficial as a baptismal font. Life there would have been intolerable without it. The town itself was seething with heat and the small houses were like white cubes that bristled in the heat. The only haven was inside the Byzantine church, whose dun-gold quiet suggested dusk—a dusk in which moths flew about and the faces of saints carved on burnished wood looked out at visitors with a resigned and temperate beauty.

A gnarled old beggar woman presided at the church door and upon receiving a coin she ranted in ecstasy, delivering a mixture of dirge and song. The narrow cobbled streets were free of automobiles, and in the square thin well-bred donkeys were tethered to the one tree, ready to cart the scalding visitors up the steep hill to the acropolis, and if necessary down again. Once, I went there at evening time and it was as if its pillars, its spaces, and its buff stone fragments looking out to sea defied every other standard of beauty and composure. I did not do much sightseeing. It was the harbor to which I veered—the harbor with a life that varied with the hours, so that in the morning breeze its ripples were like minnows on the surface, and later on, its blue was so hard, so glittering, it resembled priceless jewelry. I used to love to watch the liners gliding in, suave and white in comparison with the ferry, which looked clumsy, like a two-decker bus. Then there were the pedal boats with their sedate passengers, and all of a sudden there would be the single sail of a surf boat, like the torn wing of a giant butterfly, dipping down as some embarrassed novice lost his bearings. Two rival groups of children made sand castles.

Walking by them, I would suddenly think of my lover's children and wonder pointlessly what games they were playing on their summer vacation. I was trying to forget him, or at least to suspend the mixed memories of our times together. The two years I had known him had brought such an artful combination of pain and pleasure that I welcomed a rest, and while forbidding myself to think of him I settled for happy ruminations about his children. I imagined how I would woo them with boiled sweets and various small packets containing whistles and water pistols and other distractions. I wondered what they looked like and if they had his eyes—eyes that can be so piercing or so mild, depending on his mood, eyes that almost always contradict the cursoriness of his manner and lead one to believe that things are sweeter than he dares to admit. I shall not meet them. It is true that I have accepted all the rules and all the embargoes. Of course these rules have not been expressly stated, but one knows them, for they are in the air, like motes. It is the same with the future. He and I do not discuss it. It is as if we were prisoners—two cloistered people for whom each meeting is the only one they can count on. Once, he raised the question of our past. He said we should have met when we were both younger, both fresher. I do not agree. I believe we should have met when we met, but I did not voice this, because I have acquired the habit of saying little—at least, little of any moment. Perhaps because there is so much to say. Or perhaps we do not venture, lest our frail edifice should topple. I cannot help but think of the sand castles the children make with such resolve and such pugnaciousness, and yet when they are called in at dusk they know that the sea in all its vehemence will wash their efforts away. And yet the next day they commence again with exactly the same hope and the same gusto.

While I was on the island, I believed that I had become indifferent to him, but now as I head for home, I am not nearly so confident. As we fly across Europe, I can feel the chill in the air, and from time to time I put my hand up to lower the draft through the ventilator. I say to myself, "This is the air of Yugoslavia," or "This is the air of Italy," or "Soon it will be the air of Belgium," and I think what a marvel to tread the air of several countries, to have one's body borne forward while one's mind harks back to another place. I did not want to leave my little villa. I felt such a pang, and I thought, Why abandon all this beauty and why jeopardize this hard-won harmony? The villa, though secluded, had a fine view of the bay, a terrace with splashes of bright bougainvillea in clay urns, and at night the smell of orange blossom was so strong and so heady that it was like another presence, pleasing and drugging the senses. Then, in the morning, the flutes of morning glory, so blue and so ethereal, were like heralding angels. Then, too, life in the harbor recommenced. The visitors would file down the dusty tracks and appoint themselves under the straw umbrellas, and soon there would be bodies, or, rather, heads, bobbing in the water alongside the pink buoys, as the sun became hotter and hotter and the sand began to glisten, then sizzle.

Down there, though I was among people, I had a sense of space, of aloofness. The sun shone with such a merciless dedication that even one chink in the straw umbrella could lead to a bad burn. It was a question of lathering oneself with cream, taking a dip, and then hurrying back to the shelter that seemed like a little ark redolent of straw. Across the harbor there were two mountains facing each other, and each in turn had the benefit of the sun. When one was bathed in gold, the other was gray and pitiful, like a widow gathering her weeds about her for the night. This contrast brought to mind his wife's situation and my own: one in a state of happiness at the other's expense, yet the happy one always knowing the precariousness of her situation, just as the mountains had to settle for alternations of light and dark. Still, I was able to banish those thoughts, to rout out those daggers and apply my eyes and thence my mind to nature. In the glaze of sunshine one could wrest one's mind from thought, and it was just like pulling a blind down and shading a room. It was a sparse island, with no crops and with stunted trees that teetered on the barren slopes. There were no dogs, and the cats were thin and ratlike.

When evening came, I would sit on my terrace admiring the stars, so clear and so particular, like flowers on an immense soft navy-blue down. Music from the two rival discotheques and the ceaseless mechanical creak of the cicadas were the only jarring sounds. The lights from the other houses and the bracelet of lights from the three restaurants reminded me of the life of the town—a life that I could partake of had I the inclination. But I did not stir. I used to sit there and think that I was free of him, and tell myself that I had arrived at that sane and happy state of detachment. Indeed, had he sent a telegram to say that he was arriving, I would have sent one back to say that it was impossible. I did not want him there—not then. But now, as I near home and I see precisely the soft spill of his brown hair or one hand in his trouser pocket as he enters my house abruptly, or a look that for all its prurience is also priestly, I know that I am being dragged back to a former state, and it is as if the reins have slipped from my grasp. These forgotten gestures start up a rush of other moments that I can scarcely call memories, since they are more palpable and more real than the passenger next to me. I see the moment when my lover looked at my new dress on its hanger, looked at it with such longing, then reached out almost to touch it, as if imagining or dreading the delight that it would give others to see me in it. For some reason I am reminded of dull suburban gardens and how from packets of spring seeds so randomly scattered the hollyhocks come up tall and defiant, parading their strength and causing one to think that nature is indeed sovereign. In my garden last spring it was a tulip, a red tulip with a black center, and when the petals opened and I saw its fiendish black face, it was like seeing a caricature of a painted devil. "Oh, you little strange devil," I used to say to it, and wonder how it came to be there—if the birds had planted it or if its seed was in the bag belonging to the Breton hawker who sells onions. He knocks on my door three or four times a year, and holding the bunches of onions aloft, he is like a bishop waving a censer. In the morning light the skins are a beautiful pink, like pearls that have been lightly tinted, whereas in contrast the garlic he carries is the color of raw dough. He always reeks of cognac, and out of embarrassment or pity I give him another, and then fret over his progress on his push bicycle. One time he asked me if he could leave an empty sack in the garden, and it is possible that as he shook it out the seed of the red tulip lodged there.

Last night I was free. Last night I was certain that I had conquered rashness, and today I am proven wrong. Last night something happened to strengthen my conviction, to make me thankful for my independence. I wanted to buy some figs to bring home, so I went on an excursion to the town. You can't imagine how I avoided the town for the whole week. It was like a furnace down there, with people bumping into each other and more people spilling from coaches and clamoring for cold drinks and souvenirs and shade. I found a shop away from the main square, where there were all kinds of fruit, including the figs that I had hoped for. There were two kinds of figs, and guessing my dilemma, the proprietor, who was pale and extremely gentle, told me to help myself. He touched my wrist as he gave me a paper bag, and the touch seemed to say, "Be generous. Take both kinds." After I had paid him, I dallied for a moment, though I do not know why. Perhaps I was a little lonely at not having spoken to anyone for a week, or perhaps I was rehearsing my reemergence into the world. All of a sudden, he did a charming thing. He took a little liqueur bottle from a glass case and opened it with one wrench. It was a red liqueur, like a cordial, and we drank it in turn. As other customers came in, he weighed tomatoes or peaches or whatever, and spoke to them in English or German or Italian, then resumed his conversation with me. He spoke of the contrast between life on that island in the summer and in the winter. All or nothing, he said. In the summer he worked eighteen or twenty hours a day, and in the winter he did indoor tasks, such as painting or carpentry, and played cards with the men in the café. An old woman came into the shop, laughing and licking her lips. She was not the customary old woman in black, with a bony face and legs like spindles; rather, she was fat and lascivious. She turned her back to me and pointed to her open zipper, then gestured to me to do it up. I tried, but it was broken. She kept gesturing and laughing, and I think in reality she asked so that he and I could see her flesh. Her flesh was soft and brown, like a mousse. Some children came in and stepped behind the counter to help themselves to cold drinks from the refrigerator, and I assumed that they were his children or his nieces and nephews. He must have always avoided the sun to have a face so pale, and he had very beautiful smooth eyelids, which he kept lowered most of the time. He did not ask me to stay, but I felt that he did not want me to go just yet. I had already told him that I was leaving the following morning and that because of a bungle in my air ticket I had to go to another island, and he had smiled and said that with my coloring I would like the other island, as it was green and leafy. He liked it, he said. It was as if we had a bond, disposed as we were to a bit of shade, to tillage, and to fields. He pulled an airmail envelope from a new packet and started to draw on it in order to show me where the other island was. I had stepped behind the counter and was standing next to him, studying this funny little drawing, when a woman glided in and at once asked me sharply how the owner of my rented villa was. She was a small woman wearing canvas shoes, and everything about her was pinched and castigating.

"Your wife," I said.

"My wife," he said.

In an instant I saw their story; it was as if a seer had unfolded a scroll and told me how the man had come from the city, how he had married this thin woman, how the shop was in her name, and how he worked eighteen hours a day, had sired these lovely children, and was always watched. His wife gathered up a sheaf of the brown paper bags that were strewn all over the counter and started to put them in order, and by doing so she told him that he had no right to be slacking, that he had no right to be talking to foreign women. Then she sniffed the empty liqueur bottle and with a grunt tossed it toward the rubbish bin. Thinking that I would probably never see them again, I shook hands with them both and muttered something about the beauty of the island, as if to temper her spleen.

I went alone to the nearest restaurant, ordered a half bottle of white wine, and drank it slowly, and ordered grilled prawns, which I peeled and ate at my leisure, musing about this and that, thinking how lucky I was to be my own mistress, to be saved the terrible inclination of wanting to possess while being possessed, of being separated from myself while being host to another. I so relished my freedom that I even remarked to myself how nice it was that no other fingers dabbled in the glass finger bowl. I thought, I have arrived at a new state, a height which is also a plateau. To drive the matter home, as I walked up the hill to my secluded house I overheard an English couple having a ghastly drunken row behind an open door. Four-letter words were hurled from one to the other with such vehemence and such virulence that at each utterance the selfsame word carried different and mounting degrees of hatred; I was afraid they would come to blows, and perhaps they did. I went and sat on my terrace, and found to my surprise that a liner had anchored for the night. Its tiny windows were like strips of gold, and all of a sudden I was reminded of the interior of the Byzantine church, and for some reason, alone in the hushed night, I genuflected and said a prayer. Never had the bay seemed so beautiful or so safe, with the pair of sable mountains enfolding it. Now at last they were identical, consumed yet distinctive, in the dark. I delayed going to bed, even though I knew I must be up at five.

When I wakened this morning, the cocks had not yet begun to crow. The driver came to collect my luggage, and we went on tiptoe through the town, past all those tiny fortresses, with owners bound in sleep and countless dreams. Driving along, we witnessed the dawn, and at first sky and sea were merged, a pearled vista so pale and so fragile that one knew that it could—indeed, that it would—be vanquished. Its beauty brought to mind every intrepid, virginal thing. Even as one looked it was vanishing, or at least altering, becoming a vision or a passing dream. The little churches perched on the hilltops were like tiny beehives, and the earth gave off a breath of moisture and repose. But it was to the sky one looked, and as I looked at it the realization of my love came back to me in one unheralded burst of sadness. Beauty and sadness must be what love is founded on, I thought. Then the sky became rosier, the light seeming to flaunt itself, no longer tentative, as a river of red shot across the heavens, making a gash. The dawn itself was bleached and milky, with scarcely any light at all, and the sun rose, shy and timid, bringing that discharge of emotion inseparable from any birth. At the airport, the driver and I had coffee, and then he conveyed me to a small twin-engined airplane whereby I was whisked to that other island, which by comparison was tropical. There were white goats tethered in the fields next to the landing strip, and the sight of these and the little trees and shrubs reminded me of my native land. I had a four-hour wait, and so I sat outside on a step, and presently some young soldiers came to talk to me and tried to inveigle me to dance by putting on their transistor radio and performing some idiotic capers. They plied me with offers of coffee and cigarettes. They were dark, their dark eyes small and busy, and from the sun's constant glare they had wrinkled like raisins. Even then I did not believe that I was going home. I felt I would be detained there, and I did not in the least object.

It is evening when our plane lands. It is not dark, but it seems so in comparison with that far-off scorching island. It is as if all the sun has been snatched from here, and involuntarily I think of autumn and the hexagonal streetlights in my square, which will go on a fraction earlier each evening. My fellow passengers and I wait for our luggage, stare at the monitor to see which bay our bags will arrive at, and sometimes looking at each other involuntarily look away, as if we have done wrong. We are slipping back into our old lives. He is not here, nor did I expect him to be, but it has started up, not quite as pain or fret, but as a sense of resumption. Already I feel the imminence of his next visit, and I think how it will appear as if he had vacated the place only minutes before. The future looms, mirroring the selfsame patterns of the past—his occasional visits, the painful vigils in between, the restraints we have imposed upon ourselves—and I wonder how much longer I shall be able to endure it.